DUEL OF SORCERY

Camber could feel himself slipping even deeper into trance. Images formed and reformed on the blackness of the spell-bound water before him, only to fade before he could read them.

But he *must* read them. He dared not fail.

At the very limits of awareness, he touched Ariella's sleeping mind. And abruptly he knew the location of all Ariella's strength.

He was almost ready to withdraw, when suddenly the picture blanked and he caught an almost mind-splitting explosion of rage. A wrenching pain lanced behind his eyes, blinding him. He had been detected! His touch had been too clumsy, too direct!

Ariella was awake and aware of his link—and she was trying to sustain the link he had created, to surge back mentally across that link . . . and destroy him!

Also by Katherine Kurtz
Available from Ballantine Books:

SAINT CAMBER

Volume II in the Legends of Camber of Culdi

Katherine Kurtz

A Del Rey Book

BALLANTINE BOOKS • NEW YORK

Library of Congress Catalog Card Number: 78-16702

ISBN 0-345-30862-X

Manufactured in the United States of America

First Edition: October 1978

Paperback format
First Edition: September 1979
Fifth Printing: March 1983

Cover art by Darrell K. Sweet

Map by Bob Porter

This one is for

JOHN H. KNOBLOCK

who started me on my intellectual love affair
with the medieval world and its church,

and for all the other men and women
of whatever faith
who helped to turn that cerebral fascination
into an affair of the heart,
whether or not they were aware of it.
In our own ways, we all feed our sheep.

Contents

Prologue

*Behold, the former things are come to
pass, and new things do I declare: before
they spring forth I tell you of them.*
— Isaiah 42:9

It was the spring of 905, half a year since the crowning of Cinhil Haldane at Valoret; half a year since the last Deryni king, Imre of Festil, had been deposed and defeated by Cinhil's new-won magic; since Imre's sister Ariella, heavy with his child, had fled the halls of Valoret to seek sanctuary with the hosts of Torenth to the east.

The Deryni Lord Camber MacRorie had been the hero of that day—Camber and his children: Joram and Evaine and Rhys—and Alister Cullen, proud Vicar General of the Order of Saint Michael, which had made the physical fact of the Restoration possible.

Now the Haldane throne was steadying, Cinhil's queen safely delivered of twin sons to replace the one murdered by Imre's agent before Cinhil's emergence. King Cinhil, though reluctant still to set aside his former monkish life, was perhaps beginning to understand his role as monarch.

But Camber was ill at ease, for he knew that the last Festillic chapter had yet to be written, nor would it be written so long as Ariella lived, and Imre's bastard with her. All the winter long, there had been no word out of Torenth, though all knew that to be her

1

place of refuge. She was biding her time. The child would have been born by now. Soon, soon, she would make her move. Perhaps she was beginning, already.

And in a high solar room of a castle called Cardosa, remote in the mountains between Torenth and free Eastmarch, the woman in question stood before a tabled map of the Eleven Kingdoms and plotted her revenge. A babe suckled at her breast, but she paid him no mind as she stared at the map and sprinkled water from her fingertips onto the lands of Gwynedd, the while muttering words beneath her breath, her mind locked on one ill-willed purpose.

Each day for a week she had worked her magic now; soon she would see its fruition. Her army was gathering, even as the spring rains washed the mountain passes clear of snow and bogged the plains her enemy must cross to try to stop her. Soon, soon, she would make her move. Then the upstart Haldane priest would wear the Gwynedd crown no more.

CHAPTER ONE

By long forbearing is a prince persuaded,
and a soft tongue breaketh the bone.
—Proverbs 25:15

Rain was falling steadily in the city of Valoret. It had been falling for the past four days, unseasonable for June. Outside the precincts of the royal keep, the cobblestone streets ran with mud and flood-borne refuse. Standing pools of rain and mud rose higher with each hour, threatening and sometimes inundating the doorsills of shops and houses.

Inside the keep, it was spirits which were dampened instead of mere physical surrounds. Chill, moisture-laden air rose foully from the middens through walls and garderobe shafts to rot the rushes underfoot in the great hall and waft among the rafters. Though fires blazed on three enormous hearths, their heat could not warm the icy apprehensions of the handful of lords assembled there.

No formal summons had gathered them. King Cinhil had been avoiding structured councils of late, much to the dismay of his would-be advisors. The men who now sat around a table before one of the side fireplaces were the same who had placed Cinhil on the throne six months before—men who now feared for the king they had made—feared for all whose safety and well-being they had thought to ensure by ousting a Deryni tyrant and restoring a prince of the old, human line to Gwynedd's throne.

3

They were an odd assortment—all, save one, of the same race of sorcerer-magicians whose scion had lately ruled Gwynedd:

Rhys Thuryn, the young Deryni Healer, bending his shaggy red head to study a map whose strategies he did not really understand.

Jebediah of Alcara, Deryni Grand Master of the militant Knights of Saint Michael and acting commander in chief of King Cinhil's army—if the king could be persuaded to use that army to proper advantage.

Alister Cullen, the graying, ice-eyed Vicar General of the Michaeline Order, and Jebediah's technical superior, also Deryni, leaning with hands clasped behind his head to study a cobweb high in the beams above him—though the seeming casual posture concealed a tension shared by all of them.

Guaire of Arliss, young and earnest, and sole human member of the group. Heir in his own right to a considerable fortune, he was one of the few men of the last regime to retain a position in the court being formed under the new king.

And of course, Camber MacRorie, Earl of Culdi—chiefest Deryni of them all.

Camber had aged but little in the months since the Haldane Restoration, neither appearance nor manner betraying his nearly threescore years. The silver-gilt hair still gleamed bright in the light of torch and fire, and the clear gray eyes showed only a few new wrinkles at the corners. In all, he was as fit as he had been in the last decade—hardened and refined, if anything, by the privations and adversities all of them had endured since making their decision to replace the anointed king of Gwynedd.

But Camber, kingmaker that he was, was no more at ease than the rest of his colleagues. Though he had not wished to alarm them, Deryni or human, he suspected that the rain which fell so unceasingly outside was more than ordinary rain—that the enemy who had eluded them last year at the moment of triumph plotted still more grave offenses from afar; that the coming encounter on the field of battle, no longer to be postponed by winter snows and the enemy's indisposition, might be fraught with far greater dangers than steel and spear and arrow. The rain could be but a warning token.

He had confided his suspicions about the weather to the gentle Dom Emrys, Abbot of the Gabrilites—one man who might know for certain whether such things were possible, even for Deryni. The Order of Saint Gabriel was renowned and respected, even among humans, for the purity of its discipline, for its preservation of ancient wisdom and teaching of the healing arts.

But even Dom Emrys, that pale paragon of Deryni calm and sagacity, had only been able to suggest a way by which Camber himself might explore the question further—and that way was not without its dangers. Camber was familiar with the procedure at which Emrys hinted, but he had not yet brought himself to use it. He wished there were some less-hazardous method of investigation.

A movement at the table caught his eye, and Camber tuned back in on the conversation which had been continuing around him. Jebediah had been leading a discussion of their military preparedness, and was cursing the weather anew as he pushed troop markers around on the map. His scarred fingers were surprisingly agile on the delicate markers.

"No, even if Jowerth and Torcuill do manage to get through, I don't see how we can field more than five to six hundred knights," he said, replying to a question Rhys had raised. "That includes all the royal levies, the Michaelines, and few dozen more from the other military orders. Perhaps twice that many mounted men-at-arms. For foot and archers, say, five hundred and two hundred, respectively. We'd have more, but most of the main roads are flooded out. Many of the men we could ordinarily count on won't be able to reach us in time to do any good."

Rhys nodded as though he actually understood the

significance of the numbers, and Guaire studied his clasped hands, understanding all too well.

Camber reached out to shift the map board to a better angle.

"What's our most accurate estimate of Ariella's strength, Jeb?"

"About half again what we've committed, so far as we can tell. Her mother was related to the royal house of Torenth, you know. She's drawing heavily on those ties. Also, it apparently isn't raining east of the Lendours."

"Which means," Guaire began tentatively, "that if we could get our men together and get through those mountains—"

"We could meet Ariella somewhere in Eastmarch." Jebediah nodded. "However, getting the men there is the key problem."

Guaire toyed with one of the extra map markers. "What about one of your Deryni Transfer Portals? Might that be a way to get some of our extra men there?"

Alister Cullen, the Michaeline vicar general, shook his steel-gray head. "We daren't use magic that openly, Guaire. Cinhil has made his feelings all too clear on that subject, of late. Besides, the men we need most are the foot soldiers from the outlying regions—humans, almost to the man. After just escaping the yoke of a Deryni tyrant, I doubt they'd willingly cooperate with any Deryni working, no matter how benign."

"You make it sound, well, ominous," Guaire murmured, "as if there were something sinister about your Deryni powers."

His expression was very serious as he spoke, until he realized the irony of those words coming from his human lips and became aware of how far he, himself, had come in his estimation of the Deryni. Faint amusement registered in the eyes of the men around him, not unkindly, and Guaire colored a little in embarrassment.

Camber chuckled sympathetically.

"It's all right, Guaire. That's how *many* humans view our powers. And between the humans who distrust us because we're Deryni and the Deryni who distrust us because we deposed a Deryni king in favor of a human one, I suppose we're lucky to have the support we do."

"And if Cinhil doesn't unbend a little," Cullen snorted, "the two peoples are going to be driven even further apart. One wrong word from him could lose us half our army between dawn and dusk."

Rhys, who had been listening without comment, leaned forward and prodded the map.

"So, what can be done about it? And what about the more immediate crisis? Do we even know for certain where Ariella will launch her attack?"

Jebediah nodded thoughtfully. "Alister and I have come up with three likely locations, Rhys, two of them fairly close together. If Sighere sides with us and brings his Eastmarch levies to join us, we can eliminate one of the three."

He bent over the map and began moving markers again, and Camber permitted his attention to wander to the dancing fire, slipping back into his own private reverie.

Cullen's comment about Cinhil had struck a sobering chord. Cinhil's growing rigidity was becoming a major problem, and Camber himself was having to bear more and more of the king's resultant uneasiness.

Cinhil, immature in many ways, despite his forty-plus years, had waxed philosophical in the months since his coronation, increasingly believing that his acceptance of the Crown had been a mistake. He was a priest, not a king, despite the archbishop's dispensation of his priestly vows. Had he not forsaken those vows and left the priesthood, and compounded that sin by taking a wife, there would not now be the two tiny heirs, ill-starred twins, the elder sickly and frail, the younger fair and healthy, but with one deformed foot to remind his father forever of the sinfulness of his begetting.

Cinhil saw the infants' condition as a sure sign of divine wrath, the withering hand of God smiting that which should have been most dear, because Cinhil had deserted God's priesthood.

And who was to blame, in Cinhil's skewed perspective, shaped until a year ago within the walls of an abbey? Why, Camber, of course. Was it not the powerful Deryni earl who had induced Cinhil to forsake his vows and take the throne? What more natural than that Cinhil's resentment should fester even now within his breast? Weighed against God's anger, of what possible importance was a token loyalty to the Earl of Culdi—even if that man *was* one of the few who stood between him and oblivion?

Camber glanced away from the fire to see his daughter, Evaine, crossing the hall. Though heavily muffled against the chill in a fur-lined mantle, still she was slender and graceful as she made her way across the rush-strewn hall. Revan, her young clark, picked his way carefully after his mistress, his usual limp even more pronounced from the dampness.

Evaine's face was worried, her blue eyes stormy beneath the coiled hair, as she bent to kiss her father's cheek.

"How fares the queen?" Camber asked in a low voice, leaning back from the table so that they would not disturb the others' discussion.

With a sigh, she turned to dismiss Revan, who was waiting attentively a short distance away, and watched him limp across the hall to join several pages huddled by the opposite fireplace. Her pretty brow furrowed as she bent to her father's ear again.

"Oh, Father, she is so unhappy. Revan and I have spent the past hour and more with her, but she will not be cheered. 'Tis not right that she should be so listless and depressed, almost a full month after the birthing. Her labor was not difficult, and Rhys assures me that her physical injuries are mended."

"Unfortunately, 'tis not physical hurt which torments our little queen," Camber replied, so low that Evaine had to bend very close to hear him. "If the king gave her even a small part of his attention—but, no, he must brood on his imagined sins, and condemn himself and all around him for—"

He broke off as loud voices caught his attention in the corridor outside the far entrance to the hall. One of the voices was his son Joram's; another, angrier one was the king's.

But there were two additional voices—a man and a woman—and the woman's voice was high-pitched and nearly hysterical. All conversation at the table ceased as the king and Joram and two strangers entered the hall and began to cross the dais.

The woman was slender and fair, and even younger than Evaine. The man, husband or brother by his bearing, was obviously a military man, though he wore no sword in the royal presence.

The royal presence was flashing warning signs which should have been apparent to anyone. The Haldane eyes were hard with anger, the lines of the proud body taut with forced control. Joram was a sober splash of Michaeline blue against the crimson and sable of Cinhil's kingly garb, looking as if he wanted to be anywhere but at the king's side.

Cinhil drew his hand away in distaste as the woman threw herself on her knees and reached up in supplication.

"Please, Sire, he has done nothing! I swear it!" she sobbed. "He is an old man. He is sick! Have you no pity?"

"There is no pity in this one!" the man broke in angrily, jerking her to her feet and thrusting her behind him protectively. "How can there be pity in an apostate priest, who wages war on innocent old men? What are you, Haldane, so to decide the fate of your betters?"

In the same breath, the man's hand moved in the pattern of an arcane attack, casting a blinding flash which lit that end of the hall as if the summer sun had come inside. Instantly, all at the table were on their feet and running toward the king, Jebediah and Guaire drawing swords as they ran. Evaine hiked up her skirts and dashed frantically after her father and Rhys and Alister Cullen.

Time seemed to stand still in the afterimage of that flash. The atmosphere grew thick with the huge exchange of energy on the dais, as both Joram and Cinhil countered the assault. The would-be rescuers moved with limbs seemingly encased in lead, trying desperately to reach the king.

Joram, with the aid of Cinhil, managed to wrestle their attacker to the floor. But their wild thrashing in the rushes continued to be punctuated by flashes of light and wisps of frightful apparition as the assailant fought on. Joram nearly disappeared under the attacker's body, fighting for his own life as well as the king's. The pandemonium continued as reinforcements swarmed onto the dais.

Camber's eyes had not yet fully recovered from the initial flash, but he could just make out another, more immediate threat than the attacker's magic—an unsheathed dagger in the woman's hand. In a timeless instant, he saw that Cinhil's back was exposed as he knelt to wrestle with the man on the floor, and that the king was not aware of his danger.

Guaire, youngest and fleetest of them all, had seen the threat and was reaching for the woman, too close and too fast-moving to use his sword to advantage. But his feet tangled with those of the downed man as he lunged, tripping him directly into Cullen and Rhys.

Camber screamed, "Cinhil!" and launched one last, desperate leap between his king and the woman as the knife flashed upward.

The events of the next instant were never clear, afterward, though the results were plain enough. One second, the knife was driving unchecked toward Cinhil's back, toward Camber's body—the next, blood was showering them all, and Camber was sprawling half stunned at Cinhil's feet, in a growing pool of blood. Cinhil whirled in killing rage to see the woman crumpled over Jebediah's broadsword, her body cut nearly in two. The dagger, its blade snapped by the force of Jebediah's blow, spun through the air in several pieces, the bright steel catching Cinhil's glance with almost hypnotic fascination.

Cinhil reacted like a man gone mad. With a scream of fury, he spun and loosed a last, vicious attack on the woman's companion—a blast of magical force so powerful, and at such close range, that Joram, trapped under the man's body, was only barely able to deflect its killing power from himself.

Then Cullen was hurling himself against Cinhil and pinning his arms to his sides, subduing the king's efforts to break free and wreak yet more vengeance on his attackers.

Camber lurched dizzily to his feet and caught his balance on Cullen's arm. Then, seizing the king's face between bloody hands, he forced Cinhil to look at him, shook the royal head to break the killing concentration.

"Cinhil, stop it! For God's sake, let it pass! It's over! You're safe! They can't hurt you now!"

In that instant Cinhil froze and blinked, taking in Camber's tone and expression and bloodstained visage; then he seemed to sag a little in Cullen's arms. He closed his eyes and took several deep breaths as guards clattered to a halt around the group and glanced at one another uncertainly.

"It's all right," Camber repeated, his nod and eyes signaling the guards to withdraw from earshot until he was sure Cinhil was in control again. "It's all right, Cinhil," he whispered one more time.

With that, he released Cinhil's head and stepped back a pace, his own breathing still ragged, recovering. He could feel blood running down his left side, and knew that some of it was his own.

"Is anyone hurt?" Cullen said softly, still supporting the now-shaking Cinhil against his chest.

The murmurs of negation sparked a response in Cinhil, and he opened his eyes and stared blankly at the sea of concerned faces around him.

Rhys got shakily to his knees and started toward the bloody Camber, but the earl shook his head and indicated that he should see to the others. Rhys glanced at the woman—obviously beyond even his help—then turned his attention to the man.

Joram struggled from under the limp form until he could sit up, as pale against his cassock as Rhys had ever seen him; but he did not relinguish his grip on his now-stirring prisoner.

"Joram, are you all right?" Rhys murmured under his breath as he drew his hand across the prisoner's forehead.

"I will be," Joram whispered. "What about him? He took a terrific jolt. It was all I could do to shield myself."

The man's eyes had fluttered and tracked automatically to Rhys's hand at his touch, but it was obvious that he was deep in shock.

Rhys looked up at the king.

"What did you do to him? He's dying."

"He would have killed me," Cinhil replied sullenly.

"Well, you nearly killed Joram, you know. And I don't think I'm going to be able to save this man."

Cinhil's expression darkened at the implied accusation in Rhys's tone.

"He is an assassin! I did not mean for him to live!"

As Rhys turned his attention back to his patient, golden eyes smoldering with silent resentment, Jebediah knelt down beside the dead woman. The knight's sword dangled loosely in his grasp, the blade leaving a smear of blood on the already bloody rushes. He swallowed hard, flinching at Camber's touch of comfort on his shoulder.

"Assassin or no, I do not like killing women, Camber," he whispered. "I only thought to block the knife. She was a Deryni woman. I was certain she would have arcane shields to stop my blow from further harm."

"You could not have known," Camber replied, his breathing finally almost back to normal. He pressed his left elbow hard against his side, hoping it would slow the bleeding and that Cinhil would not notice. "No one could have known."

Cullen, tentatively letting go of Cinhil, glanced at his brother Michaeline in compassion, but he did not comment for fear of setting Cinhil off again. With a diplomatic cough, he gestured toward the man Rhys was tending.

"Sire, can you tell us what started all of this? Who were these people?"

"Rabble!" Cinhil snorted, starting to turn away.

At that, the prisoner stirred and turned his head slightly toward the king and vicar general. There was no mark on his body, but pain filled the brown eyes. He pushed Rhys's hand away when the Healer made as though to ease his discomfort.

"Do you not know us, Vicar General?" the man gasped. "It was your Deryni court which tried our father and condemned him to rot in the dungeons beneath us."

"Your father?" Camber queried.

"You know him, traitor of Culdi!" the man snapped, with more strength than any would have expected. "You, a Deryni who betrayed his own to put this human tyrant on the throne, who gave him power, I know not how—"

Cinhil reddened at that, and started to raise a hand against the man, but Cullen restrained him.

"Your name," Camber demanded. "If wrong has been done, I will do what I can to right it, but I must know who you are."

The man coughed blood and turned away in agony before looking up at Camber again.

"My father is Dothan of Erne, who was a lesser minister of this court. She—she who sleeps yonder—"

His voice caught as he glanced away from the dead woman. "—she was my sister—O God, I hurt!"

Joram eased the man more to a sitting position, and Rhys tried again to assist him, but the man knocked the Healer's hand away, pointing a trembling finger at the king.

"Your traitorous Deryni friends have taught you well, King of Rats!" he gasped, bloody froth staining his lips. "But I tell you this: you shall reap no joy of what you have wrought. I curse you in your going and in your coming! I curse you in each breath you take! I curse you in the fruit of your seed, and in all you touch—may it come to naught! You—"

The litany of curses was more than Cinhil could bear. With an enraged, animal cry, he broke away from Cullen long enough to reach out his hand and clench the air with his fist.

His victim took one strangled half-breath, then jerked in spasm and was still.

As Cullen restrained Cinhil again, and the others stared in horror, their gazes alternating between the obviously dead man and the king, Rhys checked frantically for a sign of life, knowing sickly that he would find none. He looked up; and his Sight, plus the contorted expression on Cinhil's face, showed him more than he had ever wanted to see of death and vengeance.

Camber, mastering his own horror and distaste with some difficulty, stared at Cinhil for several seconds before speaking.

"Why, Cinhil?" he finally said.

"Must I give *you* a reason? He was an assassin—a Deryni assassin!"

"He was a prisoner," Camber said. "He was in custody, beyond the ability to harm anyone."

"He cursed me and mine!"

"His curse was but *words!* Can a king afford to let himself be moved to murder just because of words?"

"It was execution, not murder," Cinhil replied, in a

more defensive tone. "Assassins are always executed."

"Even assassins deserve trials!" Camber said.

"I tried and condemned him, in my mind!" Cinhil countered hotly. "Besides, it was not just any man who cursed me, but a Deryni. How am I to gauge the potency of a Deryni curse?"

"Cinhil, the man was already dying," Camber began, trying to back off from the Deryni issue.

Cinhil shook his head. "That is immaterial. Do you guarantee that a Deryni curse, especially from the lips of a dying man, can do no harm?"

Camber started to speak, but Cinhil shook his head again.

"Nay, I thought not. Oh, I know what you say, and I know that my own power is not inconsiderable— but what do I really *know* of your Deryni powers? Only that which you have chosen to reveal to me."

"Cinhil—"

"Enough. I am sore accursed already, for offenses against my Lord God, without adding Deryni damnation to my lot. One son has died already, of Deryni slaying. And you have only to look in the nursery, at my poor, ill-begotten babes, to know how my wretched fate continues."

As he gestured toward the entrance of the hall, all of them simultaneously became aware of a long streak of blood across the back of his left hand, smeared from the edge of an angry-looking cut which had hitherto been hidden beneath the fur at his sleeve edge. Cinhil saw their glance and looked at the wound almost dispassionately.

"Yes, assassins' knives do occasionally draw blood, gentlemen. Fortunately, this is slight."

"Let Rhys be the judge of that," Camber said, signaling with his eyes that the Healer should attend the wound. He eased closer as Rhys stood and took the injured hand in his.

"Cinhil, has anyone verified or disproved their story?" Camber asked, trying to lead Cinhil gently away from the subject of curses and also distract him from what Rhys was doing.

Cinhil shook his head, arrogance and defiance still flashing in the gray Haldane eyes.

"What does it matter? I remember the case vaguely. This Dothan of Erne was arrested with Coel Howell and his adherents. Coel was executed. I recall that there were mitigating circumstances about Dothan, so he was being held for a new trial. That's the law. It isn't my fault."

"He mentioned something about his father being ill, though," Evaine interjected. "Is he?"

"How should I know?"

"It is a king's business to know," Cullen replied.

Cinhil threw up both hands in disgust, and Rhys had to move fast to recapture the hand he was examining. The wound was so slight that Rhys was almost tempted to let Cinhil go on his way and allow it to heal naturally. Instead, he sighed and began to slip into his healing trance.

"I fail to understand how a crown is supposed to grant one omniscience!" Cinhil was saying angrily. "I am beset by two Deryni assassins, I am wounded in the attempt on my life, and then you try to make me feel guilty because I killed one of them. It isn't because they're Deryni like yourselves, is it?"

Had he calculated it—perhaps he had—Cinhil could not have made a remark more certain to shock his listeners. The mental reaction of those around him was so violent, even if their faces did not show it, that Rhys broke out of his healing trance before he had even begun, only with difficulty schooling his face to some semblance of professional decorum. Around him, he could sense the others shielding their own stunned amazement.

Guaire, the lone human among them, was not so adept at covering his horror, and flinched before the long, appraising study which Cinhil turned on each of them.

It was Rhys who managed to change the tenor of

the interaction, exercising the prerogative of healers to command even kings when a question of health was involved.

"Sire, if you insist upon arguing, I can't possibly heal you. Now, please come and sit quietly by the fire so I can take care of this."

As Cinhil stared at him, jaw dropping at the Healer's effrontery, Camber laid one hand on Cinhil's elbow.

"He's right, Sire. Why don't you come and sit down? We're all nervous and exhausted from what we've just been through.

"Jebediah, unless you have pressing duties elsewhere, I'd like you to go and check on this Dothan of Erne. That's the least we can do. And Guaire, please have the guards remove these bodies. See that they receive proper burial."

"No, let them rot!" Cinhil said, jerking his arm away from Camber.

"See that they receive proper burial," Cullen repeated Camber's words.

He looked Cinhil in the eye, and the king glared back for an instant before dropping his gaze and allowing himself to be led meekly to a place by the fire.

This time, Cinhil did not resist as Rhys took his hand in his. Perhaps realizing that he had behaved less than graciously toward the man who was trying to help him, he laid his head against the chair back and closed his eyes, not seeing the glances which were exchanged among the others taking seats around him.

Rhys went into his healing trance in silence this time—though Camber did not follow and observe, as was often his wont. Instead, Camber eased himself into a chair and let his own head lie back, praying that he could contain his own pain a little longer. He could feel the blood still seeping down his side. He wondered at the nausea he was feeling, hoping desperately that he could hide it until Cinhil was gone.

He opened his eyes to see Joram and Evaine staring at him in alarm—they had sensed his pain—but he shook his head and forbade their notice with a glance.

He was not able to fool Rhys, however. The Healer had been well aware of Camber's absence. As Rhys opened his eyes, the king's healing done, those eyes gazed across at Camber in accusation.

Camber shook his head again and glanced down at the hand Rhys was removing from Cinhil's. Where the wound had been, there was nothing but a slight blood-stain on the edge of Cinhil's sleeve and a rapidly fading red line which could have been a crease in the king's hand.

Cinhil sensed the completion of the work, though not the nuances surrounding it, and opened his eyes, flexing the hand experimentally.

"Thank you, Rhys. I'm sorry if I made your work more difficult."

Rhys nodded acceptance of the thanks and the apology, but could not trust himself to speak.

"And Camber," the king continued, in that same even tone, "have you anything more to say, or may I go now?"

"You need not ask my leave, Sire. You know best what you have done, and why, and whether or not it is right."

"The Devil take you, I will not be lectured!" Cinhil cried, lurching to his feet almost hysterically. "I am not a child, and I'm no longer under your control!"

With that, he whirled and left the hall. Cullen started to follow him, but Joram caught his sleeve and shook his head. Cullen was astonished to see Camber slumping in his chair, white-faced, a hand clutched openly to his left side, now that Cinhil was gone. As Cullen sank down in the chair which Cinhil had just vacated, Rhys began fumbling at Camber's bloody robe, his tongue clucking in disapproval at the pool of blood collecting in the chair.

"I thought all this blood on your sleeve was the woman's," Rhys muttered as he ripped the tear wider with both his hands. "I asked whether you were all right, and you lied to me!"

"I preferred that Cinhil not know I had been wounded in his behalf. Besides, he needed you just then."

"It was a minor wound, and you know it. Now, stop squirming. I don't want to hurt you any more than I have to."

Camber winced as Rhys's fingers located the wound and began to probe, but he did not move. Evaine, sitting at his right, took his free hand in hers and stared at him anxiously, while Joram knelt at his feet.

"It isn't *that* serious, is it?" Camber finally murmured, when it seemed that Rhys was taking an inordinately long time just to look.

"I don't know yet. Talk about something else while I find out."

Camber smiled slightly, more to reassure his children than out of any greater comfort, and glanced across Rhys's kneeling form at Cullen.

"You know, Alister, it was interesting to note to whom he did and did not listen just now."

Cullen snorted under his breath and tried to look unconcerned about Camber's paleness.

"You're implying that I might have some influence over him that you do not," he replied gruffly. "Unfortunately, I'm afraid that's rather tenuous. It may be that he identifies with me and Joram a little because of our priesthood—something we have that he has lost. If that isn't it, I can't explain it."

"Whatever the cause, the effect seems to exist," Camber said. He shifted a little and made a grimace as Rhys's touch found a more sensitive hurt. "What will happen when you're gone to Grecotha?"

Cullen shrugged. "I don't think he knows about my promotion yet. I was only told yesterday myself. Still, Grecotha isn't that far from Valoret. I'll be safely out of reach for the niggling things, but available when I'm really needed."

"And what happens when he moves the court back to Rhemuth? Then you're twice as far from him."

Cullen shook his head. "I don't know, Camber. I go where I'm sent. I think you're overestimating my influence over him."

"Perhaps. I worry about his increasing hostility toward Deryni in general, though. And from a purely selfish point of view, I worry about his changing attitude toward me. As you cannot have failed to notice, it's becoming increasingly difficult for me to work with him."

"He's becoming insufferable!" Joram muttered darkly. "There are times when I almost wish we had never found him. At least in Imre we knew what danger we faced."

"Never wish those times upon us again," Camber replied. "We are well rid of Imre and his wicked kin, even if Cinhil is not yet all we would have him. The people will grow to love him, in time."

"Will they?" Joram lowered his voice to a whisper, after casting a careful look at the soldiers moving at the end of the hall, clearing away the aftermath of what had just occurred.

"They already love you, you know. You could have been king yourself; they would have accepted you far more readily."

Camber glanced at both his children, at Cullen watching him, still as death, at Rhys kneeling by his side, lost in his Healer's trancing—then sighed.

"Is that what you truly wish, Joram? We are Deryni, and none of us of royal blood. And if I *had* taken the throne, what then? I would have been no better than Imre, whose ancestors also took what did not belong to them. One does not right one wrong by yet another."

Evaine's eyes were filling with tears. "But Cinhil is so—so helpless, Father, and so—"

"Cinhil is our rightful king—let none forget it," Camber murmured. "And despite his failings, which I am first to agree are many, I think that he can learn to be a good king."

"If he lives a hundred years, he could not be your match!" Joram said under his breath.

Camber smiled gently. "And do you think that *I* will live a hundred years, Joram? Be realistic. If I *had* become king, what then? What, when I was gone? I am nearly sixty now. My health is excellent, and I anticipate several more good years—but how many may I reasonably expect? Ten? As many as twenty? And with your brother Cathan dead, my heir now is a lad of seven. Would you wish the crown on little Davin when I am gone? Or on yourself, to put aside your vows as we made Cinhil do?"

"You could have made a difference," Joram whispered, shaking his head.

"Aye, perhaps. And I *can* make a difference, even now, God willing it be so. But it must be on my terms, serving our lawful king. The price we paid for Cinhil's kingship was too high to throw it all away simply because the way is difficult just now."

Cullen stirred slightly, leaning back to stroke his chin thoughtfully.

"What shall we do about Cinhil, then? You, yourself, have pointed out the problem. Can you work with him?"

Camber shrugged. "If I must, I must. Oh, I think this current crisis will pass. I flatter myself that Cinhil still needs me for a while—at least until the matter of Ariella's invasion is settled, one way or the other. As my son has pointed out, I have the people's favor. It is misdirected—for all of you share in the responsibility for what they think I have done—but that is neither here nor there. Imre is dead, and they think I am responsible, even though they know that Cinhil did the actual deed. In time, they will learn the truth."

"Well, it isn't time for that yet," Rhys said, returning his attention to all of them. "Camber, this is more complicated than serious—I've done a little already—

but I don't want you trying to help this time. You've lost more blood than I would have liked."

"Which means that you are not telling me everything, and I shan't be able to convince you otherwise," Camber said.

Rhys shook his head stubbornly, not moving his left hand from Camber's side.

Camber sighed and adjusted his arms more comfortably on the chair. "Very well, I won't argue. You realize, of course, that I'm never going to learn how you do this if you won't let me watch on my own body."

"If you haven't learned by now, I'm not sure it can be learned," Rhys said with a tight smile. He reached his right hand to Camber's forehead. "Let's get on with it. Close your eyes and relax. Open to me. No barriers . . . no resistance . . . and no memory of this."

Obeying, Camber exhaled softly and let himself slip away, knowing that Rhys must have good reasons for his request, and too lethargic to worry about them. In what seemed only a short time, he was rousing to a deft mental touch calling him back. He frowned as he took another breath and opened his eyes. It had been so peaceful where he was.

"How do you feel?"

Rhys's face was hovering anxiously a handspan from his own, the fingertips of one hand still resting lightly at Camber's temple.

Camber blinked slowly, deliberately—let his gaze slip past Rhys to the others on the fringe of his vision. All of them looked far more solemn than he thought they had a right to be.

"All right, can you tell me now what it was? I feel fine, if a little weak, so I assume that the Great Healer took care of it. However, the lesser Healer has a little explaining to do. Rhys?"

Rhys hooked a stool closer and settled on it. "Damaged kidney," he said matter-of-factly. "Perforated spleen. Internal bleeding. Superficial muscle damage. Other than that, there was hardly anything wrong with you." He cocked his head at Camber with a wistful look. "What I want to know is how you managed to stay on your feet so long."

"How long did it take you to put things right?" Camber countered.

"Long enough." Rhys smiled. "You're as good as new now, though—or will be when you've had some rest. Just don't do it again. I might not be around next time."

"I'll certainly try to avoid it."

Camber smiled and slid a hand into the hole in his robe where the wound had been. Only smooth skin met his touch—not even a tenderness.

"Well, where were we?" he said, relaxing in his chair with a sigh.

His daughter shook her head and sat back with relief, dropping one hand to rest on her brother's shoulder as he settled in the rushes at her feet. Joram, for all that he was bloodstained and covered with bits of straw and rushes from his tussle with the assassin, somehow managed to convey an air of elegant competence now that the crisis was over. He looked his father squarely in the eyes.

"We were talking about your not being able to get along with Cinhil—since you refuse to consider the possibility of any other king."

"Wrong. We were talking about Cinhil not being able to get along with me," Camber corrected lightly. "As all of you know, I am a very easy person to get along with."

"We also know," Joram continued pointedly, "that Cinhil holds us, and you in particular, to blame for all the misfortunes which have befallen him since he left his abbey. He'll use you as a scapegoat, Father."

"I suspect he will."

Cullen shifted uneasily in his chair. "I don't wish to interfere in what is obviously a family argument, but can we worry about that facet a little later? In case you'd all forgotten—and I don't mean to minimize your injury, Camber—but we have a war to fight, and the weather is rotten, and Jebediah and I have to be able to tell your men something besides 'Things will work themselves out somehow.' "

Camber sighed again and pursed his lips, making a steeple of his forefingers and studying them absent-mindedly.

"Sorry, Alister. Your point is well taken. Let's table the Cinhil matter for the moment, since we're not likely to resolve it by talking, anyway."

"That's more like it," Cullen murmured.

"As for the invasion," Camber continued, not looking at any of them in particular, "I think that there is something I can do, with your cooperation and assistance, to learn a great deal more about what Ariella is planning. Alister, I'm not sure you'd approve, so you're excused, if you want to be."

Cullen sat back in his chair and looked sidelong at Camber.

"All right. What mischief have you been into this time? I know that tone, Camber."

Camber surveyed them all casually, only the gray eyes moving in the placid face. "It's clean, I promise you. A power drain, and as complicated as anything I've ever attempted, but it can be done—at least, I think it can. Or rather, I know it can be done, and I think that I can do it."

"You've never tried it, then?" Joram asked.

"No, it's from an old manuscript called the Protocol of Orin. I found it with the original of the Pargan Howiccan *senache* that you were translating, Evaine, but it's far older than that—several hundred years, I suspect. At any rate, our ancient ancestors apparently used a technique like this for what we would call divination. I prefer to think of it as a direct linkage to Ariella—if we can do it."

He felt Evaine's hand on his shoulder and turned his head to kiss her fingers.

"Frightened?" he asked.

"Nay, Father, not at all, if you be there." She laughed gently. "You have but to tell us how we may help, and we are yours to command. I believe I can speak for Rhys and Joram."

The two men nodded, and Alister Cullen cleared his throat and sat forward in his chair.

"You say it's not dark?"

Camber nodded mildly, still holding his daughter's hand, and watched Cullen's battle of conscience war across his craggy face.

"Well, if you think I'm going to let the four of you go and magick yourselves into danger of eternal damnation, you've got another thought coming," the vicar general finally growled. "Sometimes I'm not certain of your judgment, Camber—and your children take after you. You'll need a level head among you."

Camber smiled and nodded, but said nothing.

"And you always manage to talk me into these things against *my* better judgment," Cullen concluded, sitting back in his chair with an exasperated sigh. "Well, go ahead. If you're determined to do this fool thing, just tell me when and where, and I'll be there."

"Did I talk him into anything?" Camber asked, glancing at his children with a look of martyred innocence.

The others laughed, and Camber reached out to clap Cullen reassuringly on the shoulder.

"Thank you, my friend. We treasure you all the more for your caution. Now, as to when and where, I think we should move quickly on this—the sooner the better. If no one has any objections, I should like to do it tonight, as soon after Vespers as possible."

"Are you sure you're strong enough?" Joram asked.

Camber glanced at Rhys, and the Healer shrugged.

"If you promise to eat something substantial and rest a bit, all right. Remember, you lost a lot of blood, and that's one thing I can't cure."

"Agreed. Any other objections?"

There were none. Joram glanced at the others dubiously, sharing some of his Michaeline superior's mistrust of what his father might be planning, then turned his attention back to Camber.

"Very well. You're going to do it anyway, so there's no use trying to talk you out of it. Where do you want to set up, and do you need assistance?"

"Ideally, I'd like to use consecrated ground, but I don't suppose that's feasible here in the keep, for secrecy's sake, and I don't think we ought to leave. That being the case, I suggest that we use the dressing chamber adjoining my quarters. I think it can be adequately secured for our purposes."

"Assistance?" Rhys reminded him.

Camber shook his head. "I'll set this one up myself, if you don't mind. I *will* need a few things that you can gather for me, though. Evaine, find me a large silver bowl, at least as big around as a man's head. I don't care about the outside, but I want the inside plain."

"Just plain polished silver?"

"That's right. Ah, Joram: incense and something to burn it in."

Joram nodded.

"And, Alister—"

"I'm not sure I really want to know, but go on," Cullen muttered under his breath.

Camber chuckled as he stood and gathered the bloodstained folds of his robe around him, putting on a special nonchalance for Cullen's benefit.

"Relax, my friend. You might even find the entire process interesting. Here's what I want you to bring . . ."

Chapter Two

*But continue thou in the things which thou
hast learned and hast been assured of, knowing
of whom thou hast learned them.*
—II Timothy 3:14

Cinhil was out of breath and panting by the time he reached his tower quarters. When he had locked himself in, he stood with his back against the door for several minutes, heart pounding, his hands resting behind him, trembling on the bolt, as if to reassure himself that he was, in fact, safe. He tried not to think about what had just happened. For a time, he even succeeded.

But when his breathing had slowed nearly to normal, mindless panic and anger gave way to guilt and fear. Fighting down a queasy sickness in his bowels, he took a deep breath and forced himself to stand away from the door, to cross slowly and with dignity to the tiny oratory built into the leaded window of the room. There he collapsed with a shudder, burying his face in his hands to pray.

God, what was he to do? He had tried so hard and for so long to do what was right, despite the awful quandary they had put him in by making him king—and then, in the same day, in the same hour, he had been cursed, induced to kill, and healed.

He shuddered, knowing he could not hope to reconcile the killing on his own—that would have to be worked out later, with his confessor, when he could think more coherently. True, the man was an assassin, and had deserved to die—had he killed him during the struggle, it would have been simple self-defense. But he, Cinhil, had not killed out of self-defense, nor even out of justice, but in anger, from fear of mere words. Though his act might have been technically lawful, he had done it for the wrong reason—and the Word of God forbade men to kill. Camber had been right to chastise him.

And the curse—had Camber been right about that, too? *Were* the curses of a Deryni enemy no more than those of ordinary men? How could he trust the word of a Deryni on such matters? After all, they had tricked him before, these men called Deryni—although, he grudgingly had to concede, he supposed they had always acted in the best interests of the kingdom.

But what of *his* best interests? What of Cinhil? Did he not matter? Was he forever to be only their pawn, their ill-made tool, to be used as it pleased them, for purposes fathomable only to them? He was a man, with an immortal soul—a soul they had already grievously endangered, almost past redemption. When they took his priesthood away, they had—

No! He must not allow himself to pursue such reasoning, to wallow in self-pity and impotent rage. This was an old battle within him, and one which he had fought many times, finally nearing a workable resolution. He must not let the pureness of his plans be sullied by thoughts of anger and vengeance. His inner peace must stay a thing apart from all of this—apart from all taint of killing and of cursing and of Camber.

Swallowing resolutely, he turned his thoughts to the set prayers of the hour, occupying himself for the next little while with the comfort of the familiar words. When, at last, he raised his head and opened his eyes, he felt far more at peace—until his gaze fell on the bloodied edge of his sleeve. Abruptly, he froze, his healed hand beginning to tremble as he recalled the events surrounding it.

He had never gotten used to the healing which

some Deryni could perform. It made him a little nervous, but also a little awed, despite his feelings about Deryni in general.

But he liked Rhys. Even the fact that Rhys had been one of those who took him from his monastery did not particularly prejudice him against the young Healer. There was something about him, and about the other Healers he had met since, which seemed somehow to set them apart from the rest of their race —as if their calling, even though sprung from Deryni origins, were somehow as divine as his own call to the priesthood.

He clenched his fist at that, noting in passing the absence of pain or other sign of his previous injury. Then he returned his attention to the bloodstain along the edge of his undersleeve. Standing, he shrugged out of the crimson outer robe with a grimace of distaste, letting it fall in a heap beside the prie-dieu as his fingers sought the fastenings of the under-robe as well.

But as he turned, his attention was diverted by a large, iron-bound chest at the foot of his bed. His breath caught for just an instant—and then, like a man in a dream, he was moving to stand beside it. His pulse rate quickened as he bent to let one hand rest lightly on its lid.

The chest—or, rather, its contents—had come to be his most cherished possession in recent months, though he dared not let anyone know that. Gathered clandestinely, sometimes at considerable risk of discovery, what lay within was an extension of that which had been forbidden to him: symbol of the life he had been ordered to abandon when he assumed the crown.

He would be gravely censured if anyone were to discover his intentions—and because of that, a little guilt nagged at the corners of his mind every time he opened the chest to add something else. But conscience mitigated that guilt to a great extent, for he was obeying a higher dictate than those which mere men might impose—even Deryni men. Nor would he be deterred from his final goal. He simply would be certain that no one found out.

Indulging a sense of secret joy, he dropped to his knees and touched hidden studs which would unlock the chest. His hands trembled as he raised the lid, and did not cease their trembling as he began to riffle through the contents.

The first layer was a distracter. He had planned it that way. He had thrown a little-used brown cloak on top of everything else so that a casual observer would be none the wiser—not that the chest was likely to be opened while anyone else was in the room.

But beneath the brown cloak lay the real treasures. He folded back the layer of brown wool to reveal a dazzling whiteness: priestly vestments, carefully gathered and hoarded and sometimes improvised—all there now, save the all-important chasuble, the outer garment worn to celebrate the Mass.

He ran his hands lovingly across the clean linen of amice and alb, the strong, well-woven cord of the cincture with its snowy tassels; brushed a reverent fingertip along the embroidery of a priestly stole before taking it out to clasp it longingly to his breast.

Someday, perhaps not too far away, he would wear these vestments and celebrate the Mass again, as he had not been permitted to do for a year and more. True, the vestments were not essential, for God would judge him by his heart, not his raiment. But the proper accoutrements were symbolic for him. He wanted his offering to be as pure, as perfect as he could make it.

He would not give up, on man's word, that which God had decreed for him from birth. No mere archbishop's formula could refute that. He was a priest forever, as the scripture said. What matter that he must be a king in public? In private, at least, he could be true to his vows and find his peace with God once more. He would be two men: King Cinhil and Father Benedict.

He reached out his free hand to fold back alb and

amice, still clutching the stole to his breast with the other, and glanced approvingly at the clean linen cloths lying beneath. Those would be his altar cloths, his maniples, his purificators and burses and veils and corporals. How his heart soared as he savored the name of each loved item!

And under all, carefully wrapped and packed away, lay his chalice and paten—a goblet of gold and a small golden plate which he had appropriated from the royal treasury only a few weeks ago, on a day when one of the lesser household servants had been in charge, and had not thought to wonder why the king might want such riches for his quarters—this king who was ordinarily so frugal and austere about everything.

He smiled as his hand patted the layers of linen back into place, touching the stole reverently to his lips before laying it on top of everything else. There would be a time, soon, now . . .

He lost himself in dreamy recollection of how it once had been, in fervent anticipation of a restoration of that time, until a knock at the door brought him abruptly back to the present.

"Who is it?"

He closed the chest and locked it and stood, in one continuous, guilty motion.

"It's Alister Cullen, Sire. May I speak with you?"

Cullen!

Cinhil gaped in dismay and glanced at the chest, almost considering whether the vicar general might be able to see through the strong wood of chest and door. Then he shook his head and smoothed his robe and moved quickly toward the door, knowing that even a Deryni could not do that.

He drew a deep, settling breath and wiped damp palms against his thighs before laying his hands on the door latch, letting out that breath and regaining control as he moved the bolt and peered through the opening he made.

"What is it, Father Cullen?"

"I was concerned about you, Sire. If you don't mind, I'd like to come in and talk. If you do mind, I can come back later."

Cinhil studied the older man's face carefully, reading no guile in the craggy features. Of course, he could not Truth-Read a Deryni, as he might an ordinary man, but Cullen appeared to intend no more than he had asked.

With a shrug, Cinhil lowered his eyes and stepped back from the doorway. Cullen murmured his thanks and entered, waiting until Cinhil had closed the door before making a short, formal bow.

Cinhil clasped his hands behind him and began pacing the confines of the chamber.

"You need not worry about my mental state, Father," he said after a moment of pacing. "As you can imagine, I was somewhat shaken by this afternoon's events. If I seemed ungrateful, I apologize."

"You did," Cullen said, not moving from where he stood. "You gave Rhys a very hard time."

"I realize that. I said I was sorry."

The king moved into the embrasure of the northern window and put a foot up on one of the stone benches. Cullen moved with him, to lean casually against the wall beside the window and study the king's back.

"You were rather short with Camber, too, don't you think? He was only concerned with your welfare."

"Was he?" Cinhil whispered. "Or was he merely concerned with the welfare of the new regime he's created? He put me where I am today, Father. If he doesn't like the way I do things, now that I'm here, he may just have to learn to live with it—as I have had to learn to live with my situation."

"And have you learned to live with your situation, Cinhil?"

The vicar general's voice was neutral in tone, but Cinhil froze for just an instant before turning his face away guiltily.

Could Cullen possibly know? Was the man reading his mind even now?

He swallowed and forced his thoughts to run along calmer lines. Of course Cullen was not reading his mind. He could not. With the powers and abilities which Cinhil had acquired from the Deryni, he was master of his own mind and of many other things. He *knew* that there was no way even for a Deryni to probe his thoughts without his knowledge and consent. There was no way that Cullen could know what he had been thinking.

He only half turned back, however, not willing to meet the vicar general's eyes, even so.

"It has been lonely, Father. But I survive."

"Only survive?"

"What more can I do?" He glanced at Cullen accusingly. "Your Deryni friends took from me what I loved most, giving the weight of a cold and heavy crown for the glow of my faith. Even those I thought I could trust betrayed me, in the end."

"Betrayed you?"

"Camber is most to blame, with his high ideals and righteous posturings. And the archbishop—he forbade me my priesthood, lulling me to duty in the world outside my monastery. And Evaine—" He looked down at his feet and swallowed audibly. "Evaine, whom I thought to be my friend, someone who understood—she used the confidence I placed in her to make me vulnerable to Camber and his magics.

"So now I stand alone and aloof—for I dare not trust again—stripped of my priestly authority, living in sin with a woman forced upon me, father of sickly babes—whose deformities I deserve for my transgressions—"

His voice caught in a sob, and he bowed his head, fighting back bitter tears. He might have succeeded, had not Cullen come and laid sympathetic hands on his shoulders.

With that, Cinhil dissolved into desolate weeping for all the terrors of past, present, and future, abandoning conscious thought to his misery, finding but little comfort clasped against the shoulder of the vicar general. Finally, when tears were spent and coherent thought began to return, he pulled away from Cullen and drew a sleeve across red-rimmed eyes. The silence grew awkward as Cinhil tried to regain his emotional balance.

"I'm sorry," he finally whispered. "I should be a better master of myself than that. For—for a moment, I almost felt that I could trust you."

Cullen bowed his head briefly, then looked up at Cinhil again.

"I want to help you, Cinhil," he said quietly. "I know this hasn't been easy for you. If there were some way I could undo what has been done, without endangering the kingdom—"

"That's the key, Father. You've said it yourself." Cinhil's tone was bitter. " 'Without endangering the kingdom.' The kingdom comes before the king—oh, I know that. In a certain, detached sense, I can even agree—if it were some other king." He sighed. "You'll have to excuse me, Father. I'm sure you mean well, but . . ."

He let his voice trail off disconsolately, knowing that no matter how sympathetic Cullen was, he was still Deryni, and bound to the course set by Camber and the others. He ran his finger along the edge of the window casement and looked out at the rain, though he did not really see it.

"Was there anything else, Father? If not, I'd really like to be alone for a while, if you don't mind."

"Nothing that can't wait until another time. Oh, there is one thing: Jebediah has called a final meeting of the war council in the morning, to finalize our battle strategies. He thinks, and I agree, that if you were there it might help morale. And try to be a bit more positive."

"As if they really needed me," Cinhil said whimsically. He turned to face Cullen. "What does an ex-priest know about fighting wars, Father? And even I, in my supreme ignorance, recognize the odds we face."

"Things change," Cullen said. "By then we may have additional information."

The words themselves were innocent enough, but there was some spark of anticipation in Cullen's tone which piqued Cinhil's further interest. Cocking his head, he eyed the vicar general curiously.

"Are you expecting some change of circumstances?"

"Not expecting—but we have hopes, of course. Why do you ask?"

"I thought I heard—some note of . . ." He glanced down at the floor, considering what Cullen had said—and not said—and looked up again, shrewdly. "No matter. Perhaps it was my own wishful thinking. Despite myself, I do care, you know."

"Sometimes thoughts are prayers." Cullen smiled. "By the way, I do have one piece of news which may not have reached you yet. I received it myself only yesterday."

"Yes?"

"As you will doubtless recall, the sees of Rhemuth and Grecotha have been vacant for some time now. Imre had declined to fill them, since he could not be assured of the election of candidates who would ignore his excesses. However, in keeping with your eventual plans to move the capital back to Rhemuth, Archbishop Anscom has decided to revive the Rhemuth archbishopric."

Cinhil nodded. "I knew of that. Robert Oriss, the vicar general of my old Order, is to be raised to the purple."

"A most deserving man," Cullen agreed. "What you may not have heard is that Grecotha is to be revived as well, and that the archbishop and synod have elected me to fill that seat. I'll be consecrated bishop with Robert in a few months' time, as soon as all this war business is over."

"*You*, Bishop of Grecotha!" Cinhil breathed. His initial glow of pleasure faded almost immediately to one of disappointment. "But that's a long way from here, and days away from Rhemuth. Then I shall *never* see you."

Cullen shrugged, a helpless gesture. "Even as Bishop of Grecotha, I expect to spend a certain amount of time in the capital, wherever that might be, Sire. But I appreciate your concern. I, too, have mixed emotions about the promotion, though for additional reasons. Certainly, I'll enjoy returning to Grecotha— I was partially educated there, you know. And I welcome the challenge of setting the diocese in order again. But it will be a grave responsibility to have the cure of so many souls in my care. And, of course, it will mean giving up my Michaelines."

"The Michaelines—that's right. I'd forgotten. You can't retain both offices, can you?"

"No, but perhaps my successor will be able to do better for them than I have done. It will take years to rebuild what we lost under Imre, even with the generous assistance you have given us."

"You lost it for me," Cinhil murmured. "Is there nothing more I can do to repay that debt?"

"Only pray for us," Cullen said simply. "And pray for *me,* if you will—for strength to know and do God's will in my new undertaking. I would value your prayers, Cinhil."

Cinhil stared at the other man for a long moment, then smiled tentatively, almost shyly.

"It is I who would be privileged to pray for you, Father—or should I say 'Your Grace'?"

" 'Father' is always appropriate. Or 'Alister,' if you wish."

"Nay, not 'Alister.' Not yet, at least. But a bishop," Cinhil repeated. "You're to be a bishop. What a wondrous thing!"

"Perhaps we can share a few of our mutual burdens, Sire," Cullen said, touching Cinhil's arm lightly as he turned to go. "You may tell me how it is to be a king, and I shall tell you how it is to be a bishop. At least that is not forbidden us."

Cinhil watched almost reverently as Cullen moved to the door and turned to bow.

"Thank you for coming, Father."

"Thank you for seeing me, Sire." Cullen smiled.

When he was gone, Cinhil sank back on the cushions of the window seat and let out a sigh.

Cullen to be a bishop, and Bishop of Grecotha at that! And just now, when it had begun to look as if he were one Deryni who might be trusted. True, Grecotha was not *that* far away, but still . . .

Even so, to have one in so high a place in sympathy, even if he *was* Deryni—that could not help but be useful. Perhaps Cullen could even be persuaded to restore Cinhil's priestly functions, after a time. Or Oriss, for that matter. As Archbishop of Rhemuth, he would be in an even better position than Cullen to permit a more suitable disposition of Cinhil's priestly status, especially once the capital returned to Rhemuth. And Oriss was human.

True, Oriss had not known Cinhil while Cinhil was a monk under his rule. Oriss probably had never even heard of the Brother Benedict Cinhil had been before Joram and Rhys spirited him out of Saint Foillan's Abbey.

Still, Oriss would be Archbishop of Rhemuth, second only to Anscom; and Cullen would be Bishop of Grecotha. Perhaps the day was not so far off as Cinhil had feared, when he might openly celebrate the Mass again!

He mused on that for a long time, dreaming of many yesterdays, then sat up with a start. The idea had flashed through his mind so suddenly that he could not even articulate it, dared not give mental substance to what was taking shape.

Quickly, before he could think about it too much and find a reasoned argument against, he scrambled to the bellpull beside his bed and rang for a servant. Sorle, his valet, appeared momentarily, breathless and anxious-looking.

"Sorle, please ask Father Alfred to join me," he

said, avoiding looking at the chest at the foot of his bed. "Tell him to bring parchment and ink. I have work for him."

Sorle bowed, somewhat mystified, and left to do his master's bidding. Cinhil threw himself on his bed and hugged knees to chest in sheer delight.

What a singular opportunity! With Cullen and Oriss slated for elevation to the purple, it was altogether fitting that Cinhil, as king, make them suitable gifts upon the occasion of their elevations. And what could be more suitable than several sets of new vestments apiece?

No one need ever know that not all of the vestments so commissioned would find their way to the two new bishops. No one would know that at least one set would find its way into the reverent and longing hands of Cinhil Haldane!

CHAPTER THREE

> For death is come up into our windows,
> and is entered into our palaces.
> —Jeremiah 9:21

Camber sat in a cushioned chair before the fireplace in his sleeping chamber, eyes unfocused in the direction of the fire, his feet propped comfortably on a padded stool.

He felt very peaceful now—ready to cope with whatever might come. After leaving the hall, alone at his own insistence, he had returned to his quarters to shed his bloody clothing and relax for a few minutes before beginning preparations for that evening's work.

Others also had plans for him, however. Guaire, who insisted upon acting as his squire most of the time, had appeared very shortly—obviously briefed by Joram or Evaine—and coaxed him to sit and soak in a hot bath, which Guaire had already had drawn. When Camber emerged, clean-clad and feeling far better than he had expected for the experience, there was a simple but hearty meal set for him before the fire: a joint of beef, cheese, crusty bread spread thick with butter and honey, and plenty of good red wine. He *knew* Evaine had had a hand in that.

He had not thought he could eat much. Besides, he had the feeling that he wanted to fast at least a little for the ritual planned later that night.

But Guaire was insistent, and Camber could not really tell him why he did not wish to eat; so Camber complied. Guaire stood over him sternly until he had consumed more than half of what had been put before him.

After, feeling admittedly restored, Camber dismissed Guaire on the pretext of wanting to rest—which was true, though not quite yet—then spent the next hour and more cleaning and arranging the dressing room to his satisfaction. Following that, he did rest, stretching out supine on the bed while he employed diverse Deryni relaxation techniques to ensure that he would be fresh and alert when the time came for him to do what he must.

When he awoke a few hours later, the room darkening into dusky twilight, he was feeling quite fit and ready. He spent the hour until the Vesper bell in more-active meditation, making the mental and spiritual preparations he felt necessary for the task approaching. The steady rain outside was a constant reinforcement to his intent, helping to drive him to ever-deeper centering points of consciousness.

What he planned tonight was not particularly dangerous, though the best-intended dabblings in this realm could turn threatening if one did not pay proper attention to what one was doing. He had checked his source document again, while he prepared the room, and the author had made the need for prudence abundantly clear.

But the prime consideration was precision, and the necessity for great concentration and a steady outpouring of energy. The results could be unsettling to anyone not anticipating all aspects, but Camber knew he would have ample support from those assisting him. There would be no faintheartedness from those four.

Their images flashed before him in the flames as he thought about them, and he allowed himself to dwell on each one lovingly: Evaine and Rhys, beloved daughter and new-found son, fearless and above reproach; Joram—not his first-born or even his eldest son, but the only son of his body now alive, dear *because* of his stubborn differences, not despite them; and Alister Cullen, gruff and often cynical, a former adversary but now a respected colleague and friend, even if he *was* sometimes suspicious of the magic which they wielded.

He yawned and stretched luxuriously, the scarlet velvet of his sleeve catching his attention in the firelight. He wondered again why the document required that he wear red for the operation he was going to try, remembering the look on Guaire's face earlier in the afternoon when he had asked the young man to search the wardrobe of the former king for just such a garment. The feel of the velvet against his body gave him a sense of comfort as he stood and moved quietly toward the door to the corridor. He opened it before the two outside could even knock.

Rhys and Evaine passed to the fireplace without a word as Camber bolted the door, the Healer settling onto a stool while Evaine curled up on the fur at his feet, her arms cradling something bulky and awkward in its wrappings beneath her cloak.

Camber moved back to his chair, but stood with

one hand resting lightly on the back as he gazed down at his daughter.

"Are the others on their way?"

Evaine nodded and began unwrapping the bundle in her lap, letting her cloak fall back from her shoulders in the warmth of the fire.

"Joram officiated at Vespers tonight, and Cinhil wanted to speak with him afterwards. Father Cullen is waiting for him in the sacristy. Will this bowl suit our purposes?"

Firelight flickered mellow and warm on the silver as she withdrew the bowl from its wrappings and put it into her father's hands, flashing quicksilver into Camber's eyes momentarily as he gazed at his distorted reflection.

"It's perfect."

He set it carefully on a chest near the door to the dressing chamber, very much aware of their eyes following his every move as he returned to the fireplace.

Rhys coughed gently to engage his attention.

"Can you tell us what you're planning now, or must we wait for the others?"

"I'd rather not have to explain it twice, if you don't mind."

They waited, Camber outwardly assuming an air of relaxation but inwardly vaguely uneasy over the delay. Finally he heard the muffled tread of footsteps approaching, and waved Rhys back to his seat as he himself went to the door. His hands were moving the latch even as the first faint knock sounded on the other side.

"Sorry we're late," Joram murmured as he and Cullen slipped through the opening which Camber permitted. "Cinhil detained us. I brought your incense."

"Thank you. Alister, were you able to get what I asked for?"

As Camber latched the door, Cullen reached into his habit and pulled out a lumpily folded packet of cloth, which he handed to Camber.

"It wasn't as easy as you thought. Some of the specific items you mentioned weren't there. Ariella may have taken them with her, or they're already being worn by the queen. I hope this one will do."

Camber sat in his chair and began unfolding the packet. Cullen, with a nod to Evaine and Rhys, dropped to one knee on the furs to peer over the arm of Camber's chair. Joram kissed his sister and touched his brother-in-law's shoulder in greeting before settling on a stool to Camber's right.

"Ah, the Haldana necklace!" Camber exclaimed.

He reached into the last folds of the fabric to withdraw a mass of diamonds and cabochon-cut rubies, none of them smaller than a pea. The stones flashed rainbow brilliance in the firelight as he laid the necklace across one hand.

Cullen leaned one elbow on the arm of Camber's chair and looked pleased with himself.

"You said you wanted something she'd worn a lot," he said in his gruff voice. "Now, would you mind telling me what you plan to do with it?"

Camber smiled and let his eyes focus through it softly, probing delicately with his mind. After a few seconds, he closed it in his hands and looked up at them.

"This will be our link to Ariella," he said in a low voice. "Using this as a focus, I should be able to project images from her mind on the surface of a bowl of blackened water. If we're lucky, I may even be able to manipulate those images a little, backward and maybe even forward in time."

Rhys's jaw dropped, and Evaine swallowed, and Joram lifted one blond eyebrow. Cullen pursed his lips and slowly shook his head.

"Are you sure you know what you're doing?"

Camber smiled. "I told you that you could be excused, if you wanted to be, and that offer still holds. But I don't really think your conscience is going to have any trouble with this one."

Cullen made a face and muttered something unintelligible under his breath, and Camber chuckled.

"Let's go into the next room, and I'll explain exactly what we're going to do."

Carrying the silver bowl, Camber led them into the room he had prepared. His clothing and other accoutrements he had put away in chests and garment presses, all of which had been shoved against one wall to block the door to another set of apartments not currently in use. The single, high window he had curtained off with a heavy tapestry, closing out the storm and the wan light of the rising moon. Even the garderobe shaft had been sealed off by a chest dragged over the opening in the floor.

In the center of the room, he had set a small, square table, covered with a white cloth. On it, a single candle lit a sea-green glass flagon of water and four new tapers partially folded in a linen napkin. A small, stoppered bottle nestled in the shadow of the flagon to one side.

Joram put down the small thurible he had been carrying and fished in the folds of his sash until he found a packet of incense. This he laid beside the thurible as Camber carefully set the silver bowl in the center of the table.

After locking the door, Camber rejoined the other four around the table, taking a place opposite the window. He laid the Haldana necklace beside the bowl, then reached inside the neck of his crimson robe to remove a small silver crucifix, which he placed on the table where he could see it.

"In a moment I'm going to ask you to help me invoke the four quarters and set wards, much as we did for Cinhil's ceremony of power," he said, giving what he hoped was a reassuring smile. "Rhys, you're fine where you are; you're our Healer, Raphael. Joram, please change places with Alister and come here, on my right; you are logically Michael. Alister, I'll ask you to speak for Uriel, in the north. Evaine is our Angel of the Annunciation, here beside me."

The appropriate shifts were made, and then an expectant silence settled around the table. The light from the single candle reflected off the bowl and cast a nimbus of candlelight on Camber's face. In front of him, between the bowl and the edge of the table, his crucifix gleamed friendly and reassuring beside the cold fire of the Haldana rubies and diamonds.

Camber took up the flagon of water and poured it into the bowl, a wistful lift to one corner of his mouth as he glanced aside at Cullen.

"This is water—nothing more. Alister, would you please bless it?"

"A simple blessing, or something more involved?"

"The latter, I think. Use the Paschal blessing with the necessary changes."

"Very well."

Taking a deep breath, Cullen extended his priestly hands flat over the surface of the water as Camber put the flagon out of the way behind him.

"I bless and consecrate thee, O creature of water, by the living God, by the true God, by the holy God, by that God Who, in the beginning, separated thee by His word from the dry land, and Whose Spirit moved upon thee."

With his hand he traced a cross on the surface of the water, then scattered some of it toward each of the four quarters so that it sprinkled each of the watchers.

"Who made thee to flow forth from the fountains of Paradise, and commanded thee to water the world in four rivers. Who, changing thy bitterness in the desert into sweetness, made thee fit to drink, and brought thee forth from the rock to quench the people's thirst."

Again he signed the water, this time bending to breathe thrice upon it, as God, in the beginning, had breathed upon the water with the Holy Spirit.

"Do Thou, with Thy mouth, bless these clear waters: that besides their natural virtue of cleansing the body, they may be effectual for the purification of minds. *In nomine Patris, et Filii, et Spiritus Sancti, Amen.*"

As he looked up, Camber handed him the four tapers.

"Now consecrate the tapers, please."

Handling the four as one, Cullen dipped the bases of the tapers into the bowl of water.

"May the power of the Holy Spirit descend into the fullness of this water, that it may purify all it touches." He removed the tapers. *"Per omnia saecula saeculorum."*

"Amen," the other four responded.

Cullen shook the excess water off the tapers, then handed them to Camber, who dried them with his napkin before giving one to each of them.

"We'll set the wards now. Rhys, when we're all ready, you can light your taper from the central one. Alister, I've purposely put you last so you can pick up the pattern and follow when your turn comes. Any questions?"

There were none—only returned gazes of varying confidence. With a brief smile of reassurance, Camber closed his eyes and bowed his head, fingertips resting lightly on the cloth covering the table. After a few seconds he could sense the new light as Rhys touched his taper to the central candle. He could feel the prickle of power beginning to build as Rhys spoke softly:

"I call the mighty Archangel Raphael, the Healer, Guardian of Wind and Tempest. May thy winds blow cool and sweet this night, to send us that which we must know. *Fiat, fiat, fiat voluntas mea."*

To his right, Camber felt Joram stirring, to reach across and light his taper from the central flame. His son's voice was firm and confident in the stillness.

"I call the mighty Archangel Michael, the Defender, Keeper of the Gates of Eden. Lend thou thy fiery sword as protection this night, that naught may keep us from that which we must know. *Fiat, fiat, fiat voluntas mea."*

The air was beginning to crackle around him now,

as Evaine brushed his left elbow in leaning out to light her taper.

"I call the mighty Archangel Gabriel, the Herald, who didst bring glad tidings to Our Blessed Lady. As we are born of water, so let knowledge be born of water here tonight, that we may learn what we must know. *Fiat, fiat, fiat voluntas mea.*"

The circle was almost complete. Camber let himself relax a little as Cullen's light joined the others.

"I call the mighty Archangel Uriel, Angel of Death, who bringest all souls at last to the Nether Shore. Mayest thou pass us by this night, and bring instead that thing which we must know. *Fiat, fiat, fiat voluntas mea.*"

As Cullen's final words ceased echoing in the dull hollow of the warded circle, Camber opened his eyes and looked at all of them again. Each face stared back at him with serenity now, even Cullen's reluctance lulled by the comfort of the gently glowing hemisphere which surrounded them at arm's length behind them.

With a smile of confidence, Camber picked up the central candle and elevated it a little.

"Air, Fire, Water, Earth—and Spirit." His eyes flicked to what was now the fifth light in his hand. "The unity of Man. All are joined in One within this circle."

He put the candle down again and took up the Haldana necklace.

"We come to the unknown portions now, my friends," he said easily. "We use something once belonging to the person with whom we hope to form a link—in this case, the necklace—and we use it as a focal point to concentrate on Ariella."

He hefted the necklace in his hand, then slid it gently into the silver bowl of water. The scarlet stones gleamed more quietly, seen through water instead of air; but none present, attuned as they were, could fail to notice a faint rush of chill as they stared at the gems—all of them already picking up residual energies of the woman who had last worn the necklace.

Camber took a deep breath, holding back his sleeve as he stretched forth his right hand and began tracing another cross above the water.

"Blessed be the Creator, yesterday and today, the Beginning and the End, the Alpha and the Omega."

The cross which he had traced glowed in aftertrail in the air above the water, the Greek letters steady at the east and west aspects.

"His are the seasons and the ages, to Him glory and dominion through all the ages of eternity. Blessed be the Lord. Blessed be His Holy Name."

As he spoke, he traced the symbols of the elements in the four quadrants cut by the cross: Air, Fire, Water, Earth. Beneath the pressure of his hand and will, the signs sank into the water and disappeared in a wisp of mist. When he looked up, the very quality of the water seemed somehow to have changed.

He could feel their eyes on him as he picked up the bottle and removed its stopper, pouring its crystal contents on the water in the form of an encircled cross. The clear liquid turned a dense black and began to diffuse as it touched the water. By the time Camber had set the empty bottle behind him, the water was completely black, the necklace totally hidden from sight, though not from mind.

Camber waited until the surface had settled, then drew breath again and glanced up at them all.

"Joram, you can start the incense now. And then I'll ask you all to hold your candles against the edge of the bowl at the four quadrants, and to link your energies so that I can draw on them. If all goes well, I should be able to see images on the surface of the water after a time. Possibly you'll see them, too."

He extinguished the standing candle at that, then waited as Joram opened his thurible and held his hand over the charcoal inside. After a moment, the charcoal began to smolder and Joram shook a few grains of incense on it. Sweet, pungent smoke began to spiral upward as he replaced the pierced top. He watched it briefly before looking up at his father.

"Do you want it here, or shall I move it behind us? It can get pretty strong."

Camber pushed it close beside the bowl, so that the smoke curled up along the silver side and rolled across the water.

"This will be fine," he said. "I want the benefit of both the scent and the visual smoke. Let's form our link now, and see what we can find out."

The other four moved closer to the table and set their tapers against the bowl, each instinctively reaching to his or her left to link with the right hand of the next person. Camber edged a little closer to Joram, so that he stood midway between him and Evaine, reaching between them to lay his hands on the edge of the bowl. His wrists rested lightly on their forearms, physically linking him into the bond which was about to be forged.

He closed his eyes and began clearing his mind, letting the incense and the stillness carry him into a state of relaxed receptivity. He became aware of the familiar minds surrounding and meshing with his own —distinct, yet blurred in the bonding which they mutually forged. He could feel their closeness, firm and supportive, yet undemanding, passive, as he slowly opened his eyes to gaze at the saltired reflection of candlelight on the silver-rimmed blackness.

Stillness. Anticipation. A crystal clarity of all senses, as he tuned his awareness and focused in on his own mental processes. He could feel himself slipping into an even deeper concentration, and he let it happen. His vision tunneled, blurring all around him until only the blackened water remained, incense smoke rolling across the surface like heavy fog.

He put aside all conscious thought, letting conscious and unconscious merge and focus on and through the blackness which was there and not. He let a mental image form of Ariella as he had last seen her—proud and arrogant—merge with his knowledge of the necklace hidden beneath the inky water.

Dimly, no longer aware of anything else around him other than the safeness, the reservoir of energy, he quested outward and inward for some thread which would draw her essence nearer. He kept his blinking to a minimum as an image began to form at the edges of his vision.

There! A face—indistinct at first, but then a wizened, ancient—no, an infant visage, which quickly expanded to include the whole body! A child of perhaps five or six months, one tiny fist clenched beside the pursed, petulant mouth. Wisps of fine chestnut hair feathered the shapely skull. The child opened slightly bulging eyes of rich, golden brown and seemed to look directly at Camber.

Could it be that he was seeing Ariella's child, through her own eyes?

The image wavered as Camber blinked, but he managed not to lose it entirely. His vision swam for a few moments, but then it cleared and a new image began to materialize—a map this time, with a ringed female hand sprinkling water on that map. The map itself seemed indistinct—he could not seem to make it quite come into focus—but then he realized that was because the person sprinkling it was not concentrating on the map, but on magic connected with the map.

He was watching Ariella work her weather magic!

He blinked again, inadvertently this time, and lost the image—tried desperately to reschool his thoughts to tranquility.

He must regain the contact! He must somehow try to redirect Ariella's attention to the map itself. Her strategies were what they most desperately needed.

He closed his eyes briefly to rest them, then stared at the blackness again, this time concentrating specifically on Ariella and her connection with the map— any map! He could feel himself slipping even deeper into trance, and let himself go. Images formed and reformed on the blackness, only to fade and be replaced before he could read them.

He *must* read them! He was so close, he dared not fail now!

Another deep breath, a stretching to his very limits of awareness, as he tried to reach across the miles and touch her sleeping mind, actually to manipulate her dreaming. Gently, he visualized a map of Gwynedd and its surrounding kingdoms, mentally marked the map with Torenth's capital, with Cardosa—and waited.

At first, nothing. And then, other markings began appearing on the map—notations and markings such as Cullen and Jebediah had been employing on their map earlier in the day. Hands moving markers, deploying troops.

Abruptly, he *knew* the location of all Ariella's strength, *knew* where and how many and what kinds of warriors she could throw into any assault!

He was almost ready to withdraw, when suddenly the picture blanked and he caught an almost mind-splitting explosion of rage. A wrenching pain lanced behind his eyes, temporarily blinding him physically as well as psychically, and he realized that he had been detected. His touch had been too clumsy, his direction too direct! Ariella was awake, and aware of his link—and she was trying to sustain the link he had created, to surge back across that link and mentally destroy him!

With a cry of pain, he blinked and wrenched his eyes from the blackened water, gasping for breath.

"Joram, get me out of it!"

He did not know whether Joram or the others had seen what he had seen, or felt the awesome menace of Ariella's retaliation; but Joram and Evaine, at least, knew exactly what to do in such a situation. Joram threw down his taper and seized his father's shoulders, pouring power and protection into his father's mind. As Cullen joined forces with Joram, protective instincts taking precedence over caution, Evaine snatched the silver bowl and hurried to where Rhys was already struggling to move the chest which covered the garderobe.

A wind roared outside, ripping the tapestry covering from the window and whistling into the room, but not inside the wards which they had set to prevent just such an incursion. The wind died as Evaine poured the contents of the bowl down the garderobe, and Camber relaxed in his son's arms.

The link was broken.

The room seemed to undulate as Camber opened his eyes, and the first thing that he saw was Joram's ashen face, the gray eyes stunned, dulled with exhaustion. Camber swallowed and managed to get his feet under himself again, but he had to lean on Cullen's arm until he could steady himself against the edge of the table. He took a deep, sobering breath, but he knew that he had nearly reached the limits of his physical endurance. His defense had drained him.

"I'm sorry," he murmured. "I'm afraid I pushed too hard. Is everyone else all right? Do you realize what happened?"

"You linked in with something bigger than you could handle," Cullen said gruffly. "What was it? Do you know?"

"You mean you didn't see?"

"See what?" Rhys asked. "I knew you were experiencing something—but until you started shaking, all I saw was candlelight reflected on that black water."

"I couldn't see anything either, Father," Evaine agreed.

"Oh."

Camber swallowed down a surge of nausea and let that sink in, finding it increasingly difficult to think coherently in his exhaustion. He tried to straighten up more, but his fatigued body refused to obey. Partially abandoning that fight, he let himself slump back against Joram again and closed his eyes, making a conscious effort to organize his thoughts.

Rhys's hand touched his forehead, and he felt the

cool touch of the Healer's mind against his, but he shook his head and opened his eyes again.

"I'll rest in a moment, Rhys—I promise. I got what I went for, though, and you'll need the information before I let myself collapse. Joram, if you'll release the wards, Evaine can get a map and pen. I have Ariella's troop strengths and deployment, and I think I'll have just about enough strength to make those notations before I have to sleep."

He gestured weakly with a hand which seemed almost not to belong to him, so heavy was his fatigue. Rhys took Joram's place, supporting him against the table, while Joram raised his arms to release the wards. As the silvery hemisphere dissolved away, the chill of the room assaulted them. Instantly, Evaine was unlocking the door to the sleeping chamber and rushing through.

Rhys and Cullen slowly walked Camber to his chair beside the fire, where Joram wrapped another robe around him. Cullen, when he had seen Camber safely ensconced, went to the earl's desk and brought back a map board. Evaine stood holding pen and ink beside a seemingly unconscious Camber. Cullen glanced at them all in concern.

"Is he all right?"

Rhys moved his fingers from his patient's pulse point to the temples and closed his eyes briefly, then nodded and motioned for Cullen to lay the map board across Camber's lap. As Evaine put the pen in her father's hand, Joram brought a lighted candle from the mantel and held it close.

Camber opened his eyes and took a deep breath.

"All right. Her main strength is here, and here, and here." The pen glided across the parchment, marking encampments and troop deployments.

"I'd say that close to a thousand men, most of them mounted, have already come through the Arranal Canyon approach and are now camped here, at Coldoire. Another eight hundred are here, at the foot of the Cardosa Defile, where she herself plans to join them tomorrow. They plan to rendezvous near Iomaire two days from now. Be sure that Jebediah studies this aspect in particular."

As Cullen and Joram nodded agreement, Camber closed his eyes and took another deep breath. His hand shook a little as he again dipped the pen in the ink which Evaine held.

"Now, this is also important. She has eighty extra knights here." He indicated a location. "And here. She's also considering a new foot route through this pass, which can accommodate several hundred men. If she uses it, we're vulnerable here and here, even if Sighere assists us. She has reports of his troop movements about a day's ride west of Iomaire, by the way.

"One last thing—she has a small body of men, perhaps as many as thirty of them, who seem to be some kind of elite bodyguard, or special shock troops, or something on that order. But they're more than that; there's something special about them that I wasn't quite able to read—only that Ariella seemed very pleased with herself about them. It may simply be that they're Deryni. I'll try to go back over that part in the morning, after I've slept, and see if I can remember anything else. They're quartered with her in Cardosa, for now, along with another five hundred of mountain cavalry."

His pen moved to the mountain city and drew a circle, with the figure *550?* in it. Then his hand relaxed and he almost dropped the pen. Evaine rescued it as he leaned back in the chair and let out a deep sigh.

"Is that all of it?" Joram asked.

Camber nodded and closed his eyes. "All that's important. More details later. Sleep now . . ."

As his voice trailed off, his entire body relaxed and he was asleep in a single breath. When Cullen removed the support of the map board from his lap, Camber slumped even deeper into the chair, his light, even breathing the only sound in the stilled room.

Rhys reached across and felt for a pulse, then glanced at his brother-in-law.

"He's exhausted, but he's only asleep—not in a coma. He'll be all right when he's rested."

Joram gave a relieved sigh. "Good. In the meantime, we ought to get this map to Jebediah and the others. Can you and Evaine stay with him? He probably ought to sleep under wards, too."

"We'll do what's necessary," Rhys replied, slipping his arms under Camber's. "Just help me get him to the bed before you go, will you?"

As Evaine ran to turn back the bedclothes, Joram picked up his father's knees and helped Rhys carry him to the curtained bed. There they laid him down gently, Evaine unfastening his belt and starting to remove his shoes and stockings as Rhys escorted Joram and Cullen to the door. When the two priests had gone, and Rhys had bolted the door behind them, Evaine glanced up at her husband, looking tired but content as she tucked the last of the blankets around her sleeping father's form.

"I've seen him this way before, Rhys. I'm sure he'll be fine in the morning."

"Don't tell me you've worked with him on these kinds of things before," Rhys said, checking his patient's pulse again while he peered briefly beneath a slack eyelid.

"On occasion," Evaine admitted. "Don't you approve?"

"You know I wouldn't dream of interfering, even if I didn't approve," Rhys replied with a grin, sitting back wearily on the edge of the bed as he watched his wife rummage in the purse at her waist. "I know how important your work with your father is to you— as important, perhaps, as my healing call is to me. Besides, I know that you take reasonable precautions."

"We try," she said with a droll smile.

Pulling out a small black suede leather pouch, she dropped to her knees beside the bed and began undoing the thongs which bound the end closed. When she dumped the contents on the bed, eight polished cubes came tumbling out, four white and four black. She glanced up at him as she began sorting them.

"Will you work the wards with me?"

"Of course."

Slipping to his knees beside her, he watched as she arranged the cubes in the necessary pattern: the four white ones in a square, all of them touching; the black ones at the four corners of the square so formed, each near but not in contact with its closest white neighbor.

"Go ahead and start," Evaine said in a low voice. "These are mine. You shouldn't have any trouble centering in."

With a nod, Rhys drew a deep breath and laid the fingertips of his right hand lightly on all four white cubes, closing his eyes briefly while he found the balance point with these particular cubes. Then he withdrew all but his index finger, to touch the cube in the upper left-hand corner of the white square.

"Prime," he said softly.

The touched cube began to glow with a ghostly, opalescent light.

"Seconde." He touched the cube to the right of the first one, and it, too, began to glow.

"Tierce." The cube below the first cube came to life.

"Quarte." As the last white cube lit, the four seemed to form a single square of milky light.

Rhys sighed and sat back on his haunches, watching serenely as Evaine drew a deep breath and brought her finger down on the first black cube. The glowing white square reflected off her hand and cast a mellow, moonlike glow on her calm face.

"Quinte."

Her low voice seemed to chime deep in the cube, which shone now with the iridescence of an ebon butterfly wing.

"Sixte."

The second cube, at the upper right, lit with the same quiet fire.

"*Septime. Octave.*"

As the last two black cubes were activated in rapid succession, Rhys came up on his knees again and picked up Prime, extending his empty left hand under his right arm to lie easily on the blanket. Evaine laid her left hand in Rhys's, then picked up Quinte and brought it toward his Prime. So joined, hand to hand, they also joined the two cubes, pouring in defensive energy as together they spoke the union *nomen:*

"*Primus!*"

A minute click vibrated through both their fingers as the two cubes touched and fused; and then they were holding a single, oblong rectoid which gleamed with a metallic brightness. Evaine laid it on the blanket and picked up Sixte as Rhys took Seconde. She closed her eyes as they brought Sixte and Seconde together:

"*Secundus!*"

Camber stirred a little in his sleep, perhaps unconsciously sensing the power being raised at his side, but he quickly settled down again as his daughter and son-in-law brought Septime and Tierce to:

"*Tertius!*"

Finally, "*Quartus*" was formed of Quarte and Octave. Of the four silvery oblongs now lying on the bed, Rhys took the last two and set them on the floor behind him, Tertius to his left, toward the head of the bed, and Quartus to the foot. Then, as Evaine moved around to the other side to place Primus and Secundus, Rhys sat down at the head of the bed beside his father-in-law, laying a sleep-deepening hand on Camber's forehead as Evaine paused at the foot of the bed to activate the wards.

Facing toward the first of them, she raised her arms heavenward and threw back her head for a moment, eyes closed, then opened them and pointed to each of the wards in succession as she spoke their names and the words of power:

"*Primus, Secundus, Tertius, et Quartus, fiat lux!*"

A silvery canopy of light sprang up around them with her final words, its edges defined by the limits laid out by the ward components. Evaine smiled as she came to join her husband, taking the hand he held out to her and touching it tenderly to her lips. Rhys sighed contentedly and leaned back against the headboard, pulling her into his lap with an arm around her waist. They had just settled into a comfortable position, she with her head smuggled in the hollow of his shoulder, when suddenly she giggled.

"A giggle at a time like this?" he whispered.

She pulled away to peer at him mischievously. "My love, you're going to giggle, too, when I tell you."

He raised one one eyebrow in question, the corners of his mouth curving up in anticipation of her explanation, as she brushed his lips with hers and laughed again.

"I was just sitting here, thinking about cleaning up Father's dressing room in the morning, and I remembered that, in the excitement, I dumped *everything* down the garderobe—including the Haldana necklace!"

"Surely you're joking!"

Evaine giggled again and shook her head. "And that means, dearest husband, that someone is going to have to go wading in the middens tomorrow and find it."

Rhys shook his head incredulously and drew her closer in amused disbelief.

"I knew things had gone far too smoothly," he chuckled, nuzzling her ear. "Now all we have to decide is who's going to do it. Let's see—who do we know who needs a little humbling?"

CHAPTER FOUR

For it is better, if the will of God be so,
that ye suffer for well doing, than for evil doing.
                                        —I Peter 3:17

In the end, it was not a humbled soul at all, but
Camber himself, who went into the middens to retrieve the Haldana necklace. He would not have
thought of relegating the task to any other man; besides, they dared not involve any outsider in what
they had done.

When Camber awoke the next morning, to find
Rhys and Evaine cuddled asleep in each other's arms
beside him, his head was clear, his body rested, and
his memory intact. He, too, recalled what had happened
to the necklace. After rousting his daughter and son-
in-law from bed, he dressed hastily and set Evaine to
straightening his quarters. Rhys he took with him.

In fact, it was not as complicated or as odious a
task as Rhys and Evaine had imagined it to be. On
reaching the dungeon level, where all the garderobes
of that range emptied out, Camber simply scanned
the moat directly beneath the appropriate shaft with
his mind, seeking lightly to reestablish the link he had
forged with the necklace the night before.

The water was almost clear from the past week's
rain, yet neither eyes nor mind could locate the necklace at first. But further investigation on Camber's part
soon revealed the necklace still inside the garderobe
shaft, caught just a yard or two inside its mouth.

Once Camber had reached up and disengaged the tangle—the jewels had fouled on weeds and other refuse—the necklace came away in his hand, intact and hardly the worse for wear. Camber flushed it with clean water from the well, when they came out into the courtyard again, then wrapped it carefully in a clean cloth he had brought for just that purpose.

He went back to his quarters to change then, giving the necklace to Rhys to return to Cullen, who would slip it back into the royal treasury later. Rhys remarked, just before they parted, that neither moth nor mite nor any other creeping thing would likely bother the robe which Camber had worn that morning; indeed, Camber would be fortunate if Evaine even readmitted him to his own chambers in such a condition.

Camber, with a delicate sniff at his sleeve, could only smile and allow that Rhys was indisputably correct.

Half an hour later, the Gwynedd war council convened in the great hall, this time with a surprisingly attentive King Cinhil present. All of the major battle leaders were there: Jebediah, sitting at the king's right hand as commander in chief; Cullen and Joram, for the Knights of Saint Michael and the other ecclesiastical knights; Camber, with young Guaire of Arliss, representing the Culdi levies; James Drummond, scion of a distaff branch of Camber's family, who brought the vast Drummond levies to Cinhil's aid; Bayvel Cameron, the queen's aging but brilliant uncle; Archbishop Anscom and four of his warrior bishops who also commanded lay forces; young Ewan of Eastmarch, eldest son of Earl Sighere, who had arrived during the night to speak for his father's allying army; and a score of lesser nobles whose varied levies had managed to reach the capital in time to give aid.

Their plans quickly solidified. Speaking with occasional prompting from Cullen, Jebediah outlined what had been learned of Ariella's strength and positioning, without divulging its source—if he even knew it—

and the war leaders haggled out a workable battle plan. Map boards were brought out, markers adjusted; and soon the clarks were drawing up final battle orders for Cinhil's signature. By the time the sun reached its zenith, winking bravely in a watery sky, the decisions had been made and appropriate orders dispatched, all under a compliant Cinhil's seal. They would leave at dusk that same day. Some of the lords left even then, to ready their men for march. Cinhil found himself left somewhat breathless by it all.

He tried to make some sense out of things, as his commanders began drifting from the hall to see to their individual responsibilities. The tide of their movements swirled around him but did not really touch him, for they knew that his approval in these matters had been largely for show. He was not, nor did he claim to be, a military man.

But even to Cinhil's unpracticed eye, the probable deployment of Ariella's army had shifted drastically since the last time he had thought to look seriously at a map board. That positions should change was not surprising, of course. And it was certainly to be hoped that their information would become more reliable as battletime drew near.

But he was amazed at the new confidence in the voices he had heard this morning. They had spoken in far more definite terms than he had been led to expect, based on the uncertainty and anxiety they had displayed the last time he had paid attention to a military planning session.

Cinhil admitted himself mystified by it all, for he did not pretend to understand a great deal of what had been discussed. And there was too much certainty around him now to think of questioning, of asking what might happen if things did not go as they had planned. Still, he worried.

Ariella was devious—even he knew this. Even if their information were correct—which was by no means certain, so far as he could tell—suppose Ariella changed her mind? Women did. Or, God forbid, suppose the information was incorrect to begin with—or, worse, deliberately false, set to mislead them? If either case were true, Jebediah and the other battle leaders were committing the royal Gwynedd levies to disastrous positions. He was surprised to find that he cared.

He asked Rhys about it later, when the last orders had been signed and sealed, and most of the others had hurried off to make final preparations for departure. He knew that, where military matters were concerned, Rhys probably knew little more than he did. Still, the young Healer had been silent but supportive all throughout the morning's long session. Cinhil wondered where he got his self-confidence.

"A word with you, Rhys?" he murmured as Rhys started to pass the chair where they had left him.

Rhys returned an easy smile.

"How may I serve you, Sire?"

"You may answer a few questions," Cinhil said, waving his squire aside and motioning Rhys to sit down beside him. "Everyone seems so resolute this morning, so certain of what is happening. Is this usual?"

Rhys ran a hand through unruly red hair and cocked his head at the king.

"Well, Sire, I really can't say, not being a warrior sort. One is supposed to appear optimistic, though. It gives the men courage."

Cinhil leaned back, unconvinced, studying the Healer through narrowed eyes.

"My studies indicate that realism is preferable, at least among the leaders. Father Cullen said something yesterday about new information which was expected. Could any new information be reliable enough to risk everything on it?"

"Those who understand these things seem to think so, Sire," Rhys said glibly. "Why, what did Father Cullen tell you?"

"That there was possibly to be some new information. Actually, he was rather evasive."

"I see."

Rhys glanced at the floor, as though considering what Cinhil had said, and Cinhil leaned forward to lay his hand on the Healer's arm.

"Rhys, you do me no service if you, too, are evasive," he said in a low voice. "What did he mean? Surely, if there was something important afoot, you would have been included."

"There was a—spy, Sire."

"A spy? For or against us?"

"For. He—glimpsed Ariella's battle plans and managed to bring them to us during the night. We—know that the plans are accurate—or were, when he saw them. So now we must move quickly, before she has time to change her strategy or consider how much we really might have learned. That is why we prepare to move out at dusk."

"A spy." Cinhil sat back in his chair and studied Rhys. The young Healer met his eyes squarely, but there was nothing there to read besides anticipation for what Cinhil might ask next. Cinhil pursed his lips thoughtfully, suddenly certain that there was more Rhys was not telling him.

"What else, Rhys? Come, now. I'm not a child. A spy at Ariella's court would have brought far more information than that."

Rhys raised a reddish eyebrow and regarded Cinhil evenly, appraisingly. "I hesitate to tell you this, Sire, but it's something you will have to learn eventually. As you know, Ariella was with child by Imre when she fled Gwynedd. What no one knew for certain, up until last night, is that she was safely delivered of a son a few months later. The child thrives, Sire."

Cinhil's mouth went dry, and he tried to keep his mind from darting, unbidden, to the children in the Valoret nursery. Why should a child of incest thrive, while his own—

He shook his head, forcing his thoughts from his own children to hers. If Ariella's child lived, it would be a menace to his throne in the years to come, even if they should manage to defeat and destroy its mother.

He tried to tell himself that it did not matter, but it did. It mattered a great deal. His sons, despite their ill-begotten origins, deserved peace when they eventually succeeded him. It was not fair that an incestuous bastard—

He hit the table with his fist, not noticing until he had done it that his nails had cut bloody half-moons in his palm. Rhys grimaced at the sound, and Cinhil took a deep breath to regain control as he looked up at the Healer again.

"Your news is unwelcome, but you did right to tell me," he said softly. "What—else did you learn?"

"That there may be arcane offenses on Ariella's part," Rhys replied. "We're certain that she's at least partially responsible for the bad weather. Now that we know, some of our more accomplished people can look for a way to counteract it."

"By 'accomplished people,' I assume you mean Deryni?"

"There is no other way to fight one such as Ariella, Sire."

Cinhil sighed, shading his eyes with his hand and shaking his head.

So, it had come to this. Despite everything, Deryni powers were to be used in this war. He shrank from that realization, as he shrank from his own recognition of the powers he himself held, given to him by the Deryni—shrank from the memory of what he had done with those powers the day before, in his undisciplined rage. His session with his confessor the night before had convinced him, more than ever, that use of those powers must be avoided whenever possible; the temptation was too great. And yet, another part of him acknowledged that their use might be required again, within the week.

He came back with a start as Rhys stood to bow, suddenly aware that someone was approaching from behind him, almost certainly Evaine and his queen. Carefully schooling his features, he turned in his chair to confirm, then also got to his feet to bow.

Megan—how she had frightened him at first, and still did. Not yet sixteen when they married, she had borne him three sons already—and she but a few months past seventeen now. But the year and a half of their marriage had not set easily upon her. The graceful, wide-eyed girl he had first seen on their wedding night was gone forever.

True, the wheaten hair still shone like mellow gold, and the dusting of freckles still played across the tip-tilted nose. But the turquoise eyes were sadder now, the fair brow furrowed in an expression of almost perpetual worry. She had dressed to try to please him, he knew, in a fur-lined gown of sea-blue wool. But the color only accentuated the drawn lines of her face, and the jeweled coif of a married woman and a queen made her chin seem pinched and gaunt.

He had ill used her, he knew—not through any physical abuse, but through his indifference, his aloofness, which hurt her even more. He regretted it, and yet he could not seem to help himself. He wanted to make amends, but he did not know how—not without compromising his own conscience even further.

He raised her up and kissed her hands, as any man might kiss the hands of his queen, then bestowed a fatherly kiss on her forehead. Megan raised her head at that, as though hoping for something more, but he turned away under the pretext of raising up Evaine.

"Greetings, my ladies," he said to all of them, as he kissed Evaine's hand and gestured for Megan's ladies-in-waiting to rise. "What means this invasion of gentleness here, in the hall of war?"

Evaine took Rhys's hand and leaned closer against him as she gazed across at Cinhil.

"I told Her Highness that you would ride out with the army tonight, Sire. She wished that we might arm you, as we did before your first battle. All is in readiness. Please do not refuse."

Cinhil glanced from Evaine to Megan, back to Evaine, and knew he was undone.

"I see I am outnumbered," he said lightly. "I surrender."

An hour later, bathed and dressed, he stood patiently in the center of his chamber while the women put the final touches on his attire.

It was similar to what he had worn that night he took the crown, though the need for real physical protection was much greater this time. Over silk and leather undergarments, he had drawn on the strange, gold-washed mail, which still retained that otherworldliness he had noticed the first time he wore it. Gold-chased vambraces were buckled to his forearms, with matching greaves over the leather breeches and boots which he had pulled on. Over it all, he donned the surcoat of scarlet silk, blazoned with the Gwynedd lion in gold. This time, it was Megan who buckled the sword around his waist, her fingers trembling as she fastened the white leather of the belt.

Sorle, his squire, was permitted to enter then, bearing Cinhil's shield and his great barrel helm with the coronet of Gwynedd. Cinhil inspected those items as if he knew what he was supposed to be looking for, then took the red gauntlets which Evaine offered and tucked them into his belt. His light, personal coronet he placed on his head before leading all of them downstairs to the Chapel Royal for Mass.

They were all there, as he had known they would be: Camber and Joram and Cullen and Jebediah and all the rest of them who had been in the war council earlier that day. Cinhil nodded to them as they fell in behind him to enter the chapel. Beside him, Megan walked with her head erect but her eyes following his every movement. Evaine had dropped back to be with her husband, and other ladies had also joined them for last moments with their loved ones. As the royal party took their places, kneeling in the now-crowded church, a choir began to sing the *Te Deum*. Cinhil bowed his head in prayer, all else put from his mind, as Archbishop Anscom began the Mass.

When it was over, and he had received his Lord in Holy Communion, Cinhil tarried for a little longer on the chapel while the others filed out—all except Megan, still kneeling at his side. One of the most difficult moments still lay ahead, he knew.

When they were alone, he stood to face his queen.

"My lord," she whispered, tears already welling in her eyes.

Cinhil shook his head and touched her chin lightly with one finger.

"Nay, little Megan, do not weep. I shall return soon. You must be brave, and guard our sons, and pray for me."

"I—will, my lord," she said, trying hard to choke back a sob. "But, if you should not come back, I—"

She bowed her head, unable to speak, and Cinhil gathered her awkwardly in his arms and held her close against his armor.

"Megan," he murmured, after a moment.

"My lord?"

"Megan, I'm sorry that I can't be exactly what you want me to be."

She pulled back to gaze up at him in innocence and trust. "Nay, my lord, do not say it. I am—most fortunate among women. Only—only, my lord is so often apart, and—"

"I know, Megan. I'm sorry. But I—am what I am."

"I know, my lord."

Her eyes were downcast, her lower lip quivering on the edge of tears again, and Cinhil knew he could not cope with that. Searching his heart, he found a possible way to ease her unhappiness without compromising his own resolution—if she would cooperate.

"Megan, will you do something for me? Something very special?"

She looked up at him immediately, her eyes alight with hope and anticipation.

Quickly, for he dared not let her raise her hopes for nothing, he knelt before her, taking her hands in his. She started to kneel, too, but he shook his head and put her hands together between his.

"Nay, Megan, do not kneel. What I ask is only within your power to give. I want—I need your blessing, to keep me safe in battle." With one hand, he reached up and removed his coronet, keeping her hands in his other. Then he bowed his head and released her hands, balancing his coronet on his upraised knee.

"Bless me with your love, my little queen," he whispered, praying that she would seize on this small act to sustain her—and him—through the rest of their good-bye.

There was a long silence, and for a moment he feared that she would refuse. But then he felt a gentle touch on his hair, the weight of both her slender hands on his head. He closed his eyes and tried to feel the emotions of her blessing as she took a deep breath.

"May the Lord our God go with you, beloved, now and forever. May He shield you in the shadow of His wings and keep you safe. May Almighty God have mercy on us all, and forgive us for what we have done. And may the Blessed Mother cloak you in her mantle and bring you back to me. In the Name of the Father, the Son, and the Holy Spirit, Amen."

Her hands left his head as she crossed herself, and he followed suit before looking up at her. Her tears were gone, a new serenity upon her face, as he stood and replaced his coronet. He took her hands in his again.

"Thank you, my lady. I shall carry that blessing into battle as a shield. But now—" He kissed one hand, then the other. "I must go."

He started to bend and kiss her forehead, as he had in the hall earlier, but suddenly she was standing on tiptoes and pressing her lips to his. He was startled and tried to draw away, but she clung the more tightly to him, a tiny sob whimpering in her throat as her mouth opened against his.

He was only flesh, he told himself a few moments

later, as he walked slowly from the church to meet his retinue. He could not have helped it—not without creating a scene and humiliating the young woman who had given so much for him already.

But another part of him yearned to turn back to her, where she knelt with downcast eyes at the altar rail. Another part yearned to take her in his arms again, and press her slender body next to his, and feel her gentle curves, even through the mail and leather he wore—to crush his hungry mouth to hers and drink so deeply—

He swallowed and glanced at the floor as he approached the doorway, grateful for the layers of mail and leather which shielded him now from view. Fortunately, it was darkening outside, an early dusk with the rainy weather, and he did not think they could see his flushed face very clearly. He busied himself with his gauntlets as he approached them, bending his head so that Sorle could remove his coronet and pull up his mail coif.

Then Cullen was laying the great, fur-lined cloak around his shoulders, and Cinhil was drawing the furry hood close around his neck and ears, striding down the chapel steps to where his war horse awaited him. Joram was already mounted on the other side, and Camber and Rhys sat their horses just ahead of his, Rhys nearest the steps, where Evaine stood with her hand on her husband's stirrup.

Cinhil nodded to Cullen as he gathered up his horse's reins, fingering the red leather thoughtfully as Cullen gave him a leg up and helped him get settled. He saw Sorle and Father Alfred mounting their palfreys, watched Cullen spring up on his own chestnut stallion.

Then the column was moving out, and a Michaeline knight bearing his Gwynedd standard was falling in ahead of him, and he was able to put her from his mind, his body already trading the anguish of his longing for the anguish of the saddle. It would be a long, long ride.

CHAPTER FIVE

*Am I therefore become your enemy,
because I tell you the truth?*
—Galatians 4:16

The royal army rode through the night, and through the dawn, and well into the forenoon, accompanied by a steady drizzle. Though the rain was not as heavy as it had been, still it soaked the horses and it soaked the men, and eventually soaked even the great lords in their oiled cloaks of leather and fur. Damp horses and men steamed in the watery sunshine as the sun rose higher in the summer sky.

They stopped just before noon to rest the men and to feed and water the horses, having traversed nearly the half of Gwynedd in their march toward the border. Though the pace had been stiff, however, not even the foot soldiers were unduly wearied; Imre had at least left a legacy of well-trained and conditioned men. It was their present king who was feeling the worst effects of the journey.

Cinhil's every muscle ached with the slightest movement, and tortured thighs and buttocks had long since lost their ability to torment him to any greater degree. Still ill accustomed to riding any great distance, though his general horsemanship had improved considerably, Cinhil had tried to catch what jolting sleep he could during the night, when the horses walked, knowing that those whose job it was would keep his horse with the others. But every session of trotting would jar his entire body anew. Compared to that, the few times of travel at the canter were sheerest bliss.

When they had stopped, Cinhil sat his horse unmoving for several seconds, wondering whether he still had the strength to swing down from the saddle without falling. He could not delay too long, for Jebediah and his lieutenants were dismounting all around him, and Cinhil knew that someone would be there shortly to take his horse.

He saw Guaire make his way among the other milling men and animals and approach, to lay his hand on Cinhil's reins. The young lord's earnest, human face was upturned in genuine sympathy.

"Do you need assistance, Sire?"

With a sigh, Cinhil shook his head and started to dismount, the sigh turning to groan as he tried to swing his right leg clear of the high cantle. He succeeded, but his face was white with the effort by the time he got on the ground, his legs trembling beneath him as he supported himself briefly against the stirrup.

"Are you all right, Sire?" Guaire asked.

"I'm fine," Cinhil whispered.

The area in his immediate vicinity was clearing rapidly, as his companions led their horses away to be watered, and almost before he realized, Sorle was beside him and unfolding a portable stool. As soon as its legs were seated in the muddy grass, Cinhil sank down gratefully, stretching out first one leg and then the other, wincing as cramped muscles protested. Guaire took his horse away, and Cinhil closed his eyes and tried to make himself relax. When he looked up again, Rhys was crouching beside him with bread and cheese and a cup of wine. The Healer looked tired but relaxed as he put the cup in Cinhil's hand.

"Drink, Sire. A little food and wine will help revive you."

Cinhil raised the cup and drank thirstily, not thinking until he had nearly drained it that it might contain something besides wine. The Healer had drugged him once before, without his knowledge or consent, and the memory still rankled.

But it was a little late to worry about that, he realized as he lowered the cup. If Rhys *had* put something in the wine, it was already in him, working its function—and this time, it could not be a sleeping potion or some such, for Cinhil must remain functional. Besides, despite Rhys's Deryniness, he was a Healer, obeying a code of ethics as stringent in its way as Cinhil's priestly vows; and by that code, he could do no harm.

Cinhil held out his cup for a refill and took a chunk of bread and cheese in the other, noting that the Healer looked across at him in faint amusement, eyes straw-amber in the hazy sunshine. The healing hand was steady as it poured into the cup and gave the flask into Sorle's keeping.

"I seem to recall another time when you ached like this, Sire," Rhys said with a smile. "Will you let me try to ease your discomfort? This has been a prodigious journey for you."

Cinhil could not prevent a smile from working its way around a mouthful of bread and cheese. Not for the first time he wondered whether a Deryni really could read his thoughts without his knowledge.

"I fear I will never be a prodigy where horses are concerned, Rhys. I also doubt that there is much you can do for me this time—unless, of course, this cup is like the one you gave me when last I rode like this."

Rhys shook his head with an easy nonchalance. "I fear 'tis only wine this time, Sire." His expression indicated that he remembered exactly what Cinhil was thinking. "However, with your cooperation, perhaps I can undo a little of what your ride has cost. If I may?"

In question, he laid one hand on the king's knee, and Cinhil shrugged and nodded. With a breath that was like a sigh, Rhys bowed his head in healing concentration.

Already fancying that he could feel the results of Rhys's efforts, Cinhil raised his cup and drank again, more freely now that he knew the wine to be untainted. He watched over the rim of the cup as Camber and Cullen and Joram approached, nodding and taking another bite of cheese as the three drew near enough to bow.

"All goes well?" he asked, looking from one to the other of them.

Camber nodded. "We make good progress. But we dare not stay here too long—only enough to rest the horses, and then we must be on our way. We should reach our campsite well before nightfall. Our scouts report that Ariella's forces should be in that vicinity at about the same time."

Cinhil finished chewing his mouthful and swallowed, glancing around thoughtfully. "You seem confident of that. Suppose she changes her plans?"

"Strategies may change," Cullen said, "but the site of battle is more or less committed by now, unless the entire timetable is drastically revised. By riding all night, we have cut off at least one of her options for other attacks. Of course, there are still enough unknown factors to keep things complicated," he added with a wry smile.

Joram gave a grim chuckle at that, and Camber studied the tips of his steel-shod boots.

Cinhil was suddenly aware that all three of them were tense beneath their calm façades, and were trying not to communicate their tension to him. Even Rhys raised his head and looked up at them, rocking back on his heels, his ministrations apparently finished.

Cinhil was confused.

"The weather seems to be improving," he finally said, gesturing toward the sky with his cup before taking another sip. "Is that your doing?"

Camber appeared reluctant to answer, but he met Cinhil's gaze squarely.

"Sire, a number of people have been working through the night for that—at considerable expense of strength and health, I might add. Since we do not know the specifics of the spell Ariella uses, we must try a number of counterdefenses, hoping one will prove effective."

"Are all of you involved in this?"

"None of us directly, Sire. As I said, it takes a great deal of energy, which we in the field cannot spare just now."

"Well, at least it's out in the open now," Cinhil said, with a grimace of distaste. "Magic. No couching of things in euphemistic terms. You employ your Deryni powers—not you specifically, perhaps—but your Deryni do these things."

"If Your Grace would rather ride and battle in a storm, that can probably be arranged," Cullen muttered.

Cinhil opened his mouth to speak, a shocked expression on his face, but Cullen held up a gauntleted hand and shook his head.

"Nay, do not answer to that, Sire. It was not worthy. I spoke in frustration and fatigue. But Your Grace must surely know me by now to be a prudent man in these matters. I would not condone wanton magic, no matter what the cause. Yet even I must realize the necessity of what is being done. We dare not quibble over methods when it is survival we fight for."

Cinhil lowered his eyes and set bread and cheese atop his cup, put all on the ground beside him, no longer hungry.

"Still, I like it not," he murmured low. "In truth, I have great reservations about all your abilities. God does not grant such powers to ordinary mortals."

"Are you not mortal, Sire?" Cullen said.

"Aye, and I like not my powers, either."

Silence surrounded them all, an ominous, palpable thing, until Joram cleared his throat with a nervous cough.

"Sire, this is neither the time nor the place to discuss such matters. We are all tired, and what seems frightening now, in the face of impending battle, may seem far less threatening in the safety of Valoret once more. For now, I would ask that you consider only a single gift sometimes granted to our people."

Laying a hand on Rhys's shoulder as though in benediction, the priest gazed across at Cinhil, the gray eyes direct, unwavering, slightly defiant.

Cinhil felt his throat constrict, and suddenly he could no longer look at them. Even he could not deny the benign nature of the Healers' gifts—especially now, in the face of combat. Without the Healers, and there were others besides Rhys in their company today, tomorrow's battle would cost even more in blood and pain and lives than war's usual wont.

He put his gloved fingertips together across his knees, and the scarlet leather was like blood on his hands. He closed his eyes, unwilling to look at them.

"You strike me where you know me to be vulnerable," he whispered. "You know that there is no argument I can make where the lives of the men are concerned. You have made me responsible for them. I cannot deny that responsibility."

"In truth, the magic which so worries you will be little used, once the fighting begins," Camber said. "In battle, there are far too many variables, all changing far too rapidly. The most potent spell can be of little use if the wielder of the spell has his head lopped off before he can craft his magic."

"Then there will be no magic used in the battle?"

"I did not say that," Camber replied. "Should any of us come to face Ariella in single combat, we will undoubtedly be forced to draw upon any and all of our various talents. In the greater battle structure, however, the menace of grand magic will certainly decrease. We're in a fairly strong tactical position, despite our lesser numbers, since we know Ariella's strength, while she can only guess at ours. Victory does not always go to the side with the larger army."

Cinhil pondered that for a moment, head bowed thoughtfully in his hands, then looked up at the sound of horses being led toward him. Guaire had retired

Cinhil's previous mount to the baggage train, where the extra horses traveled, and had brought up Cinhil's spare, a smaller dapple-gray with a smoother gait than the albino he had been riding. The gray nickered as he spotted Cinhil, and almost brought a grin to Cinhil's face.

"Ah, Moonwind," Cinhil murmured, almost to himself. He stood, slightly bowlegged, and eased a gauntleted hand against the small of his back. Every abused muscle protested as he approached the animal and held out his other hand to the soft muzzle.

"Thank you, Guaire. I suppose this means we must be off again?"

Guaire chuckled as he gentled the horse, turning its near side toward Cinhil so he could mount. The stallion was restless, and Guaire had his hands full keeping him still.

"I'm afraid it does, Sire. Lord Jebediah is most eager to reach our campsite before dark. At least Moonwind will carry you more gently, these last few hours, once he's run a little. We suspected that Your Grace would be saddle-weary by now. That's why we had you start out on Frostling."

Around them, the others' horses were being led up by grooms and squires, noble riders swinging into well-worn saddles with easy familiarity. As Cinhil gathered up Moonwind's red leather reins, not yet having summoned the strength or courage to resume his place of torture in the saddle, he watched Camber and Rhys and Joram mount. A Michaeline serving brother brought Cullen's chestnut around, but the vicar general, instead of mounting, came over to Cinhil and gave a slight bow, offering his laced hands to give Cinhil a leg up.

Cinhil accepted readily, grateful for the assistance, but even with Cullen's help, it was all he could do to haul himself back into the saddle. As he settled, searching in vain for a comfortable position, Moonwind danced and fidgeted between his thighs. Every step sent new torment lancing through his body.

There was no time to feel sorry for himself, however. As Cullen mounted up beside him, Jebediah fell into place on the other side, signaling for immediate departure. They set a much faster pace for the first little while, and surprisingly, the rolling canter helped. By the time they had been riding for perhaps a quarter-hour, Cinhil seemed to reach a plateau of pain, beyond which he could feel nothing else.

After that, his legs settled down to a dull fatigue, and Moonwind was much more willing to go easily, and he could think about other things.

He was frankly curious about what Camber and the others had said of magic—though he would never have admitted that to them. He wondered about what Camber had said of "people working through the night," wondered whether those who worked thus were with them, or safely in the keep at Valoret, or even ensconced elsewhere, in a place of which he did not know.

He scanned the men around him as they passed, sending out tentative probes of questioning; but the humans would not have been capable of what Camber described, and the Deryni were all tightly shielded, each man wound up in his own thoughts and preparations for what lay ahead. He could have forced their attention—but he did not want that—God knew, he did not want that! He was afraid to let himself become more involved, afraid that he might unleash something within himself that he could not control. No, better to keep dormant the magic he had been granted, unless there was no other way.

The sun came out in full splendor by late afternoon, the last rain clouds melting away with the sinking sun. Either Camber's Deryni cohorts had succeeded, or else Ariella had given up on that particular harassment. Whichever, Cinhil was grateful.

He had ridden alone with his thoughts for some time. Camber and the others had left him with a royal escort, perhaps an hour earlier, to ride to the head of the van and confer with the advance scouts. But as the huge column slowed and he detected signs of deployment for camp, he saw Cullen riding leisurely back along the line toward him. Cullen nodded as he fell in beside Cinhil once again, the sea-pale eyes respectful and without guile. The sun cast long, sharp shadows on the hoof-churned ground ahead of them as they rode.

"We'll be camping at the base of yonder ridge, Sire. Your commanders are riding to the top to survey the lay of the land beyond. Will you join us?"

With his crop, he gestured toward a small knot of riders detaching themselves from the main van, the banners of Culdi and the Michaelines prominent among them, as well as the Gwynedd banner designated for Jebediah's personal use as commander in chief. Cinhil sighed and gestured for his own royal standard-bearer to follow as he swung out of line and followed Cullen toward the hill.

They cantered easily in silence, the men saluting as they passed, until they reached the crest of the ridge, where the others waited. Cinhil acknowledged their gestures of respect and eased his gray between Jebediah and Camber.

Jebediah shaded his eyes against the sun as he turned to glance at the king.

"We've met them, as we hoped, Sire. All appears to be exactly as we were told. Look over there, against the far ridge—do you see the movement?"

Cinhil narrowed his eyes and tried to focus in, standing a little in the stirrups.

"What am I looking for?"

"The glint of sun on steel, mainly. We suspect they're preparing to make camp there, at the base of the ridge. I don't know whether they've seen us yet."

Cinhil let himself settle back into the saddle, not taking his eyes from the moving specks of the enemy, now that he had found them. Suddenly, he wanted it over, one way or the other. He dreaded the night, with its waiting and sleeplessness and growing terror of the dawn. Even if he died, better than this uncertainty.

"Could we attack now, and take them by surprise?" he heard himself saying.

He could sense their exchanged glances, and immediately regretted the short shrift he had given his military studies, resolved to remedy that deficiency in the future. What had made him ask such a foolish question?

"The distance is deceiving, Sire," Jebediah said, almost without a pause. "It's half an hour's ride across the plain—more, with our horses not rested. It would be nearly dark by the time we even engaged—no time to be fighting a battle such as this."

With a sigh, Cinhil nodded and glanced down at his hands, crimson gauntlets on the red leather reins. Reaching back in memory, he called forth words they had taught him, willing his panic to cease, his pulse to slow, his features to relax. When he looked up, he appeared to be in control, completely at ease. He knew the façade was deceiving none of them, but somehow the illusion helped.

"You're right, of course, Jebediah. Do whatever you think best. Do we camp here, then, and trust that she will not move in the darkness?"

"We camp, but we do not trust," Jebediah said, with grim-lipped determination. "We will set sentries on the perimeters, and keep scouting parties out all night, and be ready to move at dawn. We will also set protective wards about the camp, unless you raise strenuous objections. I want the men to have a good night's sleep, with nothing from outside to mar their dreams."

Cinhil gulped. "She could enter men's sleep?"

"She might disquiet it. I prefer not to take chances. Every man must be in his best fighting condition, come the dawn."

With a curt nod to hide his resurging fear, Cinhil backed Moonwind out of the line and wheeled to go back down the slope. He did not want to think about what Jebediah had just said—and the silence of the others only confirmed that the Deryni commander was right in his estimation of their danger. As he rode, he scanned the sea of milling men making camp below, searching for the familiarity of his own household and servants. He saw Sorle and Father Alfred supervising the setup of his pavilion near a small stand of trees, and headed toward them gratefully.

Little eased his apprehension, however. Though Cinhil talked with Father Alfred for nearly an hour, as the shadows grew and camp was made around them, the young priest was able to offer little in the way of comfort. At length, when it was obvious even to Cinhil that such conversation was not the answer, he thanked the man and dismissed him, heading slowly toward the now-ready pavilion.

Nodding miserably to the guards, boots squishing in the damp earth, which was fast turning to mud beneath the feet of so many men and animals, he came at last to the entrance. Sorle was waiting to take his helmet, and drew aside the flap as his master approached.

"You have guests, Sire," he murmured.

By the glow of rushlights already burning in shielded holders, Cinhil could see Joram and Cullen crouching beside a small brazier set in the center of the tent. Helmets and gauntlets lay on the heavy carpet beside them, and mail coifs had been pushed back from heads of gold and grizzled gray. Other than that, both men were still fully armed, well-used mail gleaming in the rushlight at throat and sleeve, broadswords buckled over blue Michaeline surcoats.

They rose respectfully as Cinhil entered, Cullen still warming his hands over the brazier. Joram nodded and moved a camp chair closer to the brazier for the king.

"The campsite is nearly secured, Sire," Joram said. "After some discussion, it's been decided to set watch-wards rather than protective ones. Watch-wards require a far lower level of magic to maintain, and aren't even activated unless something tries to pass. They'll put fewer restrictions on our own men moving within the camp. Most won't even know they've been set."

Cinhil eased down on the chair and unbuckled his sword belt, letting the weapon slide to the carpet beside him. Fatigue washed over him like a physical thing as he let his shoulders relax, almost dulling his realization of what Joram had just said.

"Is that intended as a sop to my scruples about your magic?" he asked, in a tone which did not expect answer. He stripped off his gauntlets and slapped them halfheartedly against his knee, wincing at the pressure against abused muscles. He heard Cullen sigh.

"Cinhil, I know how you feel about it, but I thought you understood why it was necessary. It would be useful if we can all wake up rested and sane in the morning. I cannot guarantee that, unless we can ensure that there will be no arcane meddling while we sleep. The watch-wards will provide that insurance."

Cinhil looked up, biting off a tart retort.

"My understanding and my approval do not necessarily coincide, Father Cullen. I comprehend the reasons for your actions, but do not ask me to sanction them."

"But you'll not forbid them?" Joram asked.

"No, I'll not forbid them. That's what you would have me say, isn't it? I have no more wish than the next man to die before my time. However, I prefer to know nothing else of your methods."

"Very well, Sire. I'll complete the arrangements and not trouble you again."

With a curt bow, Joram gathered his belongings and left. Cullen stood silently for a moment, while Cinhil stared at the carpet, before gesturing toward a campstool.

"May I join you for a few minutes?"

"If it pleases you."

"Hardly a cordial invitation, but under the circumstances I'm grateful even for that."

He hooked the stool closer with a booted toe and straddled it, settling onto its seat with a soft clash of well-oiled mail. Cinhil watched him with a mixture of curiosity and annoyance, wondering what further the Michaeline thought he could say to him, but Cullen only gazed back at him expectantly.

Irritated, Cinhil pushed back his own coif, ruffling silver-winged hair with a hand which trembled with fatigue. In exasperation, he lowered his head into both hands, mailed elbows resting gingerly on aching thighs.

"Well, Father, what is it? I'm exhausted and angry and, quite frankly, frightened. I haven't the patience to argue with you, or to indulge in an evening of soul-searching or mind-stretching."

Cullen shifted position, to the jingle of mail against leather. "Nor have I, the night before battle. We all need our rest. But I sense that something is disturbing you—something more than your annoyance that Deryni powers must be used or your fear that we may all die tomorrow. I saw you talking with Father Alfred. I also saw that you seemed to derive little comfort from his counsel. I thought an older man might be better able to ease your heart. We are almost of an age, you know."

Cinhil closed his eyes, not certain he wanted to go in the direction Cullen was leading.

"I am quite satisfied with Father Alfred as my confessor."

"I'm sure you are. He's a fine, capable young priest. Were he not already in your service, I would be greatly tempted to lure him away from you for my staff, when I become a bishop.

"But he is also young enough, almost, to be your son, Cinhil; and he has little experience dealing with the forces which you and I, for different reasons, must learn to cope with. I offer myself not as a confessor but as a friend. We are alike in many ways. Could not our likenesses help to bridge our differences?"

Cinhil swallowed, not daring to look up. He knew what Cullen was asking. It was a reiteration of the offer he had made a few days earlier, when they had talked about sharing the respective joys and woes of royal and episcopal duties. He wanted it, in many ways; he needed such a friendship. But there was that about Cullen, about all Deryni, which frightened him still—especially tonight, on the eve of battle, when God knew what powers might be unleashed in his name when the dawning came.

It was the not-knowing that frightened him most—the dreadful suspicion that the Deryni might serve another Master, to the damnation of all their souls. Suppose that all he had seen and heard was sham, staged for his benefit, to beguile him into believing their powers were benign? In the monastery he had heard tales of the atrocities committed under the Festils—their blasphemies and abominations, not the least of which was Ariella's incestuous union with her own brother. And what might he *not* have heard, sheltered as he had been?

He shuddered a little at that, glancing up quickly to see whether Cullen had noticed, but the vicar general only gazed at him expectantly, ice eyes seemingly lit by sunlight at their depths, in as open and hopeful an expression as Cinhil had ever seen on the weathered face.

Almost, and Cinhil reached out to him. Almost, and he surrendered to the temptation to trust—to open up, to put his faith in another person, to confide his fears and sorrows, all his misgivings about himself and the world which had been thrust upon him.

But the moment quickly passed. He could not do it —not now, here, tonight, surrounded by all those other Deryni, by Camber and his allies. He dared not trust Cullen. Not yet.

With a sigh, he shook his head and threw his gauntlets on the floor beside his sword. His eyes, as he looked up at Cullen at last, were red-rimmed and almost teary.

"I thank you, Father Cullen, but it grows late and I ache in every bone. If you will only keep me informed of any change of plans, that will be sufficient for now. I wish to retire early."

"As you wish, Sire."

With downcast eyes, the vicar general picked up helm and gloves and stood, glancing guardedly at the king. He started to speak again, but then he merely bowed and strode out of the tent without a backward glance.

Cinhil sat very still for several minutes after he had gone, wondering.

His discomfiture did not ease, even after supper. Though he cleaned himself, and heard Vespers, and readied himself for bed, sleep would not come. For hours, it seemed, he tossed and fretted on his pallet, dozing fitfully, dreaming horribly when he did. At one point, he even roused himself and lit a rushlight for a time, staring mindlessly into its feeble flame while he tried to school his thoughts to tranquility and his body to rest.

Finally, in the dark of early morning, several hours before he might expect the dawn, he got up and dressed in his riding leathers, omitting mail and other armoring in favor of comfort. Wincing as he pulled boots onto saddle-aching legs, he waved Sorle back to his pallet outside the entryway when the squire came to investigate his movement. He paused to strap a dagger at his waist, for he supposed it was not proper for a king to go totally unarmed within a military camp, then threw the great black cloak around his shoulders and secured it at the throat, drawing the fur-lined hood close to his head. Then he slipped outside the pavilion to prowl the encampment. The soreness in his muscles eased as he got his circulation going.

He was not challenged. Word went before him, from his own pavilion guards, that the king walked the camp, and wished to do so alone and unheralded. But he did not go unnoticed. He could feel the guards' eyes following his progress as he went, knew they must be relaying word of his passage to their fellows ahead in some manner unknown to him—though he knew it was not magic, since most of them were human.

When he headed toward the crest of the ridge, to look out at the enemy watch-fires, one of the guards detached himself from his fellows and followed at an unobtrusive distance. Cinhil ignored the man as he slipped into the shadow of a tree trunk and gazed out across the empty plain.

The silence was profound. That was what struck him first. Even the normal night sounds of the countryside seemed muted. Horses whickered and stamped their feet softly in the hollow behind him, and guards' harness clinked nearby as they shifted and paced in the night chill.

Far in the distance he could hear cattle lowing in their pens, and that reminded him that this was part of Gwynedd's heartland, the real reason for their presence here tonight. The moonlight turned the plain to a sheen of silvery frost, dew on spring wheat and tender grasses. A shudder went through him as he imagined that plain tomorrow at this time, with the carnage of battle staining its soil. He realized that he had never seen the grim reality of violent death on such a scale.

He turned away at that, wrapping himself more tightly in his cloak as he picked his way back down the slope. Eschewing the watch fires of the guards, he made his way among the picketed horses until he found his Moonwind and Frostling. Both of the animals raised their heads to whuffle greeting, and the gray butted a velvet nose against his chest in rough affection. For a long moment, he buried his face in the warm neck, losing himself and his worries in the scent of soft, dampish horse while he scratched Frostling behind the ears.

But such creature comforts did not last long. Soon his restless feet and mind took him back into the main encampment, to slip quietly and somewhat stiffly with the morning damp along the silent tent rows and mounds of equipment. Almost unconsciously, he found himself drawn toward the main Michaeline pavilion—the one assigned to Alister Cullen. He wondered whether the vicar general was sleeping better than he had been able to do, wondered whether he himself might now be sleeping soundly, had he taken the hand which Cullen had offered in friendship.

Then he realized that there were low voices coming from inside the pavilion.

He glanced at the sky. The blackness told him that it was still several hours until dawn, and the stars pinpointed the hour even more precisely—it could not be more than the fourth hour past midnight.

He paused in the shadows to listen, slowly becoming aware that the voices emanating from the pavilion were not just random conversation. Sometimes they spoke in unison, with an eerie cadence which raised the hackles at the back of his neck, haunting both in its strangeness and its near familiarity. Other times, one voice or another spoke alone. He could not identify the owners, but one of them could only be Cullen himself.

He closed his eyes briefly and tried to pick out words, but to no avail. That part of him most easily frightened began to imagine demons in the shadows—eerie hobgoblins of doubt that picked and clawed at all his confidence.

What were they doing? Who was in there? Did they perform some arcane Deryni ritual of which they knew he would disapprove? Was that why they worked this way in darkness, when all the rest of the camp was asleep? Had they thought to hide it from him, thinking that he, too, slept obliviously?

No hesitation remained in his mind. He had to find out. Glancing around casually to see whether any of the guards had marked his presence in the shadows, he used his heightened awareness in mental quest—no one even seemed to be thinking about him.

One final glance around him, and he was on his

way, gliding across a short stretch of open moonlight to crouch in the darkness at the side of the pavilion where an overlap of canvas was laced with leather thong rather than sewn. His pulse was racing by the time he got there, and for the first few seconds he could hear nothing but the pounding of the blood in his temples, the beating of his heart.

He took a deep breath, soft, and willed himself to relax. After a moment, he found the courage to raise numb fingers to the overlap of the tent fabric, to part it and peer through fearfully.

The interior was dimmer than he had expected. At first, his moon-dazzled eyes could see only that a number of men were within—a dozen or more of them, most kneeling with their backs to him.

One man, Cullen by his profile, stood with his back to the others at the far end, candlelight flaring from behind his body as he bent over something that looked like a chest or table covered with white. Another man, golden-haired, waited with bowed head at Cullen's left, and Cinhil thought it must be Joram.

As Cinhil's eyes adjusted to the inside light level, he recognized another head of quicksilvered gold—Camber, without question—and another head of wiry red—the Healer Rhys. As Cullen straightened, the other men looked up at him, and Cinhil realized that they were the majority of his war leaders: Jebediah, Bayvel de Cameron, Jasper Miller, young Jamie Drummond and Guaire, Earl Sighere and two of his three sons, and a handful of Michaelines whose faces but not names he remembered.

But he had no time to ponder that. For close upon that recognition came his realization of the reason for Cullen's vaguely familiar yet unfamiliar silhouette: Cullen was wearing priestly vestments, but they were of the deep, Michaeline blue—not a usual liturgical color—with the Michaeline cross bold on the orphrey in silver and red and gold. Mass vessels could now be seen on the table, which Cinhil at last realized was a portable altar.

Confusion flooded Cinhil's mind at that. He had expected to surprise his Deryni allies at some arcane working of magic, but he had not thought to find that magic so familiar. He felt a tight constriction across his chest and in his throat, a welling of old, ill-repressed emotions, as Cullen raised the chalice with a sacred Host above it and spoke words hallowed by a millennium of usage:

"Ecce Agnus Dei: ecce qui tollis peccata mundi."

"Domini, non sum dignus," the others responded softly, in unison. Lord, I am not worthy that Thou shouldst come under my roof. Speak but the word and my soul shall be healed.

Cinhil bowed his head and swallowed, closed his eyes, letting the timeless and well-loved words float over and around him. Even on the lips of a Deryni, *especially* on the lips of a Deryni like Alister Cullen, the words had meaning, substance, reassurance which could sustain him through whatever might befall.

He opened his eyes to see Cullen passing the chalice to Joram, who bowed and then sipped from it. Then, leaving the chalice with Joram, Cullen turned to take another vessel from the altar and begin moving among the men, distributing Communion. Joram followed close behind and allowed each man to drink from the chalice he held, wiping the rim after each use with a linen cloth.

So the rumors were true. Cinhil had heard that the Michaelines sometimes gave Communion under both species, both bread and wine, but he had thought that confined to use within the Order only. Here, there were those who were neither Michaeline nor even clergy—Camber and Rhys and Guaire and the other laymen—and they were participating in the same manner as the Michaeline brethren.

But enough of this. He must leave before he was discovered. If nothing more was amiss than irregular communion practices, then he was quite unjustified in what had now become simple eavesdropping.

He had glanced aside to be certain that no guard

had approached while he watched, when he was suddenly aware of a shadow falling across his viewing slit. His head snapped back in alarm, but it was too late. Cullen's tall form blocked the light, and he could feel the vicar general's eyes boring through the now-thin-seeming fabric of the pavilion wall, freezing him in his place like a trapped bird.

"You would have been welcome to join us openly, Sire," the voice said in a not-unkindly tone. "There was no reason to crouch in the cold and dark. All brethren in Christ are welcome at His table."

He could not seem to move. As Joram, too, stepped into view at Cullen's left, Cinhil was aware of hands untying the lashings of the flap through which he had peered, and then of Jebediah and Jasper Miller withdrawing the flap, disclosing him there for all to see.

He could feel his cheeks burning with shame beneath his beard, knew that he had been caught red-handed. What must they think? What would they do to him?

He was not given time to brood on it. Hands firm but gentle pulled him to his feet and ushered him into the pavilion, there to lead him into their midst and bid him kneel.

He knelt, mortified, head bowed and eyes closed in a futile attempt at escape. He could hear Cullen and Joram continuing their rounds among the others, their low-voiced Latin phrases and the responses of the communicants, but he dared not look up. He was huddled in the presence of God, intruder on a rite he had not initially been invited to share. He felt guilty, devious, as if he had been caught in the midst of some unclean act. His heart caught in his throat as he realized that someone—it had to be Cullen—had stopped in front of him.

"*Ego te absolvo,* Cinhil," the voice whispered. He felt a light touch on his bowed head. "Be welcome at the Lord's table," Cullen continued in a more normal tone. "Will you share this Eucharistic Feast with us on the morn of battle?"

Cinhil opened his eyes, but he could not bear to raise his eyes higher than Cullen's knees.

"D-Domine, non sum dignus," he managed to stammer.

" 'Thou art a priest forever,' " Cullen replied in a whisper.

Cinhil felt a wrench of conscience at that, but when he looked up, fearfully, Cullen's sea-ice eyes were warm and reassuring, the way they had been the night before, in Cinhil's pavilion.

Cullen removed a fragment of Host from the vessel in his hand and held it out to Cinhil.

"Corpus Domini nostri Jesu Christi custodiat animam tuam in vitam aeternam," Cullen murmured, placing it in Cinhil's trembling hand.

Cinhil nodded, unable to make the appropriate response, and raised it to his mouth. It was a piece of ordinary bread, not the formal, unleavened stuff customarily used, but it was the most extraordinary thing he had ever tasted. He swallowed, overcome with emotion, as Joram paused before him with the cup.

"Sanguinis Domini nostri Jesu Christi custodiat animam tuam in vitam aeternam," Joram said softly.

As he put the cup to Cinhil's lips, Cinhil dared to look up at him, but there was no trace of anger or resentment on Joram's face. Cinhil drank, and the sip of wine sent his spirit soaring. He bowed his head and lost himself in mindless contemplation for the next several minutes.

It was not until the others were rising around him, most of them to bow slightly to him before leaving the pavilion, that he came back to full awareness of his surroundings and his circumstances.

Cullen and Joram were putting away the last of the altar things, starting to remove their vestments. Camber was leaning on a large trunk to Cinhil's left, Rhys standing quietly beside him. All four of them were studying him, though he could not seem to catch any of them staring.

He met their eyes uncertainly as he got to his feet.

"I heard voices as I passed outside," he said, by way of guilty explanation. "I couldn't sleep. I didn't realize that folk would be about their business so early."

"The priests will be saying Mass for the men very shortly," Camber said neutrally. "It is common custom for the commanders to hear Mass earlier, lest they get caught up in battle preparations and omit that sacrament."

"I—didn't know," Cinhil stammered.

"You didn't ask," Camber replied. "Had we realized you might wish to hear Mass with us, you would have been invited. However, we were led by your actions to expect that you preferred your own chaplain to perform that office for you."

"So he would have, had I not been led to discover you," Cinhil said. "I didn't mean to pry, but—"

"But His Grace was mightily curious," Cullen said, turning to regard the king with an appraising glance as he folded his chasuble. "And when he discovered a Michaeline Mass in progress, a *Deryni* Mass, he feared the worst."

He laid the chasuble away in its trunk and began removing the rest of his vestments. "Was the King's Grace surprised, or disappointed?"

"Disappointed?" Cinhil looked at the half-clad priest incredulously. "Why, to receive the Eucharist thus again—it was, it was—my God, Alister, I would have thought you, at least, would have understood!"

Cullen had stripped down to his undergarments, and now began drawing on the leathers and chain mail of war.

"Pious words, Cinhil. But you half expected something more, didn't you? Did you distrust us so much, even in the faith we share, that you would expect some profanation of this greatest magic? Did you, perhaps, even hope for it, as an excuse to make some real break with our Deryni race, to somehow soothe your wretched conscience?"

"Alister, no!" Rhys whispered.

"What?" Cinhil appeared dazed.

"Well, did you?" Cullen insisted.

"How dare you!" Cinhil blurted out. "You—all of you—you are responsible for my state!"

"You are responsible for your own state!" Joram interjected. "You make pious noises, but your actions say otherwise. No one forced you to do what you did."

"No one forced me? How could I refuse? I was an innocent priest, knowing only the monastic life for nearly all my forty-three years. You and Rhys wrenched me from my abbey against my will, tore me from the life I loved, and thrust me among men even more ruthless than yourselves!"

"Were you ever abused?" Cullen replied. "Did anyone ever ill use you, once you were safe in sanctuary?"

"Not physically," Cinhil whispered. "You did not have to. You were the vicar general of one of the most powerful and well-respected religious orders in the known world. Camber was—and is—Camber. What more can I say of him? And then, there was the Healer." He gestured toward Rhys. "And my brother priest Joram, who commanded me to 'feed my sheep,' and Archbishop Anscom, the Primate of All Gwynedd. And even your shy, innocent daughter, Camber—ah, how she betrayed me! And all of you were telling me that it was my bounden duty to leave my state of grace, my sacred calling, and take a crown I did not want!"

"You listened," Camber said quietly.

"Yes, I listened. What else was I to do? Had I dared to defy you, you would either have killed me or wrenched my mind to *make* me do your will. I could not stand against all of you. I was only one frail human man."

"And have there been no martyrs before?" Cullen observed coldly. "That, too, was a choice open to you, had you dared to take it. If your beliefs were as fervent as you now say, why did you not continue to refuse us, come what might? We were not easy on you, Cinhil, but you cannot wholly lay the blame on us. With a stronger vessel, we could not have succeeded."

"Well, perhaps you have not succeeded yet!" Cinhil shouted.

With a sob of indignation, he lurched from the pavilion at a dead run, clutching his cloak around him like a madman.

"Open warfare," Camber murmured, when Cinhil's pounding footfalls had faded from hearing.

"He'll come to his senses," Cullen said. "He must, or I have truly set us all to ruin. I'm sorry. I suppose it was the final eruption of all my own frustration."

Joram bowed his head, toying with a stole he still held in his hands. "I'm partially to blame. I lost my temper. I goaded him. Father, I'm sorry you had to be associated with this. It will only make things more difficult for you."

He looked up at his father in sorrow, but Camber merely shrugged and smiled.

"He has a few hours to cool off. Perhaps he needed to hear that. It was truth—as was his side."

"Truth." Cullen sighed and buckled his sword over the blue Michaeline surcoat he now wore.

"Truth. In a few hours, I expect we shall all know real truth."

CHAPTER SIX

*I have fought a good fight, I have finished
my course, I have kept the faith.*
                              —II Timothy 4:7

There was no time to ponder further consequences
in the hour which followed. Final orders must be
given, scouting reports digested, horses fed and
groomed and saddled, weapons inspected and tested
one final time before the coming battle.

Camber, with a subdued Joram at his side, repaired
to his Culdi levies to confer with his captains. Cullen
gave his Michaeline knights as tough an inspection as
they had ever stood, tight-lipped and taciturn as his
second-in-command led him along the battle lines.

To Rhys had fallen the task of organizing a hospital
corps, of making optimum use of the dozen Healers
and perhaps twice that many human surgeons they
had been able to recruit for the war effort. The surgeons and their assistants would have their hands full
by the end of the day, for the Healers' ministrations
must be confined to those in mortal need, while the
surgeons took care of lesser injuries. Those who could
be helped by neither would see the priests, for the
cure of their souls, if nothing else.

But even Rhys's planning would make little difference to the majority. Battle shock, added to actual
injuries, would claim more lives than could be saved,
even had they three times the number of Healers. They
dared not risk such valuable men in actual battle, with

the result that the wounded must lie where they fell until the battle was over.

As for Cinhil, there was little that could be done. The king retreated to his pavilion precipitously after leaving Cullen and the others, and was not seen again until time for him to mount the great horse Frostling and ascend the ridge. Jebediah escorted the king, having been warned by Joram of the verbal altercation with Cullen, and he did his best to remain as unobtrusive as possible while still performing his duties. Orders were given quietly, preferably after asking Cinhil's formal permission. Cinhil responded in as few words as possible, civil but much subdued, with the taut precision of anger held rigidly in check.

Where the men were concerned, Cinhil played his part well. Though no one dared to cross him, they read his silence as quiet confidence. But within the protection of steel and leather, Cinhil was anything but calm. He clenched his teeth and willed his hands steady on the charger's reins, grateful for the shelter of his crowned helm. His innards tied in knots as he gazed down at the battle array forming on the field beneath him, and his throat constricted at the sight of the enemy assembling far across the plain. A cadre of knights surrounded him as bodyguard, mixed Deryni and human, but they afforded little comfort since he did not know most of them.

And farther along the ridge, Camber and his son also watched the forming enemy lines. Though a gray mist still hugged the plain, smudging the distances with dampness, they could see the banners and the shadows of hundreds of men, mounted and afoot, and the flash of diffused sunlight on readied weapons.

Camber glanced at Joram, then back at the pale, empty plain spread before them, suspecting that his son was thinking much the same thing he was.

"You're wondering whether it's all worth it, aren't you?" he said, an ironic smile twitching at his lips.

Joram's eyes narrowed, but he did not shift his gaze from the plain below. "He was a pompous idiot this morning," he said bitterly. "All we've worked for, all we've tried to make him understand—nothing. Is there no one he trusts?"

"Apparently not, at least for the moment. My hopes were as high as yours for Alister to gain his confidence —higher, perhaps, knowing my own total inadequacy in this area. I never thought that Alister would light into him like that—or you."

Joram snorted and glanced down at his saddlebow. "You, yourself, admitted it was the truth."

"Aye, it was. But the more I think about it, the less certain I am that he was ready for it. I must confess, I thought Alister's patience was a little longer than that, too."

"It was," Joram murmured. "I hadn't had a chance to tell you about it, but he tried again, last night, to let Cinhil know that he wanted to help. He was soundly rebuffed. It took Jebediah and me nearly an hour, after he got back, to convince Alister that his gesture had not been in vain, that it was Cinhil's problem and not his. Even then, I think he had the feeling that he was getting close, that Cinhil had almost accepted the offer of friendship. I confess, I was not so patient. I had to walk out of the pavilion last night, when Cinhil continued to raise objections about the watch-wards. I was afraid I'd say something I'd later regret, if I stayed any longer. I suppose I should have left this morning, too."

"Then why did Alister—"

"This morning? I suppose it was just the final blow, on top of all the normal tension of battle preparations, to find Cinhil spying on us. Behind his gruff exterior is a sensitive, vulnerable man."

Camber sighed. "I didn't know about last night. Do you think the breach can be mended?"

"That's hard to say. Alister Cullen is proud, as you know well, but he also cares a great deal about Cinhil, in his own way. It's a curious affection which has grown up over the past year or so. I think—I hope—

that Cinhil senses that. God knows, he's going to have to learn to trust someone, if he's to survive."

"Then God grant that this is only a temporary setback," Camber replied. "Cinhil is frightened, and he's stubborn. I don't think he realized that he was dealing with another man almost as stubborn as himself."

Joram chuckled, despite the gravity of the situation. "Aye, that's true. Alister *is* one of the more stubborn men I've ever encountered—almost as stubborn as you, at times."

Camber laughed. "No one could be that stubborn. Not even your infamous vicar general. Speaking of which, here he comes, looking as grim as the Apocalypse. What ho, Alister?" he called.

Cullen spurred his chestnut up the remaining slope and drew rein. His blue surcoat was already spattered with mud, but he wore a surprisingly cheerful expression.

"Well, it's only a matter of half an hour or so now. So far as we can tell, her troop deployment is just as you said it would be—not a sign of treachery. One of our scouting parties had a minor skirmish with one of her patrols just at sunup, but neither side lost any men. If I didn't know that there was no such thing, I'd say this has all the shape of a classic battle encounter."

Camber smiled grimly. "I didn't think she could know how much I'd found out. And there really wasn't time for her to change her plans too drastically and still proceed with the invasion now."

"Just blind luck," Cullen muttered. "And that's what it's going to be, all day. She still has us outnumbered."

"How is Cinhil?" Joram asked, abruptly changing the subject.

Cullen sighed. "Avoiding me, whenever possible. Still, I don't think it's permanent. Certainly, he's brooding about this morning. His feelings were hurt. But he's in control. I think things will smooth out, once this is over."

Camber clapped a mailed gauntlet to Cullen's shoulder and nodded. "That is welcome news, at least. As for the battle, is there anything special we should keep in mind?"

A battle horn sounded farther over on the ridge, where the king sat his horse between Jebediah and Bayvel Cameron, surrounded by his knightly bodyguard. Cullen gathered up his reins and smiled.

"Just keep your shield up and your head down," he said, guiding his horse around them to head toward his own men, farther to the left. "Good battle, my friends. God grant we meet again, at day's end!"

With that, he was off, cantering easily toward the Michaeline cavalry assembled on the northernmost portion of the ridge. Below them in the plain, the infantry of Gwynedd was drawn up in orderly companies, beginning to move out in the gray mist at a smart pace. Cullen's Michaelines streamed down the hill and started heading farther north, to attempt a pincer movement.

Camber sighed and glanced south, at the smaller army of Earl Sighere, whose Eastmarch levies had caught up with them late the day before, then surveyed his own Culdi knights waiting patiently behind him for his signal. He and Joram would lead the Culdi levies today, each of them taking a command of cavalry and half the foot. Young Guaire had also brought a small force from his demesne at Arliss, but he had elected to place his men under Camber's command as well, that he might carry Camber's personal standard into battle at his side.

The young man approached as Camber turned in the saddle, a squire walking beside his horse and carrying Camber's shield. A Michaeline brother had brought Joram's shield, and the priest took it up as Guaire fell into place at Camber's left.

"Lord Jebediah sends ready to advance, m'lord," Guaire said.

Camber took up his own shield—*gules* and *azure* impaled by a sword and coronet—and settled it into place over gauntlet and vambrace, then stood in his

stirrups and raised his arm in acknowledgement to
Jebediah, watching them from a quarter-mile farther
south on the ridge. He glanced back at his men as he
drew his sword, but they had already seen his hand
signal and knew what it meant. Reins of anxious
chargers were gathered more closely, feet set more
squarely in stirrups, lances more firmly seated in stirrup rests, shields shifted on steel-clad arms.

Camber studied them for an instant, appraising that
all were ready, then signaled advance and started
down the slope with Joram and Guaire. The foot
levies before him were already moving, banners stirring bright and graceful against the gray of morning.

Cinhil, too, rode down that slope, secure in helm
and mail, the royal Lion shield of Gwynedd on his
arm, a sword buckled fast at his side. But a battle
mace was clutched in one mailed hand, resting lightly
across his saddlebow—a weapon requiring far less
skill on his part than a sword, should an enemy actually break through his bodyguard. A Michaeline knight
bore the royal standard beside him, and the Michaeline grand master rode a little ahead with the
best of his men. At Cinhil's back followed a dozen
human knights of noble family, swords and lances
gleaming in the wan morning light.

Silken banners moved sluggishly across the plain.
Silken surcoats glowed like rich jewels in the subdued light, glittering against the damp green of spring-
flooded foliage. There was little sound besides the
muted drum of hooves and the jingle of harness and
equipment as the troops advanced. The horses' hooves
and the men's feet flattened the spring wheat of the
Gwynedd plain and ground the good grain into ruin.
The mud rose higher on the horses' legs, spattering
their noble riders and dulling weapons' shine.

They seemed to ride forever at the walk and then
at the trot, foot soldiers hanging on to the stirrups of
their accompanying knights as the pace increased.
But then, as the distance closed, the silence was shattered by war cries, and men and horses began to run,

and the order and beauty of the morning turned to carnage as the first hail of arrows just preceded the initial clash.

The first engagement lasted nearly two hours; the second, more than four. After each initial shock, the fighting settled down to close-fighting melees, strategies and tactics all but abandoned in the chaos of hand-to-hand encounter. The plain turned to a sea of mud and blood and trampled bodies of men and animals as the two armies waged their battle.

The enemy which Gwynedd faced was of a mixed lot. Most were the warriors of Ariella's Torenthi allies, kin and vassals of her mother's family in the east, strangely alien in their rune-carved breastplates and fine-wrought mail and conical helmets embellished with silks and furs. Such men fought hard and grim, neither asking nor giving quarter, with no hint of mercy in their dark, narrow eyes.

Worse than these, though, in many respects, were the Gwynedd men who fought for Ariella: once-mighty landholders of the former Festillic overlords who had fled into exile for the promise of unearned lands and riches when their unthroned mistress should regain her crown. These had far more to lose than their Torenthi allies, for capture or defeat would bring certain retribution from the Haldane king now on the throne of Gwynedd. Such men battled wildly and took many chances. Better the quick death of the battle-field than what a just Haldane would deal to captured traitors.

The fighting went hard, on both sides. By mid-morning Camber had lost fully a quarter of his knights and nearly threescore men afoot, and by afternoon those losses had nearly doubled. He himself had two horses cut from under him, only to be remounted from riderless beasts of the enemy slain. Once, it was Guaire who came to his rescue, snagging the reins of a squealing bay mare even as he struck her rider down and trampled him under the hooves of his own gray, the while keeping Camber's banner aloft. He shielded

Camber and kept the trembling animal steady until
Camber could scramble out of the mud and swing
into the saddle. Another time, an anonymous archer
in the livery of the royal guard helped him capture a
loose sorrel stallion, when his valiant little mare had
sunk beneath him with her throat thrust through by
an enemy spear.

Camber even saw Ariella once, though he was
never able to win close enough to threaten her. Surrounded by an escort of twenty heavily armored
knights, she rode among the rear lines of her army in
armoring befitting any male war leader, her slender
body encased in leather and mail, dark hair coiled
tight beneath a crowned steel cap. Several times she
attempted to bring magic into play, but it was too
risky in such close combat, and her tentative ventures
were either too destructive to her own men or could
be easily countered by the Deryni among Cinhil's men.
After a time, she abandoned arcane assaults altogether, instead attempting to inspire courage and enthusiasm among her men by her mere presence in the
rear of the lines. She wore no weapon, and the fighting never really approached her person.

The full heat of battle never really touched Cinhil,
either, though he did manage to bloody his mace a
few times, when occasional foot soldiers would break
through his guards and threaten his person. But Joram
and his men, early separated from Camber, fought
hard and with heavy losses, as did young James
Drummond and Jebediah and the bulk of the Michaeline knights.

Alister Cullen, too, sustained heavy losses among
his Michaelines, though he held his own well enough.
When, by late afternoon, the tide of battle had finally
shifted in favor of Cinhil, Ariella's forces appeared to
be in ragged retreat. The Torenthi troops, with little
personal stake in the battle other than lives, abandoned the field to Ariella's exiles and beat for home,
leaving the Gwynedd men to fend for themselves.
Cullen and his faithful Jasper Miller and a handful of

other Michaelines had harried a smaller troop of stragglers into the edge of a wood and there cut them to pieces, taking no prisoners. They were wheeling to rejoin the main mop-up parties on the plain, a few of them nursing minor wounds, when Jasper suddenly gasped and pointed toward the trees.

"Is that Ariella?"

Cullen turned in his saddle, shading his eyes to see more clearly in the murky wood, then set spurs to his mount with a hoarse cry. His men turned to follow at a gallop, soon crashing through dense underbrush to confront a cornered quarry.

Ariella's handful of knights, a flash of Healer's green among them, turned and formed a solid line to shield their mistress in this last, desperate encounter. Ariella had shed her armor in favor of lessened weight, and huddled almost childlike on the big dun warhorse, wrapped only in a thin mantle of white wool over her white shift, her face tense and anxious beneath a tumble of dark gleaming hair.

"Surrender, Ariella!" Cullen shouted, pulling his horse up on its haunches as his men formed a matching line. "Your army is routed. You cannot escape. Surrender, and pray for the king's mercy!"

"The king's mercy?" Ariella retorted. "What care I for that?"

"There is no hope of escape," Cullen repeated. His horse plunged under the restraint of the curb, and he controlled it with his knees. "Surrender now, and avoid yet more meaningless deaths. Your cause is lost."

Ariella did not speak, but suddenly the glade filled with the glow of Deryni shields being raised by all of Ariella's men. Coruscating brilliance surrounded them as they charged, the power as quickly countershielded by Cullen's Michaelines, as they took up the challenge and spurred forward as well. The glade echoed to the screams of men and beasts, rang with the clash of weapons on shields and energies being launched and parried.

The horses were among the first casualties. Grim-faced warriors, desperate to gain any advantage in a battle which could mean life itself, struck men and animals without compunction; aimed especially for the horses in the first seconds of combat—for a knight unhorsed, even a Deryni one, faced grave odds when thrown afoot among mounted men.

Cullen fought like a madman, wheeling his charger in desperate circles, trying to protect as many of his men as possible and to inflict as much damage to the enemy as he could, before he, too, was unhorsed. A man from either side and several of the horses were killed outright in the first clash of power. From there it progressed to a grim, hacking battle, shouts giving way to screams and the clang and thud of weapons striking shields and flesh.

Jasper Miller killed two of Ariella's seven before he, too, was slain; and the man who killed him was, himself, struck down by another Michaeline's avenging sword—and that man fell to the sword of Ariella's Healer, who was acquitting himself appallingly well for one of his calling.

Cullen, though unhorsed after a few minutes, fought valiantly, taking several dangerous wounds and giving many more, until at last he alone stood in the glen, blocking Ariella's only escape route like an avenging angel, his dripping sword held two-handed before him in guard.

One of his Michaelines still moaned feebly to Cullen's left, and the mortally wounded Healer was trying pitifully to crawl toward his mistress, one arm severed at the elbow and dangling by a shred of muscle. Other than those two, only Cullen and Ariella remained upright and reasonably functional.

Ariella herself was still mounted, but her stallion was plunging with terror at the noise and the smell of blood, nostrils flared and eyes white-rimmed. It was all she could do to keep her seat and still hold the animal on the side of the glade away from Cullen and his sword. Her mantle had fallen back on her shoulders with the exertion, and her hair tumbled loose down her back like a second cloak. She was not unaware of the visual impression she presented as she brought her mount under trembling control. She tossed her head pridefully as she leveled her glance at Cullen.

"You fight bravely, Vicar General," she cried. Her horse snorted at her voice, finally calming enough to stand fidgeting beneath her. "I could yet pardon your treason, if you will swear to serve me faithfully."

Cullen stared at her in disbelief. "Swear to serve you? Are you mad? You speak as if it is you who have had the victory. You are my prisoner, not I yours."

"Your prisoner?" Ariella laughed, a harsh, contemptuous rasp, and her horse danced and sidled a few steps closer, eyes rolling nervously. "Vicar General, it is I who remain mounted and unharmed. Look at you. You are sorely wounded, your men dead or dying. Be reasonable. Give me your sword, and I will spare your life."

A strangled, half-animal cry came from Cullen's throat as he shook his head, and it came as no surprise when, in the next instant, she spurred her skittish mount toward him. He had time only to throw himself to one side and lunge at the horse as it went by, flapping his cloak in the animal's face and shouting as it started to rear. The animal shied violently—right onto his sword—screamed as it tripped in its own entrails.

Ariella was catapulted into the brush, and Cullen thought for a moment, as he struggled out from under the dying horse, that she had been stunned by her fall. But as he threw aside his blood-soaked cloak, he saw her staggering to her feet, her face white with fury as her hands moved in spell.

He shielded with all his strength. He counterattacked, drawing on knowledge he had never used, knowledge he had never believed he would use—for if he could not vanquish her in the beginning, he knew he would not last long with his wounds. Already he could feel his strength ebbing, his vision blurring, as blood pumped from his body. Already he was having to pour far more energy than he should into just repelling her attack. He had not much offensive left in him.

He was dying. Suddenly, he could deny it no longer. He could feel his faculties starting to go, one by one, his vision dimming now, his hearing dulling, sensation fading from his hands. In an infinite second, he knew that if he hoped to stop her, he must wager all his life and hope and faith on one last, desperate act—must summon up the last dregs of his strength to destroy her.

It was not easy. Leaning heavily against his sword, he fought his way up from his knees—first one foot under him, then the other. With a massive exertion, he forced his knees to straighten, to bring him upright.

He could see her standing half across the clearing, her eyes closed, her arms outstretched to either side as she built her power and increased the strength of her attack. He could feel her pressing against his shields more and more relentlessly, and he knew that if he did not act in the next few seconds, he would never act—and she would be free!

He braced himself on spraddled legs, taking all his remaining strength to raise the hilt of his sword to his lips, to kiss the sacred relic in its pommel and pray as he had never prayed before.

Then he grasped the sword, spearlike, and hurled it straight and true, never noticing that the steel had cut his fingers almost to the bone.

He fell as it left his hands, eyes closing upon a darkness which became more and more profound.

He heard no other sound.

CHAPTER SEVEN

And thou shalt be called by a new name,
which the mouth of the Lord shall name.
　　　　　　　　　　—Isaiah 62:2

The shadows were lengthening and fading when the forces of Gwynedd began to reassemble. Cinhil was off with Jebediah at the base of the ridge, receiving grim preliminary reports on casualties, but Camber and Joram reached the crest almost simultaneously, and now sat their horses side by side to survey the darkening plain.

Shadows moved amid the gloom—hospitalers searching among the slain for any men yet alive, and grooms putting foundered beasts out of their misery, and lesser-wounded men limping their slow way back to camp. Away to the left, the watch fires of the infirmary tents were being kindled, bright points against the lowering dusk, and behind them the previous night's camp began to come to life.

Far across the plain, an occupation force moved through the enemy's encampment, taking provisions and occasional prisoners and securing the camp against further belligerence. Troops of Gwynedd cavalry patrolled the edges of the battlefield to guard against looting and to protect those who tended the wounded against attack by any remaining invaders. The cries of the injured and dying drifted up faintly to the ridge crest, the only sounds in the gathering twilight.

Camber and his son sat quietly for some minutes. There was a smear of blood across Joram's right glove, and another across his forehead, but none of the blood was his. His mail was still mostly intact, if somewhat bloodied, and his hair shone in damp bronzed tendrils where he had pushed back his coif. Camber, too, was relatively unscathed, save for a liberal coating of mud and a giant rip across the back of his Culdi surcoat. His bare head gleamed silver in the waning light as he handed helmet and shield to a squire who approached to take them.

"How many did you lose?" Camber finally asked, glancing below where the Michaeline banner identified a sizable troop of Joram's order escorting a train of prisoners.

"Too many—but then, that is always the case." Joram dropped his own shield on the ground beside his horse and eased steel-shod boots out of the stirrups. "And you?"

"The same." He paused. "I see that Cinhil is still functional, at any rate. Have you any idea how he fared?"

Joram shrugged. "You see him riding. One can only assume that he's all right. Right now, I'm more concerned that no one saw Ariella after midday. You don't suppose she's escaped again, do you?"

"Dear God, I hope not," Camber murmured. He raised a hand as Rhys cantered up the hill and reined in before them. Though he had thrown on his Healer's mantle against the growing damp and chill, the hem of his tunic showed bloodstains where he had wiped his hands or tried to ease an injury, and there was dried blood around his knuckles. His face was drawn and pale with exertion already, his eyes dark-circled. He took a gasping breath as he nodded greeting to them.

"I can't stay long unless one of you needs me, but I wondered whether you've seen Father Cullen recently. We're going to lose some men down there, and a few of them wanted him, in particular, to give them absolution."

Joram's face became more still, and he glanced distractedly around the battlefield again. "I haven't seen him for hours. Father, have you?"

Camber cocked his head as though trying to place the memory, then gestured toward a wooded area to the right.

"He and some Michaelines were chasing a band of stragglers over there. That's been half an hour ago, though. I hope nothing's happened."

There was a shout from the bottom of the hill, and Rhys raised a hand in acknowledgment.

"Well, I'm afraid I haven't time to help you look. My services are needed below. When you find him, would you send him down?"

"Of course."

"Godspeed, then."

As he turned his horse and started down, Joram glanced at his father, reining his own horse sharply to keep it from following Rhys's.

"Do you think something *has* happened?"

"Let's find out," Camber replied.

For answer, Joram touched heels to his mount and began picking his way down the hill. Camber followed a few paces behind, trying to ease the limp his own horse had developed.

Dead men lay in the wood—enemy slain, at first, but then the first Michaeline, his blue surcoat stained almost black in the feeble light. Camber lingered there a little, trying to ascertain what had happened, but Joram hardly paused, calling from ahead that he had found another body—this one wearing the tunic of the Festillic invaders. He rode on, disappearing from sight in the trees ahead.

Camber's apprehension grew as he followed the trail of bodies. The second Michaeline he found bore the badge of Alister Cullen's personal guard, and a glance beneath the cloven helm revealed him to be Cullen's faithful friend and aide, Jasper Miller.

Camber stiffened at that, a hand straying unconsciously to the hilt of his sword, for if Jasper had fallen, Cullen must be in serious trouble indeed not to be at his side. He caught Joram's repeated exclamations of anguish and dread surprise ahead, and impulsively he scrambled back onto his horse and urged it ahead as fast as it could manage. Even before he rounded the last turn, Camber sensed what he would find.

Gently he reined in at the edge of the clearing and dismounted, pausing to conjure a sphere of gentle silver handfire before moving closer to where the man lay.

Cullen was lying on his side, head cradled against an outstretched arm as if deep in sleep. But there was blood on that arm, and across his chest, and a dreadful gash across his ribs which had cut partway through mail and leather and all, so great had been the force of the blow which delivered it.

Camber froze fleetingly at the sight, instantly casting about for signs of lingering danger, but there were none. He caught Joram's presence, agitated but safe, rummaging in the brush far across the clearing, but there was no menace yet remaining—only the body of the man before him, and other bodies lying in the growing shadows, men and beasts alike, and the smell of blood and death.

With a conscious effort, he forced himself to relax the physical tension of his body, breathing again, flexing the hands which had clenched in readiness at the first inkling of disaster. Setting the handfire to hover like an early moon, he wearily crossed the few steps to kneel at Cullen's head, stripping off gauntlets before he held one hand above the priest's brow. A chill swept through him as he extended his Deryni awareness along the dead man's body.

Cursed be whoever had done this, for Cullen both was and was not dead! His body had been slain, but some essence of his being remained—isolated from his body beyond all reunion, yet caught still in some vicious bond which endured even beyond the death of his assailant. There could be no return of that essence to its body in this life, for the silver cord had been severed, the bond of soul and body broken. The body was already past all animation, the vaults of memory fading with the body's warmth.

With a shudder, not yet prepared to do what must be done to release the dead man, Camber closed his eyes and searched for strength. It seemed only seconds before he felt Joram's approach. He raised his head in anxious query as his son shuffled slowly into the circle of hovering handfire.

Joram's face was ashen, the strain of unspeakable tension etched so indelibly on his features that Camber dared not even ask its source. He fell heavily to his knees across from Camber, his head pitching forward so loosely on his chest that for an instant Camber feared for him—until he heard the stifled sob.

Then Camber knew that it was grief, not personal injury, which blurred his son's mind to despair. He glanced down at the body of Cullen lying between them, then reached out a hand and laid it on Joram's shoulder. The young priest flinched at his father's touch, drawing ragged breath and shaking his head when Camber moved as if to speak.

"We Deryni do not always slay cleanly," Joram said. His voice was raw and strained near to breaking, and for an instant Camber feared again for his well-being, though he forced himself to put aside his fatherly concerns for more far-reaching questions.

"What did you find?"

"Ariella." Joram stared blindly at the body between them. "Cullen and his men apparently saw her trying to escape and pursued her into this wood. Their men killed one another, and then he and Ariella fought to the death—and Ariella fought even beyond."

"What!"

"At least we need not worry further on that," Joram whispered bitterly. "She failed."

He gestured with his chin toward the brush from

which he had emerged, and Camber's eyes followed his direction. Then, pausing only for a quick glance back at Joram, Camber scrambled to his feet and ran across the clearing.

Ariella lay half slumped against a tree, her slender form transfixed by a sword, its cross-hilt swaying slightly in the breeze of his arrival. As he knelt in disbelief, drawing more handfire into being, he could see that the sword was Cullen's Michaeline blade, sacred symbols engraved on the steel, its pommel twisted and charred by a force which had all but destroyed it.

He blessed himself—not at all an empty gesture, in the light of what had happened here—then turned his attention to the woman, gingerly pulling aside the blood-soaked white mantle. At first he thought she had only tried to escape the pinning blade—the dead fingers were near the steel, and she would have struggled long before she died, with vitals thus pierced.

But then he looked more closely at her hands and knew that they were not on the blade at all, sensed instantly what she had tried to do. The now-dead hands were still cupped together on her breast, the fingers still curved in the attitude of a spell believed by most to be impossible, merest legend. No wonder Joram had been so shaken.

He took a deep breath and ran his hands lightly above her body, not touching it as he extended his senses, but then he breathed a sigh. Here was no arcane binding of life to ruined body. The life-suspending spell on which she had spent her dying energy had not worked. Power and life were gone. Ariella, unlike Cullen, was truly dead.

With steely resolution, he drew a fold of the blood-soaked mantle over her face, then wrapped several turns of his own cloak around his hand and withdrew Cullen's sword. The weapon throbbed as he touched it, even through the layers of wool between his hand and the hilt, and it sang with a deep, thrumming note as he pulled it free.

A low-voiced phrase, a stilling of all fear, and then

he touched the sacred blade to his lips in salute. At once it was only a ruined sword.

He thrust it through his belt, then gathered up Ariella's body and wrapped it in the bloody mantle as best he could. Joram's horse was cropping grass contentedly nearby, and Camber laid the body across the saddle. As he secured the body in place, he watched his son kneeling across the clearing in the circle of silver light and thought about his dead friend. Cullen's death meant a rethinking of a number of factors.

Most immediately significant, of course, was Ariella's death, which Cullen had wrought—though that by no means ended the struggles which lay ahead for the newly restored Haldane line. Ariella had left a son somewhere in safety, someday to return and grasp for the throne his parents had lost. Ariella's son would come of age at a time when Gwynedd was least able to resist him—for though Cinhil was in good health, and like to live a score of years, barring accident, his elder son was sickly, and the younger clubfooted and almost unsuitable to rule. Either would have to be extraordinary indeed, to stand against a son of Festil and his Torenthi allies.

Added to the continuing Festillic menace was Cinhil's own bitterness. Camber counted himself partially to blame for that. In an effort to keep at least some line of communication open with Cinhil, who daily grew more bitter at what life had dealt him, Camber had allowed himself to become a focal point for Cinhil's resentment—a resentment which was slowly but inexorably being directed toward Deryni in general.

This last was not yet an overt thing, though Cullen had hinted at it this morning, and might never really mature during Cinhil's lifetime. But Camber was Deryni, and Ariella's son and allies were Deryni, as were a host of others who had put Cinhil where he was instead of in his beloved monastery. If Cinhil should die before his sons were mature enough to reject by reason what their father had felt by instinct, then there could be hard times indeed for all the Deryni race.

But what could be done? Could anyone stop the backlash which seemed to loom so certainly in the future? Or, if the storm was meant to be, if the Deryni heritage must be tempered in the fire of vengeance, was there a way to soften the blow, to keep the proud heritage and talents of the Deryni somewhat intact, even through the indignity of suppression and perhaps outright persecution? Great God, might it really come to that?

It might, Camber acknowledged, as he tightened the last of the thongs binding the body of the dead princess in place. But there might be ways to stop it, or at least lessen it. Such ways would require much, though: his full-time attention, and additional help, and most of all, Cinhil's cooperation, whether he knew it or not.

And now, with Alister Cullen dead . . .

Camber cocked his head at that, the flash of a long-ago memory lighting his gloom for just a moment, as an idea began to form. It was dangerous, it was daring, he did not know if even *he* had the courage to go through with it—but it just might work. The first question was, would Joram consent?

Mentally steeling himself for resistance, Camber ran his hand along the horse's neck a final time, then moved to kneel opposite Joram again, the body of Cullen between them. After a few heartbeats, Joram crossed himself and looked up.

"What did she do to him, Father?" the priest whispered. "There's something drastically wrong."

"I know. I'll take care of it in a moment. First, I want to ask you something very important."

"More important than Alister's immortal soul?"

"In the greater scheme of things, perhaps so— though your grief may not allow you to see that clearly just now."

Joram looked at him sharply, then brushed the back of a mailed hand across his eyes and tried to suppress a sniff.

"What do you mean?"

Camber sat back on his haunches. "Would you believe me if I told you that even Alister's death may have had its place in a greater plan?"

"What are you talking about?"

"I'm talking about Cinhil—about his increasing hostility toward me and toward our people in general, with a few notable exceptions like Alister and perhaps a few others. We changed him, Joram. From a simple, pious, dedicated priest, we made a king—yes. We taught him what he must know, and he adapted as best he could.

"But the changes which we so carefully forged in Cinhil were tainted by our urgency, warped of necessity—because even a warped Haldane was better than the Deryni madman who sat the throne of Gwynedd two years ago."

"You've lost me," Joram said. "What does this have to do with Alister?"

"Because in turning Cinhil against the Deryni Imre, we have unwittingly turned him against all Deryni, even if he does not fully know it yet. And Alister was one of our few hopes to keep him thinking otherwise.

"Oh, things may go tolerably for several years, maybe even until the end of the reign—God grant that it may be long—but what then? Unless Cinhil lays the groundwork for tolerance, despite his personal feelings against the Deryni—and maybe even if he does— I see a horrible backlash coming. If that happens, I shudder at what may happen to our people."

"Can you do nothing about it?" Joram asked, eyes wide with the new-recognized danger.

"Can Camber? I fear not. You've seen how Cinhil reacts to me. You know why we've been feeding my input through you and Alister and Rhys increasingly these last few months—and even you have begun to slip somewhat in his estimation."

Joram's gaze dropped guiltily as Camber continued. "I've been doing some thinking just now, Joram.

I've reached the conclusion that perhaps I've outlived my usefulness. More and more, I'm becoming a liability rather than an asset—to Cinhil and to our cause. I'd even considered dropping out of sight, disappearing, so that I could work in secret to neutralize some of what we've inadvertently started. Only, now I think there's a better way."

"I don't think I follow you," Joram said uneasily. "I'm not sure I want to."

"I'm not sure I want to, either," Camber replied. "It scares me more than I can tell you. But it does present a solution of sorts, with potential which I, as myself, simply don't have. Other than the two of us, no one knows that Cullen is dead. Few others *need* to know. If I were to take his place—"

Joram's hands flew to Cullen's chest in an instinctive protective gesture, his face going white.

"No! I know what you're thinking, and I won't have it!"

"Joram, if I must take the time to reconvince you of the neutrality of the magic involved, then we are lost. Believe me, it's the only way. Alister Cullen must live, and so Camber MacRorie must die."

"No," Joram whispered stubbornly, even more stricken than before.

"Yes. Come, now. 'Tis not so bad as all of that. I shan't really die, you know. Besides, to be remembered kindly as the Restorer of the Haldanes is not so bad a fate. Even our Haldane, bitter though he is, would not begrudge Camber of Culdi an honorable burial, in the vaults at Caerrorie, where his ancestors lie. And I, as Alister Cullen, can continue to work at the things which Camber is helpless to do right now. I think that our old friend would not mind."

He glanced at Cullen's still face, then back at his son.

"Joram, it may not turn out to be the best way, but it's the only way I can think of right now. And if we let this opportunity slip by, who knows if another will pass this way again? Think of Cinhil. Think of

Gwynedd. Won't you help me? I can't hope to succeed in this charade unless you do."

Joram squeezed his eyes shut and bowed his head miserably, arms clutched comfortless across his chest. After a moment he looked up, gray eyes haunted by a grief which seemed to have no end in sight.

"Must you do this thing?"

"I think I must."

Joram swallowed and fought back tears, forcing his mind to reenter its customary channels of logic.

"If you—do this thing, you will be treading a very dangerous balance, especially with Cinhil. I don't see how you can hope to deceive him indefinitely—and what of all the others?"

"I shall take such memories as are left, what things you and I know of him, and pray," Camber replied gently. "I can blame most initial lapses on battle fatigue and grief at Camber's death—perhaps even go into retreat for a while."

"And what then?" Joram asked. "Father, *I* don't even know the full extent of his relationship with Cinhil. And then, there's the Order—a full-time occupation in itself, and you not even a priest—and the bishopric he was to receive— My God, it's insane even to think of it!"

"Then it's insane, and I'm a madman, and you must either help me or betray me!" Camber countered. "Which is it to be? We haven't time to argue any more. Someone could come along at any minute."

Son and father stared at each other in silence for a heartbeat, shocked and defiant, sickened and determined, each reflecting the pain and indecision of the other. Then Joram bent to begin unbuckling Cullen's greaves, a tear splashing on the polished metal as numb fingers fought with battle-gritted buckles.

Breathing a sigh of relief, Camber pulled the coif from Cullen's grizzled head and then laid both his hands on the forehead. He closed his eyes and let his awareness center and then extend, reaching out for what was left of Alister Cullen.

The remaining memory fragments were chaotic, jumbled and rent already with death-wrought gaps which he could never hope to fill; but he had expected that. Without pausing to read those memories, he let them siphon off into a closely guarded vault of his own being, slowing the flow only to sift it from the shadows of death—not to impart any kind of order or understanding. Later, he would—he must—integrate the alien memories with his own, but for now such as remained of Alister Cullen must be merely locked away, partitioned off beyond kenning. There was no time for more.

He knew the price he would pay for that haste. To take another's memories whole, without assimilation at the time of taking, was to court the throbbing, pulsing pain of all the other's dying once he did find the time to do things right. And he dared not delay to find that time, not beyond a week or two, at best—for pressure built with passing time, like a wound festering with infection, and had been known to drive men truly mad, when at last they did dare to let the pressure out.

But he would not do that. In the mourning of the next week or so, he would make the time to deal with Cullen's memories, perhaps with the aid of those precious few whose love he must rely upon to help play out what now began. There would always be blanks, and areas of gray which he could never fill, but even some of Cullen's memories were better than none—were essential, if he was to become Alister Cullen to other men.

Memories secured and locked away, the binding made, he quested outward one more time, this time to touch those other bonds—grim, slimy chains—which lingered, part of Ariella. Those he loosed with the strength of his affection, as he had loosed others before—vestiges of arcane battle, which did not always kill cleanly, as Joram had pointed out. The very air seemed to lighten around him as the last of the spell was neutralized, and he bade a final farewell to

Cullen: former adversary, fellow conspirator, intellectual sparring partner, friend, brother. He opened his eyes to find Joram staring at him.

"Is he . . .?"

"He's at peace now," Camber said gently.

Joram lowered his eyes, lips moving in prayer, then crossed himself and resumed unfastening Cullen's armor. Camber helped him, the two working in silence for several minutes. When they had nearly stripped the body, Camber began removing his own harness, giving it to Joram to place on Cullen while he, himself, donned the fighting priest's attire. When he had finished the last buckle and lace, he knelt again opposite his son, watching as Joram smoothed the battle-stained MacRorie surcoat over the still chest. As a last task, Camber removed his MacRorie seal ring and slid it onto Cullen's bloody left hand. Joram removed the silver signet of the Michaeline vicar generalship and laid it gently on Cullen's chest between them.

"How will you explain Camber's death?" Joram whispered, not taking his eyes from the ring. "When we left to find Alister, you were unscathed. Were you killed in battle with her?"

Camber picked up the cross-embellished helm Cullen had worn and settled it over the coif on his own head. "We will explain all as it was, but for it happening later. You and I came upon Alister, locked in battle with Ariella. Alister was wounded, so I took his place and, myself, took fatal wounds in the struggle which ensued—but it was Alister who finally killed her. When you and I bring back the bodies of Camber and Ariella, no one will dream of disputing our story."

Joram nodded miserably, still not looking up, and Camber leaned across to lay both hands on his son's shoulders.

"We must do it now, son."

In an impulsive movement, Joram gave his father a quick embrace, wiping tears with the back of his hand as he pulled away to crouch in place once more.

Camber smiled as he folded his hands calmly before him.

"Will you ward us, please?" he whispered.

Drawing a deep breath and closing his eyes, Joram raised his arms to either side and triggered the words which would set the wards. Countless times before, he had done this, and often in his father's presence, but never had the words meant so much or been so emotionally charged. Pale, blue-white light sprang up around them, barely visible in the growing darkness, and Joram lowered his arms, tears now streaming down his face quite openly.

Camber ignored the tears and leaned forward to touch lightly the ring lying on Cullen's chest. At his touch, it began to glow with a cool white light. Then Camber raised his left hand and matched it, fingertip to fingertip, with Joram's right, while his own right hand was laid gently on Cullen's forehead.

"Remember, now," he murmured low, the bond of his love forging the link between them as it had in a chapel at Caerrorie two years ago and more. "Match hand and heart and mind with mine, and join your light to mine when we are one."

He watched Joram's gaze waver, the flickering of his eyelids, trembling, closing, as he sank reluctant but obedient into that calm, profound Deryni trance. Then he let his own gaze drift to the ring between them, which glowed ever brighter in the ghostly twilight. After a moment, he let his own eyes close, and concentrated on the crystalline oneness of the bond they shared. Joram was ready.

No still waters here, for Joram was not that—but rather, the laugh of a sunlit spring dancing over stream-polished pebbles, bright and jewellike, rare existence—and the cool and glimmer of deeper places, soft and silver-pure, into which Camber now let his consciousness slip.

Joram was in control now; and if he had wanted to end what was to be, he could have done it. But he did not. With Camber's merging into union with his mind

came the weight of destiny and purpose which he now
realized his father had known long before, if only unconsciously, and of which Joram himself had only
dipped the surface.

No fearing now, but sharing, sureness, acceptance.

"Behold," Joram's voice whispered, green leaves
floating on gently welling waters. "Behold the essence
of thine outward form, O my father. Likewise, the
outward form of him who was our friend." He drew a
steady breath. "Let each essence mingle now, in the
cool fire which rests between you. *Be* Alister Cullen,
in all outward forming. And let the outward form of
him who was our friend become most like the Earl of
Culdi, thy dear face. Let it be done. *Fiat*. Amen."

Camber's lips formed the words, but no sound came
forth—and Joram slitted his eyes open to watch with
awe as a mist seemed to shroud his father's face. As if
through a veil, he saw the familiar features shift,
glanced quickly at Cullen's face and saw similar
changes taking place.

Then the signet ring flared brightly between them, so
that Joram flung up his free hand to shield his eyes.
When he could see again, it was not his father's form
who knelt opposite him. The visage of one who had
been dead now opened pale, sea-ice eyes to look at
him uncertainly. And at his knees, his father's face
slept the sleep of those who will never walk the earth
again.

Joram swallowed audibly as he pulled his hand away
from a stranger's touch.

CHAPTER EIGHT

Yet a little sleep, a little slumber,
a little folding of the hands to sleep.
—Proverbs 24:33

It was full dark by the time they returned to camp. Cook fires were beginning to be lit among the tents of the common soldiers, and an occasional torch burned in a cresset set into the ground along the main aisles between the tent rows.

Small groups of men bearing the wounded and dead passed several times, but to these, the sight of two more Michaelines bringing in horse-borne bodies aroused no special notice. There were many dead; it was dark; the day had been long.

Joram led the way, guarding the cloak-shrouded body which the world would soon see as Camber MacRorie. Camber led the beast bearing the slain Ariella. Though they sometimes stumbled in the hoof-churned mud, Camber had not the heart to secure a torch and disclose his son's grief to all. Time, soon enough, for that. For now, give him the kind anonymity of darkness. Too soon, their deadly game would begin in earnest.

And even now, it began. As they passed the royal pavilion, heading for the Michaeline encampment a little farther down the line, Joram was recognized, first by some Michaelines, then by a handful of his MacRorie retainers gathered by a fire near the earl's standard. A murmur went up among the Michaelines

120

as the grizzled head of their vicar general was also spotted, and Camber lowered his eyes, glancing neither right nor left.

Young Guaire of Arliss, his bright, open face expectant in the light of the torch he bore, ran toward Joram with a glad greeting on his lips which died as he saw Joram's expression. He laid a hand on the priest's mailed arm and jogged a few steps to catch up as Joram continued walking grimly toward the MacRorie pavilion.

"Father Joram, what's wrong?"

Camber saw Joram turn his face away, the proud shoulders shaking. Guaire glanced at the bundle on the horse following Joram, then looked back at Joram in alarm—stared in sudden dread suspicion at the man he believed to be Alister Cullen—before dashing back to Joram's horse. A groan escaped his lips as he drew back a fold of the mantle and held his torch near.

"My God, it cannot be! 'Tis the Lord Camber!" he breathed. He grasped Joram's elbow and spun him half around to face him.

"Nay, say it is not true!" he demanded. "Say 'tis some other lord who has been slain! Say it is God Himself, but not Camber!"

Three of Camber's men drew near, shock immobilizing their faces, and pulled the sobbing Guaire away as Joram dropped the horse's reins and began to untie the thongs securing the body to the saddle. A group began to gather, more torches joining the smoky, flickering circle. Camber, now the vicar general, gave the reins of the second horse to one of his Michaelines and came to help Joram.

Someone took off a fur-lined cloak and spread it on the ground beside the horse. The two Michaelines, young priest and older vicar general, gently bore the body from the saddle and laid it on the fur. The body of the Earl of Culdi lay cold and lifeless in the torchlight, face serene and pale and slightly drawn in death. Terrible wounds gaped in several places, matching those which had actually cost Cullen his life. Drying blood appeared black in the torchlight.

There was a flurry of whispered surprise and consternation, a few low-voiced exclamations of grief, and then the men, Michaelines and Culdi folk alike, were dropping to their knees, one by one, removing helmets and bowing battle-stained heads around the body of the man who had brought them all to this place.

Into this silence came Jebediah and the king, the latter wide-eyed with disbelief, to stand mute and stunned between Joram and the dour vicar general. The grand master, after a perfunctory glance at the body on the ground, turned his anxious gaze on his Michaeline superior. Camber tried to pretend he was not aware of Jebediah's scrutiny, knowing that here, perhaps, lay his greatest challenge of all. Alister and Jebediah had been very close.

"What—happened?" Cinhil asked, after a long silence.

Joram tried to speak, but could not; bowed his head and fought the sobs which tried to escape from between his lips. At last it was the vicar general who half glanced at the king, gruff voice forcing out the words.

"Some of my men and I pursued Ariella and her escort into a wood not far from here, Sire. There she turned and stood her ground, for she could flee no farther. We fought. Most of our men were killed, and I was wounded. My strength was beginning to fail. When Camber and Joram arrived, the balance shifted, but still we could not overcome her."

He laid his hand on the saddle as though to steady himself before resuming.

"Camber was sorely wounded slaying the last of her men, and Joram was knocked senseless for a time. Thus it fell to me, with my last strength, to fling my sword and pierce her through." He rested one hand on the blasted hilt of Cullen's sword.

"But it was too late for Camber."

He bowed his head, unwilling and not daring to say

more. Cinhil swallowed audibly and started to bend down to touch the body lying at his feet, then drew back and composed himself once more. His face was expressionless, except in his eyes, as he turned stiffly toward Joram.

"We share your grief at the death of your father," he murmured, "and we thank you for the service he has done us this day. Would to God he were here to share in our victory."

With that, he turned away and fled to his pavilion, almost running as he crossed the final steps. Quiet followed him until he disappeared, then surged into low, whispered mutterings among the growing crowd of soldiers.

"Let's take him into the tent now," Camber said quietly, taking charge.

He bent and started to slip his arms under the body of his slain friend, but then he saw Jebediah moving to assist and let himself stagger as though momentarily overcome by weakness. He must not let the grand master touch Alister's body.

"I'm all right, Jeb," he murmured, protesting as Jebediah's strong arms supported and raised him, while Joram and Guaire bent instead to pick up the body. "On the other hand, perhaps you'd better go and find Rhys for me."

"How badly are you wounded?" Jebediah asked, not releasing Camber as he searched his eyes. "I was afraid something had happened to you. I had the oddest sensation, a little while ago."

Camber closed his eyes and took a deep breath as he drew himself upright, wondering whether Jebediah could possibly have felt Alister's death, praying that Jebediah had noted no discrepancy in his words or actions so far, knowing that he dared not keep up this contact much longer.

"I'll be all right, Jeb," he whispered fiercely. "A few minor wounds, a great weariness. Now, go and find Rhys, *please!*"

With a nod and no further word, Jebediah released

him and disappeared into the darkness, leaving
Camber to worry as he turned toward the pavilion
which had lately been his own, where Joram and
Guaire were even now carrying their pitiful burden.
As they moved silently inside, two of Camber's knights
took up guard positions of honor beside the entryway,
one of them holding aside the curtain respectfully.
Slowly, quietly, the remaining men began returning to
their duties, a few reluctantly taking the body of
Ariella into custody.

Nearly an hour passed before Rhys heard the news.
Jebediah finally found him in one of the hospice tents,
and waited silently until Rhys had finished healing a
deep gash on a young soldier's leg. At Rhys' touch,
the wound had closed to a thin, moist line, and his
patient would have only a slight scar to show for his
adventure in a week or so.

But for now, the young man was in shock and pain
—pain which Rhys' dwindling strength could barely
touch. As Rhys finished bandaging the leg, he noticed
Jebediah standing a few paces behind him and
beckoned him with a hand still gory from his recent
labors.

"Jeb, can you give me a hand here? I want to save
what strength I still have for actual healing. He needs
to be put to sleep."

Wordlessly, Jebediah knelt and laid his hand on the
lad's forehead. The feverish eyes sought his for just an
instant, then fluttered and closed. Jebediah murmured,
"Sleep," and closed his own eyes momentarily, then
looked up sadly as Rhys stood.

"Lord Camber has returned to camp," he said quietly.

Rhys, washing his bloody hands in a wooden basin
held by a page, glanced down with a tired grin. "Ah,
he found Alister, then?"

"Yes."

The stark answer, coupled with the knight's solemn
expression, suddenly sent a grim shudder of foreboding
through Rhys' mind. His eyes did not leave Jebediah's

face as he dried his hands on an already damp and bloody towel.

"What's happened? What are you not telling me? Leave us, Toban," he added, sending the page on his way with a touch on the shoulder.

Jebediah glanced at the ground, at the sleeping soldier whose life had just been saved by Rhys' ministrations, then rose slowly.

"Camber is dead, Rhys."

There was a stunned heartbeat of silence, and then: "Dead? But you said—"

Jebediah swallowed, unable to look at Rhys's stricken face any longer. "I said he had returned to camp. His body did. He and Joram found Alister locked in combat with Ariella. Alister finally slew her, but Camber died of wounds he sustained in the fight."

"And Joram? Alister?"

"Alister sent me to find you. He claims minor wounds and fatigue, but I sense that there is more than that. Joram appears unharmed."

Rhys nodded numbly. "I'll come, of course. I could have done little more here, in any case, until I have rested somewhat. But Camber—it's impossible. It simply cannot be."

Jebediah clasped the younger man's shoulders in resignation, then glanced past him and signaled another Healer who had just entered the tent.

"Lord Rhys is needed at the royal enclosure, Master Durin. Can you take over for him?"

Rhys did not see the other Healer nod agreement, for he was already moving out of the tent, trying to assimilate what he had just learned. As he and Jebediah left the hospice and headed toward the royal enclosure, a waiting Michaeline brother fell into step behind them with a torch. The torchlight cast wavering, distorted shadows ahead of them as they walked. Ahead, Rhys could see the MacRorie pavilion as if through a tunnel, his vision blurring out all around it save the guarded entrance and the proud MacRorie standard hanging motionless beside.

Later, he would not remember that walk. He was aware that he walked alone, once he approached the pavilion, Jebediah having mercifully dropped back to let him be alone with his grief. But he was not conscious of his feet, or of any feeling other than unbelieving numbness, until he paused before the curtained entryway. Taking a deep breath, he laid his hands on the curtain he had drawn aside so often before and stepped inside. He let the curtain fall behind him before he could allow his eyes to raise and behold what lay within.

All of them looked up as the curtain fell. There was Guaire, kneeling at the head of Camber's sleeping pallet, and a ghostly-pale Joram, praying at his father's side, and Alister Cullen supporting himself against the pavilion's center pole, looking as taut and anxious as Rhys had ever seen him.

But what caught and held his attention, became the core of his awareness, was the body which lay between them, stretched serenely on its pallet as though only asleep, all signs of battle now washed from the white-clad body. The face was unmistakably Camber's.

He stood, they knelt, in that frozen tableau for several heartbeats, no one moving except Guaire, who resumed combing his dead master's silver-gilt hair. Joram stared at Rhys; Rhys stared at Joram, at Cullen, at Guaire, avoiding the body now that he had seen it. It was Rhys who finally broke the silence.

"Lord Jebediah came and told me," he said in a low voice. "Alister, he said that you were wounded."

The vicar general straightened wearily, ice eyes never leaving Rhys's.

"I had forgotten," he said simply. He touched a particularly bloody patch on the side of his tunic, allowing a guarded look of discomfort to cross his face, and seemed to falter just a little.

Rhys instinctively moved to his side, putting an arm around his shoulder and supporting him close. The older man's grasp on him was much stronger than he had expected.

Do not betray me, Rhys. A familiar voice spoke in his mind, blocking out all else with a force he would not have dreamed of resisting. *React only to what you see with your eyes. It is Alister who lies dead, not I. Joram knows, but Guaire does not.*

A sob escaped Rhys, despite his attempt to control his reaction, and the vicar general held him close against his chest, helping to hide any betrayal which might cross the Healer's face in front of Guaire.

"Nay, no tears," the gruff voice spoke aloud this time. "He was a soldier in a noble cause, and he would not have wished it."

For Rhys and for Joram, kneeling still beside the pallet, the words had a double meaning which Guaire would never share. As Joram bowed his head once more, Rhys drew back from Camber and gazed tearfully into the strange, sea-ice eyes. With an effort, he rearranged his features to the grieving he knew Guaire or anyone else would expect. Blinking back his tears, he sought and secured the control he must maintain.

"Aye, Father Cullen," he whispered. "I'll try to remember that. Come, let me attend to your wounds. What strength I have must be for the living."

"I am not badly hurt," Camber said.

"Perhaps not, but you must let me be the judge of that. May we go to your own pavilion, or would you rather remain here?"

Camber gestured vaguely. "To my own. The day has been weary, and I can do naught else here."

Without further words, Rhys took his father-in-law's arm, no longer quite so familiar in form, and went with him to the entryway. They paused, both of them, to glance back at Joram, at the peaceful body lying between him and the grieving Guaire, then moved out of the pavilion. The guards drew to attention and saluted, returned to rest, as the two made their way across the clearing toward the pavilion which had been Cullen's.

Jebediah had been waiting, but now he was engaged in a serious conversation with two of his undercommanders, who were obviously requesting his presence elsewhere. He raised a hand to Camber, and Camber gave a reassuring wave that he had seen Alister Cullen use a dozen times. Jebediah looked relieved as he turned to go with the commanders.

"Thank God for that," Camber whispered as they moved away from Jebediah. "I don't think he suspects, but he must not be given the chance to grow suspicious. You're going to have to help me play this part, Rhys—especially now, in the beginning, until I get oriented. I'll explain more later—why it was necessary, and such—but for now, I think it wisest that I appear to rest, and recover but slowly. I have *his* memories to clear eventually, as well. I shall need your help."

"You know you shall have it" was Rhys's only whispered reply as they drew near the Michaeline enclosure.

A blue-mantled guard bowed and drew back the entry flap as the two approached.

"They said that you were injured, Father General," the man said anxiously. "Shall I send for your servant?"

"Nay, Lord Rhys will tend me," Camber replied. "Pray, see that we are not disturbed for a while."

"Of course, Father General."

As the flap closed behind them, Rhys began shaking in reaction. Camber held him close for several heartbeats, trying to ease his tumultous thoughts, until Rhys could regain control.

"My God, but you take a chance, Camber!" the young man finally whispered fiercely. "Why on earth—"

"Hush, you must not use that name. He whom the world knows as Camber is dead. Only you and Joram know the truth."

"And Evaine—may she be told?" Rhys asked, drawing back to look into the cool, ice-pale eyes.

Camber released him and began unbuckling his sword belt, the craggy face troubled. "Aye, of course. I wish there were some way to spare her the initial news, but she is bound to hear before we reach her . . ."

He let his voice trail off as Rhys helped him pull off the blood-stiffened Michaeline surcoat. Rhys searched the bloody mail beneath with an anxious eye, but Camber merely smiled as he bent to remove his spurs.

"Nay, the blood is his," he said. "I am uninjured, I told you."

He paused as Rhys bent to unbuckle the fastenings of his greaves, then let his weary body sink to a camp-stool, let the younger man pull off his boots and ease the mail chausses from his legs. The hauberk was next, and Camber slipped out of it with practiced ease, making a wry face at the great slashes in the metal links. The quilted doublet beneath was likewise slashed and stained with blood.

"I suppose you don't call this an injury?" Rhys muttered as he undid laces, trying to get at Camber's body beneath.

Camber almost had to smile. "I told you, this is but for show. Even I can heal the wounds I bear."

He winced and closed his eyes briefly as Rhys worked the blood-caked doublet from what could now be seen as a particularly ugly-looking wound, and for a moment Rhys was sure his words were mere bravado. The wound he had uncovered looked frighteningly real, and thus far had defied even Rhys's questing mind touch to be proven otherwise.

But then he heard the sound of approaching footsteps, which Camber had undoubtedly already sensed, and knew that Camber was merely playing his part. Instantly, he slipped into his own accustomed role as concerned physician, frowning and muttering worriedly over his patient as the curtain was withdrawn and more torchlight streamed into the tent.

"Pardon, Father General, but I heard that you were

wounded and brought warm water and cloths to bathe your hurts."

The speaker was Alister Cullen's body servant, Johannes, a lay brother of the Michaeline Order who was fairly new to Cullen's service. Also, Camber and Rhys remembered simultaneously, Johannes was not Deryni. If they were both reasonably careful, they should be able to bluff their way through the next little while with the man none the wiser. In fact, a glib performance now would greatly reinforce Camber's new role in the future, if Johannes spoke to his brethren— as he was almost certain to do.

"Your arrival is well timed, Brother," Rhys said briskly, motioning the man closer. "The father general insists that his wounds are not serious, but I want to see that for myself. I think our ideas of serious may differ. Bring you that water near." He waved away the guard who was lurking in the doorway. "Thank you, Sir Beren. All is well."

As the flap fell into place once more, Rhys took the basin of water from Johannes and put it on the carpet beside him, bidding the brother stand behind Camber's stool to support him. The vicar general was now looking decidedly pale, and Rhys marveled at Camber's ability to assume the difficult role in so short a time.

He reached out with his mind as he began washing the wounds, knowing that the anxious Brother Johannes could detect no trace of their communication.

I will follow your lead in this, he thought, glancing at Camber's half-closed eyes. *But if you should seem to faint away from weakness and the pain of your wounds, that would not be unexpected. It might give you an excuse to go easy for the first few days, until you are secure in your role.*

Camber's mind reached out in answer, his thought caressing Rhys's mind with affection. *That thought had also occurred to me, son. But for now, I think we must heal these wounds convincingly enough to assure our gentle Johannes that naught is amiss with his master. Lay your hand there, above the great wound in the side, and I will ease it away.*

Rhys did as he was bidden, feeling very strange that he should have to exert no effort to have the wound melt away beneath his touch. Camber, too, caught the strangeness of the operation; for him, it was likely as close as he could ever come to actually healing, and the sensation was exhilarating. He marveled wordlessly as he bade Rhys move on to a lesser wound. The first now appeared to be no more than a narrow, slightly moist red line—for they dared not "heal" so great a wound completely, with Rhys so fatigued.

After that, Camber let himself sink back against Johannes's chest, as though half fainting, briefly touching the man's unconscious concern to confirm that he really was unaware of what was happening. The next wound and the next passed into oblivion in fairly rapid succession, and Camber let himself sag against Johannes even more weakly.

"He is greatly fatigued," Rhys murmured to Johannes as he wiped bloody hands on a towel and pushed the basin of reddened water aside. "I want him to sleep now. Help me get him to bed."

"Nay," Camber said, stirring against Johannes's body and raising a hand feebly. "I must see to my men. There is much to be done."

"Others will do it. You need to rest," Rhys said firmly, helping Johannes lift the protesting man to the sleeping pallet.

While Camber continued to protest halfheartedly, entirely for Johannes's benefit, the brother eased from his master's war-weary body the last of his bloodstained garments and drew upon him a clean singlet of soft white linen. Rhys merely shook his head at all of Camber's protestations, tucking a sleeping fur snugly around him after he had forced him back on the pallet.

"I want no more arguments, Father General. You are to sleep now," Rhys commanded, laying a hand on the older man's brow. "Do not fight me, or you will wear out both of us in the struggling, and I will be useless to the other wounded who need my attention."

The pale eyes fluttered closed, and the man appeared to sleep. But just before Rhys drew his hand away, he caught the appreciative thought of an alert and very amused Camber.

A heartless argument to beguile a fighting man! the thought chastised gently. *If I were Alister, I should be overcome with conscience, as you intended. Go now, and do what you must. I promise I shall try to rest.*

He did try, when Rhys had gone and Brother Johannes could no longer find excuse to linger in the pavilion. Camber followed Johannes's movements through carefully slitted eyelids, feigning sleep whenever the brother would lean close to study his shallow breathing. Finally, Johannes extinguished all but one of the shielded rushlights and quietly left the tent. Camber heard him conversing with the guards for several minutes, but then all fell silent save for the normal sounds of the camp outside.

Breathing a thankful sigh, Camber let himself relax in fact. With any luck, he might not be disturbed again until morning.

He took a few deep breaths to settle his thoughts and stretched luxuriously, testing the responses and sensations of his new form. In fact, few changes had needed to be made, other than to face and hands, for he and Alister had been almost of a size, both of them tall and lean—though Alister had stood perhaps a fingerspan taller.

But height was easy enough to camouflage, if anyone even noticed so slight a difference. If the present Alister Cullen walked a trifle shorter, that could easily be ascribed to fatigue, to the new weight of responsibility which would befall him, now that Camber was dead.

Facial differences were no problem at all. Now that the initial transformation was accomplished, he could even, if he wished, change back to his own form occasionally, with little exertion involved. He had already taken the necessary steps to ensure that no conscious effort would be required to maintain his façade; it would remain even when he was asleep or unconscious. Of course, any enormous outpouring of power would probably necessitate his returning to his own shape for a time, but those instances would be few and, hopefully, in places of safety. Otherwise, only an act of his own will could let his new visage mist away. Not by appearance would he be betrayed.

Behavior might be another story. Alister Cullen had been a very complex individual, with relationships extending into many areas of endeavor. Jebediah and Cinhil had been but the first of many he would have to cope with. Of course, Camber had what remained of Alister's memories— or would have, once he found the necessary privacy and support to assimilate them safely—but now was definitely not the time to make them truly his. In the meantime, he would have to rely on his own memories of the vicar general, trusting instinct and the excuse of grief and battle fatigue to cover any lapses of behavior.

One positive thing stood in his favor, at any rate: Alister Cullen, most conservative of Deryni, had never been given to public displays of his abilities. Unless he had been very different among the members of his Order, which Camber doubted, there being humans as well as Deryni among the Michaelines, Alister Cullen was known to be very reluctant to make much of his Deryniness. In addition, it was expected that clergy, especially Deryni, were naturally closeminded most of the time, since they kept the secrets of other men's confessions locked within their minds. As a bishop, Alister would be even more inviolate. In all, Camber should have little difficulty in shielding his own distinctive psychic identity, even from other Deryni. Superficial contacts would not reveal him, once Alister's memories were his.

He was thinking about that aspect of his new identity, beginning to consider how he was going to reconcile Alister's priestly status with his own, when he became aware of voices outside the pavilion again. Controlling a frown, for he had hoped not to have to face anyone else tonight, he extended his senses and listened carefully. A shiver of apprehension went through him as he recognized Cinhil's voice.

"I know that he was wounded, and I know that Lord Rhys gave orders that he was not to be disturbed," Cinhil was saying. "However, I must see him. I promise I will not be long."

There was a momentary pause, and then the whisper of the curtain being withdrawn. Camber, his face turned away from the entryway, closed his eyes and prayed that Cinhil would not insist upon speaking with him.

CHAPTER NINE

As a wise masterbuilder, I have laid the foundation, and another buildeth thereon. But let every man take heed how he buildeth thereupon.

—I Corinthians 3:10

There was silence for a dozen heartbeats. He knew that Cinhil must be standing in the entryway, and ached to turn his head and see for sure; but he dared not. Cinhil still might leave.

Finally, when the waiting had grown almost intolerable, soft footfalls approached, muffled on the thickly woven carpet. Another silence, as the footsteps stopped a few paces from his head, and then a light touch on his shoulder.

He continued to feign sleep, still hoping that Cinhil would give up, but the touch became a shake. With a grunt which he hoped was convincing, Camber grimaced and turned his head slightly. Letting his brow furrow in mild irritation, he blinked groggily at Cinhil, pretending to be still befogged by sleep, then rolled onto his back to peer at Cinhil more closely. The king looked disturbed, and old beyond his years.

"Sire?" Camber said.

Cinhil nodded quickly, swallowing, and stepped back a pace.

"Forgive me for waking you, Father Cullen, but I had to talk with someone."

With a weary sigh which was not at all contrived, Camber sat up on the pallet and drew the sleeping furs more closely around him, rubbing his eyes with one hand and stifling a yawn as his mind raced.

He was obviously committed to talking with Cinhil, much against his better judgment at this early stage in his new persona. He only hoped he could remember enough to keep himself out of trouble. Thank God that Joram had thought to tell him of the conversation between Cullen and Cinhil the night before. And the pair's stormy parting, early this morning, would lend credence to any brusqueness which Camber might have to apply to cover gaps in his knowledge.

Yawning again, he made his eyes focus on Cinhil's dim features, a resignedly patient expression on his new face.

"Forgive me, Sire. Rhys made me sleep, and resisting his compulsion is not an easy thing. How may I serve you?"

Cinhil glanced at his booted feet in embarrassment. "I'm sorry, Father. I know that you were wounded, but I—I had to ask you more about Camber. I cannot believe that he is dead."

Camber made himself look away, afraid of where

this line of discussion might lead, and decided to take the offensive.

"You saw his body," he said softly. "Why can you not believe? Is this not what you wanted, in the end?"

Cinhil gasped, his face going white, and Camber wondered whether he had gone too far.

"What I wanted? Father, I have never—"

"Not consciously, perhaps," Camber conceded, not giving Cinhil a chance to protest too much. "But all of us who have tried to be close to you, to help you, have been aware of your resentment. He was its focal point. He it was who found you, who had you taken from the life you loved, who hammered at your conscience, day by day, until you had to accept your destiny."

"But I never wished him dead!"

"Perhaps not. Outside your heart, it matters little now," Camber replied wearily. "He *is* dead. He who was responsible for your plight is gone. Now there is no one to hold you to your duty."

With a strangled little cry, Cinhil sank down on a campstool, burying his face in trembling hands. As Camber cautiously turned his head toward him, he could see Cinhil's shoulders shaking with silent sobs, the frosted sable hair gleaming faintly in the feeble rushlight.

Camber said nothing—merely waited until the sobbing had stopped and the royal head began to lift from hands which still shook with emotion. He let Alister's icy eyes soften as Cinhil lifted teary gray ones to them.

"Forgive me, Cinhil, I was over-harsh. It's late, and I am war-weary and sleep-fogged and not myself."

"Nay, in some respects you were right," Cinhil whispered, wiping a sleeve across his eyes. "I did blame him for the loss of my religious life, and I suppose that, in a way, I always will." He sniffed loudly and lowered his eyes. "But he was a man of wisdom, who loved this land and its people in ways that I will probably never understand. And in many respects, *he* was right: however much I personally resent it, there was no other candidate for the throne besides myself. For the good of Gwynedd, I must accept that —but you must try to understand, when my inner self cries out with longing for something I can never have again."

Camber bowed his head, wondering whether he could have misjudged Cinhil's true feelings for him. But though the king seemed genuinely contrite at the moment, Camber suspected that the truth might be exactly as Cinhil had painted it: a love-hate balance which would never be resolved, even with Camber's death.

Now, to determine whether Camber's end had, perhaps, at least opened the way for a further working relationship with Cullen . . .

"I believe I do understand, Sire," he finally said, after a long pause. "And what is more, I think Camber did, too."

Cinhil's tear-streaked face turned hopeful. "Do you really think so, Father?"

"Aye. He died in my and Joram's arms, but his last thoughts were of you, Cinhil: of wondering what would happen to you and to Gwynedd and to all else he had begun, once he was gone. He cared about you greatly, my son."

"I was not worthy of his last concern," Cinhil said miserably. "He should have turned his thoughts to God."

"He did that, too," Camber replied. "He died convinced that he had done the best he could with his life—as easy a death as I have ever seen. I truly believe he is at peace now."

"I pray you may be right," Cinhil whispered.

An awkward silence fell upon them both, as Cinhil averted his eyes and appeared to be lost in thought. But then Cinhil looked up again, a hopeful yet apprehensive expression on his face.

"Perhaps this isn't the time or the place to ask this, Father—but I think that Camber would approve. I wanted to ask whether—whether it was too late to accept the offer you made me last night."

"What made you think it might be too late?" Camber asked quietly, wondering what, specifically, Cinhil was referring to.

Cinhil pleated an edge of his cloak between nervous fingers, not looking up. "We—were both very angry this morning."

"We were both anxious for the day," Camber replied, "with not enough sleep and too much imagination for either of our good. I should not have lost my temper."

"No, I said hateful things," Cinhil insisted. "You were right, and I didn't want to believe you. Had I been stronger in my faith, I might have chosen differently. God did not will it so."

"God gives us all the will to make choices," Camber pointed out. "He does not necessarily compel us to make the right ones."

"Alas for that." Cinhil sighed and stood. "But I made my choice, for whatever reason. Now I must learn to live with the consequences of that choice. Good night, Father."

"Good night, Sire," Camber murmured as Cinhil headed slowly toward the entryway, not looking back. "So must we all learn," he added when Cinhil had gone.

They did not start back to Valoret for several days, for men and beasts were battle-weary, and there was much still to do at Iomaire. While Healers of both the physical and spiritual kind worked their craft among the living, others saw to the needs of the dead of both sides. The grave mounds erected in the days which followed would forever change the face of the Iomaire plain, for only the bodies of the highest nobility would be returned home for burial. The scarred hills of Coldoire would be a grim reminder of the realities of war for generations to come.

Other work there was that first night, and all the

day after, as yet another group of men—crack soldiers, all—scoured the hills and glens of Iomaire for remnants of the invading army which had escaped their grasp in battle. Most of the enemy not actually taken during the fighting had scattered with the evening winds if they could, but there were many more who were too badly wounded to flee. These the royal troops ferreted out, bringing the living to the ministrations of the surgeons and the dead to the tendering of the priests and burial details.

In the end, prisoners of actual Torenthi allegiance numbered more than fivescore, most of them of the Torenthi nobility who had family or feudal obligations to the slain Ariella of Festil. These Cinhil immediately declared eligible for ransom, realizing, rightly, that ransom could help to replenish Gwynedd's war-depleted coffers. The Torenthi prisoners would be marched back to Valoret with the victorious army, there to be detained under strict but honorable conditions until arrangements could be hammered out for their release with agents of the King of Torenth.

But for the men of Gwynedd who had taken arms against their lawful king—no matter that they had sided with the representatives of their former liege lord—Cinhil could not afford to be so lenient. The point must be made, and firmly made, that Gwynedd's new master was exactly that, and would tolerate no further rebellion, under whatever guise. An object lesson was required, and it was Cinhil who must decide how it was to be administered.

It was not a task which the king relished, but Jebediah and Earl Sighere impressed upon him its necessity. At Cinhil's request, his advisors outlined a wide selection of fitting and just punishments, describing them in terms which left very little even to Cinhil's naive imagination. After much learned discourse, and more than one tearful session at prayer, Cinhil made the first truly independent decision of his reign, settling upon a disposition which was at once harsh, just, and merciful.

The surviving Gwynedd prisoners, numbering nearly two hundred fifty, would be decimated, each tenth man being chosen by lot, without regard to rank, for public hanging along the way home, as a vivid lesson on the fruits of treason. But for those spared the gallows trees, a more clement fate was destined—though those men would not be told of the king's mercy until they reached the capital with the Torenthi prisoners. Though they would be marched home in bondage, wrists lashed to spears across their shoulders and stripped of all titles and lands, at Valoret they would be pardoned and released, free from that moment to build new lives without further prejudice for what they had done.

As for the slain Ariclla, her severed head was mounted on a spear and given to the Royal Archer Corps to carry back to Valoret—Sighere's suggestion—the rest of the body being divided and pieces sent to various of Cinhil's cities for display on their gates. In this way, it was hoped, future malcontents would observe and learn the true mettle of their new king, and future rebellions would be discouraged. Cinhil had a kingdom to settle. He could not afford another war for some time.

The decisions made, camp was struck. Sighere bade farewell to his erstwhile allies and took his army back into Eastmarch's heartland to lick his wounds, while Cinhil and his army started on the road to Valoret. At five-mile intervals, Cinhil's sentence was carried out on the chosen prisoners, so that the trees of Gwynedd bore strange, dangling fruit which jerked briefly and then was still until the carrion birds came. Local peasants and nobles were forbidden to cut the bodies down until thirty days had passed, under pain of attainder and banishment. Cinhil forced himself to watch the first execution, but after that he had Jebediah oversee the operation.

As for Camber, Cinhil was apparently still contrite over his recent harassment of the dead lord and his other Deryni mentors, and had decreed that Camber's body should be given all honors during the journey back. The shrouded body, magically preserved by Rhys to prevent decomposition in the late June heat, was borne on a litter carried by two cream palfreys, escorted by six of Gwynedd's highest-ranking lords in full battle array, the assignments changing twice a day to accommodate all those who wished so to serve.

Clergy with candles and incense and processional crosses marched before and behind the bier, chanting psalms and prayers for the repose of the dead man's soul; and Camber himself, in his guise of Alister Cullen, was obliged to lead the Michaeline contingent just behind the procession, with Joram sometimes riding at his side as a Michaeline and sometimes marching afoot in a closer position of honor as Camber's son.

Camber disliked the experience intensely, and made a point of engaging, or appearing to engage, in deep meditation whenever possible, that he might not be drawn into unnecessary conversation and risk betraying himself. But his self-imposed mental isolation had its drawbacks, for it gave him too much time to absorb and analyze the reception the cortege was meeting along the way.

Not to many men is it given to observe the reaction to their own death. For Camber, it was an illuminating experience. He was, in turn, amazed, flattered, and a little disturbed—though he could not put his finger on the reason for that last reaction.

He had expected sadness. For that, he was prepared. He could hardly have been unaware of the gratitude of the people for his restoration of the Haldane line, after the excesses of Imre. But he had not thought to find so much personal affection for Camber among the common folk, who could hardly know much of his actual role in bringing Cinhil to the throne. Apparently, news had traveled more quickly, and with far more embellishments, than he had dreamed. Though he was certain he had never done anything to warrant it, he found himself being lauded as a new folk hero. That realization made him distinctly uncomfortable.

But if the ride back to Valoret was difficult, the arrival, on the Calends of July, was even more traumatic. Because of the slow progress of the funeral cortege and the train of wounded, and the necessity to execute the requisite prisoners along the way, word of their coming and the outcome of the battle had reached the capital several days before they did. Into a strangely silent city they rode, past throngs who cheered halfheartedly and bowed as Cinhil passed, but fell silent, some kneeling in respect, as Camber's bier went by.

Camber, from his vantage point at the tail of the procession, watched Cinhil's reaction farther on ahead, wondering as the king grew more and more subdued. He could almost sense that Cinhil was feeling pangs of jealousy.

But then they were entering the castle itself, under the eyes of all the assembled court, and Camber had something new to worry about. For among the queen and her ladies and Archbishop Anscom and a host of other clerics, there was Evaine, standing stricken and small and very lonely-looking, though Cathan's Elinor plucked at her sleeve and the folk of the court pressed at her from either side.

Her, Camber saw first, as he drew rein in the crowded yard; but at the same moment he was also aware of Anscom moving toward him, toward the MacRorie bier. Helpless to go to Evaine under the circumstances, he dismounted and waited for Anscom, at the same time catching Rhys's attention and signaling him to go to Evaine. He kept his eyes averted as he knelt to kiss the archbishop's ring.

"Your Grace," he murmured.

With a distracted nod, Anscom raised him up, his eyes only for the bier beside them. Blinking back tears, the old archbishop brushed a hand across his eyes, then knelt solemnly beside the bier and bowed his head for several minutes, the others of his party joining him. Silence fell on that part of the courtyard, slowly spreading through the rest of the company.

As Camber, too, knelt, feeling Joram slip into place at his right elbow, he knew that Joram was also aware of Evaine with the royal party across the yard. On the steps, he saw Rhys make his way through the crowd to Evaine, cradling her head against his shoulder as he took her in his arms. Cinhil's greeting to his queen was cooler and far more restrained, as if he were much more interested in what was happening around the bier.

Camber had a queasy sensation as he watched Cinhil out of the edge of his vision, the king's face staying set and expressionless as he and his party turned and went into the hall. His only comfort was the certain knowledge that Rhys had, by now, ended Evaine's grieving with his glad news. He wondered how long it would be before he could comfort his daughter himself.

At length, Anscom finished his prayers, blessed himself, and stood, and suddenly things were moving again. As his clergy took the body from the charge of the lords who had escorted it into the yard and moved with it into the Chapel Royal, Anscom turned straight toward Camber, moving deftly between him and Joram to lay a hand on either's shoulder. The pressure of his touch urged both men toward the chapel where the cortege had disappeared, though they lagged well behind the actual procession. Joram stumbled a little as they climbed the shallow steps—an unaccustomed moment of clumsiness for one such as Joram.

"Joram, I think you can guess how deeply grieved I was to hear of your father's death," the archbishop said, his voice low and strained as they stopped in the chapel's porch. "I need not tell you how like brothers we were, or how much his friendship meant to me. I hope you will accept my offer of whatever assistance I might be able to render in the future, for love of his memory as well as the affection I have always held for you."

Joram murmured a suitable sound of thanks and bowed his head. Camber knew how difficult the charade must be for him.

"And Alister," the archbishop continued, glancing sidelong at Camber, "I know how you, too, will miss him, and in what high regard his whole family has held you of late. Therefore, I hope you will not take it amiss that I dare to ask a great favor of you."

Camber nodded, not trusting himself to speak as he wondered what Anscom had in mind.

"First, you should know that I have scheduled the funeral for the day after tomorrow," Anscom continued. "Joram, it may comfort you to learn that the news reached me before it reached your sister, so that I was able to ease her initial grief at least a little. But she is a very practical young woman, as you know, and her next thought was to ask whether I would permit both of you to assist in the Requiem Mass. Joram, I think that I need not ask your answer."

"No, Your Grace," Joram whispered. "No power in heaven or earth could keep me from that Office."

"I thought not," Anscom said gently. "And you, Alister? Your participation is your choice, of course. Though Evaine did request it, Camber was not of your Order, and I will certainly understand if you wish to decline, under the circumstances."

Camber drew a thoughtful breath, wondering whether he dared accept. Of course, Evaine had not known the truth of the situation when she made the request—though she had read the relationship between himself and Alister Cullen sufficiently well to realize that he would have wanted Alister to be asked.

But the overriding question in his own mind, at this point, was whether, even for form's sake, he could validly assist at *anyone's* Mass. As a deacon only, in his own right, and one who had not, in some years, exercised that minor but holy office, he had hoped to avoid any religious observances which were not absolutely necessary to maintain his new identity. Still, if he could validly assist—Anscom would be the principal celebrant, after all—he would be one more person who could, at least in his heart, bid proper farewell to the real Alister Cullen. For, unless other arrangements could be worked out later, this would likely be the only funeral which the good vicar general would receive.

He glanced at Joram to find his son's eyes full on him, and knew that Joram must already have guessed what was going through his mind. Now he must trust that he could question Joram without Anscom's knowing what was happening.

"Joram, I will defer strictly to your wishes in this matter," he said softly, making his craggy face look as stricken as he could. "If you had rather keep this smaller and more private, I will certainly understand."

Joram shook his head, a touch of resigned but bitter mirth touching the gray eyes in a way that only Camber could read, after years of intimate acquaintance.

"Thank you for your offer, Vicar General, but I think that my father would have been honored to have you assist us. Whatever differences he had with our Order were long ago reconciled, and I know he valued your friendship greatly in this last year or so."

"Then I shall be honored to accept," Camber said, inclining his head graciously.

"My thanks as well, Alister," Anscom replied.

"There is one thing which *I* would ask, Father General," Joram continued. There was something in his tone which alerted Camber to the fact that this, too, was important. "I should like your permission for him to be buried in the habit of a Michaeline. Though not of our Order in his lifetime, he would have made a noble member, had he chosen so. It is not an uncommon request, and I believe my sister would approve."

Camber lowered his eyes, appreciating anew the skill with which his son so often moved. What Joram had said, supposedly about his father, was certainly true—but it was also a perfect way to ensure that

Camber provided properly for Alister, who most definitely would have wanted to be buried in the garb of his Order. Still, on the outside chance that he had misread Joram's intentions . . .

"I have no objections," he said, meeting Joram's eyes squarely. "Unless the Chapter should object, which I would not anticipate, I see no reason not to grant your request. Your Grace, have you any thoughts on this matter?"

"It's your Order, Alister," Anscom replied. "However, I suspect that Camber would have been pleased at the gesture. He and I studied together for the priesthood, you know, when we were only boys. After his two brothers died, his father took him out of school at the seminary, and I went on alone." Anscom sighed. "He would probably chide me for saying so, but he would have made an excellent priest."

"Nay, I think he would be flattered, Your Grace," Joram said, shooting a glance at Camber which was totally unnoticed by the archbishop. "If there is nothing more, sir, I should go to my sister."

Anscom came back from his reverie with a start. "Oh, forgive me, please, Joram. I've been most insensitive. And both of you will be tired from your long journey.

"One last thing, Alister, and then I'll let you both go. Perhaps this is not a good time to ask this, either, but I wonder whether you've made any decision yet on your successor as vicar general? While you were en route back, I conferred with Robert Oriss, and we've set a tentative date of Sunday a week for your mutual consecrations. Will that impose any particular strain on you?"

Camber raised bushy eyebrows in consideration. "I don't think so. Joram, do you?" He had no idea who Cullen might have had in mind, or even how the selection was made.

Joram shrugged and shook his head, and Anscom nodded with satisfaction.

"Good, then. I'll tell Robert that you agree, and

have the masters of ceremonies begin making preparations." He started to go, then turned back to face them.

"By the way, who *are* you going to name as your successor?"

I was afraid he'd ask that, Camber thought, glancing at his feet in an effort to gain time.

"In all honesty, I haven't given it much thought for the past week or so, Your Grace," he answered truthfully. "However," he continued, glancing at Joram and seeing no sign of disagreement, "I'll certainly inform you, as soon as a final decision has been made."

"Good enough." Anscom's tone seemed to indicate complete satisfaction. "I'll leave you, then. I know that both of you will have much to do."

When both Camber and Joram had bent to kiss his ring again, Anscom turned and rejoined his secretary to go into the chapel proper. As their forms receded down a clerestory aisle, Camber glanced apprehensively at Joram.

"Well, how did I do?" he murmured under his breath, mentally and visually scanning around them to ensure that they would not be overheard.

"It just may work," Joram replied. He, too, glanced around with a deceptive casualness. "By the way, even I haven't the foggiest notion whom Alister had in mind for his successor. Jebediah might, but I don't think you want to spend too much time with him, at least until you learn where he and Alister stood. And the successor is chosen by the vicar general, but ratified by the entire chapter of the Order. At least your answer was sufficiently vague to allow for that—a very good guess."

"Worthy of your own, about the habit," Camber acknowledged. "It's something I never would have thought of, until it was too late—though it's an obvious point that Alister would have appreciated."

Joram nodded curtly. "If it has to be this way, I'll do everything I can to keep things going smoothly.

But you know I don't like it, even though it's beginning to look like you might carry it off."

"This is neither the time nor the place to discuss that," Camber murmured, glancing around nervously once again, though he knew there was no one nearby. "However, the conversation we just had with Anscom points up something which is urgent—and that's for me to get Alister's memories integrated with my own as soon as possible. God knows, there weren't many left, but I need all the help I can get. Besides, I'm starting to get the expected headaches. How soon do you think we dare get together with Rhys and Evaine?"

Joram glanced at the tiled floor. "Getting Evaine to you will be the main problem. Rhys and I have ample legitimate excuses for being seen going to and from your quarters—which are in the archbishop's palace, by the way. Don't forget and go back to your own."

"I'll remember. Any suggestions?"

"Well, it can't be tonight," Joram said. "That's totally out of the question. What you have in mind will take a lot of energy, and none of us have had a decent night's sleep in weeks."

"I'll grant you that. How about tomorrow night, then?"

"Tentatively, yes," Joram agreed. "In the meantime, I think you should plead extreme fatigue, which is not far from the truth, and take to your bed. I'll send Rhys to see you, and have him order you excused from your official duties for as long as he can get away with it. I'll also try to arrange for Brother Johannes to be temporarily reassigned or something, until you've learned the ropes well enough not to get him suspicious."

"I don't think he's a problem, but do what you think best. When will you send Rhys?"

"How about after dinner? I think he deserves a little time with Evaine, don't you?"

Camber sighed and rubbed his forehead wearily. "Oh, of course I do, Joram. I'm sorry. I'm not really that heartless. But there are some scrolls in my old quarters which Evaine should consult before we get together. I have to give Rhys directions on how to find the right ones. That's very important."

"I know it is," Joram replied in a very low voice. "Maybe I overreacted. I know I should be trying to look at the larger plan, but somehow, I keep seeing Alister's body lying in that clearing—and then his changed one, being prepared in there." He gestured vaguely toward the sacristy door. "Sometimes, it almost seems that I'm the only one who really cares."

"You don't really believe that."

"No, but I can't help the way I feel." Joram bowed his head. "I'll send Rhys as soon as I can."

"Thank you. And Evaine?"

Joram sighed. "I'll think of something."

CHAPTER TEN

The father of the righteous shall greatly rejoice: and he that begetteth a wise child shall have joy of him.

—Proverbs 23:24

Early that evening, when Rhys had temporarily left her for the archbishop's palace, Evaine paced the floor of Camber's old quarters and wondered what her father was doing. She envied her husband, who was with him now, and she could not help feeling resentment that she was being left out of things—though Rhys had assured her that he would soon be involved all too completely.

She went to the window to peer out toward the archbishop's palace, fancying she could see the very window where her father now lay, but the night air was too chilly, even in summer, for her to stand there for long, clad only in her shift. Pulling a robe from the bed, she settled into the seat in the window embrasure and tucked her legs beneath her. The velvet and fur of the robe felt warm against her back and helped ease the cold and damp of the wall where she leaned against it, as well as the chill of the night air.

She could hardly believe now, looking back over the events of the day, that her world could change so radically in so short a time—though, of course, it had changed thus when she first received word of her father's death, almost a week ago. Then, the summer sunshine had changed to deepest gloom with the speaking of three simple and dread words: "He is dead." The kindly Archbishop Anscom, himself almost like a father to her, had brought the news, and shared her trembling grief for several hours.

She had not believed him at first; and long after she said she believed, she still did not believe him in her inner core. She and her father had been too close in life for her not to have sensed the exact moment of his death, for her not to feel the emptiness occasioned by his passing. It could not be true! It must not!

And yet, as the days passed and the news did not change, even she began to doubt. The cortege which entered the castle yard that morning had touched her heart with icy fingers, as though to underline the awful truth which she dared deny no longer. Then, just when hope was at its lowest ebb, there was Rhys in her arms, and his quick, hard kiss, and the two reviving words: "He lives!"

She could weep for joy, then, though those around her mistook it for grief which she had not been able to show in all the long days of waiting for her father's return. As soon as was decent, she and Rhys retired to

the rooms in which Evaine had taken up her domicile
while awaiting the dreaded confirmation of Camber's
death. The next hours were spent in joyous reunion
with him who, with her father, she had come to regard as the most important person in her life. As they
spoke and loved and drank each other's sight, he told
her of the past weeks' tidings, and how Camber came
to live and Alister to die. When, as dusk was falling, a
servant finally came with food, they at last parted long
enough to sit before the fire and eat. After that, Rhys
left her to go and receive instructions from her father.

She thought she understood the urgency with which
her father bade Rhys come. From what her husband
had told her, Camber's assumption of Alister Cullen's
form and memories had been extremely arduous, especially after the stresses and fatigues of an all-day
physical battle. Her brief conversation with Joram,
just after his arrival, had also hinted at other measures
which their father had had to employ in resolving all
the details of Ariella's death. Even Joram and Rhys,
younger by thirty years than her father, had not yet
fully recovered from the experience of that day and
night—and Camber was not yet finished.

According to Joram, their father had yet to complete the process he had started in the clearing there
at Iomaire, for he had not yet had a chance to assimilate the memories gleaned from the dead Alister's
mind. Now those memories festered, a continuing
drain on his strength—a process which would only stop
with the facing and whole assumption of those memories, or with madness and death.

She shivered as she thought about that, and not because of physical cold. She knew that Camber had the
ability to do what must be done, and she even suspected she knew where he had gotten the knowledge,
though she had never seen it herself. He had
mentioned, in passing, certain scrolls he had which
purported to give guidance in many varied and difficult arcane procedures, not the least of which had been
the abortive scrying experiment which they had at-

tempted only weeks before. If these scrolls were the source of his knowledge—and she thought she knew where he kept them hidden—then she ought to read them before she tried to help him.

She would not wait for Rhys to come back. She need not waste precious time. Leaving the window seat, she padded over to the canopied bed and climbed up on it, kicking aside the rumpled pillows so that she could lift the heavy tapestry hanging at the head and wriggle underneath. Not bothering with light, she ran her hands across the bare rock until she found what she was looking for, mentally articulating a series of syllables highly unlikely to be combined at random. After only a second's hesitation, a portion of the rock hinged aside.

The wood-lined cupboard behind contained half a dozen carefully rolled scrolls, each wrapped in an oiled-leather casing and bound with silken cords. Sweeping the scrolls into her arms, Evaine brought them out from under the tapestry and let them fall in a heap on the rumpled bedclothes, staggering a little as she struggled out from under the heavy hanging. As she sank down on the bed, tucking her robe around her bare feet, she took up the first of the scrolls and untied its cords, absently flaring to life a rack of candles in a standard by the bed. She held the ancient parchment to the light to scan the opening lines.

It seemed like hardly an hour before Rhys returned. Throwing off his cloak, he leaned over to kiss her and then sat beside her on the bed. The bedclothes were littered with scrolls and wrappings and partially unrolled manuscripts. Two of the scrolls had not yet been opened.

"What are those?" Rhys asked, glancing at the sight in dismay.

Evaine put aside the one she had been reading and sighed. "I don't think they're the right ones, Rhys. I haven't gotten to the last two yet, but these first ones are just the Pargan Howiccan manuscripts—valuable from an artistic standpoint, but they can't be the ones Father meant us to see."

"Where did you find them?" Rhys asked, with an easy grin coming across his face.

"Well, obviously not in the right place," she replied with a chuckle, "though, by your expression, you know where I should have looked. These were behind the arras. I thought all his important documents were here." She gestured toward the tapestry and leaned against the headboard with a sigh.

Rhys said nothing—merely smiled and leaned forward to touch one fingertip to her nose. Then, with a gesture for her to follow him, he went into the dressing chamber adjoining the room and began pulling a trunk from behind several layers of clothes on wooden pegs. With Evaine's help, he turned the trunk on its side and laid his hands on the two front corners near the feet. There was a tiny click as part of the bottom of the trunk dropped slightly, revealing a crack.

As Rhys widened the crack with his fingertips, they could see the ends of four scrolls, yellowed with age. Evaine caught her breath as the panel slid back the rest of the way, revealing most of the length of all four scrolls.

"Did he say which one we want?" Evaine breathed, reaching out a hesitant finger to touch a cord of vermilion binding one of them.

The cords on the others were black, green, and golden yellow, and it was to the last of these that Rhys pointed.

"It's this one. He also said that we were, under no circumstances, to read the other three. He wouldn't say why, but he did mention that the scrying information is in one of them, and that even he doesn't feel qualified to cope with some of the information that's in the other two."

Evaine touched the green cord, the black, then looked up at her husband wistfully. "The Tree of the Knowledge of Good and Evil?"

"Your name is close, but it isn't Eve," he said, a smile tugging at the corners of his mouth.

"True." She took the yellow-bound scroll and cradled it delicately against her breast. "Close up the rest, then, so we won't be tempted. If he kept this one in with those, I have a feeling we'll have sufficient to keep us quite busy without asking for trouble."

With a grin, Rhys slid the panel back into place and resealed the trunk. When he had replaced it and rearranged all the way it was before, he returned to the main chamber. Only the yellow-bound scroll lay on the bed now. He sat on the edge and pulled off his boots and doublet, picking up the scroll as Evaine emerged from behind the arras and settled down beside him.

"Here, you open it," he said, handing it to her and arranging the pillows against the head of the bed. "If something's going to happen when we untie the cord, it's probably safer if you do it."

"If *I* do it?" Evaine's hand, which had been about to untie the silken cord, froze in mid-motion. "Rhys, it's only a scroll."

"Probably. However, one can never tell, where Camber is concerned," Rhys said respectfully.

She looked at him curiously for a moment, as though trying to decide whether he was serious, then could not control a grin.

"That's true."

She kissed him lightly on the mouth, then untied the yellow cord and laid it aside, settling back in the curve of his arm to unroll the parchment. The script was of an ancient form, black and authoritative, the language archaic. Evaine's blue eyes skimmed across the first few lines, then skipped back to the top. She wondered how good Rhys was at reading ancient texts. Deciphering the material would be almost like translating.

"Let's see. *Herein is contained much knowledge with which a greedy man might lose his soul and wreak his will upon the weak. But for the prudent man, who loves and fears the gods, here is meat to help him grow, and drink to lift his spirits to the starry skies.*

"*Know, O my son, that what thou shalt read can slay as well as save. Therefore, be not tempted by the Evil One to use such blessings as thou shalt receive for thine own gain. All deeds, and all their consequences, come back threefold upon the doer. Therefore, do good, that thy bounty may increase.*"

She glanced at Rhys. "A timely warning. Did you follow all that?"

"I understand the language. Some of my healing texts are from the same period. This scribe's hand is a little difficult, though. Keep on reading, and I'll try to follow along."

"All right. *Part the First, being a treatise upon the taking of a dead man's shape, and the dangers therein.* I guess that's where Father got the idea."

"And then combined it with the trading of shapes, as he did when Joram and I left Crinan and Wulpher with our shapes at Cathan's funeral," Rhys agreed. "What's the second heading? Something about the minds of the dead?"

Evaine nodded. "*Part the Second, being wise words upon the reading of the memories of the dead, and grievous dangers inherent for the unwary.*"

Rhys nodded. "He's already done that, too. As nearly as I can tell, he drew out what he could and blocked off the information for later assimilation, since there wasn't time to digest it then. And unless the integration of those memories is done correctly, he could go mad trying to keep track of which part is himself and which part is Alister."

"That's what this third section would indicate," Evaine agreed, reading on. "*Part the Third, being instruction upon the safe assimilation of another's memories, with especial attention to the danger of madness, and how to avoid it.*"

"So we need the last section in this scroll," Rhys

said, helping roll up the earlier portions as Evaine worked her way past the first two headings.

The third heading came up, an exact duplicate of the indexing lines. There followed several handspans' worth of closely spaced script, in a much finer hand than the earlier lines. As Evaine bent closer to the writing, Rhys reached out and moved the candle sconce closer to the edge of the bed. He could feel Evaine relaxing and, at the same time, becoming more alert and aware, as she began reading the words of the text.

"The man sufficiently driven as to wish the memories of another is a man driven, indeed. But if there be no help for it, then one must do what is necessary to secure those memories at minimal cost to himself and those around him.

"But he must not delay overlong, for the trapped memories of another fester like a gnawing canker, and will soon destroy the holder, if he act not soon. He will be failing of energy, slow to heal physical hurts, susceptible to aching head and lethargy, all of which will increase as the pressure of alien memory grows. For this reason, it is the wise man who enlists assistance in his task, that he may call upon the strengths of others to augment his own failing ones.

"A Guide, a Healer, and a Guardian are the minimum who should assist him, and it is possible that two of these functions might be combined in the same person, though three are better, having threefold strength."

Evaine stopped reading as a chill went through her, and she glanced at Rhys. He said nothing, but his arm around her shoulders tightened reassuringly and he smiled. With a resigned sigh, she continued.

"Now, the manner of accomplishing the assimilation of another's memories is thus . . ."

They read long, well into the small hours of the morning, and when they had finished the section on memory assimilation, they skimmed the two previous sections to gain a better understanding of what Camber had done already. That information, added to what Rhys had learned in his own work with Camber, simply confirmed what Rhys and Joram had suspected almost from the beginning: that Camber was treading on dangerous ground, and must not delay any longer than was absolutely necessary to complete what he had started. Even if he later discarded the identity he had taken, the memories must be dealt with. They could not be thrown away. And whatever had remained of Alister Cullen, good or bad, noble or despicable, must be faced, mastered, and accepted—and soon. The symptoms were building. Camber had complained of a headache when Rhys had gone to him that night—something he would not have mentioned had he been able to handle it himself. And the Healer had been concerned for several days over Camber's growing weariness.

They slept late the next morning, however, for if they were to assist Camber that night, there must be energy available to all of them; lack of sleep was not likely to do any of them any good. Consequently, it was nearly noon before they stirred. When Rhys had roused himself sufficiently to ask that food be brought, he was told that Father Joram had inquired after them several times already that morning.

Rhys thanked the servant who brought the food and took the tray, asking the man to find Joram and tell him that they could see him at his convenience. They had not eaten more than a few mouthfuls apiece before there came a knock at the door.

Rhys padded to the door, a joint of capon in hand, to find Joram waiting impatiently. The priest had a cloak over his arm, and was glancing about almost as if he had expected to be followed. He gave a sigh of relief as Rhys beckoned him inside.

"I was beginning to think you two were going to sleep forever," he said, nodding nervously to Evaine as Rhys bolted the door behind them. "Do you know how late it is?"

"Approaching noon," Evaine said. She rose to kiss

her brother's cheek, her lips dusty with bread crumbs. "Have some breakfast. You look like you could use it."

"I couldn't eat. What did you learn?"

Evaine sat down and picked up a drumstick, which she inspected carefully before taking a bite out of it. "Starving won't help him, if that's what you're thinking," she said, around the bite of chicken. "If you don't eat, I'm not going to tell you a thing."

She saw Rhys's ill-concealed grin as he sat down behind Joram, and lowered her eyes. Joram snorted in exasperation, the way he had used to do when they were children, then flounced into another chair and picked up a piece of cheese.

"All right, I'm eating," he said, fingering the cheese with a nervous right hand. "What did you find out?"

"Eat your cheese."

With a sigh, Joram took a bite and began chewing. Evaine smiled and wiped the fingers of her right hand on a linen napkin, then reached behind her on the floor and picked up the scroll which had so occupied her and Rhys. She laid it on the table beside the tray of food and began nonchalantly to pour a cup of ale for her brother.

"In that scroll is a treatise from something called the Protocol of Orin. It's in three parts, the third of which is of immediate interest to us and to Father. Rhys and I read and studied that one last night and early this morning, then skimmed the other two. It's not going to be easy, but we can do it."

"Well, thank God for that," Joram breathed. As he picked up the cup of ale Evaine had poured, he reached for another piece of cheese.

"However, we mustn't delay," she continued, pretending not to notice the appetite her brother had developed. "I can't stress enough the importance of getting this memory assimilation out of the way as quickly as possible. Rhys says he's showing all the beginning signs that the scroll warns about. I know there are various things that all of us are expected to do in the next few days, but what's the absolute earliest we can all get together?"

Joram drank deeply, apparently unconcerned now, but Evaine knew that the seeming casualness was deceptive.

"Late tonight," he said, holding out his cup for a refill, which Rhys poured. "And unfortunately, I don't see how any of us can avoid our duties before that. Both of you should at least put in an appearance at the cathedral, as dutiful mourners, and I'll have to be there all afternoon and evening. At least we've managed to get him temporarily suspended from having to exercise his office."

"To avoid having to function as a priest?" Evaine asked.

"To avoid spending any more energy than he has to," Joram amended, "though I see that the sacerdotal question bothers you, too. I haven't even broached the subject of what he's going to do about the priesthood yet. He may have to fake it a few times, for survival's sake, but I don't think he can live that kind of sham indefinitely. However, that's not the issue here. I agree that we have to take care of the memory problem as soon as possible. What's going to be involved?"

Evaine worried the peel off a section of orange and popped it into her mouth. "Rhys or I can give you details when we meet this evening, since I gather we're pressed for time right now. There's no particular advance preparation to worry about—no physical accoutrements or setup, unlike some of the things we've done. The main thing is that we not be disturbed, of course. And, then, we have to figure out a way to get me into the no-woman's-land of the archbishop's palace without arousing suspicion."

"That I can solve," Joram said with a smile. Setting down his cup, he reached beside him where he had dropped what both of them had assumed was merely a cloak. A cloak there was, its blue wool badged on the left shoulder with the crimson-and-silver Michaeline insignia; but wrapped inside the cloak, so that it would have been undetectable to an outside observer, was a dark blue Michaeline habit, complete with hooded cowl and knotted scarlet cincture. As Joram pulled the habit from the folds of the cloak, he motioned for Evaine to stand up. She grinned as he held the habit up in front of her.

"So I'm to be a monk, eh, brother?" she asked, blue eyes twinkling merrily.

Joram shrugged, obviously pleased with himself. "Can you think of a better way to get you into no-woman's-land? If you knot your hair tightly and keep the cowl well down over your face, I don't think you'll arouse a second glance. The cloak over it will help to disguise your shape."

Evaine smiled as she sat down with the monkish robes in her lap.

"All right. What am I, a monk, doing in the vicar general's quarters that late at night?"

"I'll bring you," Joram said. "If anyone asks, the vicar general asked to see you on a minor disciplinary matter. No one will question that. Besides, no one has any reason to suspect that something is going on."

Rhys nodded thoughtfully. "It certainly sounds reasonable. And I can go there before the two of you, to check on the state of my patient's health. Evaine, how long is this whole thing going to take?"

"That depends on how many memories he's taken on. If Alister had been dead as long as you think he was, Joram, then Father couldn't have gotten much and it shouldn't take more than half an hour or so. If there were more memories than we think, then longer —perhaps two or three hours. I don't think any of us can last longer than that, so we'd better hope that's all there are."

"And yet," Rhys said, "the more memories he can tap, the better chance he has of pulling off the imposture. If he's determined to do it, pray God he does it right."

"Amen to that," Joram said.

The rest of the afternoon went more or less uneventfully, at least for Rhys and Evaine. Faithful to their part in the deception, the two went to pay their respects to the dead man under the MacRorie pall in the cathedral. There they even caught a glimpse of Camber, in his other guise, kneeling with some of his Michaeline brethren in the choir stalls to either side of the catafalque. The archbishop's choristers chanted the traditional psalms and prayers, and the air was heavy with incense and with grief, which was all too tangible to Deryni as sensitive as Evaine and Rhys.

Camber watched them enter the choir and kneel beside the bier, and from Evaine's expression he almost wondered whether she really knew that he still lived. She walked slowly, leaning on Rhys's arm with far more than the weight of her twenty-three years, eyes dark-circled with grief and fatigue. Rhys looked resigned, but even the fire of his rumpled red hair seemed somehow subdued in the candlelight of the choir, as if it dared not shine too gloriously amid such grief.

Camber watched his daughter through slitted fingers for several minutes, yearning to reach out with his mind and touch her tension yet knowing that he dared not. Nor could he go to her as Alister Cullen and offer even that old friend's comfort, for Joram, kneeling at his side, had cautioned him not to strain Evaine's composure with a reunion both secret and public. Far better to wait until the night, when they need not play their roles before the watchful eyes of humans and Deryni alike. He must not let an impulse rule his better judgment.

But neither could Camber bear to stay and watch her thus, though he knew her grief to be but feigned. Leaning toward Joram, he whispered that he was returning to his quarters, feeling somewhat faint, while his hand on the other's arm reassured that the faintness was but an excuse to leave. As Camber made his way out of the cathedral, leaning on the arm of one of his knights, Joram went to kneel beside his sister.

Camber allowed himself to relax a little as he and

Lord Dualta made their way back to his quarters. He was safe enough with the young Michaeline, for Dualta was fairly new to the Order and a human as well. Nothing in Camber's adopted manner was likely to betray him to one such as this—though even as a human, Dualta was more than normally observant, having had the benefit of Michaeline military training.

No, it was not Dualta whom Camber feared to meet. The king, perhaps. Or Anscom. Or—

Jebediah. Just when he thought he had gained the comparative security of his quarters, he saw the grand master rounding the corner at the opposite end of the corridor. Dualta was reaching for the door latch, but it was already clear that Camber could not graciously escape before Jebediah had reached him. Though they had met numerous times in council in the past week, he had not spoken alone with him since assuming Alister's identity. And Jebediah was Deryni.

"Good afternoon, Jeb," Camber said, in a tone he hoped was sufficiently weak to discourage lengthy conversation.

Jebediah bent to kiss the vicar general's ring, more for Dualta's benefit, Camber thought, than out of any real sense of formality on Jebediah's part.

"Good afternoon, Vicar General. I expected you to be in the cathedral for the rest of the afternoon. I trust nothing is wrong?"

As Dualta stood aside and bowed, Camber moved into his room.

"It's nothing. I felt a little faint—that's all. The heat, the incense . . . I'll be all right when I've rested."

"Are you sure that's all?" Jebediah replied. There was a look of genuine concern on his face as he followed Camber and Dualta into the room. "Dualta, you can go," he continued, moving to take the younger man's place as Camber was helped to a seat before the darkened hearth. "I'll take care of the vicar general."

The young knight glanced at Camber for approval, and Camber nodded, wishing he dared send both of them away. When Dualta had gone, Jebediah moved closer to the fireplace and knelt by the hearth. He did not look back at Camber as he began rearranging the dead embers with a piece of kindling.

"Something is wrong, Alister. Why won't you let me help you? You've been . . . distant since the battle."

Camber twined his fingers and glanced down at the ring on his finger, one thumb absently rubbing the engraved silver in a gesture which was patently Alister's. He was not yet willing to reveal his true identity to anyone else, and certainly not until he had assimilated Alister's memories and discovered the extent of his relationship with the grand master. If only this meeting could have been postponed for a few more hours, a few more days . . .

He looked up, very much aware that Jebediah was watching him in his peripheral vision, wondering why the man seemed so uneasy. He sensed no real suspicion. More like . . . watchfulness? Concern? Empathy?

"I'm sorry, Jeb. There has been much on my mind. And my health, as you know, has been less than I would have wished since the battle."

Jebediah's answer was so low that Camber nearly had to lean closer to hear him.

"You're still a comparatively young man, Alister— only five years older than I. Can the Healers do nothing?"

Camber shrugged. "Rhys says that I show steady improvement. However, there is more to heal than body."

"What, grief at Camber's death?" Jebediah snorted in faint derision. "Come now, I know that the two of you became fairly close, but you have lost friends before. Jasper died, too, and others sadly too numerous to mention. Besides, 'tis not so long ago that you and Camber were adversaries, if not enemies."

"We were never enemies," Camber whispered. "Never that. Besides, it is not the deaths which continue to disturb me."

"No?" Jebediah looked up, hand and stick poised

over the designs he had been tracing in the hearth ashes. " 'Tis nothing I've done, I hope."

Camber shook his head and smiled. "Nothing you have done, my friend. You have ever been a strength and comfort to me. Nor is it Camber's shade, though a little of his presence will be always with me, I think. No, the things which trouble me are more personal demons, I fear."

"Demons?" Jebediah started, then tossed his stick into the fireplace and stood. His handsome face was troubled as he moved to crouch at Camber's knees. "What demons, Alister? What superstitious nonsense is this? A legacy of Ariella? But tell me, share this haunting with me, and I will help you overcome it!"

Camber averted his eyes, wondering whether he had already said too much. Unwittingly, Jebediah had stumbled on the very excuse they had agreed to use in explaining any discrepancies in Alister's behavior, but which they had hoped not to have to use. Now Jebediah would have to be told more, and yet not so much that more dangerous suspicions were aroused than he already entertained. At least the suggestion of an ongoing struggle against Ariella's influence might be one which Jebediah could accept without feeling shut out —a feeling which Camber sensed was almost as strong as his very real concern for Alister's well-being. But how to strike the proper balance?

"Nay, I cannot ask that of you." Camber touched Jebediah's shoulder lightly as he stood and went to stare into the dark fireplace. "More happened on that day of battle than even you may know. It was not without cost that Ariella was slain, and I do not refer to mere physical deaths. Now payment is mine, and mine alone, to be resolved between myself and Him who made us all."

"But, I could help, if you would only let—"

"I cannot share these things with you, Jeb, even if I wished to subject you to my own peril. I can share them with no man."

Jebediah sat back on his heels, his gaze following

Camber's every move, and Camber forced himself to continue staring at the blackened hearth, aware of Jebediah's intense scrutiny. For a moment he feared that Jebediah would fight him, that he would refuse to accept what had been said; but Jebediah did not. At length, Camber turned to smile brightly at the younger man and sigh, as though in resignation.

"I'm sorry, but that's the way it has to be, at least for now. For the present, until I have either escaped my experience or paid for it, my words must be only for my confessor—and even he may not know the whole of it."

Jebediah lowered his eyes, his throat working painfully. "I was once a confessor of sorts to you."

"And shall be again someday, perhaps," Camber said softly. He wondered more than ever just what the relationship had been between the two men. "But for now, that cannot be. Please, let us not speak of it again."

"As . . . you wish," Jebediah replied in a low voice.

There was a silence which seemed interminable, and then Jebediah lurched to his feet and managed a feeble smile. "You should rest now, Father General, and I have duties which require my attention. If you have need of anything, you know you have but to call and I shall come."

"That I have always known," Camber said kindly, wishing he might say more. "God bless you, my friend."

Jebediah nodded, somewhat jerkily, then turned on his heel and left the room, head bowed in dejection. When he had gone, Camber sighed and returned to his chair, swinging his feet up on a broad, padded bench. At least he would know more after tonight, he thought as he let himself drift into sleep.

He woke several hours later to the sound of the draperies being drawn across the wide window embrasure to his left. A fire had been laid and started on the hearth, and candles lit in a floor sconce at his left elbow; he had to peer around the candles to see who was in the room. The silhouette against the darkening sky seemed familiar, but his mind was still too fogged by sleep for him to be certain.

"Rhys?" he called. He smiled as the figure finished its task and turned to chuckle.

"Now, who else could enter without waking you?" The Healer gave the draperies a final pat and crossed into the circle of candlelight. "I can personally think of two others, but they're not expected for nearly an hour. So for now, you'll have to settle for me. How are you feeling?"

As he sat down beside Camber, he laid a cool hand on the other's wrist. Camber smiled, knowing exactly what the young Healer was about.

"I feel fine—or as well as can be expected, under the circumstances. My headache has greatly diminished, and I feel considerably rested after my nap. Does that report agree with your diagnosis, O mighty Healer?"

Rhys released Camber's wrist and sat back in his chair. "You'll do. I'd like to see you stronger, of course, but that isn't reasonable to expect until we've taken care of tonight's business. Tomorrow I want to see a more definite improvement."

"I shall be perfect tomorrow. I promise you. Incidentally, by way of a non sequitur, who's on watch at the end of the corridor tonight?"

"That young Michaeline who escorted you from the cathedral this afternoon. I think his name is Dualta. Why?"

Camber sighed. "That's a relief. I was afraid it might be Jebediah."

"Why afraid?"

"Oh, he cornered me in a private conversation when I got back from the cathedral. Apparently I've been acting a little out of character, at least in his eyes. I have the growing impression that he and Alister were closer than we realized. He could turn out to be as big a problem as Cinhil, if we're not careful."

"He's Deryni, too," Rhys replied.

"Believe me, that thought never left my mind. I think I finally satisfied him. I blamed my present weakness on the battle with Ariella, hinting that I'd had to pay some mysterious price for victory—and all of that is true, of course, though not in the way he understands it. But just at the end I got a hint of hurt feelings, that I'd seemed to reject a former closeness. God knows how I should have reacted. Perhaps Joram knows. Or maybe there's something in these elusive memories."

As Camber tapped his forehead, Rhys cocked his head thoughtfully.

"What are you going to do if neither source sheds light on the relationship?"

"Operate on intuition, I suppose, and do the best I can. Becoming a bishop will help to keep us apart, other than in official contacts. If his unhappiness eventually turns to real suspicion, despite all our efforts, we'll have to consider taking him into our confidence. On the other hand, if he and Alister were as close as I begin to suspect, I don't know if he could ever forgive me for taking his friend's place and deceiving him."

Rhys pursed his lips. "Tread warily on that one, Camber," he said in a low voice. "And I want you to promise that you'll make no such disclosure until you've consulted with all three of us. This entire thing is going to be too precarious, as it is."

"Insofar as that's possible, you have my word." Camber smiled. "But on to more immediate considerations. I assume that you and Evaine located the proper scroll?"

"We read it last night. It appears to be fairly straightforward."

"However?" Camber urged, sensing hesitation in the other's words.

"However what?" Rhys said lightly. "My part is easy enough. I simply have to make certain that you remember to breathe, and that your heart keeps beating. You and Evaine have the hard part."

"Then what's bothering you? Surely you don't doubt your clever wife's ability after this long?"

Rhys chuckled mirthlessly. "Am I that transparent? No, I'm not worried about Evaine—or about myself or Joram."

"But you're worried about me."

"Not exactly that, either. It's the whole procedure, and the delicate coordination required of all four of us. Singularly, we've all done more difficult things before. God knows, some of the healings I've worked have been . . . awesome. But somehow, this is different. And you're not as strong as you should be. I wish we could have done this sooner."

"Well, there's no help for that," Camber murmured. "But come. I haven't looked at that scroll in months. Refresh my memory, in as much detail as you can. We'll both be far less anxious if we occupy our minds while we wait."

With a little sigh of resignation, Rhys reached his nearer hand across the space between his chair and Camber's, laying his fingers on the other's bare wrist. Camber closed his eyes and took a deep breath, let it out slowly. He could hear Rhys's shallow breathing at his side.

As they had done so many times before, they forged the master link between them—a deep, peaceful stillness rippled only faintly by the disorder locked away in a corner of Camber's mind. The bond was maintained for some little while, as Rhys opened the channels of memory and let his information flow into the consciousness of his friend and mentor. When it was done, and the two had blinked back to the present, Rhys looked a little sheepish. Camber tried a reassuring smile, but it did not quite succeed.

"That was fine," he said, patting Rhys's hand before rising to move restlessly to the fireplace. "It's always good to confirm that at least one's own memories aren't slipping."

"And *his* memories?"

Camber rested his hands on the mantel ridge and

laid his forehead against the cool stone between them. "Is it that obvious?"

"Yes."

"I'm sorry."

"There's no need to be. Your head hurts again, doesn't it?"

"A little. No, a lot. How long before Evaine and Joram . . . ?"

"Soon. Is there anything I can do to ease—"

A slight knock sounded on the heavy outer door, and both men froze and glanced at each other. The knock was repeated. Instantly, Camber sat down and pulled a blanket over his lap, laying his head against the back of the chair and closing his eyes. Rhys, when he was certain that Camber was settled convincingly, crossed to the door.

"Who's there?"

"Father Joram," came the reply. "On official business."

Rhys shot the bolt and yanked the door open. Joram stood directly before the opening, his cowl pulled close about his golden head and shrouding his face in shadow. At his elbow and a pace behind stood what appeared to be another, younger monk, cowled head bowed and hands tucked piously inside the voluminous sleeves of a Michaeline habit. Had Rhys not known better, he would never have guessed that the monk was, in fact, his wife.

He looked at Joram, very much aware, since Camber had pointed it out, that Dualta was on guard at the end of the corridor. As much for his own mind's calming as to set the stage for Dualta's belief, he spoke a little louder than was necessary, and with a little more formality than he might otherwise have used.

"Father Joram, I wasn't expecting you. The vicar general is resting."

Joram did not even blink. "I hope we won't disturb him too much, Rhys. The father general asked to see this monk. It's a minor matter of discipline, which should not tax him unduly."

Rhys glanced inside, as though confirming that the vicar general was, indeed, expecting the visitors, then stood aside to let them pass. As he closed the door, he saw that Dualta had turned his back and resumed a normal guard stance. That detail, at least, seemed to be taken care of.

But there decorum ended. No sooner had Rhys slipped the bolt back in place than he was treated to the sight of his wife, cowl slipping back from tightly bound hair, dashing to embrace a white-faced man who nearly staggered with the exuberance of her greeting. Husband and brother watched indulgently for several seconds and then, as if by mutual assent, turned back to the door to determine how it might best be warded for the coming work. Father and daughter held each other wordlessly for several heartbeats, until her arms had confirmed what her heart had never doubted.

"I knew you could not be dead!" she whispered fiercely, when at length they parted far enough to gaze into eyes made blurry by tears of joy. "I would have known! I surely would have known!"

"I would have spared you if I could," Camber murmured, holding her head close against his breast and touching her hair with his lips. "O my dearest child, how much I longed to spare you—but there seemed no other way. Rhys has told you something of what it was like."

"Aye, and that we can help you, Father," she said, drawing away to look at him from head to toe again, though she still did not release his hands. "We are ready to do what must be done—all of us."

"I thank you more than you can know," he replied. Releasing one of her hands, he sank back into the chair he had lately vacated, glancing to where the two young men had turned from their labors at the door.

"Gentlemen, are we warded?"

Joram nodded, coming with Rhys to stand beside Camber's chair. "No one will be able to sense our magic from without, especially considering the concentration around you. We've shielded against escape of sound, as well. As an added safeguard, I will be on guard throughout."

"Good. Have you a plan, in case we're interrupted?"

"Dualta has the watch, as you know, and is aware that 'Brother John' and I are here." Joram gestured toward his sister with a wry half-smile. "He's been led to believe that it's for disciplinary reasons, so I don't think he'll let anyone approach. However, if he should, Evaine and I will simply retire to your private oratory." He nodded toward a closed door leading off the main room. "We'll feign some act of penance. Rhys will stay with you and try to keep things from falling apart altogether, depending on what's happening at that point."

"That's a real danger, you know," Camber said. "Things falling apart, that is. If we *are* interrupted, I'm not certain I'll be able to hold up my end of things."

"Then God grant that we will not be put to that test," Evaine breathed.

With a nod, Camber leaned his head against the back of his chair and took a deep breath, let it out slowly. He allowed his pale Alister eyes to rest on each of them in turn: daughter, son, and son-in-law. Then he nodded again.

"Let's begin."

CHAPTER ELEVEN

*Grant unto thy servants, that with all boldness
they may speak thy word, by stretching forth
thine hand to heal.*

—Acts 4:29–30

As Rhys came to stand behind Camber's chair,
Joram moved to the door and set his back against it.
Evaine shed her Michaeline mantle and laid it across
a vacant chair before sitting on the bench beside her
father's feet. One hand patted the embroidered slippers
in affection as she reached into her habit with the other
and withdrew a jewellike object the size of a hen's
egg. Candlelight glinted amber on the smoothly polished surface as she burnished it against her sleeve.
Deep in the heart of the crystal, tiny inclusions reflected
fragmented fire against her Michaeline blue.

"I wish I had the one you gave me," she said, breathing on the crystal to warm it. "Unfortunately, I gave it
to Cinhil. This was Rhys's gift, though."

As she put it in his hands, she glanced behind him
at her husband, her blue eyes mirroring his answering
smile. Camber, with a contented smile of his own, held
the crystal lightly between his fingers and propped his
elbows on the arms of his chair. For a moment he
gazed profoundly into its depths, seeking the release
from tension which the *shiral* crystal usually facilitated.
Then he shook his head lightly and let his gaze skip
back to his daughter.

"I can't do it in this form," he said. "I mean, I could now, but I won't have the strength to maintain my shape illusion and still accomplish what we must. I'm taking back my own form."

As he spoke, a mist seemed to pass across his face and then to clear. For the first time since the clearing at Iomaire, he became Camber MacRorie once more. The familiar face was etched with fatigue and tension, but signs of these began to disappear almost immediately as he sighed and resumed his concentration on the *shiral* crystal.

Evaine bit her lip as she watched the beloved gray eyes grow glassy, paler, more otherworldly, though the phenomenon was comfortingly familiar. Camber's voice, when next he spoke, was a little hollow, flat, indicative of the profound relaxation he had already achieved.

"That's better," he murmured. "Rhys, I'm ready for you now."

Behind Camber, Rhys laid his hands gently on the other's shoulders and let himself sink into the special healing place from which he would keep watch over Camber's body. At his touch, Camber breathed deeply and exhaled again, the last lines of tension ironing out of his face. The gray eyes, half-lidded now, did not flicker as Evaine, with a steadying breath of her own, stood and spread her arms to either side in readiness, palms turned toward him at shoulder level in an attitude of blessing.

"*I am the key which opens many doors,*" she intoned softly.

Camber could see her through and behind the crystal in his hands, firelight from the candle sconce at his elbow dancing light and shadow on her hands and face. Rhys's touch was light and unobtrusive as the proper response flowed unbidden into his mind.

"*I am the lock which yields to light alone.*"

"*I am a candle burning in the dark,*" Evaine countered.

"*I am a twig, for feeding flame from spark.*"

Called forth by the mnemonics of the litany they re-cited, he could feel new channels opening in his mind. He had rarely been so deep before, and knew he must go deeper still. He sensed Evaine leaning forward to take the now-unnecessary crystal and slip it back in-side her robe, but his hands remained at chest level, still cupped around an ovoid space, until she pressed them gently into his lap. His universe was now encom-passed by his waiting. He could not seem to think beyond his expectation.

"I am the light, condensing from the stars," Evaine whispered, *"which brims the silver bowl of conscious-ness."* She leaned both hands on the arms of his chair to stare deeply into his eyes.

"I am the vessel, opening my will," Camber mur-mured, now almost past speech. *"I turn the key, and torch the twig . . . and fill."*

His eyes remained open, and his mind was still vaguely aware of his surroundings, but now almost all within his field of vision was obscured by the blue of Evaine's closeness. He could hear the soft rhythm of his breathing, but all other sound around him seemed suspended. Even the raising of his daughter's hand to-ward his face was silent, no rustle of cloth confirming whether the hand actually moved or only appeared to do so.

You are on the brink now, Evaine's mind whispered in his. *Let go. Let all the memories flow, and live them to the full. Each one must be acknowledged and ac-cepted and become a part of you. Let go now. We will keep you safe.*

He let himself take a deeper breath—though not so deep that it required any great effort—then let it out slowly, feeling himself slide deeper and deeper into a quiet he had never experienced before. As his daughter's hand touched his forehead, his eyelids closed of their own weight, trembling for only a heartbeat be-fore they were still. Now the shallow sound of his breathing was his only contact with the outside world. He did not even sense the moment when Evaine's hand left his forehead, and he had long ago lost the sensation of Rhys's touch.

Let go . . . let go . . .

He let things slip, starting to obey, and he could feel the tendrils of alien memory brush his own. Part of him was afraid, but he knew he must not shrink away. Abandoning all defenses and resistance, he loosed the final ties and let it happen. Immediately, thoughts not his own began to wash across awareness.

Sunlight. The warmth and heady perfume of a summery field. His Alister eyes drank in the greens and golds and pinks of summer growth: long-stemmed grasses and fertile soil and colors of a hundred different blossoms. Wildflowers sprang white and pink and lilac by bare toes. The rich blue of his habit was hiked up past his knees as he stepped through a rivulet of chill stream on water-slicked stones. He was a much younger Alister than Camber MacRorie had ever known, and he had abandoned his studies for an hour to celebrate the joy of mere existence.

He sank down in verdant clover grass and laid his head among pastel blossoms which tickled his ears; plucked a stem and sucked its sweet juice as he watched clouds pile up against a sapphire sky. A grasshopper bounded into his field of vision, and he put out one idle hand to let the creature crawl across his thumb. The delicate touch of the creature's legs and feelers, the subtle shadings of color, were so beautiful it almost hurt.

A skip, a beat, and he was no longer lying in the field.

He was slightly older now: a newly ordained priest, helping some of his older brethren to dress the altar in the Commanderie chapel at Cheltham. Dust motes shimmered in a shaft of glass-stained sunlight, and a little of the sunshine smell was in the bleached linens which he and another man shook out and laid across the smooth stone of the altar top.

He sniffed the pungent fragrance of cedar oil as he rubbed and polished the carved-oak Michael at the altar's right, remembering the feel of each burnished whorl beneath his fingertips. He inhaled the familiar scent, and when he exhaled, he was in darkness.

Terror! Somehow, he knew that he was on his sleeping pallet, alone in his cell—but he was also struggling with someone or something which was trying to suffocate him! Nightmare hands pressed close around his throat, choking off his breath, and he knew that there were claws attached to those hands which could rip both life and soul from him. He thrashed on the narrow pallet, fighting desperately to escape, to wake up, to overcome the enemy, to save his life!

A dizzying explosion of blackness, and he was no longer in bed, fighting for his life, though still his breath came tight. *He was a grown man, Vicar General of the Order of Saint Michael, and the writing in his hand spelled out the names of possible successors to his office. Four now-familiar names formed the list, penned in the precise hand of the Michaeline grand master.*

Alister knelt at the hearth and held the parchment to the flames, aware that Jebediah was crouched approving at his side. As the parchment caught and blazed, he let it fall into the fire and stood, steadying himself on his friend's shoulder with an easy familiarity. He was comfortable, contented . . .

And troubled. The novice monk kneeling humbly before him and the assembled Order was a bright young man: human, but apparently gifted with a natural empathic intuition which was uncommon even among Deryni, with the possible exception of Healers. From Alister's abbatial throne, beneath the ribbed vaulting of the chapter house at Cheltham, it would have been easy to let himself react according to his own occasional uneasiness at special abilities, to impose some harsh regiment of regularization which would forever stifle this young man's talents and make of him an ordinary monk, no different from a dozen of his fellows. The boy gazed up at him with blind, unqualified trust, and Alister knew that the boy would willingly give up the pursuit of his talent if his vicar general commanded it.

But for the Order to provide proper training and guidance for the development of that talent would be far more difficult, time-consuming, and would require his personal commitment to the task. Dared he make such a decision?

A blink. A change of time and place. *He was a brand-new Michaeline knight, receiving his consecrated sword from a grand master now many years dead. Another shift, and he was tending minor wounds sustained by one of his men in the assault on the keep a year ago, a younger and less worldly-looking King Cinhil looking on in dreadful fascination.*

The memories were coming faster now: shorter, but with a far greater intensity. There was a flash of a woodland clearing which was familiar to Camber as well as to him whose memories he read, but he pushed that aside. Later, for that last memory.

He was vaguely aware of his own body, as well as the one he was remembering, and that his lungs were filling very shallowly now, his heart rate slowed to a bare minimum. He vaguely consigned himself to Rhys's careful watch as the next image steadied for his attention.

He was a much younger Alister, sword in hand, hacking at a pell in the Commanderie training yard; a younger man still, almost a boy, jumping a heavy bay destrier over a succession of obstacles in an open field, five other riders following the same course behind him.

At night, and he knew this was no training exercise, he and another knight slipped through the shadows of an enemy periphery by moonlight. He knew the dry, metallic tension in his throat as he realized his quarry was also Deryni, though not yet aware of his presence —and the grim satisfaction of drawing dirk across the man's throat, the body crumpling without a warning sound . . .

Sitting beside a night-shielded campfire with Jebe-

diah and two other knights, fishing hot pebbles out of a leather traveling cup, the scent of mulled wine sweet and pungent in his nostrils. The peaceful relaxation of the night, leaning against Jeb's booted knee to gaze dreamily into the fire as the flames gradually turned to ashes and the four of them talked on and on.

Suddenly, he was wrenched from his adopted memories and struggling to breathe, and he could feel Rhys's hands on his face, Rhys's mouth forcing air into his protesting lungs.

His ears were ringing, and his fingers tingling, and he was vaguely aware of what seemed like a slow, insistent drumming, pulling him back from wherever he had been. As he forced heavy eyelids apart, he realized that the pounding was coming from the door, that Joram was looking from him and Rhys to the door as though in slow motion. Evaine seemed frozen beside her husband, mouth caught in a surprised *O,* and Rhys was pulling away to stare urgently into Camber's eyes as he felt his patient begin to breathe again on his own.

Camber's head reeled, pain lancing behind his eyes and at the back of his head as he coughed and time settled back into place. Dimly he could hear the pounding on the door again, and a familiar but dreaded voice calling his adopted name.

"Father Cullen, may I come in?"

It was Cinhil.

With great difficulty, Camber forced himself to focus on Rhys, not needing to tell the Healer of his alarm. Any other man but Cinhil might be denied admission without explanation, but Cinhil would persist until his own need for comfort was satisfied.

And here sat Camber, in the guise of a man supposedly dead, about to be revealed to the very man for whose sake he had already risked so much. It must not all end now!

Gathering all his reserves in a massive effort of willpower, Camber gestured for Evaine and Joram to go to the oratory as they had originally planned, his hand aching like lead at even that slight movement. To Rhys he murmured, "I have been very fatigued, and you worry that I may be battling some residue of Ariella's influence. I'm going to take back my other shape and try to hold it."

As Rhys started to protest, Camber was already triggering the return to Alister's shape, forcing the other's memories into abeyance with all his might. He did not know how long he dared hold the two together, but he knew he had to try. When he let his eyes flicker open again, he could see Evaine through the open door of the oratory, lying prostrate before the tiny altar. Joram knelt beside her with his golden head bowed. Rhys was striding toward the door, his eyes hardly leaving the now-changed Camber as he laid his hands on the latch and loosed the wards. In all, the delay had not been more than half a minute.

Camber closed his eyes and hoped.

"Father Alister . . . ?" Cinhil asked, his voice trailing off as he saw Rhys filling the doorway.

Dualta was standing at the king's elbow, and gave Rhys an apologetic nod.

"Sorry to disturb you, m'lord. I explained to His Grace that the father general was engaged."

"You said it was only a disciplinary matter," Cinhil interjected, trying fruitlessly to peer past Rhys. "I need to talk to him, Rhys. Where is he?"

Rhys did not move his hand from the doorjamb at Cinhil's eye level, and the king had to continue trying to look past it.

"It's all right, Dualta," Rhys murmured. "Your Highness, Alister is not really up to seeing any more visitors this evening. I shouldn't even have let Joram in. He's extremely tired. I'm trying to get him settled down for the night."

Concern sparked the gray Haldane eyes, and then Cinhil pushed his way past Rhys and started toward the bowed gray head, just visible over the top of the high chair back. Rhys managed to keep up, half a pace behind, but even he could not move fast enough to stop the king.

Dualta, uncertain just what to do under the circumstances, stepped inside the room and waited uncomfortably. As Joram appeared in the doorway of the oratory and signaled with his hand, Dualta closed the door and stayed there at attention, intelligent brown eyes following king and Healer curiously.

"Sire, he's drifting in and out of consciousness," Rhys was saying. "He'll probably be all right in the morning, if he gets a good night's sleep, but the important thing now is rest." He almost caught his breath as Cinhil leaned closer to stare at the still form.

Camber had managed to return completely to his Alister shape, but now he appeared to have lapsed into real unconsciousness. Quickly Rhys knelt to touch a hand to the older man's wrist, not daring to look at Cinhil now.

"I don't understand. What's wrong?" Cinhil asked, in a very small, frightened voice. "Ever since we got back, he's been so weak."

"He paid a high price for your safety, Sire," Joram said, appearing at Cinhil's side almost without warning. "He would not have told you himself, since he did not wish to trouble you, but his defeat of Ariella cost him a great deal. I was there. I know."

Cinhil, his attention momentarily diverted to Joram's solemn face, swallowed awkwardly and glanced at his feet.

"I—sensed that something had changed, from that very first night. But I thought he was only exhausted, and that he would get better."

"He dreams," Rhys whispered. "In his mind, he fights her still. It was not a clean kill."

Urgently he took Camber's slack hand between his own and held it hard against his forehead, closed his eyes and tried to will energy through the connection.

"Hold strong, Father!" he murmured, so low that Cinhil could barely hear. "Fight it! *God!* Give him strength!"

As Camber's eyelids trembled, Joram, too, knelt, crossing himself with a heavy hand. As though a bond had been forged between him and Rhys as well, he laid his hands on Camber's other arm and bowed his head.

And Cinhil, opening spontaneously to the emotional currents now flowing in the room, staggered and caught himself against another chair, so shaky that Dualta came rushing to his side to catch him under one elbow and lend support. The king was not picking up the specifics of what was occurring, but the sheer surge of power was coming through. Neither he nor Dualta noticed a small, seemingly frail monk come to stand apprehensively in the doorway of the oratory.

Camber stirred sluggishly to awareness within his borrowed form, becoming conscious once more of the forces at odds within him. He had secured control of his shape again, but only at the cost of temporarily damming up the flood of memories. He did not know whether he could slow the process and control it once he let it start again—not and still retain his physical façade. And the pressure was building again.

Try one—one at a time, he told himself, not knowing whether that was even possible, yet certain that he had to relieve the pressure soon or lose everything.

Try one—just one . . . easy . . . easy . . .

He was in the classics school at Saint Neot's. He was fifteen, and he was the most promising of his class. As he stood to recite, he could feel Dom Eleric's proud eyes upon him, knew that he had mastered everything the good Gabrilite brethren were permitted to teach him. He had been here for nearly two years, the maximum time allowed for young men not intending to enter the Gabrilite Order. In the summer he would go to Cheltham for further training under Michaeline masters. And in a few more years, if God willed it, he would be knighted and ordained . . .

There. That hadn't been so bad. Try another one. Let it—

He was wounded, though he felt no pain. He knew

the wounds were bad, that they would probably kill him, but he knew he would not fall until he had suc-ceeded. The Evil One could not stand against him in this fight, for he fought with the strength of the Light.

My God, he was reliving Alister's final battle with Ariella!

He felt a sword slash into his thigh as he was un-horsed, cleaving leather and mail, but still he fought on. Another part of him struggled to pull away, to avoid this last confrontation at any cost, but the exultation of battle against Her minions was tonic to his tortured body, rendering him invincible, invulnerable to pain. One of Ariella's men went down beneath his blade, and then another.

And what he felt now, in the extremity of his striving, both as Alister and as Camber, was echoed in the chamber, there for the psychic listening of anyone with the wit to ken it.

Rhys felt it, and tightened his grip on the master's hand, pouring out all the strength he could to aid the struggle.

And Joram, apparently in prayer against more usual devils, laid both hands on his father's knees and willed him power, his head drooping low between his outstretched arms as he reached to the bottom of his being to call forth strength.

Cinhil was reeling under the onslaught, senses com-pletely overloaded, trying in vain to cope with emo-tions of an intensity he had never had to deal with before. He sank limply to his knees as his staring eyes watched Alister Cullen's trembling body.

Neither he nor the petrified Dualta was aware of the final contribution: of the slender monk standing in the doorway of the oratory, hands now raised in benedic-tion, lips moving silently but with the force of mind behind, in the renewed words of a litany she and Cam-ber had shared before.

I am the key . . .

I, the lock . . . Camber managed to respond.

A candle in the dark . . . Evaine sent.

A twig, for feeding flame . . .

I am the Light, Evaine willed. *Let it be!*

The vessel, came Camber's faint response. *Key . . . twig . . . I—fill . . .*

The floodgates opened again, more sluggish this time, since a part of him must struggle to maintain his shape; and then he was barraged with a new set of memories in rapid succession—shorthand, telegraphed images, each with its wealth of information which did not have to be consciously examined but which slipped into his own memory and to greater depths with a force which could no longer be withstood.

Poring over a brightly painted map board with a handful of newly dedicated Michaeline knights, listening approvingly as one of the most promising, a blond young priest named Joram, explained the strategy for a hypothetical attack on . . .

Dhassa, the holy city, seat of the Prince-Bishop Raymond, his maternal uncle, who laid consecrated hands on his head in ordination, while his parents proudly watched . . .

He was a child again, running and shouting at games with the other boys his age at Saint Liam's Abbey school, tanned legs flashing beneath the blue uniform robe which all of them wore, whether or not destined for the Church . . .

A massive leap forward in time, and he was once more the Michaeline vicar general, rising to give guarded greeting to a tall, gilt-haired Deryni Lord who was an older, more mature version of the beloved young priest at his side, who would serve as intermediary in this first face-to-face meeting.

And later, much later, standing guard in full armor before a secret chapel door, as a woman and a Healer and that same High Deryni Lord approached, guiding a glaze-eyed man no longer priest and not yet king. He could feel the quillons of the greatsword cold beneath his gloved hands, and bowed his helmed head in homage as he passed them through the door. He knew and did not know what else occurred that night, for he was, in fact, two men now, seeing that door through two minds intertwined.

A gasp of pain, a searing crunch of bone within his mailed side, and he was back in the clearing at Iomaire. The great warhorse reared and plunged beneath him, striking out with steel-shod hooves to maim and kill Ariella's men, and this time Camber knew he would have to let the memory run its course. The horse screamed and died beneath him as he took another wound in the thigh, but he managed to throw himself clear and gut another of Ariella's men as he rolled and scrambled to his feet. His Michaelines were dying all around him, as well as Ariella's men, and at last he alone still stood, to face the deceptively innocent-looking Enemy across what seemed an infinity of blood-soaked clearing.

He hurt now. No blessed numbness of battle fever any longer. Yet he knew that the worst was surely yet to come. Standing shakily in the only path which Ariella might take to freedom, sword gripped tightly in his two gloved hands, he saw her spur her stallion toward him as though in a dream. A tangle of hurting hooves and saddle and steaming horse entrails as his sword ripped upward, and then he was struggling from beneath the dying animal to search desperately for Ariella, who raised her hands in killing spell.

He knew the awesome certainty that death was near. He could feel his physical strength ebbing as his body pumped blood from half a dozen wounds. Pulling from his deepest reservoirs of strength, he reversed his sword and brought the gilded cross-hilt tremblingly to his lips, with that kiss imparting all his will and resolution to the sacred blade.

As he hurled it toward her heart, he felt himself falling, sinking psychically as well as physically into a darkness which could no longer be denied.

Another part of him realized, at least vaguely, what was happening, however, and that part was not ready to succumb. Even though he could not seem to make his body respond, Camber knew still, through the fog of alien memory, that he must keep hold of the last shreds of the identity his body wore.

But he was not breathing any more, and could not seem to make himself resume! And if he diverted energy to that, he would not be able to hold his shape!

He felt Rhys's presence strongly, then, and Joram's, and knew that they would not let him die—but there was a reason why he must not lose his shape, though he could no longer remember what it was. A few more seconds, and someone would have to do something, or he would be in control of nothing—and the memory assimilation was not *yet* complete, though the pressure of the remaining recall was not nearly as insistent now, after the reliving of Alister's death.

Suddenly there was motion around him, and he knew that the decision had been taken out of his hands. He felt his body being pulled to the floor amid the soft fur rugs, felt firm hands tilting back his head as Rhys once more blew life into his lungs. His heart was pounding now, trying to get oxygen to his starved brain, but it could not hold that pace for long. Rhys must also have realized that, for abruptly Joram replaced him on the breathing so that Rhys could concentrate on slowing the racing heartbeat, pressing healing hands against the barely moving chest and willing the heart to slow.

He thought he could feel someone staring at him, but the effort to open his eyes and see was far too great.

Then Evaine's presence was strong within him, though she had not moved from her place in the doorway of the oratory, hands resting above shoulder level on the edges of the doorjamb. He could feel her reaching out to someone else's mind in the room, though he did not know how he knew that. And then he heard a young voice which should have been familiar but was not, gasping in desperate supplication:

"O God, if only Camber were here!" the man cried. "O God, Camber could save the vicar general!"

Camber was too weary to worry about the implications. Indeed, he would never really quite remember

what actually happened next. At Evaine's word of reassurance, he gathered a mammoth surge of strength
and willed himself to settle back into the proper functions of his body, forced himself to inhale on his own
—once, twice, a third time—letting other controls
waver, if they must. Joram drew back to watch,
pleased at first—then tried to hide his panic as he realized what Camber was doing.

For Camber's face was changing, misting over, shifting subtly from the gaunt, drawn features of Alister
Cullen to Camber's own, as though the one were superimposed on the other.

Rhys saw it coming almost as soon as Joram did, but
he dared not allow its recognition to hinder his healing
function. Now was the only chance he would have to
mend the damage already done and to get Camber
back into balance. He closed his eyes to shut out the
distraction, and prayed as he set things right.

But Cinhil went even whiter as the change became
apparent, hardly feeling the iron grip of Dualta, who
stared in awe at what he believed he had called up.

The entire illusion did not last more than a few seconds, but it was long enough. Long enough for Rhys to
work his healing, and for Camber to regain control;
long enough for the stunned Dualta to be certain,
for the rest of his days, that he had just witnessed a
miracle; and for Cinhil to doubt his sanity for just a
moment.

Quickly the face Camber wore solidified into the
familiar visage of Alister Cullen and resumed a slow,
steady breathing, seemingly at peace now; and behind
them all, a slender monk let fall her arms and sank to
her knees in exhaustion.

Camber, as he let the last of Alister Cullen's memories slip into place among his own, had a final fleeting
image of Alister standing in the window of his study at
the Michaeline Commanderie, arms crossed casually
on his chest as he stared out at the dying day. There
was someone else standing at his back who had al-

most always been there, and whose arm was laid across his shoulder now in simple, mindless companionship.

It was Jebediah; and Camber knew, as he slipped into healing sleep, his identity now secure, that he could never hope to duplicate the bond the two had shared.

As Camber relaxed in sleep, Rhys drew a long, shuddering breath and lifted his head, catching himself on hands and knees as his own fatigue washed over him. Joram, who had been kneeling by Camber's head, rocked back on his heels and then collapsed with his face in his hands, bowed over his trembling knees, shoulders shaking with silent weeping.

Cinhil swallowed noisily, the only sound in the hushed room, and glanced from Healer to priest and then, almost as an afterthought, at the sheet-white Dualta kneeling beside him.

"Did—" He had to swallow again. "Did the rest of you see what I think I saw?"

"The Lord's Name be praised!" Dualta whispered. He crossed himself and clasped his hands reverently. "He sent the Blessed Camber to help us! The Lord sent Camber to save His servant Alister!"

Rhys saw Joram's shoulders stiffen a little at the obvious conclusion Dualta had reached, but he was far more concerned with Cinhil's reaction. As he glanced groggily at the king, he could see that Cinhil's face had gone set and stony, that the previous man of faith, who could easily have accepted a miracle in the course of a day's experience, was warring with the present man of more cynical persuasion.

As much to distract Cinhil from too much thinking as anything else, Rhys reached out to touch Camber's forehead. The inference of divine intervention was unfortunate, but it was certainly more desirable than the truth. If necessary, he must foster the lie to guard the greater lie. Cinhil must never suspect that it was a mortal Camber who had made an appearance a few minutes ago.

"He appears to be out of danger now," he managed to croak. "I—can't explain what happened. All of you are far more knowledgeable about these things than I. But I do know that he was fighting a terrible battle within himself, and that from somewhere he found the strength to persevere."

"From Camber?" Cinhil whispered.

Rhys smoothed the iron-gray hair on Camber's forehead with an absent gesture and shrugged. "Perhaps. That is not for me to say."

That much, at least, was the literal truth, though he knew that Cinhil was not reading it that way. The king got to his feet and turned away, passing a hand over his eyes as though to convince himself that his senses had not lied. Too late Rhys realized that Evaine was still kneeling in the doorway of the oratory—knew that Cinhil could not help but notice her, and question her witness of what had just happened.

He glanced hurriedly at Joram, but the priest was still huddled beside the now-sleeping Camber, face bowed in the shielding shelter of his hands. Evaine, too, had her head bowed, face invisible beneath her blue cowl.

He saw Cinhil freeze, as though becoming aware of the additional person in the room for the first time, to stare for several heartbeats, hands clenched rigidly at his sides. He held his breath as Cinhil started toward Evaine, for he knew without any benefit of Deryni talents exactly what the king must be thinking.

"Rhys, who is the monk?" Cinhil asked, pausing to gesture toward her jerkily with his chin.

Rhys projected as much fatigue into his voice as he could, hoping he might yet distract Cinhil.

"Joram said his name was Brother John," he sighed. "There was some disciplinary matter. Alister had asked to see him."

"Has he been here the whole time?" Cinhil insisted.

"I suppose so. Frankly, I'd forgotten about him."

He prayed that Cinhil would not pursue the matter, though he knew that plea was hopeless.

Cinhil turned back to "Brother John" and then glanced at the floor uneasily.

"Brother John, did you see what just happened?"

Evaine's shoulders stiffened just slightly, and she hesitated the merest instant before straightening to a more conventional kneeling posture and tucking her hands into the folds of her sleeves once more.

"If it please Your Grace, I am but an ignorant monk," she murmured, in a low, muffled voice. "I am not learned in such matters."

"You don't have to be learned," Cinhil snorted, clasping his hands together and beginning to pace back and forth nervously. "Just tell me what you saw. And *look* at me when I'm speaking to you!"

CHAPTER TWELVE

I am made all things to all men,
that I might by all means save some.
—I Corinthians 9:22

The king's back was to Rhys as he spoke, so he could not see the look of horror which flashed across the Healer's face at his words. Nor could he note how Joram's head snapped up and the priest nearly came to his feet in sheer reflex. Dualta had also turned to stare curiously at the young monk, so he, too, missed the reactions of the two Deryni.

But by the same token, Cinhil did not see their other reactions, as "Brother John" raised a young but bearded face to gaze at him with eyes of smoky black—not blue. Those incredible eyes flicked guilelessly to the king's for just an instant, forever establishing the differentness from any other identity which Cinhil might have suspected or even dreamed of, then dropped decorously under long black lashes. Lips far narrower than Evaine's moved hesitantly in the bearded jaw, speaking in a voice which bore little resemblance to any which Rhys or Joram could have foretold.

"If—if it please Your Grace," the monk replied, "it did seem to me that some other . . . person . . . was in the room . . ."

As the voice trailed off uncertainly, Cinhil's eyes flashed and he leaned closer to grip the young man's shoulder.

"Another person? Go on, man! Who was it?"

"It—it was *him,* Sire. And he drew *his* shadow across the vicar general."

"Name him," Cinhil whispered dangerously. *"Name me his name!"*

The monk's hands wrung within the royal blue sleeves, and the black eyes glanced furtively at the king once again.

"It—it seemed to be the Lord Camber, Sire. Yet, he is dead. I have seen him! I—I have heard of goodly men returning before, to aid the worthy, but—p-please, Sire, you're hurting me!"

Cinhil's eyes had gone almost glassy as he stared at the monk, but at the man's last words, he blinked and seemed to shake himself free of some inner compulsion, murmuring an apology as he released the monk's arm. He stared at his hand for several heartbeats, as though still not totally in touch with the real world, then slowly turned back to Rhys and Joram. The monk bowed his head and said nothing.

"I . . . must retire to think further on this," he said haltingly. He wrung his hands together and would not meet their eyes. "It—cannot be, and yet . . ."

He swallowed and made a visible effort to regain his composure.

"Please tell Father Cullen that I shall speak with him later, when he is stronger," he said briskly. "And I should prefer that none of you speak of—of what has happened, until we have all had time to think further on it. If only . . ."

With a shake of his head and a gesture of futility, he turned and let himself out without further words. The sound of the closing door was the trigger which released them all.

Dualta sank back on his heels and glanced at his hands—white and bloodless from clasping them hard for so long—then turned frightened eyes on Rhys and Joram.

"Father Joram, I don't understand."

"I know, Dualta," Joram whispered, studying his own folded hands.

"But I *must* speak of this with someone," Dualta insisted. "It—it was a miracle! May I not tell even my confessor?"

Joram shuddered, unable to look up at his brother knight. "Only if I am that confessor, Dualta," he said in a low voice. "The king is right. Word of this should go no further until we have had time to assess it." He forced himself to look up at the younger man. "Are you agreeable to that?"

"That you should confess me? Certainly, Father, if you wish it. But—it *was* your blessed father! I saw him!"

Joram closed his eyes in resignation for just an instant, then sighed and got slowly to his feet, stiffly, like an old man. As the Michaeline knight also rose, Joram touched his shoulder lightly, at the same time extending his mind to touch Dualta's, undetected.

"I know what you think you saw," he said wearily. "But for now, and until I give you permission, you are to speak of this to no one except the people in this room. Is that clear?"

"Yes, Father," Dualta murmured, eyes downcast.

"Thank you." Joram dropped his hand. "You'd best go now. The father general needs his rest, as do we all. You can wake Lord Illan and tell him that Rhys thought you should be relieved of duty for the rest of the night. You must be very tired."

Dualta glanced at Rhys at that falsehood and started to protest, but Rhys only sat back against the legs of the chair behind him and nodded agreement, golden eyes catching and holding Dualta's brown ones.

"Joram is right, Dualta. We're all tired. And if it hasn't actually hit you yet, it will." At the very suggestion, Dualta's eyelids drooped and he swayed on his feet, opening and closing his mouth several times in bafflement.

"Ask Illan to relieve you, and then go to bed," Rhys ordered.

Dualta, with a murmur of assent and a perfunctory bow, turned and staggered toward the door. Rhys and Joram both held their places until the door had closed. Then, as Joram rushed to bolt the door behind him, Rhys scrambled to his feet and raced toward the monk still kneeling in the oratory doorway. As he grasped the blue-clad shoulders, Evaine raised her own familiar face to gaze at her husband tiredly.

"Are you all right?" Rhys demanded.

With a contented sigh, she slipped her arms around his waist and let him help her stand, a cryptic smile lifting her lips as she laid her head against his shoulder.

"The question is, are you all right?" she replied. "And is Father?"

She pulled back to look at him, then glanced at her brother as Joram came to take one of her hands and press it fervently to his lips, as though to reassure himself that it was really there. There was no mistaking the disapproval in his gray eyes.

"You shape-changed," he said accusingly. "How?"

"I managed." She pulled away from both of them and crossed to kneel beside the sleeping Camber, Rhys dogging her footsteps. "When Rhys and I read the scroll last night, we reviewed the information before the memory assimilation, too. I thought it might help if we understood a little of how Father got the way he did. I must confess, I never thought I'd have to use that knowledge myself."

Joram was scowling as Rhys again bent over Camber, but he said nothing until the Healer looked up. Then: "You realize what she's done, don't you?"

"By shape-changing? I don't think it did any harm. Besides, what else could she have done, under the circumstances? If the ruse has to be given up eventually, I certainly don't want to do it when Camber is unconscious and helpless."

Joram sat in one of the chairs and laid his hands precisely on the arms. "That's not the point. Dualta thinks he witnessed a miracle. The Church has very strict laws regarding such matters. And Cinhil—God knows what he thinks!"

Evaine rocked back on her heels and stared up at her brother in surprise. "Is that what you're worried about? Better they should think there's been a miracle than that they should guess the truth! Rhys is right. Besides, this is only one isolated incident. What harm can it do?"

"I suspect we shall find out, eventually," Joram replied softly. He laid his head back against the chair and closed his eyes. "I wonder whether Father will agree. I wonder whether he'll even remember. You can rest assured that Cinhil will."

And in another part of the archbishop's palace, in the flickering light of death-watch candles, a frightened and resentful Cinhil made his way down the long aisle of the cathedral and approached the bier of Camber of Culdi. Royal guards stood at rest with their backs to the four corners of the catafalque, spears reversed at their sides, eyes downcast, not moving as the king came near. From the choir, the chanting voices of a score of monks drifted eerily on the incense-laden air, the only sound in the vastness of the great church.

Cinhil approached the bier slowly, reluctantly, almost as if his feet were hampered by some new weight which he must drag behind him. He moved along the left of the great catafalque, where kings of Gwynedd had lain in state, and let his gaze pass slowly from the feet toward the head, taking in all the somber splendor of the funeral pall which covered the body to the chest.

The MacRorie arms on the pall glowed satin-rich in the flickering light, *gules* and *azure,* with the ancient sword impaling the Culdi coronet in a profusion of gold and silver threads. Above the pall's black velvet, rich Michaeline blue continued to the corpse's neck and framed the silver-gilt head with shadow. Still hands clasped a crucifix of rosewood and carved ivory. The seal ring of the Culdi earls gleamed on a finger of the left hand, the silver changed to ruddy gold in the candle glow.

Cinhil laid his hands on the edge of the catafalque and stared at the familiar face for a long time. He was only vaguely aware of the preserving spell which surrounded the body like an invisible shroud, keeping it temporarily from corruption. He was not aware of the spell's other function, to mask residuals of other magic which an adept might otherwise have detected.

What is it you want of me? he asked as he studied the once-handsome features. *You're dead. Why can't you stay dead?*

The waxen lips made no reply, and Cinhil glanced down with eyes which were rapidly filling with tears of frustration.

You can't come back! he thought stubbornly. *You're dead. Haven't you done enough?*

The monks' chanting broke through his consciousness in a paean of joy for the soul's promised ascension to God. Cinhil, with a stifled sob, sank to his knees and laid his feverish forehead against the back of one white-knuckled hand.

O God, you let him take away my life, he thought. *You let him take me from Your house. Now he is gone, yet still he keeps me from Your service. Will he never give me peace?*

He raised tear-blurred eyes to stare at the still profile, but there was no answer in any of its lines.

Though he waited for the better part of an hour, vaguely aware that the guards were becoming uncomfortable, the monks a little curious, still no answer came. When finally he rose from numbed knees and bowed his head toward the High Altar, there was desolation in his heart.

He returned to his quarters in the keep after that; but he found little sleep.

Of them all, it was probably Camber who slept best, once the night's crisis was past. He it was who woke first the next morning, to find Rhys curled up under a blanket in a chair beside his bed and no sign of either Joram or Evaine. By the light slanting in through a mullioned window, it was not long past dawn.

He lay motionless for several minutes, letting consciousness settle slowly into place. He had not yet moved, other than to turn his head toward Rhys, but so far he seemed to be completely recovered. All traces of headache were gone, and he was experiencing none of the disorientation or grogginess he might have expected.

Even his body felt resigned to its adopted shape, almost as if he had always worn it. He seemed to recall a slight problem with control last night, but most of the experience was a blank haziness. However, he must have made no serious slips, else all would not now be so peaceful. When he got the chance, he would have to ask Joram or Rhys for a full report.

With a contented yawn, he flexed his limbs experimentally beneath the blankets and withdrew a strange yet familiar hand, spreading the fingers and turning them to and fro before his pleased eyes. Barring extreme stress and conditions requiring massive outpourings of energy, he knew that the shape was truly his now. Alister's signet was cool and a little loose on his finger.

And just as he knew the security of his physical identity, so he knew that the mental aspects of

Alister had also sorted themselves out during the night. As he reached into the depths of recall, he found the other's memories no longer alien, and as accessible as his own.

To be sure, there were some gaps in his adopted memories. He had known, when he first probed the dead Alister's mind, that much was gone already. But he had gained far more than he had expected, and with what remained, he knew he could function as Alister with only reasonable attention to detail. What had been done before on sheer acting skill could now be trusted to instinct.

He turned his head and glanced at Rhys again—no need to wake him yet, after all the Healer had been through for his sake the night before—then eased himself slowly to a sitting position and swung his legs out from under the blankets, touching bare feet luxuriantly to the furs spread beside the bed. He paused a moment, to be certain he could trust his newly rested body, then leaned to study Rhys more closely.

The Healer slept soundly, but he seemed to be cramped in the chair. Dark circles smudged the hollows of his eyes, and the fiery hair seemed to draw all hint of color from the gold-stubbled face.

With a smile, Camber touched Rhys's brow and deepened his sleep, then stood and slipped his arms under the relaxed body, shifting it gently to the bed which he had just vacated. After tucking a blanket around Rhys, he padded barefoot into the garderobe, emerging a short while later dressed in a clean cassock of midnight blue and with his toilet complete. Before anyone came to help him vest for the funeral at noon, there was much to be done.

At least he now knew Alister's candidates for the vicar generalship, he thought, as he sat down at the writing table which had been his alter ego's. And those, plus the future of the Michaelines, must now become a prime consideration.

As he took a sheet of parchment from a stack at his elbow, his other hand was dipping a well-used quill into an inkstand. His hand moved automatically in another's writing as a list of names flowed onto the page, adding to Jebediah's nominees two additional names which he knew Alister had been considering.

Then he put that sheet aside and began drafting a second piece: insurance, in case he had inadvertently omitted anyone he oughtn't. Half an hour later, after recopying his second missive, he pushed his chair away from the table and took both pieces of work to the outer door.

A tired-looking Dualta had been leaning against the wall opposite the door, talking in low tones with Brother Johannes, Alister Cullen's former aide, and both men came to smart attention as Camber appeared in the doorway. Each of them wore the formal blue mantle of their Order, Dualta with the full Michaeline badge on the shoulder, Johannes with only the silver cross moline fitchy of the lay brotherhood. They appeared surprised to see him.

"Father General, you're awake early," Dualta said, looking a little guilty.

Camber controlled the urge to lift an eyebrow in surprise, for he had not expected the young knight to be there. Johannes, yes. Johannes was waiting to conduct him to the cathedral for vesting, as he did before every major celebration. Besides, Camber now knew exactly where Johannes had stood with Alister, and knew that he could continue the relationship without alteration.

But Dualta—had he not been on guard duty last night? He seemed to remember something about Dualta coming to the door with Cinhil, but beyond that, he did not know. What had Dualta seen?

"Good morning, gentlemen," he said, warm yet reserved. "Johannes, I've missed your helping hand. And, Dualta—you haven't been here all night, have you? I must confess that much of what happened last night is a blur, but I cannot believe that Joram expected you to guard all night and still be here this morning."

"No, sir, he didn't," Dualta admitted sheepishly. "He told me to ask Lord Illan to relieve me—and I did," he added, as it occurred to him that the vicar general might think he had disobeyed an order. "But I couldn't sleep very well, sir, so I came back after Matins. I thought you might need something before you go to the cathedral."

With as much of a smile as Alister usually permitted himself, Camber clapped the younger man's shoulder —he was a boy, actually, even younger than Joram or Rhys—then gave Johannes a conspiratorial wink.

"He's as bad as all the rest, for all his newness to the Order," he said lightly. "All of you spend far too much time and energy worrying about a crotchety old man."

"Vicar General!" Johannes exclaimed.

"Oh, I know you'll deny it to my face, so what's the use?" He sobered. "Actually, each of you can do something to assist me this morning, if you would. Johannes, how much time do we have?"

Johannes looked doubtful. "You should be at the cathedral within an hour, Vicar General. May I ask what you have in mind?"

"That's ample time. I intend to go there almost immediately," Camber answered, ignoring the question. "Dualta, I should like you to convey this summons to the grand master with my greetings. It instructs him to assemble all available members of the Order in the chapter house this afternoon, after the funeral. The meeting concerns the status of the Order and the selection of my successor. I'll inform the archbishop about the use of the hall when I go to vest."

He handed over the summons, authenticated at the bottom with his ecclesiastical seal, then held up the second missive, this one folded and sealed closed with the blue wax.

"Now, this is a list of those I especially desire in attendance this afternoon. Give this to Jebediah as well,

and ask him to ensure that as many as possible are
there, given the relatively short notice."

The knight nodded. "I understand, Father General."

"Good. Now, Johannes."

"Yes, Vicar General?"

"Johannes, I want to ask whether you would be
willing to give your time and talent to someone besides
myself this morning. Yon Healer in there got little
sleep last night because of me." He gestured behind
him with a grim smile. "So I want him to sleep as long
as possible. In the meantime, see about fresh clothing
for him, and make certain his lady wife knows where
he is. Tell her that I regret having taken him from
her side at a time like this, and assure her that he will
join her in time for the funeral. Then make sure
that he does."

"What about yourself, Father?" Johannes asked. "I
had thought to help you vest for Mass."

"Many can help me with that, good Johannes. I
had rather entrust Lord Rhys to your care."

He took Johannes's elbow and drew him into the
doorway, himself moving into the corridor.

"When he does wake, assure him that I am well
and tell him where I've gone. I'll rely on you to get
him to the cathedral on time."

"Very well, Father," Johannes said dubiously.

Camber could feel the eyes of both men on him as
he turned and strode briskly down the corridor, but
there was no suspicion in either's mind—only genuine
concern, which was being rapidly allayed by their
master's apparent return to robust health.

So far so good. Now, by arriving at the cathedral
early, he should be able to spend a few moments collecting his thoughts for the funeral ordeal ahead.
Though he knew there was no help for it, and that
he would be in no technical violation of his personal
ecclesiastical authority as a deacon, he still could not
help feeling a little uneasy about filling Alister's
sacerdotal functions.

Cinhil was in a grim mood after his sleepless night, and the promised heat of the day did little to soothe him. Like Camber, he had abandoned his bed at first light; but his desertion had been in name only, for he had but tossed and turned anyway.

He roamed his chamber restlessly for nearly an hour, his mind still churning with the events of the previous evening, before finally putting the turmoil from his mind for a while and calling the servants to draw his bath. He suffered their ministrations in silent detachment while they washed and groomed and dressed him. By mid-morning, garbed in the unrelieved black he had chosen for this morning of mornings, he was finally able to dismiss the servants and settle down, to really prepare himself.

The stark facts were easy enough to accept. This noon would see the funeral of Camber MacRorie, and tomorrow his grieving family would take his body home to Caerrorie for burial in the family vaults. By all rights, that should make an end to all. It did, for ordinary men.

But Camber was no ordinary man, another part of Cinhil reasoned. He was Deryni. Still, even Deryni could not return from death. Or, could they?

Fighting down an icy shudder, Cinhil sat on the chest at the foot of his bed and laid a hand on its polished surface, assuring himself that it was still there, with its precious contents.

His faith told him that there *were* exceptions. Very holy men had interceded in the lives of the living before, else there would be none of those creatures whom his religion called saints. And there was no doubt that something had come over Alister Cullen last night. Whether it was Camber or not, a part of him could not help but be intrigued. He had never been witness to a miracle before.

But Camber was not a saint! The rational part of him recoiled at that, shrinking from the possibility that even a sainted Camber might continue to take an interest in the affairs of Gwynedd, and its king in particular. If Camber *had* returned from the dead to aid Alister Cullen, what else might he return to do? And what must he *know,* from the other side of that dark veil of death? Perhaps he even knew of Cinhil's forbidden cache of vestments, and the secret, rebellious thoughts within his heart—and if he did, what might he do?

A whimper caught in Cinhil's throat, and he clutched at the edges of the trunk to stabilize his world.

No! He must not think of that! Camber could not touch him now. Camber was dead. Cinhil and a host of others had seen him dead, and would soon see him buried. Then he *certainly* could not return!

Shaking his head, he forced himself to take a deep, relaxing breath, willed his hands to unclench on the oak edge at his knees. His brow was dripping with perspiration, his upper lip and chin beaded with moisture beneath mustache and beard. Screwing his eyes shut against the runnels of sweat, he wiped a sleeve across his face.

He was overreacting, and a rational part of him knew it. Mindless panic could serve no useful purpose. Camber was dead, and could no longer rule him. It was time to bury him.

With another deep breath, Cinhil stood and arranged the folds of his robe around him, tugging his belt into place with hands which were steady and without tremor. Moving briskly to the polished glass beside his bed, he took up the coronet the servants had left and placed it firmly on his brow—though he would not meet the eyes which stared back from the glass.

Minutes later, he was joining the procession which was forming in the castle yard to walk the quarter-mile to the cathedral. He even managed to find a gentle smile for his queen, as he took her arm and they began to move. He could barely see her tear-swollen face beneath the heavy veil she wore, but for that he was thankful. He knew he could not cope with both Camber and his queen this morning.

The funeral of the Earl of Culdi began on the stroke of noon precisely, in a cathedral filled to capacity by those who had loved, respected, and sometimes feared him. Three Deryni priests celebrated his Requiem: the Primate of All Gwynedd, who had been his boyhood friend; the Vicar General of the Order of Saint Michael, who once had been his enemy; and his only surviving son. The three moved through the ritual in flawless harmony, permitting no faltering of voice or movement to mar any part of this last sacrament for the dead man.

And Camber himself, secure and outwardly serene in a form both known and alien, prayed for Alister Cullen: both the man who had been and the man who had become. Only when it was over, and he had followed Anscom and Joram back into the relative privacy of the sacristy, did any reaction ruffle his outward calm. Brushing aside those who waited to help him from his vestments, he fled to a far corner of the chamber and pressed the heels of both hands hard against his eyes, as much to still his trembling as to shut out what he had seen.

Mere participation in the funeral had not unnerved him. Anscom's priestly role had been the essential one, with Camber and Joram only giving support to the prayers which the archbishop offered in the name of the deceased. Camber had functioned as a deacon without difficulty, bolstered by his own long-ago memories as well as the more recent ones of his alter ego. No, it was not that part of the charade which set him shaking now—though he knew that was something with which he must deal eventually.

He drew a deep, shuddering breath and forced his conscious mind to slip down deep inside his fears, touching the real reason for his reaction almost immediately. There, beyond the reach of normal reason, a simpler, more primitive part of him howled and gibbered in mindless terror, cowering from the remembered image of his own body on the bier before the altar.

He was not really afraid of death—not normal death, at any rate, for that must come to all men, in time. Even Ariella, in all her arcane knowledge, black and white, had not been able to cheat real death indefinitely—though Camber thought he knew why her last spell had failed.

But there were many ways to die, not all of them so final or so clean. The visual image of his own face, so still in death, was concrete symbol of his own quite different death and rebirth in another's life, as well as body. From here, there could be no casual turning back. For better or for worse, he was now Alister Cullen. Except for rare occasions when he might dare relax his hold, Camber MacRorie was truly dead.

That acknowledgment made, he found that he could let go of his fear. He took another deep breath and felt himself relax; breathed again as his pulse slowed and his trembling ceased.

He would not have to look on that face again. Even now, Anscom's monks were waiting for the last of the mourners to leave the cathedral, so that they might seal the body in its coffin and wrap the whole in leaden foil. Tomorrow the body would go to Caerrorie and be buried, and that would be the end of it. And he, Alister Cullen to the outside world, would go on.

Squaring his shoulders and breathing again, he turned and went back into the center of the chamber, delivering himself to the ministrations of Johannes and another monk. His movements, as he helped them take off chasuble and other vestments, were automatic, Alister's; and he allowed that other part of him to take over his physical movements as he scanned the chamber for the first time since entering it.

Anscom was gone. He suspected that the archbishop had returned to his own vesting chapel almost immediately, sensing that both of his colleagues would wish to be alone with their grief. Anscom had always been a man of practical sensitivity—only one of the traits which had first drawn him and Camber into friendship, more than forty years before.

But Joram was there, eyes averted, deep in thought, changing back into his accustomed Michaeline raiment with movements as automatic as Camber's. Camber held his arms away from his body as he watched his son, letting Johannes knot the broad white sash of Michaeline knighthood around his waist. As the other monk draped his shoulders with the formal, badge-embroidered mantle of the vicar generalship, Camber ducked his head to permit donning of the silver pectoral cross which Johannes brought. Lastly, Camber picked up the skullcap of royal blue and put it on his head, adjusting it automatically as he moved closer to Joram. Johannes motioned for the other monk to leave and withdrew to stand against the door, there to wait until his superior was ready to go.

Camber shifted the folds of his mantle to a more comfortable arrangement as Joram looked up. One of the cathedral monks was fastening Joram's cassock, a second standing by with his white sash. Joram's eyes were hooded and unreadable.

"I meant to speak to you before this, Joram, but I thought you would want the time alone," Camber said. He was well aware that he dared not speak too openly in front of Joram's dressers. "I'm sure you're aware of the Grand Chapter. I fear it may seem precipitate, but I knew that you would be occupied with family duties for the next few days, and scheduling this meeting for today seemed the only way to permit your attendance. I value your counsel, you know."

Joram averted his eyes as he fastened his own cloak at his throat. "Thank you, Father General. I appreciate the thought."

"Will you accompany me?" Camber continued, laying his hand gently on Joram's elbow and gesturing toward the door with his eyes.

Joram, helpless to resist under the gaze of so many

curious observers, could only murmur assent and
move with him. Though Camber knew that Joram
must be yearning for some time alone, under the double burden of grieving the loss of Cullen and pretending to grieve for his father, there was simply no help
for it. Camber dreaded facing his first Cullen-
encounter with the Michaelines without Joram at his
side, and Joram must leave in the morning to escort
"Camber's" body back to Caerrorie.

Just outside the sacristy, Gellis de Cleary, the acting
precentor, was waiting to conduct them to the chapter house. Reentering the cathedral by a north door,
they made their way along the ambulatory aisle and
across the south transept, exiting through the processional door into the warm brightness of the cloister
walk. At least a score of Michaelines, clergy and
knights mixed, were milling outside the entrance to
the chapter house, catching a last breath of cooler air
before joining their brethren in the closed, circular hall.
The stragglers picked up their pace as they saw their
vicar general approaching, the scrape of sandaled and
boot-shod feet shuffling and echoing on the tiled
floor.

As Camber appeared in the doorway and was
seen, a respectful pathway opened before him and
the chamber began to quiet. Those already seated
rose at his entry, crowding together on the tiers of
stone benches to make room for their more tardy colleagues. All conversation ceased as the tall, gray-
haired figure moved among them.

Smiling faintly, nodding greeting and recognition
to those whose eyes he met, Camber made his
way through the center of the hall, knowing in a
flash of dual memory that he had always come this way
among his brothers in faith, reaching out to touch a
hand here, a shoulder there in comfort, fingers moving
in benediction above numerous bowed heads. He was
aware of Joram following a few paces behind—
comfort to the part of him which was Alister as well as
to himself—and then another jog of memory brought

a wave of unexpected sorrow: for it was Nathan who approached to conduct him to the abbatial throne, not the beloved Jasper Miller, who had performed that function for him almost from the beginning of his tenure as vicar general.

A part of him knew that the real Alister had never faced the emptiness of Jasper's absence, and that Alister himself had died only minutes after his friend fell in battle. But there was also no doubt that another part of him was responding to the knowledge of Jasper's death as though he were Alister in fact as well as in form. His dual memory seemed to be functioning forward as well as backward in time, progressing almost as if there had been no ending to Alister at all. He had not expected that.

He faltered for just an instant as he mounted the three low steps to the chair which was temporarily his, vividly aware of the sea of royal blue around him, of the brightly muraled walls, the high, hammer-beamed ceiling, the smudge of rainbow light cast from the windows far above his head. His eyes met Jebediah's, staring down at him hopefully from the right of the chair, the grand master's strong hands resting steady on the quillons of the sheathed sword of the Order.

Camber spared him a weary, reassuring smile before turning to face the others. To the left, Nathan stepped up behind a narrow table where two clarks were shuffling sheets of parchment and checking lists of names. Johannes stood directly behind the chair, and Dualta beyond, in place of a knight named Lauren, who had been slain. Joram moved quietly to his accustomed place beside Jebediah, eyes downcast.

Camber waited until all of the stragglers had found places around the sides of the chamber, then sat, signaling for the last man in to close and bar the door. The dull shuffle of feet and sheathed swords against stone briefly disturbed the stillness of the chamber as the rest of the company took their seats and settled down.

"Dearest brethren." Camber let his hands rest gently on the arms of the chair, trying to scan all of them by vision and intuition. "I apologize if the timing of this meeting appears to follow too closely on an event which has touched us all profoundly." He took a deep breath. "Except for the urgency of our own situation, and the familial duties which will call one of our most beloved brethren to other responsibilities for a few days, I would have risked delaying this speech for yet a little while." He glanced at Joram. "However, under the circumstances, I do not feel that any of us would be well served by further postponement of the inevitable. I apologize that my recent ill health did not permit any earlier meeting."

He glanced briefly at the signet on his hand as he searched for words to tell them what he must. He could hear no sound but guarded breathing in all the packed chamber. The air was close already, tight with anticipation. A part of him wished he were anywhere but here.

"My brothers and friends, I personally face as grave a responsibility in the next few weeks as has ever come to me; for I must leave you in another's care at a time when change will be but one more disruptive factor in a year already fraught with tragedy for our Order. Beginning with our decision to support the Restoration, with its concurrent dispersal of you all to places of safety; continuing through the capture and subversion of our lamented brother, Humphrey of Gallareaux, may his soul rest in peace—" He crossed himself, a movement which was mirrored immediately by his audience. "—and not ending with Imre's wanton retaliation against us, because we would not abandon our just cause—we have given much for what we believed. The cost has been high, yet I think we could not have done differently, even had we foreseen the eventual outcome as it is."

He sighed. "Perhaps the highest price has been paid in human lives. Our battle casualties alone were staggering. Most of you are aware of losses as individuals—the friends and comrades you have lost—but some of you may not be aware of what these losses mean to the Order: yet another legacy of our dispersal to separate places. Jebediah, would you please give us your latest estimation of our precise losses in men?"

Jebediah's face did not change expression—he was too good a soldier for that—but Camber could see his tension in the whitened knuckles on the sword beside him.

"More than forty knights were killed outright in the fighting or died on the battlefield of their wounds, Father General," he said in a low voice. "Another score lie at the brink of death even now, with surgeons and Healers battling to save their lives. Some who will live will never fight again. Our present battle-ready strength, including those on light duty because of still-healing injuries, is perhaps one hundred ten, of nearly two hundred who rode out to Iomaire."

There were murmurs of surprise and consternation around the chamber. Camber kept his eyes averted until conversation had ceased, then resumed without looking up.

"Barely half our previous strength, brethren. Nor is our domestic situation much better. Nathan, please report on the state of our lands and properties."

Nathan stood and moved to stand beside Camber's chair, resting a hand lightly on one turned finial as if to underline his support of his superior.

"Of the twelve major establishments functioning before Imre began his harassment of the Order, ten were looted, burned out, and razed. Even the foundations were uprooted, in some cases. The lead was stripped from the roofs and windows, and most of the usable stone and timber at each site was carried away by Imre's men for his aborted building project at Nyford.

"What little remained after the soldiers finished has been well scavenged by the local peasants, and can currently be seen in scores of cottages and walls and sheep pens. In order to rebuild at any of these sites, it would be necessary to bring in almost all new materials."

He consulted a page lying at the end of the table. "Further, we estimate that some forty-five hundred head of cattle, sheep, and horses were appropriated by the Crown or, in some cases, slaughtered and the carcasses left to rot. All standing crops were seized, the stubble burned and ploughed under, and the whole sown with salt. If any of these fields yields a crop in the next fifty years, I will be very much surprised."

There were rumbles of anger and bewilderment, until Camber held up a hand for silence. Porric Lunal, one of the men whose name had appeared on Jebediah's list, stood in his place, eyes blazing.

"Father Nathan, you've accounted for ten of our twelve houses. What of the other two?"

"They are somewhat better off," Nathan conceded. "After being stripped of their lead and timber, Haut Eirial and Mollingford both were burned out and salted, but their wholesale dismantling was interrupted by the Restoration. Though some scavenging took place, the basic fabric of the stone buildings appears to be intact. Our masons feel that sufficient stone remains to rebuild smaller establishments on these sites, but I personally believe we would be better off to build elsewhere. The salted fields could not support even a small community for some years. We would be totally at the mercy of anyone who decided to cut off our supply lines."

He glanced down at Camber, his last words and his expression leaving little doubt, at least in Camber's mind, just to whom he was referring, but Camber chose to overlook the intended implication. Nathan, like many other Michaelines, was well aware of the tenuous balance currently in effect between Deryni and the king; and the Michaelines were Deryni, in large part.

Wearily, Camber dropped his forehead against one

hand and closed his eyes, in a typically Alister gesture.

"I share your concern, Nathan," he murmured.

"What about the Commanderie?" another voice called, from somewhere on the right.

"Jeb?" Camber replied, not looking up.

"The Commanderie cannot be salvaged," Jebediah said. His voice was bitter, and Camber could visualize the expression on his face without even having to see it.

"Imre's butchers were thorough, especially since Cheltham was the first of our houses on their list. I see no hope of ever restoring Cheltham to its former prominence, had we twice our numbers and five times our present financial resources, which we do not."

There was silence as Camber raised his head to face them all again. Every eye was on him now, waiting for him to tell them that it was not true, for him to make things right. That he could not do—though he could give them hope. But once he had done that, he must turn discussion to his real reason for calling this meeting, and hope that he could read them all correctly.

"You have heard the reports by our esteemed brethren, my friends," he said, in a voice which penetrated to every corner of the chamber. "I wished you to know the whole of it, that you may harbor no illusions as to where we stand.

"On the other hand," he continued more confidently, "we are not totally bereft of resources. We still command more than one hundred knights—some of the finest in Christendom." He glanced at Jebediah, who lowered his own gaze in bitter acknowledgment. "We have nearly three hundred professed brothers and priests, albeit most are presently scattered to places of safety and refuge across this wide land.

"Also, I have in my possession certain new grants of land, made to us by King Cinhil before ever we gathered for battle a few weeks ago." He held up a hand for silence as reaction threatened to interrupt his speech.

"We have two superb choices for the site of our new Commanderie: Cùilteine and Argoed, both of which will be handed over to the Order by royal charter upon the succession of your new vicar general. Which brings us to the most important reason for this meeting."

CHAPTER THIRTEEN

For though I be absent in the flesh,
yet am I with you in the spirit,
joying and beholding your order.
                                  —Colossians 2:5

The sun had set, and the cathedral bells were ringing Compline, when Camber finally adjourned the Grand Chapter. All afternoon he had listened to their discussion, with various candidates and their adherents advancing and refuting numerous opinions and concerns. By the time Camber thanked them for their attendance and dismissed them, he had a fair comprehension of the consensus of the Order, and a clear picture of the task facing him in the next few days. Already, in his own mind, he had narrowed the field of possible successors to three. He would rely upon private interviews in making his final selection.

A few of them lingered when most of the rest had gone, making it clear that they would have liked to stay and talk further, but Camber did not encourage them, and they soon departed. Not even Jebediah tried to force further communication after the long day; besides, he had duties in the hospice where some of his men lay a-mending, and that was foremost in his mind just then. Joram had been among the very first to leave—to join Evaine and Rhys and bolster himself for the trip to Caerrorie tomorrow, Camber suspected.

And so, when he had sent away even his own attendants, Camber was able to slip into the solitude of the cloister garth for some much-needed quiet. Leaning his back against the rough bark of one of the trees, so that he blended with the lines of the sparse grove there, he gazed sightlessly at the night sky and let the afternoon sift into place. Only when the last of the Michaeline voices had faded from hearing did he stand away from the concealing tree and reenter the cloister walk. He headed purposefully toward a postern door in the south transept, for his quarters lay on the other side of the cathedral.

The murmur of chanting voices met him softly as he slipped inside. He melted back against a column to survey. Aside from the monks in the choir and a few people kneeling in the nave, the cathedral was deserted. Far across the transept, he could see brighter candlelight streaming from one of the north chapels, filtering softly through the carved wood screens, and he reasoned that they must have laid his alter ego's body there for the night.

Drawn by a need to bid one final farewell, he moved across the dim nave with bowed head, soft-soled shoes making no sound on the glazed tiles. No one marked his passage, but he felt a profound sense of relief when he had crossed that expanse of vaulted openness. Slowing his pace, he glided along the back of the chapel toward its doorway, trying to appear nonchalant as he glanced through the wooden screen.

At least he would not have to look upon that face again. During the afternoon, the monks had laid the body away in a plain oak coffin, sealing that within the traditional wrapping of leaden foil. The MacRorie pall lay over the coffin now, the sword and chased coronet of the Earldom of Culdi resting near the head, closest to the altar. At the corners, four fat candles stood flickering vigil, taller than a man in their bronze holders. Two royal guards whom Camber did not know stood watch outside, reversed spears at rest, as much to protect the valuable sword and coronet as to keep watch over him who slept within. Now that the formal obsequies were over, the Earl of Culdi was no different from anyone else who had died in the faith and received the blessings of the Church on his passage to the Nether realms.

The guards did not move as Camber approached, but as he started to step through the doorway, one of them turned slightly toward him and caught his eye.

"Father?" the man whispered.

Camber nodded acknowledgment.

"Father, there's someone in there, praying by the coffin. We didn't want to intrude, but he's been in there for several hours now. Maybe you could make sure he's all right?"

With a glance inside, Camber nodded and moved into the chapel, studying the mourner.

The still, kneeling figure would not have been noticeable to the casual observer. He was huddled at the left of the coffin near the head, cloaked shoulders shaking with silent sobs, hooded head bent in shadow. Grayed, trembling hands rested on the corbeled edge of the catafalque on which the coffin rested, moving occasionally to reach up under the velvet pall and touch the lead wrappings. The candlelight did not penetrate far enough to reveal any other details.

Pursing his lips thoughtfully, Camber moved close enough to crouch down beside the man. From the way he started at Camber's touch on his shoulder, Camber knew that he had been so deeply immersed in his grief that he had not heard Camber approach.

"Be at ease, son," he murmured, trying to send a whisper of reassurance into the troubled mind. "There is nothing you can do for him here. We shall all miss him, but the grief which you feel will pass, in time."

A pale, tear-swollen face turned toward him in the

shadows of the hood, and watery eyes gazed across at him in misery. Camber's hand almost withdrew in shock as he realized it was Guaire.

"How can there be peace or ease when he is gone?" Guaire whispered, before Camber could respond. "My Lord Camber was the architect of all which we now support in the king's name. Without him, there would have been no Haldane king. Without him now—"

As the young man broke into weeping again, Camber glanced up at the velvet-draped coffin, at the fringe of gold bullion, the earl's coronet resting near the head. How to explain to Guaire, without revealing all, that Camber had served his purpose, that he had fulfilled his outward work and must now serve in other ways?

Useless. He could not explain. He could only hope to comfort.

"I know, son," he said. "We shall simply have to try to carry on his work. He would have wished it thus. Can you not see a purpose in that?"

Guaire hung his head and swallowed hard, as though something constricted his throat. "I loved him, Father General. He was—very special to me, in ways I can't begin to explain. I would have died for him— gladly—and now—"

"Then now you must live for him," Camber said gently, trying to keep his own emotions out of his voice. "You can, you know."

"Can I?" Guaire laughed—a grim, humorless croak —then got to his feet. "Perhaps you're right, Father General. But right now I can't accept that. Now I feel only an emptiness and loss of purpose inside. Why couldn't *I* have been the one to die?"

His despair brought on another bout of weeping, and Camber rose to lay his arm gently around the young man's shoulders and begin drawing him away from the coffin. The guards stood aside respectfully as the two of them left the chapel, but Camber kept Guaire's face turned close in the protective circle of his arms, shielding him from the men's well-meaning but prying curiosity.

He tried to ease the troubled mind as they moved into the bosom of the summery night, but it was soon clear that Guaire's grief was far more profound than he had first imagined. By the time he and Guaire had reached the comparative shelter of his own corridor, Camber knew he dared not leave him alone in this condition. On the other hand, he himself needed time alone after the day's strain. He could not keep the boy with him all night.

Continuing past the door to his own quarters, he walked Guaire farther along the corridor until he came to Johannes's door. Johannes was used to odd requests from his vicar general. He would take Guaire in.

Camber's light knock was answered almost immediately.

"Vicar General, what—?"

Shaking his head in warning, Camber drew Guaire into the room and sat him down in a chair beside the small fireplace.

"Johannes, this is Guaire, who was Lord Camber's squire," he said, stroking Guaire's hair in comfort as Guaire sobbed against the hand he would not release. "Can you fix a pallet for him, and let him stay the night?"

"Of course, Father General. Is there anything else I can do? Would a cup of wine help, do you think?"

"I'll bring some from my quarters," Camber said, extricating his hand from Guaire's and beckoning Johannes to come and take his place. "Sit with him while I'm gone, will you?"

Back in his room, Camber thought about Guaire as he gathered up a wine pitcher and hunted for clean cups. He supposed he had known, or at least suspected, Guaire's devotion to him as Camber. The boy had been a close friend of his son Cathan, though Camber had not actually met him until after Cathan's death.

But Camber had not realized the extent of the attachment Guaire made, even at that first meeting; and the attachment had grown during the long months of confinement in the Michaeline sanctuary with Cinhil. Now Guaire's earnest, faithful trust had turned to near hysteria at Camber's supposed death. Whatever was Camber going to do with him?

He found the cups he had been searching for, then took a small casket from beside his bed and began searching for a sleeping powder. A good night's sleep was first on the agenda. Unless he had greatly misjudged, Guaire's grief would not abate with the mere passage of time. He was despondent, without comfort or purpose. His grief must be turned to more constructive ends. Rest would set the stage, but what then? Perhaps if he had it from Camber's own mouth: the message of hope, of courage to go on, even in his hero's absence . . .

Camber sat thoughtfully on the edge of his bed and fingered a small packet of folded parchment as he reviewed how that might safely be done, concluding that neither the risks nor the difficulties seemed overly great. After a moment, he consulted his medicine chest again and took out another packet. The first he emptied into the pitcher of wine, for Johannes would have to be provided for, as well as Guaire. He slipped the second packet into his sash before taking up pitcher and cups and returning to Johannes's room.

Johannes was stirring the fire on the hearth and looked up worriedly. Guaire sat unmoving where Camber had left him, tear-swollen eyes staring sightlessly at the stone floor beneath his feet. Ruddy firelight danced on the finely chiseled features but brought no life to them. Had Guaire been carved of stone, he would have been a masterpiece of grief and dejection, but as a man, he was pitiful to behold.

"I've brought wine for all of us," Camber said. "I thought we could use it, after the day we've had."

He set three cups on the hearth and filled them, then casually took the packet from his sash and emptied its contents into one of the cups. What he did was shielded from Guaire's vision, but he knew that Johannes was watching with interest, and would think that *that* was the sleeping potion, not realizing that all the wine had already been doctored.

"You'll feel better when you've slept, Guaire," Camber said, glancing over his shoulder. "Shall I heat yours?"

He did not wait for reply. He did not expect one. Swirling the wine in its cup, he pulled a hot poker from the flames. The wine sizzled as he plunged the glowing metal into it, and the spicy aroma began to fill the room. As he took Guaire's cup and rose to go to him, he saw that Johannes had taken up one of the others without prompting and was drinking deeply. Camber smiled gently as he put Guaire's warm cup into his hands.

"Drink this, son. It will help you sleep."

Though Guaire's hands closed around the cup, he did not otherwise move. With a slight sigh, Camber put one hand on the young man's shoulder and with the other raised hands and cup to Guaire's lips.

"Come on, son. Drink it down. You'll feel better."

Guaire obeyed, each automatic swallow loud and labored in the quiet room. When he had drained it to the dregs, Camber took the cup away and helped him stand. Guaire's eyes were already becoming heavy as Camber and Johannes walked him to a pallet which Johannes had pulled out from under his own bed. His knees buckled as he collapsed on the padded mat. Camber adjusted a pillow under the lolling head, then pulled a sleeping fur from the bed and tucked that around him.

Johannes yawned and sat down in the chair Guaire had just vacated, his own eyelids growing heavier and heavier as he watched Camber tending Guaire. Guaire seemed to be having trouble focusing.

"Sleep, son," Camber murmured, brushing hair back from the glazing eyes. "You'll feel much better when you've had a good night's sleep. Go to sleep now."

Camber had not dared to use his Deryni mind touch on Guaire before, for he had used it several times as Camber, and the young man might have recognized that touch. But Guaire was too far gone for it to matter now; and in the future, he would no longer be able to make the connection. Camber would see to that.

But for now, the drugged wine was doing its work, lulling Guaire into a deeply receptive mental state where Camber could move without fear. As the red-rimmed eyes closed and the breathing rhythm changed to that of slumber, Camber sat back and watched for several minutes. He could hear Johannes snoring softly behind him, oblivious to everything, and he knew that the monk would not stir for the rest of the night.

He smiled and gave Guaire's forehead a last, fleeting touch, then rose and glanced at Johannes, deepening his sleep as well, before tiptoeing silently out of the room. In a little while, when the drugs in Guaire's system had had a chance to take effect completely, he would return. Camber MacRorie would see that all was made right.

Guaire turned and moaned in his sleep, then became aware that, though his eyes were still closed, he was suddenly alert and aware of himself again—of the warm, drowsy comfort, snuggled under the sleeping furs, of the flickering firelight playing on his closed eyelids, of the faint smell of burning wood, the lingering aroma of spiced wine.

He remembered the wine, then, and was aware of the warm glow still permeating his stomach and, indeed, his whole being. Slowly the day's events began filtering back to him. Strangely, they did not hurt him now as they had earlier.

There was still the sense of loss, and his throat still ached from the continual constriction it had suffered for the past eight days since Camber's death. But he felt strangely at peace. He wondered idly whether Father Cullen had put something in the wine to make him feel so calm.

He was mulling that idea around, vaguely aware that he seemed to be thinking somewhat more slowly than usual, when he suddenly began to sense that something in the room had changed. A cold draft stirred his hair, and he started to huddle down under the furs to escape it. But then it suddenly struck him that the draft had come from the door, and that someone else was in the room.

He rolled over and opened his eyes, expecting to see Brother Johannes or Father Cullen; but Johannes snored softly in his chair beside the fire. And somehow he knew that he would not see Father Cullen as he turned his head toward the door.

What in—?

He blinked, thinking that perhaps his eyes were playing tricks on him, then stared in amazement as a tall, light-shrouded figure began to move slowly toward him. He was not afraid, though the thought crossed his mind that perhaps he should be. He was feeling rather a sense of expectation—and that, too, seemed odd. He could not see the figure's face—it wore a long gray cloak, the hood drawn close about the head. A silvery glow extended around the whole figure, wispy, amorphous.

Childhood fantasies swept through his mind then, and the thought occurred to him that this could very well be a ghost—it certainly did not appear to be of this world. He started to sit up straight at that—then froze halfway up, leaning on one elbow, as he saw the face.

"Camber!" he breathed, awe wiping his face of all other emotions.

The figure came a few steps closer, then stopped. The gray hood fell back from the well-remembered silver-gilt hair. The face was serene and untroubled, the pale eyes glowing with an intensity which Guaire could not remember having seen before.

"Don't be afraid," the figure said, in a voice astonishingly familiar. "I return but for a moment, to ease your grief and to assure you that I am at peace where I now dwell."

Guaire swallowed and nodded, but could not quite find the courage to reply.

"I have seen your sorrow these past days," the figure continued, "and I am saddened that you should mourn so much for me."

"But—I miss you, Lord," Guaire managed to whisper. "There was so much to do—and now it will go undone."

The figure smiled, and to Guaire it was as though the sun shone in the darkened chamber.

"There are others who will do it, Guaire. You, if you only will."

"I?"

Guaire finished sitting up and stared at the apparition in disbelief.

"But how can that be, Lord? I am only a human. I have not the resources, the talent. You were the heart of the Restoration. Now, with you gone, the king will endure unchecked. I fear him, Lord."

"Pity him, Guaire. Do not fear him. And help those who remain to carry on our work: Joram, and Rhys, my daughter; Evaine—my grandsons, when they are older. And Alister Cullen, who brought you here. He, most of all, has need of your support, if you will only give it."

"Father Alister? But he is so gruff, and sure of himself. How could I possibly help him?"

"He is not so self-sufficient as he would have men think," the apparition replied, the familiar smile playing about his lips. "Gruff he may be, and sometimes far too stubborn for his own good. But he, even more than my children, will miss that companionship we used to share. Will you help him, Guaire? Will you serve him as you served me?"

Guaire dropped his gaze to the figure's feet, which he could not see beneath the voluminous cloak, then glanced up shyly at the shining face once more.

"I could truly help him?"

"You could."

"To serve him, as I served you?"

"He is more than worthy, Guaire. And too proud to ask you for your help."

Guaire swallowed.

"Very well, Lord. I will do it. And I will keep your memory alive, I swear it!"

The figure smiled. "My memory is not important. The work we began *is*. Help Alister. Help the king. And be assured that I shall be with you, even when you are least aware. I count on you to carry out my work."

"I will, Lord."

The figure turned to go, and Guaire's eyes grew round.

"No! Wait, Lord! Do not leave me yet!"

The figure paused to gaze at him in compassion.

"I may not stay, my son. Nor may I come to you again. Be at peace."

Guaire stared at him in despair, then slid out of the sleeping furs and knelt with hands upraised.

"Then leave me with your blessing, Lord. Please! Do not deny me this!"

The figure's face became more serious, and then a graceful hand was emerging from the folds of the cloak to trace the sign of blessing. Guaire bowed his head.

"Benedicat te omnipotens Deus, Pater, et Filius, et Spiritus Sanctus."

"Amen," Guaire breathed.

And for an instant, as a hand touched lightly on his hair, his senses reeled.

But when he raised his head and opened his eyes, the figure was gone, the air dark and empty where before there had been light.

Guaire gasped and scrambled to his feet, staggering

unsteadily to where the figure had been. For a moment he stood there as one dumb, holding himself up against the door frame, silently reliving what he had just seen—or thought he had seen. Then he was struck by a soaring sense of joy and jubilation.

Camber had come back to him! Abruptly, he wanted to run through the corridors of the archbishop's palace, shouting to wake the dead, that Camber had returned, if only for a little while—and that the great Deryni Lord had charged him, Guaire of Arliss, a humble human of very little worth, with the awesome responsibility of carrying out the great man's work!

But he could not do that. Camber had judged wisely, at least in this, and the drugs which Guaire had ingested would not permit him to do anything that decisive. Already, the details of the encounter were fading, transforming themselves into a blurrier, dreamlike set of memories far more in keeping with what the actual occurrence was supposed to have been.

No, he could not announce his wonder to the world. As Guaire mulled the problem in his sluggishly functioning mind, he realized that what had happened was far too precious to share with just anyone. Besides, who would believe him?

Not Brother Johannes. That pious and devoted monk had not even stirred while the miracle took place. If Guaire woke him and tried to explain, Johannes would say that it had been but a drug-induced dream. No, he could not share this treasure with Johannes.

Then Cullen. Of course! Father Cullen would understand. Father Cullen would *have* to believe him! After all, it was Cullen himself whom Camber had named as the one Guaire should serve. Surely Cullen had a right to know.

Joyfully, Guaire wrenched at the door, careening down the corridor toward Cullen's quarters.

And inside, Camber hunched down under his blankets and feigned sleep as footsteps hesitantly approached the bed. He could hear Guaire's breathing, quick and agitated, as the young man paused to look at him, and then the footsteps receded slightly. A few seconds later, brightness flared from the direction of the fireplace.

Camber waited, listening carefully, as the footsteps approached again, this time with brightness as well.

"Father General?" Guaire called softly. "Father General, are you asleep?"

Camber rolled over and leaned on one elbow to peer at Guaire, blinking and squinting in the flickering light. Guaire's face glowed with more than candle-light as he dropped to one knee beside the bed.

"I was," Camber grunted, stifling a yawn. "Why aren't you?"

Guaire shook his head. "I was, too, but—please don't be angry with me, Father. I'm sorry to wake you, but I had to tell someone, and I think—I think *he* would not mind."

"He?"

Guaire swallowed, a shadow of doubt flickering in his eyes. "The—the Lord Camber, Father. He—he came to me in a dream—I think—and—and, he told me I must not mourn—that I had important work to do—*his* work—helping accomplish the things he did not get to do."

His words came tumbling out breathlessly, as though he feared he might not dare to speak them if he delayed too long.

Camber nodded wisely and yawned again, remembering to keep sufficient gruffness in his voice.

"Well, of course you have important work to do. I told you that before. Camber relied greatly on you."

"He did? Oh, yes, I know he did, Father!" Guaire positively beamed. "And he said—" Here his face went more serious. "He said that I should serve you, Father. He said that I should serve you as I served him, that you would need my help. Do you, Father?"

Camber sat up slowly, drawing the deep blue of his Michaeline mantle around him as he swung his feet to the fur beside the bed.

"He told you that?"

Guaire nodded solemnly, not daring to speak.

Camber looked long into the earnest brown eyes, and finally spoke very slowly. Guaire seemed to have made the necessary transferrence of loyalty. Now Camber must cement that new alliance in Alister's distinctive style.

"You realize, of course, that serving me would not be like serving Camber. Camber was a great secular lord, surrounded by the luxuries of his class. There's nothing wrong with that," he added, as Guaire started to raise an objection, "but it's different here."

"Because you're a priest, Father?"

"In part. And you will find, if you do serve me, that a cleric is often bound by things which do not concern a secular lord like Camber. Soon, by the grace of God, I shall be a bishop, potentially wielding a not-inconsiderable power, even in secular affairs. In many respects, that is a princely office, and some men make it so. But I am not that sort, as I think you know. The panoply of a prince's court, or even an earl's, will not be found within my walls."

"I have no need of that, Father," Guaire whispered, drawing himself up straighter as he knelt.

"Very well, then. I never had a secular aide before, but—we shall give you a try. For now, though, suppose you go back to bed. Perhaps you can go without sleep, but I cannot."

With joyful tears in his eyes, Guaire nodded and started to rise, then seized Camber's hand and kissed it. When he had gone, Camber stared after him for a long time before lying back on his bed.

CHAPTER FOURTEEN

I am afraid of you, lest I have bestowed upon you labour in vain.

—Galatians 4:11

No immediate repercussions arose from the night's work—at least none of which Camber was aware. Guaire settled into the routine of serving his new master without a whisper of difficulty or friction, gently weaning the solicitous Johannes to other duties. He even adopted a semi-clerical attire to fit in better with the other staff which Camber would be acquiring with his episcopal office. Johannes would be remaining with the Michaelines to assist the new vicar general, when his former master left for Grecotha the following week, so Guaire temporarily functioned as valet as well as clerk and factor to the incipient bishop. Nothing more was said about the conversation he and Camber had shared the night before; indeed, it was as if nothing had occurred.

Nor was there reason for Camber to give the matter further thought during the rest of the week. Those others who might have sensed what was developing, had they been able to assemble all the pieces of the mosaic—Joram and Evaine and Rhys—were, themselves, too busy trying to settle Camber's affairs in Caerrorie and get back to the capital by Friday to see the full scope of what was building. On that day, the seven-year-old Davin MacRorie, Camber's grandson and heir, must be formally recognized by the king as the new Earl of Culdi, doing homage for his titles and lands with nearly a score of other nobles, young and old, who had come into their inheritances through the death of predecessors during the recent war.

That, and the feverish collection of such of Camber's important manuscripts and other possessions as he would continue to need, tended to blur the true significance of what was happening at Caerrorie itself. Camber's children noticed but did not react to the growing numbers of mourners who came daily to kneel and pray in the chapel above the MacRorie vaults, where "Camber" slept beside his long-dead wife and other family; saw but did not comprehend the meaning of the floral and prayer offerings which began to appear in increasing numbers with each day's visitants.

They certainly did not connect these things with the uneasiness which Camber himself had felt as he rode back to Valoret and watched the people's reaction to his funeral cortege. And Cinhil's fleeting glimpse of Camber's face on that night of memory integration was far from any of their thoughts.

And so, alone and on his own in his new role, unknown in his true identity to any person in the castle at Valoret, Camber settled into his new life. He could not know that his tomb in Caerrorie was fast becoming a pilgrimage spot for the faithful of the area; that an embittered king brooded long hours into the night on what he had seen in a vicar general's bedchamber; that a Michaeline knight already fretted under the restriction not to speak of what *he* thought had happened that night. In temporary and blissful ignorance, Camber pursued the duties and cemented the relationships which would be increasingly important to the future Bishop of Grecotha. Camber of Culdi and all that he had been were far from his mind in those days.

One of his most immediate tasks was the selection of his successor as vicar general. He spent nearly three days at that, interviewing candidates and others and learning more with each passing hour about the inner workings of the ecclesiastical mechanism of which he had lately become a part.

Much of his learning was on the strictly verbal level, from what people actually told him. That was important, and its value not to be denied. However, with his Deryni skills, he was also able to glean information from his human cohorts which they never intended to volunteer, sometimes to their detriment. Even the Deryni often gave off unsolicited surface information, which any of their race might read without undue effort—or detection.

But the human candidates were ripe for deeper probing, wanting only the touch of a master to release all to a questing mind. From them, Camber gained a great deal of insight into how Alister Cullen had been seen and would be expected to function in the future. He did not often go unbidden into others' minds, but in this case, the end surely justified the means. He was making a selection which would affect the whole of Gwynedd for many years to come.

He settled finally on the brilliant and human Crevan Allyn, a polished soldier as well as a pious priest, who had served outstandingly under Jebediah during the war effort. Crevan had been one of the unheralded masterminds behind the planning involved in putting the Michaelines safely underground during that year of hiatus during which Cinhil trained for kingship and Imre tried to track them all down. He had no enemies that anyone knew of, no vices, no taint of unorthodoxy. He did have that sort of intuition and perspective which allowed him to move with the times, flexible in the lesser things while remaining true to what could not be compromised, no matter what the temptation. Also, King Cinhil liked him.

That last was vitally important, and had carried due weight in Camber's deliberations. In fact, another man of almost equal talent had been eliminated from consideration precisely because of the fact that Cinhil did *not* like *him*.

But Crevan, increasingly in Cinhil's favor, and

human, could perhaps command a growing trust as Deryni influence waned. This was the sort of man the Michaelines, and Gwynedd, would need in the years ahead, as they trod the increasingly precarious path which all Deryni needs must travel, now that Cinhil would be settling down to get his kingdom in order.

Already Cinhil was gathering human allies to his side, some of them with far older grudges than his own against the race which had kept them from lands and titles and riches throughout the Interregnum. Cinhil's restoration had already brought the scions of several formerly powerful families back to court. A few of them who had fought for Cinhil in the war would be confirmed in their old titles along with young Davin, when Cinhil held his first formal postwar court on Friday afternoon. The human Crevan, though in deep sympathy with his Deryni brethren, hopefully would not have to face the kind of opposition that a Deryni vicar general eventually might.

But there was another, even more important factor in Crevan's selection; and that was that Crevan, as the unique human individual that he was, could be subtly guided by Camber himself, in ways which even he would never suspect, unless Camber was entirely heavy-handed. In addition to the obvious ties of Michaeline brotherhood and obedience to a bishop's higher rank, Crevan would be bound by more invisible links of Deryni crafting. Camber made sure of that during his last interview with Crevan, after informing him of his intention to name Crevan as his successor.

His touch was subtle but irresistible; and Crevan left none the wiser. Nor would any other Deryni be able to detect the signs of Camber's binding, without forcing Crevan to the question and destroying the man in the process. No one would lightly enter the mind of a Michaeline vicar general against his will, human or not.

The announcement of Crevan Allyn's selection was made to the assembled Grand Chapter, minus Joram MacRorie, on Thursday evening. It was followed by a solemn Mass of Thanksgiving, celebrated by the vicar general—elect and assisted by the incumbent. At the homily, an appropriately humble Crevan addressed the Order quietly but with great feeling, briefly outlining his yet-tenuous plans for the beginning of his tenure.

Afterwards, Camber dined with his successor and eight other of the highest-ranking officers in his Order, including Jebediah and Nathan. During the course of the meal, plans were completed for installing Crevan as vicar general on Saturday at noon, the day before Alister was to be elevated to the episcopate. The part of Camber that was Alister drank in the evening as bittersweet dregs, for Alister had known only the life of the Order of Saint Michael for many, many years.

The next day brought all of them to Cinhil's hammer-beamed great hall to vie for places in the crowd which assembled to witness the king's recognition of his newest nobility. Eighteen heirs, from earls and barons to lesser lords, ranging in age from sixty years to six months, came forward in serried processions, banners and regalia gleaming richly in the torchlit hall, there to kneel in homage to the king from whom all honor flowed, at least in theory— though some of the lords being confirmed today could have bought and sold Cinhil's personal holdings, had they thought to take such a course.

Young Davin was among them, of course, next to the last of those who would be confirmed in their titles today. He was accompanied by his family: his mother, Elinor, Cathan's widow, who would act as regent for the earldom until he should reach his majority at fourteen; his uncles, Joram and Rhys, brilliant in Michaeline blue and Healer's green; and his Aunt Evaine, whom he adored. His younger brother Ansel, heir after him, carried a blue velvet cushion bearing a scaled-down earl's coronet. The *gules/azure* banner of Culdi was carried by his cousin, James Drummond.

Only his aunt and uncles paid particular attention to the blue-garbed men who stood ranked to one side, among a host of other clergy, or to one particular Michaeline who watched the boy Davin with haunted eyes. Fortunately, it was the incipient vicar general, and not the incumbent one, who elicited attention among those who wore or watched the blue. Crevan Allyn played his part to perfection, never guessing how he helped screen Camber from too close a scrutiny as Camber's grandson came forward in his turn, to kneel tremulously before the king.

The seven-year-old Davin was grave and dignified as he placed his small hands between those of the graying king. After reciting his oath of fealty in a clear, piping voice, he stared solemnly into the royal eyes as Cinhil gave the return oath to protect and defend young Davin and his new-come earldom.

Nor did the lad flinch as Cinhil gently dubbed him on shoulders and head with the great sword of state, which the constable, Lord Udaut, had already handed to the king a full sixteen times in the past hour. Only when Cinhil raised him up and kissed him on either cheek did his composure waver—for the king's beard and mustache tickled, and Davin had been long enough solemn for so young a child.

He fidgeted a little as Queen Megan buckled the jeweled earl's belt around his little waist. But when Cinhil took up the small coronet and lifted it a little above Davin's head before settling it on the sunny hair, Davin stood without a quiver, his pretty face going a little pale. He made his final obeisance with the gravity of one many times his years before backing into place to witness the final oath-taking.

Shadows were long, the light diffused with the coming sunset, by the time the ceremony and attendant court had been concluded, but Camber tried to linger a little as people came pouring out of the great hall. While making small talk with his brethren, he surreptitiously watched his grandsons and their mother being escorted to a group of horses and servants waiting to conduct them to quarters which had been arranged in the city, managing to bow gracefully as

Evaine came to extend a formal dinner invitation which both of them knew he could not accept. Even had he not been committed to a night-long vigil with Crevan, in preparation for the transfer of office the next morning, still he would not yet have dared to face Elinor and the boys in so intimate a surrounding. There was no need to involve them in his intrigues. Later, perhaps, when the boys were grown . . .

He thanked Evaine graciously and, as she moved away to join Rhys and the others, returned his attention to the men who had waited while he spoke to her. He even managed to exchange a few words with Joram before they all dispersed, when Joram came to offer his congratulations and obedience to his new superior, who stood at ease at Camber's side.

Then the young priest adroitly turned the conversation to the topic of the present vicar general's health, suggesting that Father Cullen, to satisfy the anxiety of many who were concerned for him, might like to consider inviting the Healer Rhys and his lady to dine with him the following evening, the night before Cullen was to assume his bishop's miter. In fact, since Cullen had not seen his illustrious physician for several days, and had still been recuperating when Rhys left, Joram *insisted* upon the event, and would himself make arrangements and join them, to ensure that Cullen did not try to avoid the issue. Once Cullen left the loving attention of his Order and friends to pursue his new duties in Grecotha, he would be on his own, but the Michaelines could at least guarantee that he *started* his new assignment in good health.

Camber, after the expected feeble protests, accepted the invitation gracefully, secretly delighted at the ease with which his son had turned a much-desired meeting of father and children into an ecclesiastically expedient dinner engagement, and before decidedly partial witnesses. Days had passed since he had last been able to talk with any of these three who loved him most; and there were many details yet to be decided, before he left for the relative isolation of his new see in Grecotha. He allowed a resigned smile to shape his mouth as he and Crevan headed for the archbishop's private chapel to begin their night's vigil.

The investiture of Crevan Allyn went off without incident the next morning, and it was with some relief that Camber finally put away the last of the vestments he had worn and started back to his own quarters with Joram. Again, he had managed not to be the principal celebrant at the accompanying Mass, thereby avoiding—at least technically—the exercise of priestly functions to which he was not entitled.

But the moral issue he had been putting off for several weeks now would soon have to be faced—tomorrow, in fact, when Bishop Cullen would be required to celebrate his first Mass. Camber was glad that he and Joram would have some time this afternoon to discuss the matter in depth. And dinner tonight would bring the added comfort and insight of Evaine and Rhys.

But an afternoon of such soul-searching was not to be his. No sooner had he and Joram stepped from the cathedral doorway than he was met by one of the king's pages, conveying Cinhil's invitation to ride out from the city for the afternoon. Apparently, Cinhil had decided that the former vicar general needed physical activity to occupy his mind and body; for no excuse of fatigue or pressing duties or prior commitment elsewhere could persuade the page to let him decline the invitation.

Half an hour later found Camber riding out of Valoret at the king's side, hard pressing the tall bay courser he rode in order to keep up with Cinhil's fleet Moonwind. Eight mounted knights accompanied them, for it was not seemly that the King of Gwynedd should ride out unattended. But the riders hung back a score of lengths to the rear, giving their royal master the illusion of privacy he wished. The effect was as if the two men rode alone, only a cloud of dust and the muffled sound of following hooves reminding them that they were guarded at reasonable call.

After an initial gallop, the two rode at a gentle canter for some minutes, each man alone with his thoughts in the breeze which their passage stirred in the warm summer air. When at last they pulled up in the shade of an oak grove to let the horses blow, the knights stood by just out of earshot. For all practical purposes, they were alone. Camber wondered what was on Cinhil's mind, for him to insist so strongly on this meeting, but he knew better than to speak first and break the mood.

Cinhil let the reins slide through his gloved fingers and lie slack on Moonwind's neck as the stallion stretched to steal a mouthful of grass. Oddly, the king had begun to acquire a taste for riding since the war, and appeared far more at ease astride a horse than Camber had ever seen him.

For several minutes, the only sounds were the rustlings of breeze-stirred leaves and the soft, horse noises of snuffling breath and muted harness jangle. Leather creaked, a rich, comforting comment on the laziness of the summer's day, as Cinhil gave a contented sigh.

"So, we have a new master of the Michaelines," Cinhil finally said. "How does it feel to be just plain Father Cullen, if only for a few hours?"

The king's smile was open and friendly, genuinely curious, and Camber allowed himself to relax just a little.

"I feel a little naked, if the truth be known, Sire. And sad, too, in a way," he admitted. He leaned his elbows on the high pommel and echoed Cinhil's sigh. "I shall miss my Michaelines. The Order has occupied some of the best years of my life."

"Aye, that's probably true—though you have many more good years ahead, I'll warrant."

"God willing," Camber agreed idly.

"And your successor—he is a competent man," Cinhil replied, after only a slight hesitation. "I've had numerous occasions to speak with him since we returned from Iomaire, and I confess I am impressed. I was a little surprised you chose a human, though."

Camber gave Cinhil one of Alister's sidelong glances of appraisal. "Are you disappointed, Sire?"

"Disappointed? Nay, of course not. But I thought —I thought that you would surely choose another Deryni," he finally blurted, at last betraying his anxiety. "You weren't jesting, were you, about wanting to help me?"

"I would never jest about that, Sire. Crevan Allyn is the best man for the job in these troubled times, were he Deryni or human. He will be a uniting factor, not a divisive one. That will be increasingly important as potential enemies begin to test you in the months and years ahead."

"You begin to sound like Camber," Cinhil snorted. "Perhaps he did touch you that night."

Camber coughed and then sneezed to cover his alarm.

What was Cinhil talking about? He *could* not know that Camber was now Cullen—at least his tone did not indicate that he was in any way suspicious.

But what night was Cinhil talking about? It almost had to be the night of the memory integration. What had happened? He had always assumed that everything had gone well, that no suspicions had been aroused—else Joram or Rhys or Evaine would surely have found a way to warn him.

On the other hand, he knew he did not remember all of that night. He had a vague recollection that Cinhil and someone else had at least come to the door, but he had lost consciousness shortly after that. Could it be that something *had* happened—something minor, but disturbing to Cinhil, nonetheless—and his children had merely assumed that he knew?

He turned in his saddle to look at Cinhil squarely, letting a little of his puzzlement show on his face. Honest dismay should not arouse suspicion. He knew that Alister would have been similarly curious in such a situation.

"Perhaps *who* touched me that night, Sire?" he

asked in a low voice. "And *what* night? What are you talking about?"

"Why, the night you were so ill—Sunday, it must have been. The night before Camber's funeral." Cinhil looked back at him in surprise. "You don't remember?"

Camber shook his head slightly, his gaze not leaving Cinhil.

Cinhil drew a deep, shuddering breath and glanced away, trying to hide a haunted look in his eyes, then looked back at Camber quickly.

"You really don't remember?"

"What happened, Sire?"

Almost without thinking, Camber had let his voice take on a harder, more demanding edge—still Cullen's, but far more harsh than Camber had intended. Fortunately, Cinhil seemed wrapped in his own reluctant remembrance, gray gaze fixed unseeing on the reins slack in his gloved hands.

"I—I guess I just supposed you were aware of what was going on," the king finally whispered. "But I realize now that you were like one possessed. Alister . . . what demon *were* you fighting that night?"

Camber closed his eyes briefly, as if to shut out a painful memory, chilling at the image of possession Cinhil had touched. In a way, he *had* fought a demon, *had* been possessed—but in no way that he dared explain to Cinhil.

Still, what connection had Cinhil made between Camber and Cullen, if any? Camber had to know.

He shook his head. "It—is nothing I may speak of here, Sire," he said softly. "But I sense now that my memory of that night is even less complete than I dreamed. Pray, tell me what happened. I—seemed to sense that you were there at some point, but beyond that, I remember very little. When I awoke the next morning, Rhys was asleep beside my bed and I had not the heart to wake him; and there was no time to ask him after that."

Cinhil drew breath again and tried to regain a more objective tone.

"You—had stopped breathing. Rhys was trying to keep you alive. He said you were fighting some vestige of Ariella. We thought you were dying."

"Go on."

"Well, your young Lord Dualta was with me, watching as all of us got more and more afraid for you. Even I could feel a little of what you were fighting— the fear and terror of it, anyway. And then, suddenly, Dualta—fell to his knees and invoked Camber to fight for you, to make you live."

"He—invoked Camber," Camber repeated.

Cinhil gave a reluctant nod, not meeting Camber's gaze. Each word seemed to be dragged from deep inside him, almost against his will.

"He said—he said something like 'Oh, if the Lord Camber were only here, he could save Father Cullen!' And then—" Cinhil swallowed, and enunciated each word carefully. "Then a shadow seemed to come across your face, and I—seemed to see—the face of Camber on top of yours, shifting in that shadow."

"Camber's face!" Camber breathed.

Instantly he knew what must have happened, though he still could not remember it; the temporary relaxation of physical controls as his beleaguered mind fought to resolve the inner chaos of another's memories—a few seconds only, but long enough to leave an indelible impression on those who saw.

With a blink, he was back with Cinhil again, sea-ice eyes searching the king's with dismay appropriate to Alister. He opened his mouth, but no sound came out. He swallowed and, with a hand sign, bade Cinhil continue.

"I—gather—that you, too, find it hard to believe," the king murmured. "Nonetheless, I assure you that we saw what we saw. For a few seconds, the image wavered—and then you began to breathe, and the face disappeared, and you were yourself again. Dualta said it was a miracle."

Camber felt Alister's memories tugging at his own, and this time he let the cold shudder pass through his body as he crossed himself in the gesture he had seen Alister use a dozen times.

A miracle. Was that what Cinhil thought, too? How that supposition must gall the poor, guilt-ridden king, who could not seem to escape Camber's influence, even with the man's death. No wonder he was troubled. Camber had not foreseen this complication.

"I wish someone had told me sooner," he said, after a few seconds' pause. "I had no idea."

"And Rhys or Joram didn't tell you?"

Camber shook his head. "They must have assumed I would remember. Besides, I told you that I found Rhys asleep by my bed the next morning, and I left for the cathedral before he awoke. And what with the funeral and the chapter meeting, I didn't really have a chance to speak with either of them in private before they left for Caerrorie. It's not the sort of thing one discusses in front of just anyone, you know."

"Certainly not," Cinhil agreed. "Besides, I forbade them all to discuss it further, except among themselves. That reminds me, I should find that young monk who was kneeling in your oratory and question him further. Is he attached to your household?"

"The monk?" Camber realized with a start that Cinhil must be referring to Evaine. "No, I think he was from one of the outlying houses, quartered with another order until our facilities can be rebuilt. I suspect he's been sent back by now. I don't even remember why he was brought to me. It all seems so long ago."

"No matter. I'll find him."

Oh no you won't, Camber thought. At least that was one thing he need not worry about—though now he wondered how Evaine had managed to keep her identity a secret, especially if Cinhil had spoken to her at all.

But for now, he must worry about the king himself, and Dualta—and Guaire, he also realized. After all,

Guaire's little "dream" had deliberately been staged to look like a supernatural visitation. At the time, there had seemed no reason to play it otherwise. Now, if Guaire should get together with Cinhil or Dualta and compare notes . . .

He suddenly realized that Cinhil had fallen silent and was looking at him strangely. He stole a glance at Cinhil's face, then turned his attention to his saddle-bow, wondering where he and the king stood now. He dared not speak.

After a moment, Cinhil sighed.

"You believe it, too, don't you?"

"Believe it, Sire?"

"That he came back. That it was a miracle."

Camber exhaled slowly. "I—don't know, Cinhil. Do you want me to say I do or I don't? It's—beyond all reason, all rational explanation—and I still don't remember any of it. I haven't even the delusion of memory to go on."

"It's called 'faith,' Father," Cinhil said grimly. "Once, I thought I had it. Very recently, I thought I had it. Now—God, will I never be free of him?"

A fist came down on the pommel of the saddle, its force checked only as gloved flesh made contact with tooled leather. The royal head bowed in a soundless, choking sob, and the red-clad shoulders shook.

Camber dared not answer that response, beyond a lowering of his own gaze and sympathetic silence. Cullen would not be expected to share Cinhil's hostility toward Camber, for Cullen and Camber had been friends, and Cinhil knew that. But until Camber could find out from Rhys or Joram or Evaine just what happened that night, he must not let the discussion go back to Camber MacRorie. To do so could only risk inviting even more dangerous speculation than what had already passed between him and the king. Better to feign quiet sympathy, which was not altogether manufactured, and try to turn their conversation to more neutral subjects.

After a moment, Camber gathered up his reins and

urged his bay into a slow, ambling walk, leading a withdrawn and silent Cinhil quietly along a grassy path which skirted the oak grove. He commented on the warm weather, on the high water level of the streamlet through which they guided their mounts; and soon they were discussing politics, and arguing the fairness of the ransom Cinhil was considering for the Torenthi prisoners, as if nothing had happened.

They did not return to the subject of Camber, much to Camber's relief; but he was secretly pleased to note that many of Cinhil's ideas for the future of his kingdom seemed to come almost directly from the reading which he and Joram had forced on Cinhil in the early months of his rehabilitation from priest to prince. Gone were the tantrums and sulks of a few weeks ago. It was as if the war and the events of the past fortnight had burned out that streak of emergent obstinacy which had so worried Camber before.

The rest of the afternoon gave him much insight into how Cinhil was assimilating into his duties, and seemed to open the way for an increasing intimacy between king and future bishop. Almost, the price of his own transformation from Camber to Cullen began to appear justified. If only there were not that nagging question, constantly worrying at the back of his mind.

What had happened that night? What had Cinhil *actually* seen?—no matter what he *thought* had occurred. And would that event come back to haunt him?

He had to wait several hours for even a partial answer to that question—until he and Cinhil and their escort had returned to Valoret, hot and dusty, and he had escaped to his own quarters to wash and change for dinner.

He greeted Joram, then Evaine and Rhys, as Alister Cullen should—the perfect host in front of Guaire and the two servants who brought their meal and laid the table. The four of them made suitably inconsequential small talk while the food was served, the goblets filled with wine, the meal begun. In no word or nuance of manner or movement was there anything

to suggest that he was anything but the gruff former
master of the Michaelines, soon to be a bishop and
prince of the Church.

But as soon as Guaire and the servants had left the
room, all pretense fell away as Camber asked his
question. The faces of sons and daughter confirmed
what he had suspected: they had *not* known that he
did not remember. All of them had assumed too much.

When, after hurried preparation, Camber entered
Evaine's mind and relived that night from her point
of view, seeing the facade his daughter had felt constrained to put on the incident, he could understand
why Cinhil had been so unnerved. So far as Cinhil
and the trusting Dualta were concerned, a miracle
had occurred.

And since Cinhil had forbidden all to talk about it,
the incident should go no further. Unfortunate that
Evaine should have to use a deception involving this
particular explanation, but better that than to betray
the greater good for which so many had already given
so much. Even Joram was reluctantly forced to admit
that her solution had been brilliant, under the circumstances.

Still, what Camber next told them did not help to
alleviate the general unease which their discussion
had already raised. The matter of Guaire was related in terse, half-apologetic phrases, Camber hardly
daring to meet their eyes as they listened with growing
disbelief. Certainly, his well-meaning intervention
was understandable, especially in the light of what he
had not known; but it did complicate matters further.

Nor could the mistake be easily remedied. It was
too late for Camber or anyone else to reenter Guaire's
mind and try to erase his memory of the "dream" he
thought he'd had. Guaire's experience, even blurred
by the drugs Camber had given him, was by now far
too fully integrated into his memory of Camber as a
whole. To tamper at this point would alert even the
fully human Guaire to the reality of psychic interven-

tion, and might drive him to inquire further as to what had happened, and who had done the meddling.

But it was Joram who finally stumbled on a real cause for alarm, almost as an afterthought, as he speculated gloomily on all the possible things that could still go wrong. Like his father, he quickly drew the deduction of disaster if Guaire and Cinhil and Dualta should get together and compare notes. But from there, he went one step further.

Suppose any two of them did compare experiences? Even if they did not see through the sham of both events and uncover the deceptions, suppose they accepted what they had seen as fact, corroborated each by the other? Suppose the word spread? Camber MacRorie had always been popular among the common folk, and never so much as since the Restoration. "Kingmaker," they called him. And "Defender of Humankind," since he had helped to throw down the evil excesses of the Deryni Imre. Two miracles attributed to the man already called hero could start a cult of Camber.

Joram's voice trailed off at that, for suddenly he was remembering the throngs of people he had seen but not particularly noted in the chapel at Caerrorie, above the tomb where "Camber's" body lay. His expression reflected his growing suspicion as he began mentally to put things into new perspective. At Rhys's urging, he told in disbelieving phrases of what he had seen. Soon Evaine was adding her own stunned observations, describing the gifts of flowers left near the tomb, the increased offerings, the looks of reverence in the scrubbed country faces. Was it starting already?

Silence fell heavily among them for a long, endless moment, as each of them declined to put into words what they all were obviously thinking. Finally, Camber brought the flat of one hand down hard on the table, jarring the dinnerware and making Joram start. The alien face of Alister Cullen was grim as Camber pushed himself back slightly from the table with a sigh.

"Very well, you've convinced me. It's getting out of hand. I hadn't realized—none of us had realized, obviously. The question is, what are we going to do about it? There's enough blind superstition in this world without deliberately adding the hypocrisy of make-believe miracles. God knows, I certainly don't qualify for sainthood."

Evaine gave a quick, nervous smile. "*We* know that, Father—but convincing your devoted followers may not be that easy. Frankly, I'm not nearly so worried about Cinhil and Guaire at this point as I am about what's happening at Caerrorie. If we don't do something, we're going to have a full-fledged cult of Saint Camber on our hands. All the signs are there."

"We *could* tell the truth," Joram muttered darkly.

Rhys shook his head. "You know we can't, at this late date." He glanced at all of them. "But what would happen if we simply closed that part of the chapel, so people couldn't get near the tomb? For that matter, is it necessary to keep the chapel open to outsiders at all? The villagers have their own church, where Cathan is buried."

Evaine shook her head wearily. "We can't, Rhys. That chapel has always been accessible to our people, and to anyone who wanted to come there and pray. The only time it's closed is at night, when the manor gates are closed, and then it's still accessible to the staff. If we shut it down, we admit that there's something unusual about the place. We give credence to what they think is happening."

"This is incredible!" Joram exclaimed. "How could we have been so stupid?"

"It isn't a matter of stupidity," Camber replied, a little sharply. "No one could have foreseen the way things would come together. Evaine is right, though. We don't dare prohibit free access to the chapel. That being the case, I think we need to consider how we're going to protect the tomb—especially since the occupant isn't who they think it is."

"Just pray that they never find out who it *isn't*,"

Evaine murmured under her breath. "Father, what if they should try to steal the body?"

"Then, we would *really* have a problem."

Rhys laid a distracted hand on his wife's in reassurance, but his eager eyes and attention were on Camber. "Suppose we set up wards, then? Deryni wards on a Deryni tomb aren't unusual. At least they might discourage casual snooping."

"Why don't *we* steal the body and eliminate the problem entirely?" Joram countered, beginning to recover his perspective and humor. "Go ahead and ward the tomb," he added, as all heads turned toward him in surprise, "but move the body to another burial place. Wards wouldn't prevent a Deryni from breaking in unless they were so powerful that he'd be *sure* something was unusual. I don't think we want anyone to take that close a look."

"He's right," Rhys agreed. "Neither the preservation spell nor the shape change will last indefinitely. Even though the lack of one will tend to cancel out the lack of the other, what's left still won't stand up to really close inspection by anyone who knows what he's doing, especially a Deryni. We could move the body to that hidden Michaeline chapel, next to Cinhil's little son and that monk, Brother . . ."

"Humphrey," Evaine supplied.

"That's it, Humphrey of Gallareaux. Joram, I think it was always your intention to rebury Alister as himself, in Michaeline soil, eventually, wasn't it?"

Joram gave a grim, humorless chuckle. "Well, I don't know that it will make any difference to Alister, but it will certainly make me feel better. Once he's moved, though, if someone does break into the empty tomb, it will fall to you and Evaine or whoever is at Caerrorie to explain. We don't want anyone to think that the body was assumed into heaven or anything. All we need is a third miracle."

Camber, who had been listening to all their exchange with a growing wistfulness, could not restrain a wry smile. "I'm happy to see that you're all thinking again, instead of merely reacting. Rhys, I don't think we need to complicate this further. Whether it's you, or Evaine, or even Elinor who must explain, this is one case where you can simply tell the truth: that the body was moved to another, safer burial place, because you feared that vandals might desecrate the tomb. Camber did have enemies, after all. There's no need to be more specific, even if you're pressed. It's no one's business besides family."

There was no dissent to that. While they discussed ways and means of accomplishing what they had decided must be done, the four of them picked half-heartedly at their now-cold meal, too keyed up and preoccupied by their potential dangers to do more than nibble. The details were finally resolved to the satisfaction of all; but by the time they had finished both dinner and discussion, it was within an hour of midnight, and the subject of Camber's impending consecration as bishop still had not been broached. Evaine and Rhys had carefully avoided the topic, perhaps in deference to Joram's personal involvement in the issue, and Joram himself had overlooked several obvious opportunities to introduce the subject.

Camber could only conclude that the three of them had reached a prior agreement as to how the situation was to be handled, and guessed that Joram was waiting for Evaine and Rhys to leave. To facilitate that probability, Camber rang for the servants to come and clear away the meal, then retired to a chair by the fireplace with a fresh cup of mulled wine so that Joram could exchange whatever signals or glances were necessary to get Evaine and Rhys out of the room. As expected, the couple followed close on the heels of the servants bearing away the dinner things, bidding Father Alister Cullen good-bye with formal courtesy.

When they all had gone, Joram brought his own new-filled cup and settled carefully into a chair beside his father. The wine in his hands seemed to occupy all his attention as he sipped and listened to the retreating footsteps in the corridor outside.

After a few seconds, Camber glanced sidelong at his son, reading the tension in every line of the taut young body. He wondered what Joram was thinking, knew that the young priest was finding it difficult to begin. For, whatever the outcome of their discussion, both of them knew that Camber must go through with what was planned for the morrow. Camber MacRorie, as Alister Cullen, must be consecrated a bishop and assume all the priestly and episcopal functions which that office entailed, whether or not he was entitled to them in his own right.

As Camber gazed at his son, Joram looked up and met his eyes, then glanced quickly back at the cup in his hand. He took a deep breath before speaking.

"We haven't had much chance to talk lately, have we?"

Camber turned his eyes but not his attention to the steam curling from the cup in his hands, hoping that would make it easier for Joram.

"No, we haven't. I had hoped we would have this afternoon together, but—"

He shrugged, a helpless, weary movement, and Joram's eyes flicked nervously to the low-burning fire before them.

"I know. Cinhil." Joram hesitated a beat and then continued. "Tell me, have you thought much about tomorrow?"

Camber controlled the urge to smile.

"If you understand me at all, after all these years, you must know that tomorrow has not been far from my thoughts these many days," he replied gently. "I share your distress, son. I simply see no way around what I must do."

"Perhaps not." Joram's eyes were hooded beneath blond lashes. "The end result is unavoidable, I suppose. But, have you considered that there might be an alternative means to that end? You don't have to base *everything* on deception, you know."

"No?"

"No. You could make your status legitimate."

"How?" Camber whispered.

"Be ordained a priest," Joram replied, turning desperate, heartsick eyes on his father. "Do it now, tonight, and you enter the cathedral tomorrow with a clear conscience. You can! God knows, we've talked about it often enough in the past. You were made a deacon as a young man. You've been a widower for years. You certainly have the vocation for it. Under the circumstances, I'm sure Anscom would do it."

"Anscom?"

Camber took a deep breath and let it out slowly, feeling his heart pound as the impact of Joram's words sank into all his being.

Actually to be a priest, not just a sham. The thought excited him and, at the same time, chilled him. Certainly, it had always been in the back of his mind finally to take priestly vows. His early monastic training had taken far better than he or anyone else had thought.

But that had been before, when he had still walked the world in his own skin, and a man named Alister Cullen had still been alive in fact as well as in name. Could Camber MacRorie, having taken that other man's identity—even though he had not taken that life—presume to approach the altar of God and ask the precious gift of priesthood? Dared he base so holy a calling on a further deception?

On the other hand, could he allow Archbishop Anscom, Primate of All Gwynedd and a friend for many years, to confer the bishop's miter upon him when he was not properly prepared? Of course, if he told Anscom and Anscom agreed to ordain him, then Anscom would be actively guilty of duplicity in concealing Camber's true identity—unless, of course, he refused to have anything to do with the situation at all, and renounced Camber publicly instead of going through with the consecration. That, too, was a possibility.

But, if Camber did not take the matter to Anscom, and tried to continue as he had been, what then? After tomorrow, he would no longer be able to avoid the exercise of the priestly functions of Alister Cullen without arousing dangerous suspicions. Yet it was either that or perform those offices for which he was not ordained, and be in peril of his soul.

CHAPTER FIFTEEN

*I will pay my vows unto the Lord
now in the presence of all his people.*
—Psalms 116:14

He returned to the room with a start, aware that Joram was watching him, unable to say how long he had been off on his own reverie. His fingers were clenched tightly around the earthenware cup in his hand, on the verge of shattering it, and illogically he wondered how he would look at his consecration tomorrow with a bandaged hand, if the thing did break.

With a conscious effort, he willed his hand to relax enough to set the cup on the floor beside him. He took a deep breath before looking up at Joram again.

"You certainly caught me off guard with that one," he said in an uncertain voice. "I suppose I had refused to consciously consider that alternative. You and I understand why I have to do what I'm doing, but I guess I didn't want to face the possibility that Anscom might not. If he didn't, I can't say I would blame him."

"Do you really think he wouldn't understand?" Joram said softly. "*I* know him better than that, and I've known him for less than half the years you have."

Camber lowered his gaze, watching his finger systematically trace along the carving on his chair arm.

"You know *me* pretty well, too, son. And you're certainly right, in the final analysis. The priesthood and what it stands for mean far too much to me to degrade that special magic by practicing the forms without the substance."

He looked up and smiled. "It's just that I never thought it would be like this, when I finally asked him to ordain me. I suppose I always thought it would be some years in the future, when all my children were grown and I could settle the earldom on Cathan.

"But that's all changed now. Cathan is dead, and his son and heir is only a child, and a new king is on the throne who is a child himself, in many ways." He sighed. "And we're here and now, and like Cinhil, I'm going to have to learn to live with what I've chosen to become."

Joram looked away briefly, then met his father's gaze again.

"You'll talk to Anscom, then?"

"I think so. I want to ponder it a bit more, but if you could make sure that Evaine and Rhys are available, I'd appreciate it. The three of you can be my only witnesses, even if Anscom agrees."

When Joram had gone, Camber stood staring into the dying fire for several minutes before moving into the adjoining oratory. Only the ruby Presence light burned in the little chamber, and Camber smiled wanly as he lit the other candles on the altar, taking pains to perform all as a human might.

No arcane manifestations of flame for the thinking he must do. He must not let the difference of his Deryniness color the decision he must make.

He covered his eyes with both hands as he knelt at the prie-dieu, letting his conscious mind occupy itself for the first few minutes with the recitation of standard prayers and meditations—anything to let himself settle down so he could move on to this most important consideration.

From there, he turned his attention inward, seeking out all possible ramifications of the subject at hand. Slipping into the profound, introspective trance which he had mastered so many years before, he allowed the deeper facets of his being to explore the situation, drawing upon Alister's memories and knowledge as well as his own.

When he at last raised his head, the altar candles were shorter by a fingerspan, guttering and quaking in a wayward draft which whispered through the half-open door behind him. Above, the smooth, gentle face of the carved Christus gazed down with compassion from its cross of wood and ivory.

He cocked his head and searched the blank, shadowed eyes as he had done so many times before, mouth set in stubborn questioning, then let the alien lips of his alter ego relax in a little smile, bowed his head in surrender. In the flickering candlelight, he could almost imagine that the figure inclined its head slightly, and that the ivory lips smiled in return.

Very well. He would take it as a sign. He would go to his old friend and mentor, Anscom. He would reveal himself as Camber, and would lay the entire matter at the feet of the man who was at once brother and spiritual father. Then, if Anscom agreed, he would be properly ordained a priest. Only in that way could he go through with the consecration as bishop which must be the lot of Alister Cullen, and his own.

He was knocking on Anscom's door, a torch-bearing monk at his side, before the full emotional impact hit him of what he was about to do. His breath caught in his throat, his mouth went dry, and his hand jerked spasmodically before he could control it.

Anxiously he wondered whether the monk had seen—tried to fathom the man's reaction as the silence of waiting began to stretch on interminably. He prayed that the man would merely ascribe his nervousness to the natural apprehension of any man about to be made a bishop. Surely the monk could not see beyond his Deryni facade.

Then the monk's gnarled old fist was pounding on the door instead of Camber's, and he was murmuring something about the archbishop's hearing perhaps not being quite as good as it once was.

Camber, grateful for the timely if erroneous excuse, let his hand fall awkwardly to his side and said nothing as he heard the bolt being shot from the inside. Anscom himself opened the door, his disheveled appearance and bleary eyes bespeaking much of the sleep he had just left.

"I'm sorry to disturb you at this hour, Your Grace," Camber murmured.

"Alister." Incomprehension and sleep slurred the archbishop's voice. "I had thought you abed hours ago. Is anything wrong?"

"I was unable to sleep, Your Grace. I wondered whether you might hear my confession."

"Your confession?" Anscom's eyes flicked down the figure of the former vicar general and were back on his face in an instant, all drowsiness now completely gone. "I was of the impression that you had your own Michaeline confessor, Father. Was he not available?"

Camber averted his gaze, his words low and careful.

"He is not a bishop, Your Grace. There are certain things I may ask only of you."

As Camber glanced meaningfully at the monk beside him, Anscom reacted with a start, as though he had forgotten that the man still stood there, overhearing every word of their conversation. With a wave, Anscom dismissed the monk, standing aside to admit his visitor as the monk's circle of torchlight slowly receded down the corridor.

Camber kept his eyes lowered as he stepped past Anscom, standing awkwardly in the center of the room until the archbishop had re-bolted the door and turned toward him. Even after his long introspection, he was surprised at how apprehensive he felt, now that the moment of revelation was almost upon him. He followed Anscom into the archbishop's private oratory, much more ornate than the one in his own quarters, and watched him pick up a violet stole from the prie-dieu.

"I thank you for seeing me at this hour, Your Grace," Camber murmured. "I would not have disturbed you, but what I have to say could truly be trusted to no other."

Anscom inclined his head slightly and raised an eyebrow as he touched the stole to his lips and draped it around his shoulders. Gesturing toward the prie-dieu and straightening his sleeping robe, he started to turn toward the altar.

Camber caught at Anscom's sleeve gently, then backed off a pace and let his alien identity begin to slip away.

"What in—!"

Anscom shrank against the wall beside the altar steps and stared, aghast, one hand groping with protective instinct for the pectoral cross which customarily lay on his breast. As he watched, his visitor's face began to waver, mist, then to alter to features long loved and well remembered—features which Anscom had thought forever buried for many days now. His mouth moved several times before he could whisper the single word: *"Camber!"*

Camber, his face wreathed momentarily in a nimbus of light, smiled a gentle smile and let himself sink to his knees on the prie-dieu as Anscom had originally directed.

"Forgive me, old friend," he murmured. "I know how difficult it must have been, and will be."

"But how—? You were dead! I saw you! I celebrated your Requiem!" Anscom shook his head and looked again, brushing a hand across his eyes as though to clear away a veil.

"You will not like my explanation," Camber replied. "And you will like it even less when I tell you that I must continue in what I am doing, and that I must enlist your aid. It was Alister who killed Ariella, and was killed—not I."

"But, you—"

Sudden comprehension dawned on Anscom in that instant, and he collapsed to a seat on the altar step as though physically struck.

"You've shape-changed with his body," he finally managed to choke out. "You knew that your effectiveness was waning—you even talked with me about it, long before the battle—and you saw Cullen's death as a chance to try again. Cullen was dead, after all— he *was* dead, wasn't he?"

An appalled look had flashed across Anscom's face before he could hide it, but the thought was obvious. Instantly, Camber was on his knees beside the prelate, gray eyes locking with the frightened blue ones of Anscom.

"Dear friend, dismiss it from your mind! Can you really conceive, even for a second, that I would murder a friend and colleague merely to ease my own difficulties?"

Anscom looked away. "Murder is a very strong term," he whispered. "Some, in your circumstances, might simply have chosen not to help a gravely wounded man. The effect would be the same."

There was a long silence before Camber breathed, "Am I that kind of man?"

Anscom drew a deep breath and let it out slowly.

"I—think not. But, then, I would not have expected you to shape-change with a dead man, either." He looked up. "Tell me what I want to hear, Camber— and pray God that it be the truth."

Tension grew as the two searched each other's eyes. Finally, Camber sighed and let out a tiny smile.

"I cannot fault you for your doubts, dear friend. Your conscience and your office demand them. But believe me when I say that I had no part in Alister Cullen's death, directly or indirectly. He was dead when we found him. Joram can verify. He was with me throughout."

"Joram?"

Anscom gave a relieved sigh and wiped a sleeve across his face, swallowing uncomfortably as he tried to make himself untense.

"My God, Camber, you're going to have to give me a few minutes to get used to this," he said, half turning away and nervously rubbing his hands together as he thought out loud. "You shape-changed with Alister's body, and you've been playing his part for—nearly two weeks, now." He paused and glanced at Camber with a sickly expression on his face. "You've been functioning as a priest, too, haven't you?"

Camber shook his head. "Technically, no. I've managed to avoid o'erstepping the bounds of my long-ago deacon's vows. You needn't worry on that account."

"But you've been playing the vicar general of the Michaelines. Do you mean to tell me that you've not once said Mass, or heard a confession, or anything else you're not entitled to do as Camber MacRorie?"

"So far. However . . ." Camber sighed. "I realized this evening, with some not-so-gentle prodding from my priestly son, that there's no way I can keep up that particular sham after tomorrow, unless I have your help. Even I, as audacious as you probably think I am right now, would never dare to accept consecration as a bishop when I'm not even a proper priest."

Anscom stared at him for several seconds without saying anything, as if trying to pierce beyond the veil of Deryni complexity to the real man beyond, then lowered his eyes.

"Then you've come to me for ordination?"

"Yes. And it must be now, tonight. I'll accept any penance you like for what I've done up to this point; and perhaps I've been too bold in wanting the best for Gwynedd at whatever the price. But I'm willing to risk that for this land. I had a son, Anscom—and

Cathan was not the only one to suffer under Imre, God knows.

"But that's past now. Will you do it, Anscom? Will you ordain me?"

"Camber . . ."

Anscom's voice trailed off as he glanced at the crucifix above the altar.

"Camber, have you thought about what it really means, what you're asking? It's forever, you know—once it's done."

"I had always intended to become a priest, even as a child. You know that. If both my brothers hadn't died when they did, I would have remained in the seminary, and you and I would have been ordained at about the same time. By now, and I say this in all modesty, I probably would have been a bishop, too. Who knows? I might even have had your job."

He gestured fancifully toward the archbishop's signet on Anscom's hand, and Anscom held out that hand to glance at the violet stone. The old blue eyes shone as he looked up again.

"You might, at that," he whispered, lips curving in a reluctant smile. "You would have made one hell of a bishop."

"I hope I *will*," Camber murmured. "With your blessing, at least I have a chance."

Anscom turned away, not really seeing anything as he fingered the embroidered end of his stole. Then he studied the amethyst on his hand for a long time. When he raised his head, it was to let his eyes meet Camber's squarely. Much of the archbishop's old twinkle was back in his voice as he got determinedly to his feet.

"You drive a hard bargain, Camber. But, very well. I'll ordain you."

Camber let out an enormous sigh of relief.

"I don't intend to make it easy for you, though."

"I would be disappointed if you did."

"Good. We understand each other, then. It will take me an hour or so to prepare. I assume, from what you've said, that at least Joram knows your true status?"

"Joram is waiting for your instructions. Also Evaine and Rhys. No one else knows about me."

Anscom nodded. "A small band of witnesses. You deserve better. However, under the circumstances, I suppose that quality will answer for quantity." He paused. "I don't suppose there's anything else you haven't told me, is there? I've had enough surprises for one night."

"Just one." Camber smiled.

"I was afraid of that."

"It's a matter of names," Camber added quickly. "Perhaps it won't seem important to you, but I'd like to be ordained under my old name in religion."

"Kyriell? I see nothing wrong with that. You've often used it as a second name, haven't you? Besides, no one will know except the two of us and your children."

"I'd also like to add that name to Alister's, when I'm consecrated bishop," Camber replied. "That *is* my right, isn't it, to take an additional name upon assuming my new office?"

Anscom raised an eyebrow. "Are you certain you want *that* name associated with Alister's? What if people start adding things up?"

"What is there to add?" Camber countered. "You can say something about it being Alister's gesture of remembrance for an old friend."

"And suppose that isn't enough?"

Camber shrugged. "As a priest and bishop, guarding the secrets of the confessional, I'll have immunity from submitting to a Truth-Read unless you, as archbishop, require it. Apart from that, there is no way anyone can prove I'm not Alister Cullen."

"So you hope," Anscom muttered. "Very well, I'll do it, since you insist."

He moved into the doorway and stood silhouetted against the candlelight in the outer chamber. His sleeping robe and rumpled hair contrasted sharply with the determination on his face.

"One last thing, and then I'll leave you to wrestle with your conscience while I make preparations. Since you've obviously thought all of this through, do you have any preference for where we hold this ceremony? I obviously can't ordain you in the cathedral, as should be done."

Camber cocked his head in thought, then nodded.

"Yes, the chapel in the Michaeline stronghold, where we first acknowledged Cinhil as the lawful heir. I think it's fitting, don't you?"

CHAPTER SIXTEEN

For every high priest taken from among men
is ordained for men in things pertaining to God,
that he may offer both gifts and sacrifices for sins.
—Hebrews 5:1

Two hours later, the chapel of the Michaeline stronghold was ready. Abandoned and arcanely sealed since Cinhil's restoration the year before, it had been hastily cleaned and prepared by Rhys and Evaine in the hour just past, under Joram's relieved supervision. Camber, central figure in the drama which would shortly unfold, had seen neither the chapel nor his children. As Anscom had promised, things were not going to be made deliberately easy.

Camber himself now waited in a small anteroom near that chapel, striding back and forth restlessly, as he had for nearly the past hour. Cold permeated the little chamber, for though enough dust had been cleared that he might dress and wait in reasonable cleanliness, no one had taken the time to light a fire. A single rushlight glowed yellow on the table where his vestments had been laid out, but it provided scant warmth to the icy hands which Camber held over it. Though Camber knew that the cold he felt was not entirely from the temperature, still he was human enough to be uncomfortable because of it—and Deryni enough to be annoyed that his best efforts were not enabling him to fully control his body and its apprehensions.

He had tried to isolate the cause for his apprehension, but rational thinking, he suspected, was not the answer in this case. He wondered whether every candidate for the priestly initiation grew so anxious as his time approached.

He felt he was prepared, God knew, not only in his soul, with which he had already wrestled, but in the mechanics of the rite which he was about to undergo. His Deryni learning ability at least had not failed him in the latter, and he had the memories of Alister's long-ago ordination to draw upon, as well.

In the hour which had preceded his arrival here at the Michaeline stronghold, he had watched Anscom pore over the standard ritual of ordination and shake his head, then produce a copy of an alternate rite which he assured Camber was of far more ancient origin, and much better fitted to a Deryni, such as Camber, about to be priested.

Camber had spent the next hour in deep Deryni meditation, committing to memory every nuance of word and gesture and knowing that, even in his understanding of the words and the significance of the movements, there was much which simply would not occur to him until he experienced the rite.

He glanced down at the white alb skimming his body from neck to floor, from shoulder to wrist; at the deep blue Michaeline stole laid over his left shoulder, baldric-style, and secured at his waist by the cincture of white linen cord.

How long had it been since he had assumed the deacon's stole of his own accord? Had it really been as long as forty years?

Fingering the silk of the stole meditatively, he turned toward the table where the rushlight burned. There lay the snow-white chasuble with which he would be vested as part of his ordination, the most significant outward sign of the priesthood. Beside it was the unlighted taper he would carry into the chapel to begin the rite—a pure offering with which to approach the altar of God.

A gentle rap on the door brought his head up with a start.

Was it time already?

Joram slipped in quietly, a candle in his hand illuminating an expression somewhere between awe and guarded joy. Almost involuntarily, Camber moved toward him, not taking his eyes from his son's face, until they stood an arm's length apart, father and son staring at each other as though truly seeing for the first time.

A shiver swept through Camber, in recognition of the soon-to-be-shared bond between them; and Joram, mistaking that slight shudder for apprehension, put aside his candle and flung his arms around his father, disregarding all else in the sheer closeness of the moment.

Camber hugged his son, stroking the golden head as he had when Joram was a boy. He caught a prickle of Joram's concern as he drew back and held him at arm's length.

"I'm not afraid, son," he said, searching the younger man's face as though to memorize every detail anew. "Really, I'm not. Did you think I was?"

Joram shook his head proudly, tears starting to well in the pale gray eyes despite his best efforts to the contrary. "No, sir. I just—felt like hugging you—*Brother*."

Camber smiled and began straightening his garments. "Brother. What a wonderful word, the way you say it." He glanced fondly at Joram. "I think that may be an even greater honor than having been your father."

Joram bowed his head, forcing the tears back, then looked up and smiled broadly.

"Come along—Father. 'Tis time to give a second meaning to that title."

Proudly, then, and without further words, he took up the folded chasuble and laid it across his father's arm, lit the taper and put it in the hand of the candidate for priesthood. Together, they started toward the chapel.

The little chapel was ablaze with light—candlelight, not the less-expensive fire of rushes. The tiny, faceted chamber gleamed gold and stony silver-gray, thick yellow tapers burning in sconces on each of the eight arching walls. Six more candles glowed on the altar, three to a side, illuminating the rood on the eastern wall. Additional candles stood unlit in freestanding holders at the four quarters of the chamber: at the back of the altar, against each of the side walls, and beside the door. These alone bespoke the difference of this ordination from the customary.

All of this Camber absorbed in an instant, to be filed in memory only as a setting. For it was the occupants who captured his attention from the start—three whose stature somehow made the chapel seem far smaller than he remembered.

Archbishop Anscom dominated the room, standing to the left of the altar in the full resplendence of his episcopal vestments, his face set and unreadable. Rhys and Evaine waited at the right side of the Kheldish carpet before the altar steps, each cloaked in a borrowed Michaeline mantle, Evaine's golden hair spilling from beneath her hood to reach nearly to her waist on either side. The two of them smiled solemn welcome as Camber and Joram entered.

Joram closed the door and laid the great bar across its supports as Anscom came down the three altar steps and beckoned Camber toward the jewel-toned carpet. When Camber had knelt to kiss the archbishop's ring, Anscom raised him up.

"Be at ease while we set the wards, my friend. Since you and yours originated this particular warding, you know what's involved. Your children insisted upon using it."

Camber controlled a smile as he straightened from his bow, remembering the last time they had set such wards in this chamber. That night, they had hoped to give Deryni powers to a priestly prince; tonight, it was a Deryni to whom they planned to give priestly authority. The parallel both cheered and awed him.

He stood straight and let his head tilt back slightly, half closing his eyes, the better to isolate outside distractions. He could feel the warmth of the taper in his right hand, the different warmth of the chasuble across his left arm. Beside him, Joram bowed to the archbishop and then ascended the altar steps. To his right and behind him, Rhys and Evaine stood with eyes closed and minds stilled. He was aware of Anscom's quickened breathing to his left as he turned his thoughts inward in preparation.

After a moment, Evaine moved from behind him to kneel at the bottom of the altar steps, as Joram bent to kiss the altar stone. Then the young priest held aloft an unlighted taper with his left hand—passed a graceful right hand over the virgin wick.

Fire flared, and Joram turned to invite Evaine to join him.

Now came the time for true concentration. For, as Evaine mounted the altar steps to take the taper and light the great eastern candle, they must all begin pouring their respective energies into the wards which were being formed.

The eastern candle caught and steadied, and Evaine turned to make her way down the steps and toward the candle on his right, shielding the flame with her hand as she walked.

Closing his eyes, Camber let his mind begin working

on the construction of the wards, sensing now, rather than seeing, the concentration of energy around them as Evaine lit the candle to his right and continued on behind him. He could hear the gentle hiss of incense being spooned into an already smoking thurible—let himself become immersed in the words which Joram spoke as he censed the altar.

"Incensum istud a te benedictum . . ." May this incense, blessed by Thee, ascend to Thee, O Lord. *"Et descendat super nos praesidium tuam."* And may Thy protection descend upon us . . .

Evaine had lit the last candle on the left, and Camber could hear her moving back to the altar. A pause, and then the sound of the thurible swinging on its chains again as Joram censed his sister and then turned to the right to begin retracing her steps. Evaine returned to stand behind her father as Joram's voice floated in the stillness.

"Terribilis est locus iste: hic domus Dei est, et porta caeli . . ." Terrible is this place: it is the house of God, and the gate of Heaven; and it shall be called the court of God . . .

Joram finished censing the circle, and now censed all inside it with the sweet smoke which spiraled from the thurible. He replaced it beside the altar, then returned to stand at Camber's right, as Rhys moved to the Healer's place, directly before him.

Camber, though he kept his eyes closed, the better to feel what was happening, was aware that Evaine was rousing now, to lift her hands and eyes and shining voice to That which they had called. Images of her last performance of this office mingled with present sounds and sensations as her words began to weave the crystal spell.

"We stand outside time, in a place not of earth. As our ancestors before us bade, we join together and are One."

All bowed their heads in unison.

"By Thy blessed apostles, Matthew, Mark, Luke, and John; by all Thy holy angels; by all Powers of

Light and Shadow, we call Thee to guard and defend
us from all perils, O Most High," Evaine continued.
"Thus it is and has ever been, thus it will be for all
times to come. *Per omnia saecula saeculorum*."

"Amen," all murmured as one voice.

Without opening his eyes, Camber eased himself to
his knees, steadied by Joram on his right. He could
hear and feel Anscom brushing past him to ascend the
altar and begin the Mass.

"Introibo ad altare Dei," Anscom intoned. I will go
up to the altar of God.

"Ad Deum qui loetificat juventutem meam." To
God Who gives joy to my youth. Those words were
Joram's, as he joined Anscom at the altar.

"Judica me, Deus . . ." Judge me, O God, and dis-
tinguish my cause from the nation that is not holy . . .

The Mass continued in its familiar form until
Anscom had finished the Collect. As the final words
died away in the stillness, Camber opened his eyes at
last, once again allowing visual input to join other
heightened senses.

Rhys and Evaine stood to his left now; and Joram,
on his right, helped him to stand. Anscom, moving to
the faldstool which had been set to the left of the altar,
sat down quietly, the miter on his head winking jewel
eyes in the candlelight as he took up his bishop's
crozier. His seamed face was ruddy in the glow of the
Presence lamp. His tone was curiously quiet, almost
thoughtful, as he spoke.

"Dearly beloved, now stand we all in the house of
the Lord, at the center of a universe which is not ours
as we know it. Here, before the Lord of Hosts and
those other Powers which we have summoned, we call
before us Camber Kyriell MacRorie, who would be ordained a priest."

"Adsum," Camber murmured, inclining his head. I
am here.

With Joram still at his elbow, he moved forward
three steps and knelt again. The taper he held trembled a little in his hand.

Joram made a deep reverence. *"Reverendissime Pater . . .* Most Reverend Father, for the sake of Holy Mother Church and of those of our kind who have gone before us, I ask you to ordain the deacon Camber Kyriell MacRorie, here present, to the burden of the Deryni priesthood."

"Do you know him to be worthy?"

Joram bowed again. "So far as mortal frailty permits one to know, this I know; and I affirm my faith that he is worthy to undertake the burden of this office."

With a curt nod of acknowledgment, Anscom turned his attention to Rhys and Evaine, speaking ritual words to which he expected no reply.

"Brothers and sisters, know you that with the help of our Lord, we have chosen for the order of priesthood the deacon Camber Kyriell. If anyone has ought against this man, let him speak now, in the Name of the Holy One."

When there was no response, Anscom turned his eyes back on Camber, still kneeling on the Kheldish carpet with his candle held before him.

"It is the duty of a priest to offer sacrifice, to bless, to preside, to preach, and to baptize. Also, because a Deryni can truly see into the hearts and souls of men, there are additional responsibilities imposed upon a Deryni priest. Will you, in the Name of the Lord, receive the rank of priest?"

"Volo." I will.

"And will you be obedient to your bishop, according to justice and the grade of your ministry?"

"I will, so help me God."

"Then may God vouchsafe to bring your good and righteous will to the perfection that is pleasing to Him."

"Amen," Camber responded.

Rising, Anscom took Camber's candle and set it on the altar, Joram likewise taking the folded chasuble from his father's arm and laying it on the altar as an offering.

Then Camber was lowering his body to the carpet to prostrate himself, as the others knelt and began the various litanies for the day. Camber let the phrases ripple over him and carry him to an even more profound inner stillness.

"Kyrie eleison."

"Christe eleison."

"Christe audi nos."

"Sancta Maria . . ."

"Ora pro nobis."

"Sancte Michael . . ."

"Ora pro nobis."

The litany droned on in a lulling, monotonous cadence fully intended to assist the listener to a heightened state of awareness—for the Church fathers had long ago learned of the mental state which one should achieve to experience fully a sacrament such as ordination. By the time Camber consciously focused back on the ritual, Anscom was finishing the litany with a final prayer, directing the Divine Attention to the man prostrate before the altar.

"So, look Thou with favor upon Thy servant, Camber Kyriell, O Lord, whose hands are stretched out before the throne of Thy Majesty. Clothe him with the mantle of Thy priesthood, wherewith Thou didst adorn Thy faithful servants in ages past. Strengthen him, that he may ever serve Thee, by night and by day, O Giver of All, Lord of All, God Most Mighty . . ."

When the prayer had ended, Anscom moved quietly to his faldstool, there to wait in all his sacerdotal splendor as Joram assisted his father to stand. The priestly initiate was brought to kneel before the archbishop, Joram taking his own place at Anscom's side—for, as a priest, he, too, would share in the imminent transmission of priestly authority.

Camber drew a deep breath and let it out slowly as Anscom's hands were raised above his head. This was the heart of the ordination: the mystical laying on of hands. Resolutely, he let his defenses slip away, opening every channel of awareness that he could, that he might feel the Forces of Creation flowing through Anscom and Joram.

"O Lord of Hosts, Who hast made me, Thy servant Anscom, an instrument of Thy will and a channel of Thy power: now, according to the apostolic succession passed in unbroken line by the laying on of hands, I present to Thee this, Thy servant, Camber Kyriell, that he may become Thy priest."

The consecrated hands descended gently on Camber's head, and Camber felt a faint tingling sensation, the building of a flow of pure energy against the outer edges of his mind. His immediate instinct was to withdraw, to shut down, to raise every defense and ward against the awesome Power whose potential he could already sense. But he dared not hold back—not if tonight was to have any meaning.

He felt another hand join Anscom's, gently touching the side of his head, and knew Joram's cool and gentle probe on his mind. Forcing himself to relax and remain open, and reassured by Joram's presence, he closed his eyes and let out another deep breath, surrendering to whatever might come. He sensed his control slipping as Anscom continued speaking.

"*Accipite Spiritum: quorum remiseritis . . .*" Receive thou the Holy Spirit. Whose sins thou shalt forgive . . .

There was more, but Camber swiftly lost the meaning of mere words as he concentrated instead upon the sensations he was beginning to experience at Anscom and Joram's hands. A subtle pressure grew inside his mind, a gradual filling and expanding with Something which was so powerful, so awesome, that no corner of his being escaped Its insistent touch.

His hearing went first, and he knew that his vision also was gone—though he could not, to save his mortal life, have opened his eyes to test that knowledge.

Then all awareness of having a body at all began to fade. He was pure consciousness and more, centered in a bright, shining point, bathed and immersed in a golden brilliance, cool and fascinating, which was unlike anything he had ever experienced or imagined experiencing.

He was no longer frightened; he was engulfed in an emotion of peace and joy and total oneness with all that was and would be and once had been. He stretched and soared on rainbow wings, exulting in the certainty that there was far more to being than a mere mortal body and lifetime—that even when this human body died, whatever guise it wore, he—the essence of him—would continue, would grow, would move on in the fullness of eternity.

In a sparkling instant, he saw his past, and other pasts, in shimmering, quicksilver glimpses, immediately lost to memory; and then his present experience, as though observing his own body from above, silvergilt head bowed unflinching beneath consecrated hands whose touch was both delicate and relentless.

The thought whisked across his consciousness that perhaps he was fantasizing all of this; and a rational remnant of himself agreed. But another part of him banished that notion almost before it could take definite form.

What did it matter, at this point, whether he was experiencing true reality or one created, born of his own emotional need and reaching? No mere mortal could hope to experience the Godhead in *all* Its many facets. Man the finite could but glimpse the filmy shadow-trails of the Infinite, and that only if he were very fortunate.

But in his present mode, given all the weaknesses and strengths both of human and Deryni resources, was this not as close as he had ever brushed the Power which governed the wheeling of the universe?

He was marveling at what seemed to him an awesome piece of logic, part of him already wondering how much he would be able to retain when he returned to his normal state of awareness, when he sensed a drawing back, a lessening of the flow of power.

For the first time since Anscom's initial touch, he

could sense the archbishop's own consciousness, warm and reassuring, respectfully curious as to what Camber had just been experiencing—for, truly, Anscom had been only what he had said he was: a channel for some greater Force.

Neither had Joram experienced exactly what Camber had. He, too, was but a channel, a conduit, however dear and beloved.

As the archbishop withdrew, first mind and then hand, and Joram also drew back, Camber settled gently back into his body and reluctantly let sensation sift back into its proper perspective. With a sigh, he opened his eyes and let his gaze rise to meet Anscom's, glanced briefly at his son standing awed before him.

But he knew instantly that there was no need to tell them what had happened—not the generalities, at any rate. They knew. They, too, were priests, touched by the same Forces as he in their own ordinations. Now the three of them shared that knowledge; Camber even understood a little of the frantic grief Cinhil must have experienced, to give this up. And Camber, like Anscom and Joram—and Cinhil—and all the others who had gone before, would never be quite the same.

He took a deep breath and sighed again, and Anscom, too, relaxed a little and smiled. Sitting down again, the archbishop untied the linen girdle around Camber's waist and brought the far end of the Michaeline stole across Camber's right shoulder so that the silken strip now lay about his neck. Crossing the ends of the stole on Camber's chest, he secured them under the cincture again as he spoke.

"Accipe jugum Domini . . ." Take thou the yoke of the Lord, for His yoke is sweet, and His burden light.

With a bow, he took the snow-white chasuble which Joram brought from the altar and pulled it over Camber's head, settling the folds gracefully around his body.

"Accipe vestem sacerdotalem . . ." Take thou the garment of the priesthood, which signifies charity; for

God is able to advance you in charity and in perfection.

Another prayer was recited, with Joram making some of the responses as Anscom went briefly before the altar. Then the archbishop returned to sit and remove his gloves and bishop's ring. Camber remained kneeling before him, laying his open hands on Anscom's knees to receive the anointing with holy oil. The archbishop's thumb traced a cross on the upturned palms, right thumb to left index finger, left thumb to right index, as he intoned:

"Consecrare et sanctificare digneris, Domine . . . " Be pleased, O Lord, to consecrate and hallow these hands by this anointing and our blessing.

He made the sign of the cross above the hands. "That whatever they bless may be blessed, and whatever they consecrate may be consecrated and hallowed *. . . In nomine Domini Nostri Jesu Christe. Amen."*

With that, Anscom closed Camber's hands and bound them, palm to palm, with a white linen cloth. Then, as Joram brought the new-made priest to kneel before the altar once more, Anscom approached the altar and took up a chalice. Joram poured wine and water into the chalice, then placed the paten with its Host on top of the chalice. Anscom descended the three steps to Camber and extended the symbols of priesthood to the new priest.

"Receive the power to offer sacrifice to God, and to celebrate Masses for the living and the dead, in the name of the Lord. Amen."

Camber touched chalice and paten with the fingertips of his bound hands, then bowed his head as Anscom returned them to the altar and Joram removed the bonds and wiped away the holy oil. When Joram had finished, he raised up his father and led him to kneel before the archbishop on his faldstool once more. Camber bowed his head as he placed his hands between Anscom's to pledge his obedience.

"Promittis michi et successoribus meis obedientiam

et reverentiam?" Anscom asked. Do you promise obedience and reverence to me and my successors?

"Promitto." I promise.

"Pax Domini sit semper tecum."

"Et cum spiritu tuo."

"Ora pro me, Frater," Anscom whispered, with a tiny smile.

Camber returned the smile. *"Dominus vobis retribuat."* May the Lord reward you.

Anscom glanced up at the others, Joram and Evaine and Rhys, watching so proudly, then glanced down at Camber once more with affection.

"The rubric indicates that here I am to warn you of the potential danger of that upon which you are about to embark. However, I think you know that, and that you will exercise prudence. You will find, if you have not already guessed, that the rituals authorized by the conferring of the priesthood are no whit less powerful than any of our strictly secular Deryni operations, 'secular,' in the Deryni sense, being a somewhat nebulous term. Perhaps that is why, even in our 'secular' affairs, we are careful to perform our works according to specified and formal procedures. We know, or at least suspect, the length and breadth and height and depth of the Forces we draw upon."

He glanced up at the other three again, then returned his attention to Camber.

"And so, my dearly beloved son, I will not admonish you as I would any common priest—for you are one of the most uncommon men I know. I will simply wish you all fulfillment in the new responsibilities which you have undertaken here tonight, and will ask you to bear with me as we complete the last portion of your priestly investiture before allowing you to celebrate your first Mass. Joram, will you please bring the Book?"

As Joram brought the Gospel from the altar, Anscom stood and signaled Camber also to rise. Taking Camber's right hand, the archbishop turned him to face his daughter and son-in-law.

"Hear ye, all present: Camber Kyriell has been set apart, consecrated, and perfected for the work of the Lord, and for the office of the Aaronic and Deryni priesthood. *In nomine Patris et Filii et Spiritui Sancti, Amen.*"

Joram bowed and gave the Gospel to Anscom, his eyes never leaving his father's face as Anscom placed the book in Camber's hands.

" 'The Lord hath sworn, and will not repent. Thou art a priest forever, after the order of Melchizedek,' " Anscom announced. " 'The Lord at thy right hand shall strike through kings in the day of His wrath.' "

With the words graven upon his soul, Camber kissed the book and gave it back to Anscom with a bow.

"And now, let us make a joyful noise unto the Lord!" Anscom said, breaking into an enormous grin and taking Camber in an enthusiastic embrace. "Joram, come and embrace your father, who is also a Father and your brother now."

He relinquished his hold on the new-made priest as Joram took his place. Soon Joram was supplanted by Evaine, whose tears of joy dampened his shoulder, and then by Rhys, whose Healer's hands he took in quiet affection.

"All happiness and honor, Father Camber." Rhys smiled. The merry, sun-gold eyes danced in the fair, freckled face. "And now, if you're quite finished taking in all this congratulation, we've been waiting quite long enough to receive a special gift from your hands. May we assist you to celebrate your first Mass?"

With the help of those he loved, Camber celebrated that first Mass. Joram and Anscom gave their calm assurance as support during the ritual, reinforcing an office they both had performed countless times before, while Evaine and Rhys watched with wonder.

Camber even felt they understood, in part, what it meant to him; and what they could not understand, they took on faith. He could sense that faith in their response as they knelt to receive Communion from his newly consecrated hands; and he could see it in his daughter's joy as she and her husband embraced him a final time before going back through the Transfer Portal to their own quarters.

Of Joram, of course, there was no question. He understood perfectly. Camber knew that without even asking, from the glow in Joram's eyes and the new way he looked at his father now that they shared this common bond.

But they did not speak of it until Anscom had also gone and the two of them were packing up the vestments and altar furnishings, preparing to leave the little chapel as they had found it. Joram finished folding the vestments he and Camber had been wearing, laying them carefully into a leather travel satchel, then looked across at his father with a relaxed smile.

"Well, Father, how does it feel?"

Camber, kneeling to scrape up congealed wax from around the base of the western ward candle, glanced up with a wide grin.

"Do you realize how different your voice is, when you say that word now?"

"Father?" Joram chuckled and came to take the candle and put it with the others beside the door.

"Well, aren't *you* different?"

"I hope you don't really expect an answer to that." Camber laughed. "Joram, I haven't been this happy in years."

Picking up the last of the wax from the floor, Camber compressed it in his hand and watched it vaporize in a sparkle of sputtering fire. A wistful smile was still on his face as he dusted his hands against the blue of his cassock and joined Joram in the stripping of the altar.

"You know," he continued, as he shook out an embroidered linen cloth, "it's something that I don't think I'll ever be able to explain in words, even to someone like yourself, who knows exactly what I'm talking about. Does that make any sense at all?"

"Oh, yes." Joram put aside a cloth he had already folded and took the other end of Camber's, smiling warmly across the folds of linen as he met his father's eyes.

"Well, I'm glad it does to you," Camber replied, "because I'm not sure *I* understand. It was awesome, wondrous, weighty—and, frankly, a little frightening, in the beginning."

"Frightening? Yes, I suppose it is, in a way," Joram agreed. "We take on quite a responsibility when we enter into this kind of commitment." He stacked their folded cloth on top of the one he had already folded and leaned both elbows on them as he gazed across at Camber.

"It's worth it, though. And the scary part recedes after a while, I've found—at least most of the time. The awesomeness never does, though. Nor am I sure I'd ever want it to."

Camber nodded. "Perhaps even the fear is important, in the long run. A recurring reminder of the weight of responsibility, to keep us humble. That's surely as it should be."

"True."

With a sigh, Joram glanced around the chapel in survey a final time, then gathered up the altar cloths and vestment satchel and headed toward the door.

"Well, I'll take these and leave you now. I suspect you'll want a few minutes alone, before you go back. I'll collect the candlesticks in the morning."

Camber nodded. "What about the altar vessels we used? Should they be left here overnight?"

Joram glanced at a leather-bound box lying on the floor beside the candlesticks, then lowered his eyes.

"Those were Alister's, Father," he whispered. "I guess that means they're yours now. If you don't mind, though, I'd rather not watch you change back into him —not tonight."

"Joram, I know you don't approve—"

"No, it isn't that—not any more." Joram shook his head and finally looked up. "I understand what you have to do, and why. And I'm more delighted than I can ever tell you, that you did what you did tonight."

His eyes shifted from Camber's for just an instant, then held steadfastly. "But the times when you can be simply Camber Kyriell instead of Alister Kyriell are going to be somewhat rare. I'd like to remember you as yourself tonight."

For just a heartbeat, Camber gazed at his son in a mixture of shock and amazed revelation, then hugged him close in a wordless embrace. Joram was smiling, his eyes sparkling with unshed tears, as they drew apart, and the smile changed to a grin as he gave a quick nod and turned to go.

Camber stared fondly after him for several seconds, then stooped to pick up the box containing Alister Cullen's altar vessels. With a sweep of his free hand, he conjured a handful of silvery light as he rose, at the same time extinguishing all the other lights around the walls except the Presence light.

Then, bowing to that Presence a final time, he turned and glided from the chamber. Only one task remained before he returned to his quarters and the world of Alister Cullen.

The room he entered was a familiar one. For nearly a year, it had been the refuge and domicile of the then-Prince Cinhil, dominated in those days by a life-sized portrait of Cinhil's great-grandfather Ifor, to remind the prince of his origins. A darkly gleaming mirror hung on the wall beside the door, and before it Camber now stood. Once a mirror of truth for Cinhil, a confirmation of the potent Haldane blood, now it must serve a similar purpose for the man who tonight searched its depths.

He set the handfire to hovering and stood at arm's length from the polished surface, carefully studying the face which peered back at him.

Camber Kyriell MacRorie. *Father* Camber Kyriell, now. How long had it been since he had last looked upon that face? How long until he looked upon it again?

How long could he be another man, wear another man's guise, live another man's life? Would there ever be time to pursue his own ends, to live awhile for himself instead of for others?

He was fifty-nine years old. How much longer did he have? And things to do—so much to do!

He sighed and shook his head, pressing palms briefly to his eyes to force back the moment's indulgence in self-pity. He had not come here for that—only to remind himself who he really was, despite and because of what had happened tonight. That must be what sustained him, whatever the outward form he wore. As Alister, he should be able to gain the time he needed, if not immediately, then at least in the foreseeable future. And as a priest, and soon a bishop, no one would think odd the long hours alone which he so sought.

In the meantime, he thanked God for the dimension which had been added to his life tonight. It would make tomorrow, and the days which would follow, far more than merely bearable.

Calmer, then, he gazed into the mirror at his own visage, once again memorizing the familiar features which stared back. He noted the roundish, smooth-shaven face; the steady, pale eyes which glowed like wisps of fog in the gleam of the handfire; the silver-gilt hair framing those eyes like a cap of quicksilver; the sensitive mouth, set in a line of stubborn determination.

But he dared not dwell on anything just now. Though he felt not at all like sleeping, he must at least be in his bed by the time Guaire came to dress him in the morning. And to return to that bed, he must resume his disguise, must don again the outward form of Alister Cullen.

With an impatient sigh, he closed his eyes and settled into the stillness of Deryni trance, hesitating as he realized that he could watch the transformation this time, if he wanted to.

Slowly, he allowed his eyelids to drift apart, willing the shape-change to begin. A luminosity began to grow around his face, a slight buzzing to fill his ears; and then his features began to waver, to shift, to change.

He resisted the impulse to blink, for the sensation was not unlike fog, or the blurriness of recent sleep. But he knew that a mere blink would not change his perception of what was happening now. He held his eyes open and watched his hair coarsen and darken to Alister's familiar iron-gray, watched his brows thicken and extend, the eyes beneath them go bluer—greener, and the lines around them deepen. His face elongated slightly, the features becoming more prominent and his complexion weathering from pale to tan. His body, too, became more weighty-looking, stooped just a little; and his hands grew more wrinkled, the knuckles more pronounced.

He finally blinked as the transformation was completed, the action bringing him back to his normal state of awareness. He shook his head, an involuntary disbelief at what his eyes told him.

Camber was gone. Alister was there. Kyriell, he realized, could be the bridge of sanity between them.

A few minutes later, comfortably settled in his new body, he was standing in the Michaeline Transfer Portal and closing his eyes to visualize his destination in the archbishop's palace. Soon, Alister Kyriell Cullen would be safely in bed.

Chapter Seventeen

Wherefore gird up the loins of your mind,
be sober, and hope to the end for the grace
that is to be brought unto you.
—I Peter 1:13

Guaire knocked at Camber's door early the next morning, long before Prime and sufficiently before first light to startle Camber initially.

Camber had not been asleep. He had not particularly felt the need for sleep after his experience of the early-morning hours, though he had realized he must at least feign sleep, if only for Guaire's benefit.

Camber had to smile as he recalled Guaire's fervent, almost childlike exuberance of the past week, how the young man had spent nearly all the previous afternoon preparing and laying out appropriate raiment for to-day's ceremonies, while Camber rode with the king. Somehow—and Camber had no idea how—Guaire had managed to gather the impression that his new master was, if not helpless, at least absentminded when it came to details of ceremony and protocol—a notion which Camber deliberately did nothing to dispel. Guaire's self-esteem, badly eroded by the loss of his former master, was being considerably bolstered as he came to realize that his new master did, indeed, need him. Almost, Guaire was the way he had been before "Camber's" death.

As a consequence, Camber did not stir at the first knock on his door, choosing instead to burrow even farther under the blankets and close his eyes to merest slits. Very soon, the tap-tapping was replaced by the muffled click of the latch being worked, and then the soft pad of approaching footsteps. A brightening glow of yellow warmed the wainscoting by his face, and he knew that Guaire bore a rushlight. As the steps stopped a few paces away, Camber heard a perplexed-sounding sigh.

"Father Alister? Your Grace!" The voice was soft but insistent. "Are you not awake *yet,* my lord?"

At Camber's incoherent grunt, Guaire sighed again and began lighting additional rushlights around the still-dark room. When he had knelt to rebuild the fire, Camber rolled over lazily to peer at Guaire's back, gradually becoming aware of a plainsong melody which the younger man was humming under his breath. He watched curiously as Guaire fed the fire, noting how the black monk's robe which Guaire wore became him. He suddenly wondered whether there was more to the adoption of the garment than mere comfort and convenience. Guaire had been wearing it yesterday, too.

"Guaire?" Camber sat up and leaned on both elbows. Guaire turned at the call and grinned, though he continued tending the fire.

"Good morning, Father. Did you sleep well?"

"Um, I spent some time with the archbishop before retiring. It was a very late night. You're up early, aren't you?"

"You're to be consecrated bishop today, Your Grace. That's a very important event, and there's much to do if we're to leave for Grecotha tomorrow," the young man answered cheerfully. "You can't have forgotten?"

"No, hardly that."

With a yawn, Camber stretched and sat up, but when he started to get out of bed, Guaire was there with a warm mantle before he could even get his feet on the rug, sporting a broad grin. Camber pursed his lips thoughtfully as Guaire laid the mantle around his shoulders, tilting his head back so that Guaire could fasten the clasp at his throat. As Guaire knelt to put soft slippers on his feet, Camber watched the top of his head thoughtfully. Something was different this morning, and it had nothing to do with Camber.

"You're awfully cheerful this morning," Camber observed.

Guaire did not look up from what he was doing. "This is a momentous occasion," he returned easily. "It's going to be a long day, though, sir. I know you daren't break your fast until after the ceremony, but do you think you might stretch a point and have some mulled ale? It would steady your nerves. You told me that, one time."

"What makes you think *my* nerves need steadying?" Camber shook his head and tried to keep back a smile as Guaire stood and dusted his hands together.

"Guaire, may I ask you a question?"

"What question is that, Father?"

"Why are you wearing a monk's robe? Is there something I should know?"

"This?" Guaire touched the edge of the hood where it lay on his shoulders and flashed a worried half-smile. "You're not angry, are you, Father? I meant no harm. I just thought I'd blend in better with the others if I wore religious garb. The place will be swarming with monks and priests and bishops."

"Ah." Camber breathed a mental sigh of relief. He had no objection to Guaire's eventually taking religious vows if he wished, but for a moment he'd had the disturbing suspicion that his "miracle" with Guaire might have triggered a premature or unwarranted conversion. The religious life was fine, but only if it was Guaire's own idea.

Allowing himself a faint, gruff smile, Camber moved to the fireplace. Guaire followed him and hovered with an expectant air as Camber warmed his hands above the flames. Even as Guaire opened his mouth, Camber realized that the matter was not finished. The robe *was* more than camouflage for today's ceremonies.

"I *have* thought about the religious life, Your Grace," Guaire admitted, almost shyly.

Camber nodded patiently. "I suspected you might have. Is it because of the dream you had?"

"I—don't think so, sir."

"No? Well, with your family connections and military training, I could probably get you into the Michaelines, if you like," Camber offered, seeing a military order as the lesser of two evils. "You'd make a fine Knight of Saint Michael. I know Jebediah would take you. The Order lost a great many men, you know."

"I—don't think I want to be a Michaeline, Your Grace—with all due respect. I don't think I want to be a knight at all. Maybe I've just outgrown my fighting days."

"At—what?—twenty-two?"

"Twenty-five, sir, a month ago. I'm just—tired of fighting."

"Then what did you have in mind?"

Guaire shrugged. "I'm not certain. I have a better-than-average education. My copy hand is as good as most. Father Alfred, the king's confessor, thinks I might make a fair clark, or even a priest—though I'm not so sure about the priesthood, myself. Besides, you'll need a clark with military background, once you no longer have the Michaelines to draw upon. Perhaps I could help you with that."

Camber snorted, forcing himself to put all of Alister's gruffness in his next words. "Well, if you do it, don't do it out of expediency or loyalty to me— only for yourself, and for God. Silliest thing I ever heard, taking holy orders just because you think you can serve me better!"

"Sir, I wouldn't—"

"Promise me you won't?"

"Of course," Guaire agreed. "Only for the right reasons."

"I'll hold you to that. In the meantime, let's see to my bath." Camber nodded, smiling just a little as he motioned in the direction of the open door. "And, Guaire—"

"Your Grace?"

"If you do, and it *is* for the right reasons, I would be pleased."

Guaire tried, unsuccessfully, to hide his relief as he stood aside for his master.

An hour later, bathed, dressed, shaved, and hair trimmed and brushed to as tame a semblance as Alister Cullen's gray thatch was likely to get, Camber was finally able to sit down and begin going over the rubrics of the coming ceremony, taking refuge in the recess of an eastern window where the light was strong and the cushions could be arranged to ease his back against the lime-washed stone.

There had been no time to review the night before, of course. In fact, in the past week he had not had time to even open the scroll which Anscom had sent for his perusal. He could draw on Alister's memories of similar ceremonies seen at various times in the past, but watching was a different matter from doing; and the sacramental nature of the rite was something which could not be denied, which must be prepared for. He needed sufficient time and quiet to commit the rudiments, at least, to memory.

That task was not as easy as it might have seemed, though, for he kept getting interrupted. People were continually coming in and out, all of them on legitimate business—delivering gifts and well-wishes and taking out items to be packed for the trip to Grecotha tomorrow—and many of them required direction which only Camber could give.

He did not even glance up as Guaire went to answer yet another knock at the door. Not until he became aware of someone watching him did he break his concentration and look up.

"Sire!"

In one movement, Camber laid aside his scroll and got to his feet, wondering as he bowed whether anything was wrong. Yesterday he had gotten the impression that the king would be engaged this morning until just before the ceremony. That was still more than an hour away.

"Good morning, Alister," the king said, favoring the older man with a complacent smile and a nod of his head. "You're not still learning your lines, are you?"

"Only reviewing, Sire. Time has been in short supply this week, as I'm sure you're aware." He gestured toward the bench opposite his own. "Will you join me?"

Cinhil shook his head. "Not this morning, I'm afraid, though I'll expect you for dinner after the ceremony. I merely wished to make my own small contribution to this momentous occasion. Sorle?"

At his call, his squire Sorle led in two servants carrying something tall and almost the size of a man, covered with a black cloth. Sorle bore a large bundle wrapped in crimson, which he laid carefully on one of the chairs beside the fireplace before supervising the setting down of the object the other two men carried. As Camber moved closer, he could see that the object was a garment rack, similar to one already waiting, vestment-laden, near the foot of his bed. However, he was quite unprepared for the sight which met his eyes as Cinhil pulled off the outer covering.

Vestments. Creamy textured silk so richly worked with jewels and bullion that the cloth almost could not be seen. A bishop's cope, stiff with needlework, clasped with gold and diamonds over a chasuble and stole with orphreys worked in a pattern of wheat sheaves and pomegranates, all picked out in ballasses and crystal. Camber had never seen such vestments.

Finally remembering to breathe, Camber let out a slow, wondering sigh and reached out to run one reverent finger along the edge of the cope. He started to turn toward the king, but Sorle was there, holding a matching miter of gold and jewels which he had withdrawn from the package on the chair. At the edge of his vision, he could see Cinhil watching him, studying his reaction with a pleased smile.

Camber shook his head disbelievingly.

"Sire, I—they're magnificent. A princely gift. I don't know what to say."

"A simple 'thank you' will suffice," Cinhil replied, looking very smug. "I actually find it rather hard to believe, myself—not the vestments, for they were made to my specifications, but the fact that I seem to have you finally at a loss for words."

"I— You do, indeed, Sire. But, these are far too rich for me. They should belong to a great cathedral, or—"

"Or to the master of a great cathedral, such as you are about to become," Cinhil interjected. "Don't argue with me about this, Alister. Of course, I realize that such vestments cannot be worn just every day. For one thing, they're entirely too heavy and beastly hot, as you'll discover. So Sorle has also brought some more-usual sets."

At his signal, Sorle unwrapped the rest of the package and stood aside. Rich silk brocades of emerald green and white gleamed in ordered folds from the fire-lit chair, touched here and there with more sedate embroidery. Camber could only shake his head.

"You do me too great an honor, Sire," he finally said, fighting down the guilty feelings he was experiencing—for it was Alister to whom Cinhil had just made so revealing a gift—Alister to whom Cinhil had, in effect, finally offered a trusting hand. Alister, not Camber.

Yet, who was Camber, now?

Cinhil, unaware of the inner conflict of the man he had just honored, merely signaled the servants to withdraw.

"I give you only what is your due," he said quietly, "and perhaps share a little selfishly what can never be mine in fact again. Nay, I am resigned to that, Father," he went on, as Camber looked disturbed. "I told you that before. And you offered to share a little of your priesthood with me, if I would share my king-ship with you. Do you remember?"

Camber nodded, drawing the memory from the part of him which was Alister. "I meant it," he said softly.

"Then I intend to hold you at your word," Cinhil murmured. "I will not stop you from going to Grecotha. You may go and set up your diocese. You may have several months, if you like. The archbishop will expect it, and it will take me that long to get things straightened out here—the prisoner ransoms, formation of a council—all the things I should have done on my own before, the things a king should do.

"But, when they're done, I shall call you back. I shall call you back to sit at my side and help me make the laws by which I'll govern this kingdom that your Deryni colleagues have given to me. I didn't want it, Alister. God knows I didn't. But now that I have it, even I can recognize my responsibilities. And, some-what selfishly, I admit, I can ask you to help me through some of the difficult times, when I sit alone and brood in my chambers about all the things I've already told you far too many times. Will you do that for me?"

Camber laced his fingers together and studied them with downcast eyes. "Is that what you really wish, Cinhil?"

"I think so. Things will certainly be more pleasant for everyone else if I settle down and start doing my job."

"And what of the king's pleasure?" Camber asked quietly.

"The king's pleasure?" Cinhil laughed bitterly. "The king's pleasure will have to be confined to mere satisfaction that I'm doing the best I can—even if I would rather be anywhere else, back in my monastery, where we both know I'll never be allowed to go again."

"If you could go back, would you?" Camber asked, looking up wistfully. "I mean, if, right now, this very instant, with all other things as they are, you could be magically transported back to your old cell at Saint Foillan's—would you go?"

Cinhil lowered his eyes. "No," he whispered. "Because it could never be the same—I realize that now. If, in the beginning, I'd refused to go along, if I'd been steadfast—but, not now. I made my choice, even if it seemed like no choice at that time, and now I have to pay the consequences. One day, perhaps God will forgive me."

"You still insist that you sinned, by taking up your crown?"

"What else? You've seen my babes, Alister. You've seen that sad young woman who came to be my bride —I, whose only bride should have been the Church. Now, in my own poor, bumbling way, I have to go on, and make the best of things for them, too, at least so far as that's possible. Perhaps one day my sons will learn to rule more wisely than I am likely to do, with this frail, flawed clay."

As he held out hands which trembled now, Camber sighed and laid an arm around Cinhil's shoulders. After a moment, Cinhil looked up again.

"Forgive me, Father. I didn't mean to bring my maudlin moods to this most happy of days for you. Perhaps you see why I need you near me."

"I shall try always to be near when you need me, Sire," Camber said. "When you call, be assured that I shall come as soon as I can. I could count no greater worldly honor than to serve my Lord and King."

"Thank you. I shall try not to let that service interfere with that other duty which we both owe to a higher Lord," Cinhil said, finally managing a smile. "But I should go now and let you finish your preparations. You *will* wear the new vestments this morning, will you not?"

"If you wish it, Sire." Camber smiled. "I only hope I shan't outshine my brother bishops too much. Archbishop Anscom, I know, has access to the cathedral treasures, but poor Father Robert may be totally overshadowed."

"You need not worry for Robert Oriss," Cinhil returned smugly, pausing in the doorway. "After all, the revival of the second archbishopric in Gwynedd is also a momentous occasion. I've already delivered a similar set of vestments to him."

"I see."

"Of course, they aren't the same as yours. You and he are very different men."

"I shan't argue with that."

"And frankly," Cinhil concluded, just before he disappeared behind the door, "I think it's just as well. I don't think I could cope with two of you, Alister."

"Bless you, Sire!" Camber chuckled as the door closed with a click.

He wondered what Cinhil would think if he ever found out there *were* two Alisters, at least after a fashion.

An hour later, on the stroke of Terce precisely, Camber squinted in the sunlight of the cathedral close and waited for his part of the procession to begin moving. To either side of him, Joram and Father Nathan stood respectful attendance, ready to escort him when the time came. He eased the weight of his new vestments on his shoulders and stifled a yawn as he watched the beginning of the procession start filing up the steps and into the church. The voices of the cathedral choir, deep inside the reach of stone and glass and timber, were discernible only as a low, muffled echo. Conversation in the close itself had ceased as the column started moving.

Cinhil had been right about the vestments, Camber decided, as he shifted from one foot to the other and tried not to appear as uncomfortable as he felt. The robes *were* heavy, and they were hot—and Camber did not even wear the great jeweled cope and miter yet. The heat of the day was still to come, with the sun burning in a cloudless sky. Already he could feel sweat forming beneath the heavy alb and chasuble.

With a stoic sigh, he turned inward to seek and find

the controls which would lower his body temperature just slightly. He wondered how his human compatriot, Robert Oriss, was faring in the heat—Oriss, who had no recourse to Deryni disciplines.

Ahead of them, feet shuffled and the line began to move. Most of the other bishops of Gwynedd and the neighboring areas had come to attend the ceremony, many of whom Camber had just met for the first time today, as Alister as well as Camber: Niallan of Dhassa, the traditionally neutral and essentially independent bishop who would be working closely with the new Archbishop of Rhemuth; young Dermot of Cashien, whose uncle had been bishop before him and was whispered to have been more in kinship than uncle to his brother's child; Ulliam of Nyford, head of the southernmost diocese, who must cope with the ruin left by Imre's abortive attempt to build yet a third capital in Ulliam's port city—and four of Gwynedd's six itinerant bishops, with no fixed sees, whose faces Camber was just beginning to associate reliably with names: Davet and Kai and Eustace and Turlough.

All of the assisting prelates wore full pontificals, carried the stylized shepherds' staffs of their offices with the crooks turned inward, since they were in Anscom's jurisdiction.

And ahead of the bishops, just now disappearing through the vast double doors, were others of the procession in colorful array: candle bearers and crucifers, thurifers swinging fragrant censers on long golden chains; the ecclesiastical knights, Michaelines and others, in their mantles of azure and scarlet and gold; surpliced priests bearing the regalia which would be bestowed on the two bishops to be made.

Next came the mitered abbots of Gwynedd—Crevan Allyn of the Michaelines in his cloak of blue; Dom Emrys of the Order of Saint Gabriel, white-haired, white-robed shadow of a man, gliding wraithlike in the invisible mantle of his Deryniness; the masters of the *Ordo Verbi Dei*, the Brotherhood of Saint Joric, and a handful of others—and then the bishops.

Finally, it was Camber's turn, to climb slowly the worn cathedral steps and pass into the shade, Joram and Nathan catching up the edges of his chasuble as he walked, to follow two small boys who bore their golden candlesticks as though these were the most precious objects they had ever touched. Hands folded reverently before him, eyes downcast to minimize visual distractions, Camber stilled his mind and prayed for grace and guidance. As they moved up the aisle, followed finally by Oriss and then by Anscom and his attendants, the strains of the introit reverberated joyously among the columns and arches and galleries:

"Fidelis sermo, si quis episcopatum desiderat . . ." Faithful is the saying, If a man desire the office of bishop, he desireth a good work. A bishop then must be blameless . . .

And from his favored place in the right of the choir, a restless King Cinhil watched and brooded, dreaming of days gone by, longing to be even the humblest part of that sacred company.

But on his head was a royal crown, and at his side stood a wife and queen, and all around was the panoply of a regal court—worldly glory, for him who would have preferred a homespun habit and a simple monkish cell.

He shifted impatiently as the bishops came into view, watching until one grizzled gray head stood out among the others, near the end. On him the king fastened his attention, studying the seamed, craggy face and wondering what really went on behind the pale, sea-ice eyes. As the bishops passed him, to pause before the High Altar and genuflect before taking their places, he breathed a prayer of thanksgiving for his new-found friend and confidant. He bowed his head and knelt as Archbishop Anscom mounted the steps to the altar and began the Mass.

The liturgy progressed apace through the Gospel readings. Then, when the choir had sung the *Veni Creator,* invoking the presence of the Spirit upon those about to be consecrated, Robert Oriss and Alister

Cullen stood before the throne of the Primate of All Gwynedd and were examined on their fitness for the offices they were about to assume:

Would they be faithful and constant in proclaiming the Word of God? Would they sustain and protect the people of God and guide them in the ways of salvation?

Would they show compassion to the poor and to strangers and to all who were in need? Would they seek out the sheep who had strayed, and gather them back into the fold?

Would they love with the charity of a father and a brother all those whom God placed in their care, even at the cost of their own mortal lives?

They would.

Laying their hands upon the cathedral's most sacred relics, they vowed to discharge to the end of their lives the office about to be passed on to them by the imposition of hands. Prostrating themselves before the High Altar in humility, as all priests had done from time immemorial before assuming further holy orders, they prayed for the grace to keep their promises, while the archbishop and his clergy knelt and recited the traditional litany of saints.

Then, rising only long enough to move before the archbishop's throne, the two men knelt again, side by side, there to receive the sacramental imprint of prelacy, the apostolic laying on of hands, first by the archbishop, and then by all the other attending bishops.

With the open Gospel laid across their shoulders by two assisting bishops, they were sealed with holy chrism on head and hands, then invested with the symbols of their new offices: the Gospel, that they might teach; the ring of amethyst, as a seal of faithfulness with the Church they served; the miter, crown of earthly authority, but also weight upon the brow to remind that the title of bishop derived not from his rank, but from his duty—for it was the part of a bishop to serve, rather than to rule.

And last, the crozier, the pastoral staff—sign of the

Shepherd's office, to watch over and guard the flocks given them to govern in God's Name.

Following a Mass of Thanksgiving, the new bishops were led through the cathedral to bless the congregation for the first time, while the triumphant strains of the *Te Deum* reverberated among the vaulted arches.

Afterward, in the great hall of the castle, King Cinhil held a reception and feast for the new bishops and their brethren—as lavish a celebration as had yet been held during his reign. The event was not the glittering spectacle of the Festillic years. Cinhil instinctively shied away from any hint of that; and besides, the ways of worldly formality were still alien to him, and would always make him a little uncomfortable. Still, for Cinhil, it was festive.

Seating Bishop Cullen to his right, and Archbishops Oriss and Anscom to his left, on either side of his queen, Cinhil presided over a hall of all Gwynedd's highest clergy and baronage, drinking the health of his two new bishops and appearing almost happy, especially once his queen had retired and he was left to the company of his male friends.

Camber left for Grecotha the next morning—a long day's ride stretched out to three, because of the panoply in which a prince of the Church was expected to travel for the first entry into his new benefice. Cinhil had granted him an escort of a dozen knights to guard him on his way, and these were augmented amply by a score of the archbishop's own crack household troops, who would stay on at Grecotha to become his own. In addition came a full staff of chaplains, clarks, and other servants who would assist the new master of Grecotha in setting his domain in order. Domestic servants had already been sent ahead, a week before, to reopen what served for a bishop's residence and to provision it for occupation.

The next weeks passed quickly, as summer eased into autumn and the daylight hours diminished. The Diocese of Grecotha, one of the oldest in the Eleven

Kingdoms, was centered in the heart of the great university town of the same name, and had been without a vicar for more than five years. As a consequence, its new bishop found himself much occupied with pastoral duties.

There were ecclesiastical courts to convene, confirmations to be administered, priests to ordain. He must make official visitations to every parish and abbey and school under his jurisdiction, to ascertain that all were in competent hands and running as they should, and take steps to correct, if they were not. He had also to perform the routine duties of any ordinary priest: daily celebration of Mass, administering of other sacraments—baptism, confession, marriage, extreme unction.

All of these, well-known to Alister but new and awesome to him, Camber performed, and learned much of himself and his fellow man in their performance. He found himself falling into bed at night to sleep a dreamless sleep, his physical strength continually shored up by his Deryni abilities. He wondered how ordinary men functioned under the pressures of the job, with only their human resources to rely upon, and decided that it could only be through the gift of Divine grace. He marvelled, under the circumstances, that he was able to keep abreast of it at all.

And when Camber was not traveling, he was spending the bulk of his waking hours reviewing the administrative records of his diocese and directing his assistants in the setting up of a more efficient governing system. The office of Dean was reinstated almost immediately, the appointment going to a quiet but competent human priest named Father Willowen, who seemed singlehandedly to have stood between the diocese and total administrative collapse for the entire five years of the see's vacancy.

One of the most appalling discoveries which Camber made, and which was in no way Willowen's fault, was the deplorable state of the cathedral archives. To Camber, reared with a reverence for the written word which approached that of his religious faith, the state of neglect of these important records was inexcusable.

The fault, he soon discovered, was not a recent one. It lay with the confusion which had followed the separation of the famed Varnarite School from the cathedral chapter more than a century and a half ago, when the ultra-liberal Varnarites had taken their library— and, Camber suspected, a great part of the cathedral's —to new quarters in another part of the city. Never really properly reorganized since then, the present records showed glaring lapses, and infuriating juxtapositions of fiscal, canonical, and secular material. Some of the disorganization seemed almost methodical.

He turned Willowen and a handful of monks and clarks loose on the project, and order slowly began to emerge from bibliophilic chaos. Willowen was a martinet when it came to overseeing a task of this magnitude, and hounded his compatriots unmercifully if they did not work with enough speed or accuracy to please him. Oddly enough, no one seemed to resent Willowen's manner, perhaps realizing that he acted thus because he cared; and the work got done.

Camber took to spending time alone in the older archive sections himself, for his skill in ancient languages was useful in deciphering some of the more obscure entries buried on back shelves. One find which he did not share with Willowen and his monks was a very ancient cache of scrolls dating from long before the Varnarite separation, in a language which even Camber could read only with difficulty. He had no time to explore these in detail when he found them, but the few words and phrases which he had managed to scan during his initial examination were enough to convince him that no human should ever see these scrolls. One of them, of a somewhat later date than most of the others, seemed to tie in with some of the ancient records which he and Evaine had been studying while still in Caerrorie. In another, he had found mention of the Protocol of Orin!

But the Bishop of Grecotha dared not indulge these

interests overmuch. Winter was fast approaching, and with winter would come the summons from Cinhil, commanding attendance at the capital. In light of that priority, all personal pursuits must pale, though he would try not to let that keep him from sending word to Evaine of his discovery.

And that was one thing he *was* able to do: to stay in relatively close touch with his children. Beginning with the first week after his arrival in Grecotha, he had been receiving regular fortnightly communications from the capital via Joram, whom Cinhil had decided was the ideal confidential messenger between himself and the new Grecotha bishop. Cinhil had perceived Joram as a dual-purpose messenger, able to transmit news of Alister's old Michaeline Order as well as missives from his king. Joram and Alister *had* been close, after all. Who more fitting?

Of course, Cinhil did not know that Joram also brought reports to and from Archbishop Anscom, in addition to his own astute observations on the state of Cinhil's progress; or that Evaine and Rhys, too, were funneling royal intelligence to Camber in their own ways. Cinhil knew only that Joram's return reports indicated considerable progress in the revival of Grecotha as a functioning arm of the ecclesiastical hierarchy and that Bishop Alister Cullen was proving as able a diocesan administrator as he had been of the powerful Michaeline Order. That boded well, in Cinhil's mind, that the said bishop would be able to do the same for a kingdom, come the first snows of winter. Accordingly, he left Alister in peace through the summer and early autumn. Besides, Cinhil was busy getting his own life in order.

Grecotha was a time of personal ordering for Camber, as well, not only from the standpoint of learning to function as an ecclesiastical administrator, but as an experience in being alone. Of course, he was truly alone only rarely, but there was a loneliness nonetheless, for there was no one he could really talk to here in Grecotha.

Of all those who had come with him from Valoret and stayed, only Guaire had he known before—and the human Guaire was busily trying to find his own spiritual balance. As autumn approached, and the harvest was reaped and garnered, Guaire spent an increasing amount of time under the tutelage of the priests and brothers of the episcopal household, growing somewhat distant from Camber. He also began to make a point of chatting with each messenger who came to the Grecotha residence, especially those in orders, Deryni as well as human.

Camber first became aware of Guaire's growing Deryni attachments one day late in October. He was strolling with his breviary in the newly cleared gardens of the fortified manor house which served as bishop's residence, savoring the last dregs of sunlit autumn, when he noticed Guaire at the other end of the garden, in animated conversation with a short, wiry man in the habit of the Gabrilite Order. The man's back was to Camber, the peculiarly Gabrilite braid of reddish auburn hair hanging almost to his cinctured waist, as thick as a man's wrist. Camber thought he saw the green of a Healer's cloak behind the man's body. The man looked vaguely familiar, but there were several Gabrilites who were also Healers.

Curious, he started to go toward them, the better to discover why Guaire should be talking with a Gabrilite, when he realized that he did know the man —and that the man had known Camber MacRorie. The Gabrilite priest and Healer was Dom Queron Kinevan, Deryni like all members of his Order, and a particularly gifted one, at that—a Healer of minds and souls, as well as of bodies, acknowledged as a skilled retreat master. While he and Camber had not been intimates, still, Camber knew the man's abilities. It made him all the more curious as to why Queron was spending time with Guaire—Guaire, who was bright and pleasant, but hardly in Queron's class. By their expressions and relaxed manner, this was not the first time they had talked thus.

Pausing in the lee of a leafless tree, Camber opened his breviary and pretended to read, reflecting on the possible reasons for Queron's presence in Grecotha. But even though something rang strange about the apparent relationship, he could hardly come out and ask Queron why he was talking to Guaire. Nor did he dare probe Guaire's mind for an answer, so long as Queron was present. He dared not risk the possibility that Queron might recognize his unique mental touch.

With a sigh, Camber closed his book and turned to make his way into another part of the garden, away from Guaire and Queron. He was probably being overly sensitive anyway. The meeting was likely quite innocuous. Perhaps Queron had business with the canons of the Varnarite School, and Guaire, in the bright-polished zeal of a burgeoning religious vocation, had seized on the Gabrilite as a mentor. Perhaps he had even known Queron before.

Foolish for Camber to let himself become apprehensive over an incident which was probably as innocent as Guaire's new-found faith!

CHAPTER EIGHTEEN

*Even the mystery which hath been hid
from ages and from generations, but now is
made manifest to his saints.*

—Colossians 1:26

Camber never got a chance to follow up on
Guaire's visitor, for it was only a few days later that
the summons from Cinhil finally came.

Camber, comfortably perched on a stable gate in
worn Michaeline riding leathers, had been watching
the farrier put new shoes on a favorite dun mare.
The ring of hammer on anvil had temporarily blunted
his hearing, so he did not hear the two men approaching from the stable yard until Andrew the smith broke
his rhythm to glance curiously up the stable aisle.
Camber turned to see Guaire escorting a familiar
blond figure in Michaeline blue. He jumped down
from his perch as Joram approached to kiss the
episcopal ring.

"Joram, it's good to see you!" he said, allowing one
of Alister's infrequent grins of pleasure to crease his
face. "I fear you've caught me playing truant from
my duties. I should be preparing Sunday's homily, but
instead I thought to watch Falainn shod and then
slip away for an hour's ride. I'd ask you to join me,
but I doubt you have any great desire to put backside
to saddle again today."

Joram returned his father's grin, slipping easily into
that relaxed façade which the two of them had built

over the past months for the public side of their relationship. He was dressed almost identically to his father and superior, except that he also wore the sturdy Michaeline mantle, hood pushed back from his gleaming yellow hair. Though he must have ridden many miles to arrive so late in the day, he looked as he usually did: unruffled and composed, hardly a golden hair out of place.

"Your Grace is too observant, as usual," he murmured, bowing slightly in acknowledgment. "And I fear that someone else may have to deliver your homily on Sunday. The King's Grace requires your presence within the week."

"Within the week?" Camber glanced at Guaire, then back at Joram, who was pulling a sealed letter from the pouch slung across his chest.

"Aye. He's convening Winter Court early, since so much must be done—on the Feast of Saint Illtyd, six days from now." He handed across the letter with a formal bow. "With this he names Your Grace to his first officially constituted royal council, commanding you to make preparations to absent yourself from your present duties at least through Twelfth Night. The commission is countersigned by Archbishop Anscom, granting you leave to delegate such duties as you may to another during your absence."

With a raised eyebrow, Camber returned Joram's bow and broke the seal, but stopped short of opening the parchment as Joram produced a second letter, which he tapped against the fingers of his opposite hand to regain his listener's attention.

"It is also His Highness's pleasure," Joram continued with a sly grin, "to create a new office of chancellor in this, his kingdom. To said office, he likewise appoints Your Grace, charging you with duties specified in this warrant and certain others which he shall impart to you in person, when you reach Valoret." He handed the second letter to Camber and smiled smugly. "My Lord Chancellor, your warrant."

Jaw dropping in amazement, Camber took the letter and stared at the familiar seal for a moment, glanced at Joram speechlessly, then broke the seal and scanned the contents. As Joram had said, it was a warrant as Chancellor of Gwynedd, which amounted to primacy in the royal council which the first letter supposedly appointed. A hasty inspection of the first letter confirmed the summons to Valoret which Joram had already conveyed.

Camber sighed and began refolding the letters.

"Well, Andrew, it seems I'm not to have my ride this afternoon after all. In fact, you'll have to check with the constable to see what other horses need shoeing before the journey. Guaire, is it at all possible that we could leave tomorrow?"

"Tomorrow? I doubt it, sir. The day after, certainly. Shall I inquire of the seneschal?"

"Do that, please. I'll need only a small escort: the household troops and perhaps one other clark besides yourself. Father Willowen will remain as provost during my absence. You can tell him for me, if you will."

"Yes, Your Grace. Will you take supper with your curia this evening, then?"

"Yes. Please so inform them. And you can start packing and have the apartments next to mine made ready for Father Joram for tonight. We'll be up in Queen Sinead's Watch for the rest of the afternoon, if you need me—but try not to."

A few minutes later, Camber and Joram were high in the interior of the bishop's residence, climbing the last of the one hundred twenty-seven steps of the tower stair to enter a small, enclosed chamber. The aerie was lined with stone benches and partially screened from the elements by a timber roof and carved screens of alabaster in the windows. Camber had stopped to fetch a flagon of wine from his own apartments on the way up, and he set it on one of the benches as he stepped from the rampart walk into the chamber.

Joram glanced out at the vista of the city spread at their feet as he caught his breath.

"What did you call this place?"

"Queen Sinead's Watch. Are you familiar with the name?"

Joram nodded. "Queen to the first Aidan Haldane, who was the great-grandfather, several times removed, of our present king." He watched expectantly as his father poured wine into two cups and passed one to him. "She's buried somewhere here in Grecotha, isn't she?"

"She is." Camber smiled. "You've remembered far more than most people. There's a legend that Sinead and Aidan were extremely devoted to each other and that when Aidan rode off to his last battle, as a very old man, his queen took refuge with the Bishop of Grecotha for safety, and would watch from his tower each day at dusk, praying for his safe return.

"These window spaces were open in those days, and when Aidan's army finally came back one evening, bearing the body of their slain lord with them, Sinead was so distraught that she threw herself from these ramparts and fell to her death. Her grieving son named the tower in her memory, and had the windows filled in with this tracery so that such a thing could never happen again."

"Did that really happen?" Joram looked skeptical.

"It makes a good story, anyway." Camber smiled. He held his cup moodily before him and stared at its contents, then sighed.

"So, tell me how things progress, son. What's really behind this appointment as chancellor?"

Joram glanced at the doorway leading back to the ramparts, then at his father. "Is it safe to talk here?"

"We won't be disturbed. Was the chancellorship Cinhil's idea?"

"His and Anscom's, I think," Joram replied. "Anscom has been trying to ease the pressure from me and Rhys in the past few months, making himself increasingly available to spend time with Cinhil. He's worried, and so are we all, about the new men who have begun cultivating the king—many of them displaced nobility of his great-grandfather's reign and their descendants, and most of them with definite anti-Deryni leanings. Anscom thought it would be a good idea if a few Deryni in positions of influence got appointed to high-enough offices to counteract some of what the human lords will undoubtedly try to do. You're one; and he's also convinced Cinhil that Jebediah should be retained as general in chief of the armies. Crevan Allyn has given his permission for the present, but it's almost inevitable that that will be but a temporary measure. There's bound to be a conflict of interests between royalists and Michaelines eventually."

Camber nodded. "That's so. However, it was a wise move for the present. And Cinhil—I take it he's well?"

"Well enough, I suppose. He's mellowed a lot since you left—I'm not sure exactly why—but he's still moody and impetuous at times. Some of his new human friends have been talking up the idea of another heir, almost pressuring him, really—and I think he's starting to weaken and doesn't much like himself because of it."

"What does Rhys say?" Camber asked. "Is Megan up to another pregnancy so soon?"

"Not really, but what else are we to do? The barons are right. Even Rhys has to admit that the two little princes aren't the best of all possible hopes to live long enough to inherit. Javan is healthy enough, but the clubfoot is going to hamper him. And little Alroy's health is still quite frail. Dynastically speaking, Cinhil *needs* another heir."

"You're right. I just wish it didn't have to be Megan. We and Cinhil aren't the only ones who have had to make sacrifices."

"No."

"And how are things at Caerrorie?" Camber asked, after a pause.

Joram tossed off the last of his wine and put his cup down very precisely. "No better than they were. We moved the body early last month—I forgot to tell you that, the last time I was here. He's been safely reinterred in the chapel of the haven, as we agreed—and in good time, I think. I don't like the feel of things."

"Have there been further incidents?" Camber asked.

"None outstanding," Joram replied. "We've tried to discourage the pilgrimages, without being hostile about them, but it does no good. The people seem to think that family is too shortsighted to recognize your obvious sanctity. We're even finding little devotions to 'Blessed Camber' left in the chapel by the tomb. It's—unnerving."

Camber shook his head resignedly. "It's not confined to Caerrorie, either. I've heard rumblings even here, in Grecotha. And if such talk reaches even me, as sheltered as I am now, I shudder to think what the common folk are really saying."

Joram shrugged, but said nothing.

"And yet," Camber continued, "there's an odd undercurrent, too. I don't know whether you've noticed it, Joram. Even as they laud the supposed accomplishments of a martyred 'Blessed Camber, Architect of the Restoration and Defender of Humankind,' they're also muttering about the old Deryni atrocities. I don't like the feel of it, Joram. I think we have to consider seriously the possibility of a backlash."

Joram sat and thought a minute, chin on hands, elbows propped on leather-clad knees, then spoke without looking up.

"Your tone says you see backlash as an inevitability, not a possibility. Are there no alternatives?"

"I'm not sure. I don't think so—at least not indefinitely. What you've just told me about the new factions forming around Cinhil makes it fairly certain that his reign, if not actually hostile to Deryni, is at least not going to be preferential. So long as you and I and Anscom and a few trusted others remain close to him, I doubt he'll allow any overt persecution, but the tenor of the court will be changing. We have to prepare for that. Eventually, we may even have to go underground again—and not just for a year, as we did in the haven. In case that time comes, we have to begin building safeguards now. We have to make certain that our people stay in line, that there are no more Imres or Coel Howells trying to reestablish influence through the misuse of Deryni talents. I think we might start with a semi-secret regulating body of some kind, to prevent flagrant abuses and to discipline those we can't prevent."

"A regulating body—composed of whom?" Joram asked softly.

Camber sighed. "Would it sound terribly self-righteous to suggest that some of us would have to do it? I'd also recommend men like Anscom, Dom Emrys of the Gabrilites, Bishop Niallan Trey, several others. Seven or eight, in all."

"Deryni sitting in judgment of Deryni," Joram muttered. "I'm not sure I like the implications for abuse of power right there. They'd have to have power, after all. The rulings of the body would have to be enforceable."

"That's true. I don't have an answer for you yet, either," Camber admitted. He eased his booted legs to a more comfortable position and stretched, indulging in an enormous yawn. "We'll have to find a sufficient way to bind our watchers with the very power they wield. Which reminds me of something which may or may not relate to what we've just been discussing."

"Which is?"

"Some fascinating records I've been uncovering. Are you aware that the archives of this diocese go back nearly four centuries, two of them in fair detail? They're badly disorganized, but—"

"What did you find?" Joram asked impatiently.

Camber smiled. "Well, in addition to some written materials which are probably associated with the Protocol of Orin—I say 'probably,' because I haven't had time to translate them fully yet—in addition to these, I've found some other material which may relate to some of our ancient Deryni origins. Tell me, what are the two major schools with reputations for turning out well-trained Deryni?"

"Why, the Varnarites and the Gabrilites, of course," Joram replied.

"Very good. You probably also know that the Varnarite school, now run by laymen, originally broke off from this cathedral chapter around 753, because of philosophical differences. Now, can you tell me where the Gabrilites came from?"

Joram thought a minute. "I—supposed—that they just arose as an independent Order. But I see by your expression that I'm in error. I never really thought about it before. I do know that they have only the one house at Saint Neot's."

"Correct on the last statement," Camber agreed. "They do have just the one house. However, my discoveries lead me to believe that the Gabrilite founders were originally an arch-conservative arm of this same cathedral chapter which spawned the Varnarites— who went their way even before the Varnarites pulled out, though they did it a few members at a time, not in a mass exodus. Mind you, I can't prove this yet, but I've found—well, I'll let you decide. How would you like to look at some ruins?"

"Ruins?"

With a nod, Camber rose and moved to the northwest corner of the little chamber, where he knelt and traced a large square along the edges of one of the flagstones near Joram's feet. Joram watched, thoroughly mystified, as Camber straightened up and beckoned for Joram to join him on the square.

"This is something I've already gleaned from my archival reading: how to construct a new kind of Transfer Portal—or perhaps I should say that it's an old kind that had been forgotten. The location changes from corner to corner of this area, in a deosil rotation, so that the same spot is used only once in four times. Another feature is that it's attuned so that only

I can sense its presence or use it. I'll have to take you through blind."

As Joram stepped on the square, a peculiar expression came across his face.

"There's a Portal *here?*"

"I told you, it's specific to me. And I take it as a distinct compliment to my abilities that even you can't detect its presence."

Joram could only shake his head. "You do scare me sometimes."

Smiling, Camber stepped behind Joram and laid his hands lightly on his son's shoulders.

"All right, I'm going to show you what's left of the *old* Varnarite school, before they moved to new quarters. I think you'll find this very interesting. Open to me when you're ready, and we'll go."

Joram closed his eyes and took a deep breath, letting it out with a slow exhale. As he did, Camber simultaneously forged the familiar link with his son and nudged them both into the spell of the Portal. In a blink, they were no longer in the daylit tower chamber.

"Are we underground?" Joram whispered as he opened his eyes to total blackness.

"This part of the complex is."

Light flared in Camber's hand, cool and silver-hued, to coalesce in a shining sphere a handspan above his palm. With a gesture, he set it to hovering slightly above his right shoulder, then ignored it as he moved beside Joram. The light showed them to be standing in a plastered anteroom which opened into a rubble-strewn corridor. Termite-riddled timber lined the passageway, and the tesselated tiles which they stepped out upon were cracked and uneven.

"I doubt anyone had been through here for fifty or a hundred years before I came," Camber said, gesturing toward the left as he ushered Joram into the ruined corridor. "One of Willowen's work crews broke through into an upper level of this complex when they were clearing away some collapsed masonry to get at a clogged drain—which led me to take a much closer look at the old master plans for this house. Mind your head."

As he ducked to avoid a fallen beam, he glanced back at Joram. The following handfire cast an eerie silvery wash on ancient, crumbling frescoes lining the hallway—half-glimpsed scenes of monastic and academic life so badly damaged by time and damp that little detail could be read. The air was musty and stale, and did not move except as their garments stirred it with their passage.

"Anyway," Camber continued as they walked, "I eventually worked my way down to this level through a series of passages, most of which I've since sealed. That was after I'd discovered that the corridors leading to the outside had long since fallen in—or possibly been deliberately slighted when the school was abandoned. And, of course, I'd already set up my private Portal. Unless I've badly misinterpreted the building plans, the Portal is the only way into this area now. Watch your step. What I want to show you is just beyond this next bend."

As they made a sharp turn to the right and halted, Camber's gesture caused the hovering handfire to float a little higher and ahead to illuminate a vast double door of iron-bound oak, half of which dangled precariously from one rusted hinge. Above the doorway, carved into the lintel with graceful chisel strokes, was a Latin inscription: *Adorabo ad templum sanctum tuum, et confitebor nomini tuo.*

Joram scanned the carving intently, moving a little closer in the ghostly light.

"It's from the Psalms," he said. "I forget the exact verse. It says, 'I will worship toward Thy holy temple, and will give glory to Thy Name.'" He glanced at his father. "Is this a chapel you want to show me?"

"Not exactly. I think your 'temple' is a more apt translation. Let's go inside. I want you to tell *me* what it is."

Pushing the door ajar, Camber ducked and stepped

through, holding the opening until Joram could follow gingerly behind him. The handfire, bright enough in the outer corridor, seemed to dim almost to nothing in the vastness of the inner chamber. Camber cupped his hands and breathed light into another sphere, set that to hovering an armspan from the first one with a wave of one amethyst-ringed hand.

"I'm afraid it's in a terrible state of repair," Camber murmured. "This place was old long before it was abandoned. The earliest date I've been able to locate so far is on a ledger stone there to the left of the altar dais—and that reads either 603 or 503. The stone is badly damaged. Take a look around and then tell me what it reminds you of."

Joram gave only a perfunctory nod, for he was already sweeping the chamber with sight and other senses, questing out into the sheer otherness of the place.

The chamber was far larger than he had first supposed, wider and higher than even the central transept of the cathedral in Valoret, which was said to have the largest dome in the Eleven Kingdoms. Circular in shape, its walls set with time-dulled mosaic designs of leaves and seas and golden-gleaming fire, it was vaulted by a tangle of arches and geometric patterns whose intricacies vanished in the subtleties of shadowed height.

From the dome's central boss hung a heavy metal chain terminating in nothingness. Beneath the chain, on a raised circular dais of seven wide steps, stood what remained of a square altar with black-and-white sides, its once-burnished mensa smashed almost to powder by whatever had fallen from the empty chain. Fragments of shattered stone and glass and twisted metal littered the dais around the altar. The pavement of the dais, also badly damaged, repeated the black-and-white checkerboard pattern of the altar sides, though on a far smaller scale.

Camber cleared his throat and glanced at Joram after a few minutes had passed.

"Well?"

"I think I understand the Gabrilite connection you mentioned earlier," Joram said, after a thoughtful pause. "It's—something like the chapter house at Saint Neot's, in that it's round and has a square altar in the center. I've only seen those design features at Saint Neot's before this. But this has—a strange feel to it." He glanced at his father. "Does that make any sense?"

Nodding, Camber looked around the chamber. "It does. I felt the same way, the first time I came here. And now that I've been reading some of the ancient records connected with this place—well, come and take a close look at the altar."

They crossed the rubble-strewn floor in silence, only the slither of leather soles on stone intruding on the quiet. Up the seven shallow steps they climbed, to tread gingerly on the black-and-white tile of the dais floor. The pavement was swept fairly clean on the side of the altar from which they approached, and Joram glanced around it curiously. One triangular section of the altar slab remained in place, nearly half the original top, and he could see now that an inscription had once been carved around the edge. Faint traces of gilt paint still clung to the curves of the incised lettering.

"*Benedictus es, Domine Deus patram nostrorum,*" Joram read in a low voice, filling in the sense of missing letters and parts of words.

" 'Blessed art Thou, O Lord God of our fathers,' " Camber translated. "I believe it's from Daniel. And the rest would read: *et laudabilis in saecula*—'worthy of praise forever.' It's not a usual quotation for an altar stone, so far as I've been able to discover."

Merely grunting in reply, Joram bent to pick up a fragment of glass from the tile. The piece was a clear, smokey amber, remarkably free from bubbles or other imperfections. Running diagonally across one jagged corner was a streak of cloudiness which Joram suspected was once part of an etched design. He could not quite visualize the original object it had helped to form.

"What do you suppose this was?" he finally asked, laying the glass on the altar slab.

"An unusual sanctuary lamp, I think," Camber replied. "I've found some drawings which I'm fairly certain are from this place. If so, this was part of a great lantern of eight sides, done in silver wire and amber glass etched with equal-armed crosses." He indicated the debris of glass and twisted metal with a sweep of one leather-clad arm. "But as to whether it fell or was pulled down for some reason, I couldn't say. Judging by the size of that chain, I should think it unlikely that the lamp fell by itself—but if it was pulled down, why? Or, was it blasted by some great energy? I don't think the altar was ever deconsecrated, by the way."

"No?"

"See for yourself," Camber replied. "When I first laid my hands on the altar, I thought my senses must be playing tricks on me. If I wasn't new to magic, I was at least new to priesting, and I hadn't expected— Well, see for yourself. Remember every other altar you've ever touched; remember the one in the haven chapel, after Cinhil celebrated his last Mass—and then tell me what this one says to you. In fact, don't touch the table slab at all. Lay your hands on the black stone underneath."

With a puzzled glance at his father, Joram wiped his hands against the leather of his riding tunic and moved closer to the altar. He wet his lips in concentration as he held his palms a fingerspan above the black undersurface for several seconds, then closed his eyes and let his hands rest gently on the stone. After a long moment, he exhaled softly through slightly pursed lips and raised his head a little.

"I see what you mean," he finally said, eyes a little unfocused as he continued trying to pin down the sensations he was experiencing. "There's power here still —far, far more than I would expect, after so many years—and more than can be explained even if the altar were still in use, which it clearly is not. Or is it?" He looked up shrewdly. "What was done here? You know, don't you?"

Camber smiled drolly, the expression somehow almost mischievous on Alister Cullen's weathered face, and folded his arms across his chest.

"I have my suspicions, at least in part. Look closely at the altar, at how it's constructed. Then try searching some of your earliest childhood memories. That's where I found the connection."

Frowning, Joram stepped back a few paces and eyed the mass of stone from another angle, his expression clearly proclaiming that he saw nothing unusual in its appearance. From an obsidian base, perhaps a hand-span in thickness and extending that much around the edges, side panels of alternating black and white squares rose to waist level, four squares to a face. The now-destroyed table of white marble, originally the same size as the base, had once rested on four fluted columns as big around as a man's arm, two white and two black, though one of the black ones was fallen now, its shaft snapped clean across the center by the same impact which had smashed the marble mensa.

Camber watched Joram's perplexed gaze follow the lines of the stones, then shook his head resignedly and reached into the front of his leather tunic and withdrew a small black velvet bag. Untying the scarlet cords which bound its neck, he leaned down to blow dust from a portion of the black understone of the altar. He tipped the bag gently above the cleaned ebony surface and captured the polished cubes with his right hand as they tumbled out, four white and four black. The cubes seemed to glow in the baleful light of Camber's handfire, casting hardly any shadows. Camber's bishop's ring glittered in brilliant contrast to the quieter shimmer of black and white cubes.

"Wards Major?" Joram whispered.

Nodding, Camber sorted the cubes with his finger-tip, moving the four white ones until they formed a solid square. The velvet bag he laid aside as he looked up steadily at his son.

"You remember the spell, Joram," he said softly. "It was the first one I ever taught you. Your mother thought I should have waited until you were older, but I knew that your brother Ballard would show you if I didn't, and then you both might have gotten yourselves into trouble."

With a smile, Camber moved the four black cubes so that they stood at each corner of the larger square he had already formed, black not quite touching white. Then, glancing up to be certain he had Joram's attention, he gently placed first and second fingers on *prime* and *quinte* and switched their places, repeating the process with *quarte* and *octave*. He looked up at Joram again, hoping for comprehension, though he did not really expect to see it.

"You never learned this one, did you?"

Joram studied the configuration in silence, fair brow furrowed in consternation. Then: "But—you can't set Wards Major like that."

"That is very true."

"Then . . ." Joram's eyes took on a faraway look. "You mean that—something *else* would happen if you tried to work the spell using this arrangement?"

Camber nodded.

"You wouldn't get a Ward Major," Joram continued tentatively.

Again Camber nodded.

"Which means that—the cubes can be used for more than one spell," Joram finally murmured. He stared at the cubes fixedly for several heartbeats, swallowing audibly before daring to look up at his father again.

"What—what *would* happen if you went ahead with this setup?"

"I don't know. I've not tried *that* arrangement." He picked up the white cube in the upper left-hand corner, normally named *prime,* and held it lightly between thumb and forefinger. "Without actually naming the components and risking finding out precipitously, however, I want you to consider yet another variation. If I place *prime* on *quinte,* and *sixte* on *seconde,* and *septime* and *quarte* on *tierce* and *octave*—what will I have?"

Joram stared hard at the cubes, trying to visualize them as Camber had described, then shook his head. "Go through it again. *Prime* on *quinte*—"

"*Prime* on *quinte.*" Camber nodded, stacking the two cubes, white on black, as Joram watched.

"And *sixte* on *seconde,*" Joram continued, picking up the black *sixte* and putting it on its white counterpart.

"And *septime* and *quarte* on *tierce* and *octave,*" Camber finished, suiting actions to words as he put the final two cubes into place. "Now," he said, looking at Joram discerningly once more. "We have a cube. What does that tell you?"

When Joram started to shake his head in bewilderment, Camber brought the flat of his right hand down on the altar with a slap.

"Look at the cubes, Joram! Look at the altar! What do you see?"

Joram looked, then took a step backward and looked again, this time at the altar itself. Camber watched with a satisfied nod as his son made the connection at last.

"I see—a cube made of eight alternating black and white cubes," Joram finally whispered. "And the— altar is also made of eight black and white cubes." His eyes sought his father's. "Are you saying that the altar cubes are part of a giant Ward Major matrix?"

Camber sighed and scooped up the little cubes in his palm, letting them fall, one by one, back into the black velvet bag. He did not look up or speak until he had retied the bag and tucked it back into his tunic.

"That I don't know. I don't think it's a Ward Major matrix, but I'm beginning to suspect that it *is* a matrix. At very least, I think the altar may be symbolic of the cubes we use. In fact, the very appellation of 'Ward

Major cubes' is probably a misnomer. I've found sketches of a full dozen additional cube matrices already, and there are logically dozens more possibilities. Unfortunately, I haven't yet figured out what any of them do, including this one—which appears to be the only one worked in three dimensions, by the way."

"A dozen different matrices!" Joram whistled low under his breath. "Have you tried any of them yet?"

Camber shook his head. "I'm afraid to. I haven't a notion what might happen. This one especially." He laid his hand on the altar once more. "And if the altar is symbolic of the power of the particular spell evoked by this pattern, which I think highly likely, then it must be powerful indeed—perhaps at the very heart of our Deryni abilities. We already know that there was great power associated with this altar, if we can still detect its traces after hundreds of years. Who knows what we might unleash if we go experimenting without suitable preparation? We've time to go slowly."

Joram glanced apprehensively around him, casting a furtive look into the shadowed spaces above their heads, then turned back to Camber with a shudder.

"I'm glad you're the one who's insisting on caution this time," he murmured. "I was beginning to think I was the only one to get occasional attacks of the shivers. Let's get out of here, can we? I suddenly feel really uneasy."

With a slight smile, Camber turned and led the way out of the chamber, across the rubbled, dust-covered floor and through the ruined doors. Down the collapsed passage they walked in silence, stopping finally in the plastered alcove where the Portal had brought them through before. Again Camber took a place behind his son, this time only laying an arm around his shoulders. Immediately he felt Joram's mind go slack and open, inviting a blind, trusting link such as he rarely permitted.

With a comforting surge of affection and protection, Camber wrought the Transfer link and pushed the two of them through. Both men blinked as they emerged in the daylit tower again, Joram stumbling a little in the transition back to reality. They surprised an unsuspecting Guaire, who had just been leaving what he had thought to be an empty tower chamber.

"Your Grace!" Guaire's gasp was involuntary, the young man immediately settling as he realized what must have happened.

With nonchalant ease, as if he were in the regular habit of appearing out of thin air, Camber signed for Joram to refill their abandoned wine cups, blocking Guaire's view of his son so that Joram would have time to recompose his expression. Camber's manner was casual and disarming, confidently proclaiming the everyday as he nodded acknowledgment to Guaire's astonished bow.

"Oh, there you are, Guaire. Sorry if we startled you. Joram and I were just reminiscing about the old days, and got a little carried away, I'm afraid. Frivolous, perhaps, but we seemed to have the time."

Guaire bowed again, his expression shifting to one of amused understanding. "No apology necessary, Your Grace. I only came to tell you that we *will* be able to leave in the morning, after all. Apparently the seneschal anticipated Your Grace's summons far better than we thought."

"Excellent," Camber said. "And the supper arrangements for this evening? I don't know about Joram, but I'm starved."

"In preparation, Your Grace. And hot baths are being drawn even now."

"Thank you. We'll be down directly."

As Guaire bowed once more and disappeared down the spiral stair, Camber sat down beside Joram and took up the cup of wine waiting for him. Joram had already drained his own, and was pouring a second.

"That could have been tricky," Joram said, when he was certain Guaire was well out of earshot. "Does he suspect anything?"

Camber shook his head. "He's fairly used to my

Deryni wanderings by now. There are several other Portals in the house. When will you next see Evaine and Rhys, by the way? I meant to ask earlier."

"They're at Caerrorie now, so I presume it will be sometime next month. I promised Cinhil I'd deliver you to Valoret first."

"Fine. That will give me time to get a few things together for you to take to Evaine. I'm going to need some help with the translation on some of the scrolls I've found."

Joram could not control a grin. "Are you sure you want to trust her with such things? Remember what she did with the Protocol of Orin, the night you integrated Alister's memories."

"Ah, yes." Camber smiled in recollection—not of the incident itself, but of their three retellings of the event. "I really must ask her more about that some day. I've never heard of anyone taking another shape without a model to work from—and certainly not one of the opposite sex." He shook his head.

"But, to answer your question, I see no problem. We're going to be working with disconnected bits and pieces for a while, at least—until we figure out what we've got. I'm not sure any of us could do anything with them at this point. It's rather like the difference between a sacramentary and a rubric book, one containing only the words, and the other giving just the movements. You need both to put together a proper ritual. And she's going to have to wade through translations that will make the Pargan Howiccan sagas seem like children's nursery rhymes—archaic language forms, some of which even I have never seen, and a devilishly difficult copy hand. If she can find the time to track down the more obscure references, that will be the biggest help."

Joram nodded. "You're probably right. She'll love the challenge. For that matter, let me and Rhys know what we can do to help. At the very least, we can probably make fair copies for you, as the work progresses. In fact, if you pull the proper episcopal strings, you could probably get me assigned to your staff on a permanent basis. Allyn couldn't refuse you, if you asked."

"You'd want that?" Camber said, shaggy brows lifting in surprise.

"To work with you? Of course," Joram replied lightly. "Serving as Cinhil's personal messenger is all well and good, but it looks as if things are going to get even more interesting from now on, and I don't want to miss out. There's no reason I couldn't be your liaison with the Michaelines, instead of the reverse—if you want me to, that is."

Camber's face beamed with a very un-Alisterlike grin. "Son, I would have asked you months ago, but I wasn't sure you wanted to come. I can understand if you'd rather work for the Order than for me."

Joram glanced down at his boots, a shy smile playing at his lips. "That might have been true, once. But we've come a long way in the past year, you and I. And if you'll have me, I'd be proud to serve you in any capacity I can, whatever the guise and the face you wear—Father."

As he looked up, Camber caught and held his son's gaze, searching the fog-gray eyes with an intensity which he had not allowed for some time. Then he merely reached across and laid a hand on Joram's shoulder and smiled, letting the warmth of his love surge across the bond of blood and mind. No words were necessary.

CHAPTER NINETEEN

*Order ye the buckler and shield, and draw near
to battle. Harness the horses; and get up, ye
horsemen, and stand forth with your helmets;
furbish the spears, and put on the brigandines.*
—Jeremiah 46:3–4

Camber's return to Valoret and the king took less
than two days, and would have been accomplished in
one, but for heavy rain—a hardly unexpected feature
of Gwynedd weather so close to winter. The deluge
turned the road to a river of mud and drowned the
hilltop Samhain bonfires and brought the season's first
frost, all in the space of less than twenty-four hours.
It made the journey far less comfortable than hoped,
but Camber hardly cared. The anticipated challenge
of the coming months was tonic to his eager mind. He
was anxious to see what his star pupil had been up to
during their months of separation. All indications were
that Cinhil had not been idle.

The Bishop of Grecotha entered Valoret near midday on the Feast of All Saints. He was greeted at the
cathedral steps by a far more substantial welcoming
committee than he had expected, given the rain and
his hasty response to Cinhil's summons. Archbishop
Anscom presided, of course, since it was his cathedral
and his bishop; but he had been joined by Vicar General Allyn, a score of cheering Michaeline knights, and
the visiting Archbishop Oriss, who had arrived the day
before in answer to his own summons from the king.

But most important, and overshadowing all the rest, was the presence of a damp but exuberant King Cinhil, who had not been able to curb his eagerness sufficiently to wait for his new chancellor in the dry and warmth of the castle hall. Cinhil ran down the cathedral steps to meet his returned friend, bareheaded in the rain, talking incessantly from the moment Camber swung down from his mud-bespattered mount. Cinhil was fairly bursting with ideas he wanted to try out, projects on which he wanted his chancellor's opinion. Camber could not remember when he had seen Cinhil in better spirits.

While they talked further over dinner that evening, it became more obvious how Cinhil had spent his summer and autumn. In the time between Camber's arrival and the actual convening of Cinhil's high court, Camber spent nearly every waking hour either talking with Cinhil or closeted with a clark to whom Cinhil had already dictated copious notes on what he wanted to accomplish. By the end of the fourth and final day, Camber finally began to feel that he had a grasp of the total picture Cinhil had envisioned. The plans were nothing if not ambitious.

On the morning of the Feast of Saint Illtyd, following a solemn Mass of the Holy Spirit to invoke Divine guidance, King Cinhil convened his high court and formally created Bishop Alister Cullen Chancellor of Gwynedd, himself reading the writ of appointment and investing him with the symbols of his office. Queen Megan laid the broad collar of golden H's over the bishop's purple-cassocked shoulders, never knowing that it was her former guardian who kissed her hand dutifully in thanks.

But it was Cinhil who gave into Camber's consecrated hands the Great Seal of Gwynedd, newly redesigned with the golden Lion of Gwynedd replacing the lion's claws and ermine of the House of Festil. With these, Camber received a personal seal for the Office of the Chancellor, the arms of the See of

Grecotha being impaled with the Cullen family arms and augmented with the badge of Haldane.

Camber bowed and thanked king and queen when the presentations were completed, then took his place at the king's right hand, beside the high-backed throne, as was now his right.

Nor was Camber's the only appointment to be made that day. Humans and Deryni alike received the royal mandate, as Cinhil settled down to the true business of governing his realm.

As recommended by Archbishop Anscom and a host of others, Lord Jebediah of Alcara was named Earl Marshal and was confirmed as field commander of the royal armies, second only to Cinhil himself, should he choose to exercise the royal veto—which was unlikely, since Cinhil knew very little yet of military strategy, though he was fast learning. Jebediah, by reason of his appointment, would sit on the king's council with the life-rank of earl—an almost unprecedented honor for an ecclesiastical knight.

With Jebediah would sit Archbishops Anscom and Oriss and four of the new peers created at the ceremony which had made young Davin MacRorie Earl of Culdi. The four, two earls and two barons, were humans but for Baron Torcuill—to balance the three Deryni among the clerics, Camber suspected, though he did not disapprove. Later, Cinhil planned to create four additional council seats, but the eight would do for now, until responsibilities could be parceled out according to the talents and abilities of the men already chosen. Camber wondered whether the king would be able to maintain the balance of humans and Deryni thus far established. Remembering what Joram had told him about the human lordlings flocking to court in hopes of regaining lost lands and titles, he suspected not.

Following the conclusion of the formal court, Cinhil and his council retired to a private room to dine informally, just the nine of them, with no other attendants. There he made it clear that the appointments he had just made would not be empty honors; royal councillors would be expected to work, or they would be replaced. Before the servants had cleared away the last of the meal, Cinhil had begun to assign tasks to each man, with progress reports to be presented before the council reconvened on the Feast of Saint Andrew, nearly a month away. The opening of Christmas Court should set the wheels in motion for sweeping changes in the Kingdom of Gwynedd.

The ramifications for Camber were far-reaching, for he must mastermind the overall coordination for Cinhil's plans—and those ultimately touched almost all areas, from diplomacy to military preparedness to legal reform to social betterment.

One thing the king would have immediately, and that was a cementing of alliances, or at least treaties, with Gwynedd's neighbors. While there had been no further threats of invasion during the months immediately following Ariella's defeat, this did not mean that there had been no military activity. Meara, to the west, though nominally a vassal state since the death of the last male heir, nearly thirty years before, had always been a periodic threat to Gwynedd's integrity, as were the dual kingdoms of Howicce and Llannedd, which occasionally ceased their internal bickering long enough to make troublesome incursions into the southern parts of Gwynedd. Mooryn, a powerful ally before the ouster of Imre, had been totally silent since Imre's fall, making no hostile moves, but sending no envoys, either. Cinhil had no doubt that all of these would be watching carefully for signs of weakness in Gwynedd's new master.

Of an even more immediate concern was the status of the petty princedom of Kheldour, to the north, formerly the holding of Imre's kinsman, Termod of Rhorau. Word of an anti-Deryni coup in Kheldour had reached Cinhil only a few weeks before, a wobbly cadet branch of the House of Festil having fallen to the forces of Cinhil's former ally, Sighere.

Now Sighere occupied Kheldour as well as Eastmarch, a human lord who was honest enough to recognize that he probably did not have the military or administrative ability to hold alone what he had won. The lake region of Rhendall, nominally part of the Kheldish principality, was rumored still to be a hotbed of Deryni resistance, harboring two Festillic heirs and what remained of the Rhorau strength of arms. Cinhil was aware of Sighere's plight, and saw formal alliance with Eastmarch as a sure way to crush that Festillic remnant before it could reunite with its Torenthi counterparts and pose an even bigger threat. Baron Torcuill and Lord Udaut, the constable, would ride to the earl immediately to suggest a parley.

Nor was Sighere Cinhil's only concern. News of Torenth's King Nimur had been exceedingly sparse following the ransom of his hundred captured knights. The Deryni king had redeemed them at the demanded price without even attempting to haggle Cinhil down —which might mean that he needed men more just now than he needed gold. Since Torenth faced no threat from any other of its neighbors, Nimur's Deryni abilities having been used long ago to cement unbreakable ties with the lands to south and east, might his apparent concern for his knights actually mean that he was contemplating a move of his own against Gwynedd at some time in the future? After all, a Festillic infant lived somewhere in Torenth, kin to nobles ranking high in Nimur's court, those kinsmen quite willing to press the child's claim to Gwynedd's crown when the time was right.

And Nimur? Why, what king would refuse to support his subjects' annexation of new lands to enrich his crown? No one was fool enough to think that those who helped a Festillic king back to his throne would not be handsomely rewarded.

Accordingly, military reorganization must be high on Cinhil's list of priorities. He must have reliable troops to call up on very short notice, especially in the vicinity of the Gwynedd-Torenth borderlands adjoining Eastmarch.

Granted, there was little that could be done during the fierce winter months to train soldiers, since the peasant levies had returned to their farms for the harvest and could not be called again until after the spring planting. But there were many indoor activities which could be pursued in castle yards and halls, so that if Cinhil's fighting men were not better trained by spring, at least they would be better armed.

Accordingly, armorers were set to forge new blades and spearheads and helmets. Apprentices began the tedious task of knitting mail and sewing metal rings and plates to leather hauberks. And everyone with armor of his own must see to its repair during the winter, so that all would be properly outfitted when the spring thaws came.

Fletchers feathered thousands of fine, polished arrows of seasoned wood which would not warp or split when the weather changed. Close-grained lengths of yew and hickory were cut and hung to season in the warmth of smoky rooms, to be planed and shaped and bent into longbows, the staple weapons of the Gwynedd yeomanry.

Tanners, with ample material available following the autumn slaughter of beasts against the winter, prepared caps and cuirasses and shields and other body armor of leather, boiled hard and tough, wove cords and bowstrings of gut; crafted other harness of various sorts for men and beasts of war.

And on another side, Lord Jebediah and the other two earls of the council, Fintan and Tamarron, began to develop a long-range plan for the raising and training of well-mounted and well-armed horsemen, for Jebediah saw cavalry as the reckoning force of the future. While Jebediah and the earls worked out details of recruitment and training programs, Baron Hildred and several lesser lords began making the rounds of all the best-known stud farms in Gwynedd, inspecting stallions and their progeny and acquiring brood mares to begin a new breeding program in the spring—for Jebediah would have his elite troops

mounted on taller and faster horses than had hitherto
been available. A number of R'Kassan stallions had
been captured in the war, for Ariella's Torenthi allies
had been importing the swift desert horses for generations. Jebediah and Hildred saw the blood of these
sires as a powerful factor in improving the Gwyneddan
native breed over the next decade.

Progress continued more slowly on Camber's personal projects, but it did continue. Within a few weeks,
he had managed to arrange a schedule which allowed
ample time with Cinhil and the court, yet still left an
hour or so each evening for his own inner workings.

After very little string-pulling at all, Joram was
appointed as the chancellor's confidential secretary,
with the blessings of Crevan Allyn and the king's
pleased approval, and was installed in quarters immediately adjoining Camber's in one wing of the archbishop's palace. So far as Camber and Joram were
concerned, it was an ideal arrangement.

Evaine and Rhys, too, were actively brought back
into the picture now—though it was through their own
offices and those of the queen, rather than Camber's,
that satisfactory arrangements were eventually made.
Megan had been trying for months to persuade Evaine
to accept a post as lady-in-waiting; and though there
were several other Healers at court, many of them
far older and with much more impressive credentials,
the queen preferred Rhys above all others.

At length, when Evaine finally acquiesced, the court
was treated to nearly a week of high spirits on the
part of the usually mouselike little queen. Even Cinhil
noticed the difference, and thanked Evaine for coming to Megan's aid. Soon, Evaine and Rhys had been
assigned semi-permanent quarters in the royal keep,
where both of them could be near Megan's solar and
the royal nursery. Evaine, when she was not required
to attend the queen, began work on translating the
vital documents which Camber had brought from
Grecotha.

Contrary to what Joram had feared, Evaine did *not*

appeal Camber's prohibition against lone experimentation with the material she was translating. It was evident from the first that the information was too powerful to be trifled with. Camber said little, but he thought about it a great deal; and often he and Joram and Rhys and Evaine would sit and talk until the wee hours of the morning, pushing aside goblets and the remains of spare meals to manipulate unactivated ward cubes into different patterns on the table as they tried to make sense of what Evaine told them.

And so the Feast of Christmas came and went, and Twelfth Night, too; and Camber and his family thought less and less about their old lives, caught up as they were in the wonder of their own explorations and the intricacies of beginning to forge a new social order.

Evaine maintained correspondence with Elinor in Caerrorie, who kept her informed of the boys' health and mentioned in passing that the winter weather seemed to have dampened the enthusiasm of the many pilgrims who had used to frequent Camber's tomb. Only a few folk came there now, though they still left prayers and devotions. But Caerrorie seemed far from Valoret. And as winter deepened, those in Valoret thought less and less about the now-empty tomb and all it represented.

The first intimation that the matter had not died came in early February, but a few days before Camber was to make a month-long visitation to Grecotha. He would be there until the Feast of Saint Piran—long enough to inspect the work done by his staff in his absence, to direct further activities for the spring and early summer, and to perform those sacerdotal offices which could not be handled by other than a bishop. By the Ides of March, he must be back. The king planned to convene his Spring Court early, for Sighere of Eastmarch had sent word of his intention to parley in person. For that, the king would have his chancellor at his side, bishop or no.

But on this chill February morning, the Bishop of

Grecotha was still ensconced in his apartments in the archbishop's palace—quarters somewhat more sumptuous than those he had occupied during his first sojourn, when he had been a mere vicar general. He was seated comfortably before a large but inefficient fireplace, with his head leaned against the chairback and his eyes closed and a towel of nubby gray linen draped close around his shoulders. Guaire had just finished lathering his face and was carefully drawing a razor across the stubble of the night's beard—a duty he had taken on himself ever since Camber's consecration.

Joram stood beside the hearth and read aloud from the bishop's schedule for the day, one blue-clad arm laid casually along the warm stone of the mantelpiece. His fur-lined winter cloak was pushed back off his shoulders, but he had not removed it even at that proximity to supposed heat, for he was well aware of the inefficiency of his father's fireplace at farther than an armspan. He had no intention of letting his backside freeze.

"So, after Mass and breakfast with Anscom, you have a meeting with His Highness and Lord Jebediah for the remainder of the morning," Joram explained. "I've transcribed our notes from yesterday, and Guaire drew up the revised map sections, so it should be only a matter of review—unless they want to start on something new, of course."

Camber grunted appreciatively, but did not move, out of deference to Guaire's razor.

"This afternoon, the Court is invited to go stag hunting with Baron Murdoch and his party," Joram continued smoothly. "It seems that Murdoch spotted a white stag in the forest yesterday, and insists on running it down. As coincidence would have it, his wife and sons just brought him five new couples of coursing hounds to show off."

Joram's last statement had been delivered in precisely the same noncommittal tone as the rest, but something nonetheless made Camber open one eye to glance at his son. As he had suspected, Joram's face wore a look of undisguised contempt.

Joram had never liked Murdoch. Nor had Camber, for that matter. Murdoch of Carthane was the scion of one of those old human families which had once ruled in Gwynedd, and whose lands had been confiscated when the first Festil seized the throne of Gwynedd almost a century before. In those intervening years and generations, Murdoch's ancestors had tried every underhanded scheme they could devise to regain influence with their Deryni masters.

Now that a new administration was in power, Murdoch was following in the family tradition. He had come to Cinhil's court almost three months before to petition for the return of his family's lands—which Cinhil had granted, though he had not yet given back the title of earl which went with those lands. In Cinhil's mind, Murdoch was earnest, loyal, and seemed to be sympathetic to Cinhil's personal situation. At one time, he had almost entered the same religious order as Cinhil—or so Murdoch said.

"Baron Murdoch, eh?" Camber murmured drolly. "Yes, he and his do seem to be much in evidence of late, don't they?"

"I think it no secret that Murdoch works toward a valuable and undeserved appointment at court," Joram replied, arching one finely defined eyebrow. "He may get it, too. I fear our king is sometimes too easily moved by a tale of past injustice and a pious mien."

With a snort of exasperation for court toadies in general and Baron Murdoch in particular, Camber shifted in his chair and started to make a sharp retort, causing Guaire to gasp and draw his razor hand away quickly. With a shrug of apology, Camber laid his head back again and sighed, silent as Guaire resumed his task. He was contemplating the self-seeking Baron Murdoch, and mentally reviewing how he might possibly broach the subject with Cinhil, when he became aware that Guaire seemed unusually withdrawn this morning, a trace of unaccustomed brusqueness clipping his movements as he laid aside his razor and wiped the last traces of soap from his master's face.

Camber wriggled into a more upright sitting position as Guaire began combing his hair, trying to observe Guaire unobtrusively out of the corner of his vision and wondering whether the apparent nervousness was just his imagination. His expression must have betrayed some of his curiosity just then, for Guaire suddenly glanced away self-consciously and began tugging at the thick, iron-gray hair even more awkwardly. When he had finished, far more perfunctorily than usual, he whisked the towel from Camber's shoulders and used it to dust off imaginary specks of lint and hairs from the violet cassock as his master stood. He did not seem to want to meet Camber's eyes.

"Is anything wrong, Guaire? You seem distracted this morning."

Guaire turned away momentarily to pick up Camber's skullcap of violet silk. His face was impassive as he reached up to set it in place on the wiry gray hair.

"No, Your Grace. There's nothing wrong. Should there be?"

"I don't know."

Thoughtfully, Camber turned to slip his arms into a dull, wine-colored over-robe lined with fur, which Joram held ready for him. As he turned back to Guaire, to receive his cross and chain of gold, he caught Guaire's eyes again—just a flash of an apprehensive, almost haunted look. He tried to put on a more benign expression as he bowed his head to receive the chain around his neck.

Guaire swallowed and looked down at his feet as Camber straightened.

"Your Grace, there *is* something . . ." he began tentatively.

"I thought there might be," Camber said kindly, sitting down again and inviting Guaire to a seat on a stool to the right of his chair. Beyond Guaire, Joram had returned to the writing desk and was unobtrusively rearranging the scrolls, but Camber sensed that he was now watching Guaire as well. He wondered whether Joram had picked up the same air of uneasiness.

"All right," Camber said gently, trying to put Guaire at ease. "Do you want to tell me about it?"

"I—yes, Your Grace." Guaire swallowed hard, drymouthed, and his gaze, usually straightforward and guileless, kept shifting to points around the room and on Camber's person—anywhere except the pale, seaice eyes—as he searched for words.

Patiently, Camber settled back in his chair to wait, twining his fingers before him in an Alister gesture so familiar by now that it seemed second nature.

Guaire took a deep breath and looked up again, finally managing to meet Camber's eyes.

"Your Grace, I—I seek a boon," he murmured, starting to draw confidence now that the first words were out. "It—it is not one which, strictly speaking, you yourself can really give." He paused to draw a reinforcing breath. "But I dare hope that you will choose to encourage its giving. Your opinion carries great weight with His Grace the Archbishop."

"His Grace best knows his own mind," Camber said carefully, wondering what Guaire was driving at, "though it is true that he has been known to heed my counsel on occasion. I must remind you, however, that if you have already asked His Grace this boon and been refused, there is doubtless little I can or should do."

"Oh, no, Your Grace. I have not asked him yet. I —in truth, I hesitate to approach him. That is why I came to you. If he should scoff—"

"Scoff? Why should he scoff at a request made in sincerity?" Camber asked. "Is it a matter of faith? If it is, I can tell you that he is aware of your spiritual growth. I have kept him apprised of your progress."

Guaire lowered his eyes. "Your Grace has not the whole of it," he murmured. "I fear my faith has grown in ways you have not foreseen, nor would approve. I am near to taking holy orders, Your Grace."

"And you think I'd not approve of that?" Camber shook his head. "Guaire, perhaps you have misread my earlier words. I counseled only that you not rush rashly into vows which would forever change your life. If you have found your way, and are happy in it, then I am happy, too."

"Do you truly mean that?"

"Of course. Tell me about your new-found vocation. What order have you chosen?"

"It—is a newly forming order, Your Grace." He glanced up fearfully. "And I beg you not to press me now for names and places, for I have already sworn vows of discretion. Promise you will not."

"I promise," Camber agreed. "But tell me what you can."

Guaire took a deep breath. "We—we plan to devote ourselves to a new saint, Your Grace. We will seek permission to establish his first shrine in the cathedral here in Valoret. We plan to petition the Council of Bishops for his immediate canonization. There is ample evidence of his miracles."

"A new saint?" Camber arched a bushy eyebrow, hiding a shiver of foreboding which darted across his mind. "There are channels through which one goes, Guaire. Of which saint are you speaking? I was not aware of any great upsurge of miracles of late."

Guaire bowed his head, tongue-tied now that the moment had come to reveal his plans.

"Come, now. Don't be shy," Camber insisted. "Who is it?"

"It—it is Lord Camber, Your Grace."

CHAPTER TWENTY

And the servant of the Lord must not strive;
but be gentle unto all men, apt to teach, patient,
in meekness instructing those that oppose themselves.
—II Timothy 2:24–25

Camber's head shot up in horror at the name. At the same instant, behind Guaire, he saw Joram's involuntary start.

God! Had he heard aright? Camber? Guaire *could* not have meant *him, Camber!*

"Your Grace cannot be that surprised," Guaire continued, mistaking Camber's horror for startled ignorance. "Surely you have heard how his cult flourishes at Caerrorie. The numbers are somewhat less since the onset of winter, but daily, since his death, scores of pilgrims have flocked to his tomb to seek his intercession and blessing. We would establish his first shrine there, except that his family opposes any mention of his sainthood. I beg your pardon, Father Joram."

He chanced a look at Joram, who was standing pale and mute, hands supported against the writing desk behind him, then returned his attention to Camber.

"But even they cannot deny the miracles, Your Grace," Guaire concluded, in a whisper which somehow managed to sound defiant.

Camber swallowed, fearing to ask further, yet knowing that he must. He did not dare look again at

Joram, for fear of what even Alister's face might betray.

"Did you say—miracles?"

Guaire nodded gravely. "Do you not remember how I came to you the night of his funeral, after you found me mourning by his coffin and brought me to Brother Johannes? I told you of my dream—how *he* appeared and asked that I carry on his work."

An icy chill rippled down Camber's spine at the emphasized *he,* and he wiped a hand across his face in consternation, trying to remember exactly what Guaire had told him that night. In the past months of hard work, he had almost managed to forget the incident. He certainly had believed Guaire to have forgotten it, for the young man had never mentioned it again after that night.

What was he going to do? Whatever had he been thinking, to couch his comfort in a form which could be so misinterpreted?

"Do you not remember, Your Grace?"

Guaire's hesitant voice broke through his numbed thinking, and Camber looked back at the earnest young face, schooling his own features to calm. The temptation was great to reach out and read Guaire's mind right now—to probe relentlessly for the names, the details of all involved in what had just become a waking nightmare—at least to Truth-Read him.

And yet, the last would do no good, for Guaire *was* telling the truth—at least, the truth as he perceived it. And the first temptation was equally unacceptable, since Camber—or Alister Cullen—had given his word that he would not pry. Besides, all moral and aesthetic squeamishness aside, if he did break his promise and tamper with Guaire's mind to learn what he wanted, there was a distinct chance that the very tampering could arouse suspicions he would rather not raise about Alister Cullen, if not Camber himself.

He could not afford that; and the possibility was very real. If there were other Deryni involved in Guaire's formative religious movement—and here, his

meeting with the redoubtable Queron Kinevan became greatly suspect—then Camber had to assume
that all of them, human and Deryni alike, were probably in periodic close communion of minds. Guaire,
like any other human working closely with Deryni—
especially a master like Queron—would have grown
more sensitive to Deryni contacts in general. And
while an adept like Camber might delve deep enough
to hide the signs of his probing from Guaire's human
awareness, he could not be sure of deceiving another
Deryni.

But what *could* he do? Guaire was here and now.
If Camber dared not use his Deryni abilities to change
Guaire's mind, he wondered whether there was, perhaps, some *logical* way to convince Guaire that his
miracle had been no miracle at all, but only the dream
Camber now wished it had been. Success on that front
would not solve the problem, would not end the burgeoning order devoting itself to "Saint Camber," but
it might at least provide an opening wedge.

And Guaire *might* let fall some additional clues
about his Order's plans. Anscom could be alerted; and
he, who knew Camber to be no martyred saint, would
stall and delay any official recognition of a Camber
cult for as long as he could—perhaps indefinitely.

Determined to do just that, Camber gathered the
shreds of his logic around him and looked at Guaire
again, at the same time sending Joram a stern admonition not to interfere, to let him handle this.

Camber coughed self-consciously. "Aye, I remember, son," he finally managed to murmur. "But surely
you don't really believe that Camber appeared to you
that night? You said yourself that it was a dream."

Guaire looked past him, eyes unfocused on the
flickering fire as he retreated to some inner recall.

"I remember it as being dreamlike," he said slowly,
"and yet, there was that about it which was no dream.
Just before he appeared, I remember waking and being very aware of the room around me: of Brother
Johannes snoring in his chair—and that, in itself, was

strange—of the warmth of the fire, the wavering light, the smells and textures of the bedclothes around me. His coming was no less real than those."

"Dreams can be very vivid," Camber said tentatively.

"Aye, but I do not think this was a dream," Guaire insisted, turning his gaze back on Camber with its full intensity. "I think that he was there, in some mystical way I can't explain. I think he came back from beyond. I think he continues to guide and inspire us, to the good and aid of all mankind. Do you not agree that these are the kinds of things he would have done, had not the mad Ariella slain him? To urge us to carry on the work he started?"

Camber squirmed uncomfortably in his chair. "These are the kinds of things he always espoused," he had to agree. "But he was no saint, Guaire. He was a man, like other men. He had strengths and weaknesses, and the same kinds of temptations which assail us all. Being Deryni, perhaps his temptations were even greater than we dreamed. I do not think he was a saint, Guaire."

"No? But you admired him."

"Yes."

"You admired him so much that you took his name in religion as your own, that his memory might live on."

"That is true," Camber conceded, wishing desperately that he had done no such thing. "But that hardly makes the man a saint."

Guaire bowed his head. "I know it is not always easy to see these things, Your Grace—especially when one has been so close to a man, as you were to him." He looked up, a beatific smile on his lips. "But you'll see. God willing, you and many others—even his children—will come to know his greatness as we have. That is one reason we wish to build his shrine in the cathedral, where his body lay before its last journey, so that all may pay him reverence. One day, his tomb at Caerrorie will be a shrine as well. To some, it is already. I only wish that Father Joram would permit us freer access, even if he does not yet believe."

He turned to gauge his effect on Joram, but the young priest had half turned away, face buried in his hands as he tried to get his emotions under control. With a shrug, Guaire stood and smiled again at his master, compassion glowing in his eyes.

"Camber touches him," he said softly, "and, in time, will touch all men. Forgive me for pressing the issue, Your Grace, I see now that my request was premature. I'll not speak to His Grace the archbishop, and you need not petition him on my behalf. God will find a way, when it is time."

"Guaire—"

"Yes, Your Grace?"

Camber stood, trying to decide how he was going to phrase this. He dared not actually forbid Guaire to pursue his apparent goal, for Guaire was not bound to him by any formal vows of obedience; nor did Camber think such would have held him, if they had been sworn.

Guaire must have sensed the drift of Camber's hesitation, for his next words and actions took the matter forever out of Camber's control. Dropping to one knee, he took Camber's hand and dutifully kissed his ring. His head remained bowed, but his voice was steady, leaving no doubt of his resolve.

"Forgive me, Your Grace, but I see that I've put you in a difficult position. I regret that. As you know, it had been my intention to continue serving you as Camber bade me, but I see now that I can better serve him in other ways." He looked up, meeting Camber's eyes squarely.

"I must leave your service now, Your Grace. I hope you will not take it amiss, but each of us must follow his own conscience, and my goal is clear now. You have shown me where my duty lies."

"Guaire, it isn't necessary to leave," Camber began, knowing that if Guaire did leave, it would be even more difficult to follow the progress of the incipient

Camber cult. "I will not interfere with your work. If you wish to take vows with this new Order—what did you call it?"

"I did not, Your Grace, but it will be called the Servants of Saint Camber," Guaire said calmly.

"The—Servants of Saint Camber," Camber repeated, controlling a tendency of his voice to crack with the words. "If—if you wish to do that, I shall not stand in your way. Men of many orders can work together for me. While I may not agree with your aims, I respect your right to try to do what you think you must. I should hate to think that I have driven you away by my inflexibility."

"You have not driven me away, Your Grace," Guaire said, getting to his feet and glancing at Joram again. "Nor has Father Joram. But it's time I went. There are things which must be done, which I can help, God willing it be so. My brothers and sisters have the right to expect my undivided attention. 'Tis time I made a full-time commitment to Camber's cause."

"Very well, then. If you must, you must," Camber replied. "But think about what you are doing, and why. You could be mistaken, you know."

"I do not think so, Your Grace. May I have your leave to go now? I'll gather my belongings and be away by noon."

"You have it, son, and my prayers that God will guide you in the right paths," Camber whispered.

Guaire bowed and turned to go toward the door. As his hands worked the latch, Camber made one last, desperate appeal.

"Guaire—"

"Your Grace?" Guaire paused in the doorway to look at his bishop a final time.

"Guaire, I don't know who your friends are in this venture, but please pass this on to them for me. I think you're wrong. I think you're deluding yourselves, building hopes on idle wishes. Your intentions to follow in Camber's tasks are noble, and I think he would have been pleased; but do not make of him something he was not."

"Good-bye, Your Grace," Guaire whispered, and turned away to disappear behind the closing door.

With so inauspicious a beginning, the rest of the morning could hardly have been expected to go smoothly; nor did it. No sooner had Guaire had time to get out of earshot than Joram erupted in appalled horror.

What had Camber been thinking, to let Guaire leave? The man must be brought back, his mind probed to discover the exact threat of this new order calling itself the Servants of Saint Camber. Servants of Saint Camber, indeed! It was blasphemy for such an order even to be contemplated. Guaire had witnessed no miracle!

But Camber remained calm, even in his own dismay. Forming a close but emphatic link with his son, he insisted that Joram review all the same alternatives which he himself had considered while he talked with Guaire, making him see precisely why they could not afford to interfere overmuch.

Camber's son and his very good friend must have supremely logical reasons for opposing Camber's canonization—though, obviously, those could not be the real ones—but even ordinary methods of resistance must be employed prudently. On no account must Camber's own part reach the point where Alister Cullen came into question. The chancellor-bishop was getting on far too well with the king just now to risk any hint of scandal.

Joram had to concede the wisdom of that observation. Even he could not fault the progress made by Cinhil during the past six months, much of it at his father's urging. The king's entire attitude toward the business of governing seemed to have improved greatly.

But how would Cinhil react when he learned of the movement to canonize Camber? Suppose the Servants somehow found out about *Cinhil's* version of a miracle? If they forced the matter to a formal inquiry, even the king would not be able to deny under oath what he had seen. The fact that he must be regarded as a reluctant witness regarding Camber's alleged sainthood would only tend to support the Servants' allegations.

For that matter, what of Dualta, who was far more ripe for pumping about a Camberian miracle than Cinhil? Joram was willing to bet that his father did not even know where Dualta was!

On that point, it was Camber's turn to concede. He did *not* know where Dualta was—though he had a vague impression that the young knight might have been sent along on Baron Hildred's horse-finding expedition, since he was known to have a good eye for horseflesh. Did Joram have some reason for suspecting that Dualta had talked?

Not exactly. But Dualta had spoken with Joram several times in the month immediately after the incident, and Joram knew he had not forgotten it. After those initial discussions, in which Joram tried to discourage Dualta's awed recall, the knight had come no more to Joram.

What contacts might Dualta have made in the intervening time? Suppose he, like Guaire, had met the increasingly evident Dom Queron and confessed all? By now, the story of how "Saint Camber" had healed the Bishop of Grecotha could already be part and parcel of a budding Camberian hagiography. If so, then all who were present that night could be implicated.

Reluctantly, Camber had to admit the possibility, though he did not think it likely. Had Guaire known anything of the Cinhil witnessing, he would surely have confronted the man said to be the object of the miracle. The fact that he had not, argued well for the probability that he and the Servants did not know. Of course, lack of that information would not necessarily stop the Servants of Camber. Saints had been proclaimed before on far flimsier evidence than martyrdom at the hands of an evil sorceress and supposed appearance in a miraculous-seeming dream.

The prospect of sainthood did not please Camber, and the living of a partial lie disturbed him. Still, if he must bear this cross in order to see Cinhil's education and guidance through to their proper ends, then he would do it. He did not have to like it, and did not; but, like many others, he would learn to live with it, if he must.

Joram found it difficult to understand how his father, now a priest and bishop, could dismiss deliberate religious hypocrisy. But he did agree to abide by Camber's direction and to temper his own vigorous opposition with prudence, for the greater good.

However, they agreed that further discussion between the two of them would serve no useful purpose just then. Accordingly, when they had composed themselves sufficiently to venture outside Camber's apartments, they made their way to the archbishop's chapel without delay. Anscom was waiting impatiently, so the two Deryni, father and son, did not attempt to make explanations before Mass. Vesting quickly, each used the order and serenity of the liturgy to restore his own inner calm, emerging renewed and reassured.

When all had been properly concluded, and they were seated in the archbishop's solar breaking their fast, they told Anscom everything that had happened, sharing their assorted mental impressions as well as the verbal retelling.

Anscom, who had received all without interruption after his initial shock, shook his head after sipping from a cup of goat's milk.

"Camber, you continue to be a thorn in my side, don't you? Oh, I know it isn't really your fault. You've done what you had to do. But the problem exists, nonetheless."

He made a face at the milk, for he drank it only out of duty to a sensitive stomach, which was churning even more than usual at the morning's news. Camber did not reply.

"However," the archbishop continued, "you can rest assured that no shrine to Saint Camber will be built in my cathedral while *I'm* archbishop." He set down his empty cup with a gesture of finality. "As for canonization—well, there's not much any of us can do to stop a popular folk movement, I suppose, but I *will* promise to prevent any formal petition from reaching the Council of Bishops."

"Thank you, Anscom," Camber said quietly. "I could not ask for more."

Anscom shrugged. "I wish it *were* more. Frankly, I don't see how you can be so calm about it all. I'm sure I should be a bundle of nerves if someone were trying to make a saint of *me*."

Camber gave a wan smile as he buttered a bit of fine white bread. "You've seen the rationalizations I've had to make, to achieve this state of outward calm," he said, popping the bread into his mouth. "But what else can I do?" He chewed and swallowed. "Revelation of the truth would completely undermine the progress we've made in these past few months. Cinhil is really beginning to think like a king, at last. We haven't seen his likes for at least a century, so far as potential is concerned. You should see the plans for military reorganization that he and Jeb and I drew up yesterday. They're brilliant—and most of the input is from Cinhil, not Jeb or me."

He nodded thanks as Joram refilled his cup with fragrant brown ale, pausing to drain it by half before continuing.

"And that's not all. We've only made preliminary notes so far, but some of his ideas for legal reform are truly revolutionary. He's taken the basic texts that we made him read while he was in the haven, and he's used them as a jumping-off point to devise plans I've never even thought of. Oh, some of them are too theoretical to work, but the point is that he's learning. He's starting to think independently, to synthesize new ideas from what we gave him. Sometimes even I have trouble keeping up with him, Anscom."

Anscom, who had been eating a slab of cheese with apple slices, wiped his fingers and then his knife on a damask napkin and began cleaning his nails with the tip of the blade. His eyes held a twinkle of amusement.

"I'm not arguing with you on that point. I know, from *my* meetings with him, the kinds of things he's proposing." He turned his gaze on Joram. "But, what about you, Joram? And Evaine and Rhys? Can the three of you cope with your father becoming a saint, if that's the price we must pay for our good King Cinhil?"

Joram put down the piece of bread he had been methodically turning into dough pellets and dusted his hands over his plate.

"There must be *something* we can do to stop it, Your Grace."

"I agree that there ought to be. Unfortunately, your father's life and untimely 'death' are precisely the stuff of which martyrologies are made. There's little we can do to stop the talk."

"But the hypocrisy of it all!"

"I know." Anscom sighed. "But sometimes one can't afford to be overfastidious. Moral scruples aside, can you handle the rest? For example, what if Guaire and his friends should ask Lady Elinor for permission to enshrine the tomb at Caerrorie?"

"Oh, God, she wouldn't let them, would she?"

"I don't know. I'm asking you. She'll not have Evaine and Rhys to rely upon in the future, you know. If Evaine's appointment as a lady-in-waiting weren't enough to keep them at court, then Rhys's confirmation as the queen's physician certainly will be. Megan is pregnant again, you know."

Camber lowered the cup he had been raising to his lips and looked at Anscom in surprise. "So soon? Does Cinhil know yet?"

Anscom shook his head. "Rhys only confirmed it a few days ago. It will be another boy, if she carries it to term. Needless to say, Rhys's services will be constantly on call until she's safely delivered at the end of the summer. However, Joram still hasn't answered my original question. What will Elinor say if the Servants of Saint Camber ask her permission to enshrine the tomb?"

"Without coaching, she might agree," Joram said gloomily. "She was very fond of—Camber." He looked up at his father, at Anscom, back at Camber again.

"Father, couldn't we tell her the truth? She'll have to know eventually, if you still plan to include the boys."

"Eventually, yes; but not yet. Rhys tells me that she's considering remarriage, and I'm afraid her prospective bridegroom can be a bit of a hothead. If she has to cope with my sainthood, I'd rather she knows nothing she has to be afraid of revealing."

"Cousin Jamie?" Joram asked.

Camber nodded. "Anscom, we're talking about young James Drummond. You may remember him from the haven. When Cathan was courting Elinor, James was also a suitor. Now that Cathan is gone . . ." He shrugged. "At any rate, I'll be very surprised if Elinor doesn't say yes. The boys need a father, and Elinor needs a husband. The combined resources of Culdi and the Drummond lands will make quite a tidy holding."

"But you referred to him as a hothead," Anscom said. "Do you mean that, if he knew the truth about you, he might let it slip?"

"Let's just say that I'd rather not give him that temptation just now," Camber replied. "I don't believe in husbands and wives not being able to share totally, if they want to—which means that both of them will have to learn to cope with the comings and goings at Caerrorie like the rest of us. Joram, do you think they can do it?"

"I suppose," Joram answered doubtfully. "It certainly isn't going to be easy, though."

"Nothing is ever easy," Anscom muttered under his breath, "especially where Camber MacRorie is concerned. Camber, it's a good thing that I know you as well as I do."

But the immediate future, at least, was easy. Guaire was gone by the time Camber returned to his quarters, and Joram's discreet inquiries over the next few days revealed only that Guaire had left Valoret alone and headed southeast. Now they would simply have to wait for Guaire's next move.

And so, after warning Evaine and Rhys of what had happened, Camber left for his scheduled visit to Grecotha, resolved not to worry further where worry would do no good.

He found his neglected see in good hands, and was once more nagged by the suspicion that Willowen of Treshire could get along very well without him. Though the winter had been wet and cold, the see's holdings had prospered. A bountiful if late harvest and Willowen's frugal management had left the diocesan granaries still more than half full. Sale of a portion of the excess for seed and flour would net a tidy profit for the recovering cathedral treasury. Lambing and calfing were also at a record high.

Final refurbishing of the episcopal residence had been completed only the month before, balky drains and all. Several leaks in the cathedral roof had been repaired, using lead salvaged from a collapsed and abandoned chapel in the chapter complex. Inside, the choir stalls had been refinished and repaired, and all the statues of the sanctuary and side chapels cleaned and regilded. The great nave glistened when the bishop entered to celebrate his first Mass upon his return.

But of greatest interest to Camber, personally, was the progress made on the cathedral archives. Willowen had embarked upon a library exchange program with the Varnarite rector who was his counterpart. All through the cold, dark winter, ten scribes each from the Varnarites and the cathedral chapter spent most of their waking hours in their opposites' library, piecing together chronologies and copying missing portions of important records and chronicles of interest to both groups. Their diligence did much to fill in some of the gaps in the history surrounding the original schism.

Willowen even found a chest full of manuscripts penned in the ancient script which only his bishop could readily read. These he saved for Camber, who took them into his private quarters to begin translating in his spare time.

Camber returned to Valoret on schedule, well pleased with the state of his episcopal affairs, only to find the gathering court in an uproar over the impending arrival of Earl Sighere, who all now knew had subdued the principality of Kheldour. Barons Torcuill and Udaut had brought Sighere's acceptance of a springtime visit months before; but as the time grew near, and no new word came directly from the powerful earl, reports of his actions and intentions became more varied and more speculative.

Sighere marched toward Valoret with an army at his back—no, he came in peace. No, Sighere brought only an escort with him, but his army approached by another route for a surprise attack, swelled to double its previous size by newly hired Kheldish and Torenthi mercenaries.

Camber counseled a postponement of judgment, but some there were who could not accept that. Paranoia was a very popular sport at court that spring—which was perhaps understandable, given Gwynedd's past year.

But when Sighere did appear before the gates of Valoret, bright on the morning of the Ides of March, as he had promised, he rode with only a modest escort of fifty knights. Still, their initial impression could have been construed by even the level-headed as war-like. Sighere's fifty men were heavily armed, as was their leader; even their horses were caparisoned in leather battle bardings and steel chamfrons. Earl Sighere himself did not improve upon that ominous image, riding silent and distant behind a closed war helm, the coronet of his rank nearly obscured by a veritable explosion of sable ostrich plumes. Nor were the coupled dragon heads on his scarlet shield reassuring.

But an unarmed herald bore Sighere's personal banner at his left side, while his war banner followed behind him; and that should have told them something. Also, Sighere readily consented to leave all but ten of his knights outside the city gates, if those remaining ten might retain their arms to provide suitable escort before the king.

Cinhil agreed, with apparently more confidence in Sighere's good will than most of his retainers felt, and called his court together to receive the earl. For this occasion, even Megan was at his side, though looking a little pale in the early stages of her pregnancy.

Jebediah stood in the privileged position of earl marshal, on the top step of the dais and on the king's right side, minus his helmet but otherwise in full Michaeline battle attire, one gloved hand resting competently on his sword hilt. Udaut, the constable, who had gone to treat with Sighere months before and still was unsure just what decision the earl had reached, waited midway between Jebediah and the king, likewise mailed and armed, Gwynedd's great sword at rest beneath his gauntleted hands.

Camber, wearing the full ecclesiastical vestments in which he had been consecrated bishop, with the addition of his collar of office, stood directly to Cinhil's right, clerical as well as secular advisor for the occasion, since Archbishop Anscom was abed with a digestive upset—an event which was occurring with disturbing regularity of late.

Cinhil himself sat in a long velvet robe of Haldane crimson, his golden lion bright upon his breast. Miniver showed at sleeves and neck, repeating the snow-white of the belt girding his waist. On his head was the state crown of Gwynedd, jewel-winking gold with crosses and leaves intertwined, more formal than was his usual wont, in marked contrast to the silvered sable of his hair and beard. The ruby Eye of Rom was barely visible among the strands of collar-length hair over his right ear whenever he turned his head and the great jewel caught the light of torch and candle.

Trumpets sounded a fanfare, brief but honorable, the entry doors swung apart at the opposite end of the hall, and all eyes turned in that direction.

First to enter was a company of Cinhil's own knights, lightly armed, but patently prepared to quell any disturbance which might be engendered by the men they escorted. Following them walked Sighere's knights, two by two, battle-armed and vaguely menacing in the mystery of their intentions.

Eight of the knights marched before their master, helm-shadowed eyes watchful, wary, as they approached the dais and bowed, brief inclinations of proud heads, giving no more obeisance than strictest courtesy required. As Sighere came between their ranks, herald on his left, a captain on his right, and his war banner at his back, his knights split to either side and bowed again with well-trained precision, the depth of their bows leaving no doubt as to just whom these men owed their allegiance.

Sighere, when he reached the dais steps, stopped and removed his helm with a sparseness of motion appropriate to the iron-willed man who had recently subdued most of proud Kheldour. He wore a mail coif beneath the helm; but when he handed that helm to his captain, he did not uncover to the king. Dark eyes gazed out impassively from their frame of metal links, the mind behind them shrewdly measuring the man who wore the crown of Gwynedd.

Sighere's herald footed his master's standard on the lowest step of the dais and bowed with precise formality.

"Sighere, Earl of Eastmarch and Warlord of Kheldour, brings greetings to His Royal Highness Cinhil Donal Ifor Haldane, King of Gwynedd and Lord of Meara, Mooryn, and the Purple March," the herald recited.

Sighere bowed, a stiff inclination of his upper body, but there was something in the set of his mouth, almost hidden behind a bristling red beard, which Camber could read as almost a smile, tempering the solemnity of the occasion to a game which Sighere played for the benefit of those watching, lest what was to come seem far too easy. Abruptly, Camber was certain that Sighere meant to offer a full alliance, though the exact terms still remained to be disclosed. He glanced at Cinhil to ascertain whether the king had caught Sighere's intentions, but Cinhil's nod of acknowledgment to Sighere's greeting betrayed nothing of his inner state.

"Your Royal Highness," the herald continued, "my master bids me say the following: The King's Most Excellent Grace will no doubt recall how our two hosts of Gwynedd and Eastmarch did fight side by side in war last year, and did prevail against a common enemy. After that great battle, we two did go our separate ways, to rebuild our war-torn lands and stabilize a new order, free from the Festillic tyrant's heel.

"But, while the King's Grace built his peace in Gwynedd, I and mine were forced to battle other enemies which stood to threaten Eastmarch in the north. This we did. Kheldour now lies beneath the guard of my son Ewan and an Eastmarch army, secure for now, except for its capital of Rhorau, but uneasy for want of ample troops. If assault should come from either Torenth or rebellious Rhendall, whose mountains hide many things, we are undone; and not only our Kheldish holdings, but Eastmarch as well—and with us, your border buffer which we maintained in our common struggle last year.

"I, Sighere of Eastmarch, therefore propose the following alliance—not as full equals, for you are ruler of a mighty kingdom and I, though owing fealty to no other suzerain, am yet a petty prince beside Your

Grace's might—yet, I would become Your Grace's chiefest vassal.

"If Your Grace will consent to accept my sword in liege fealty, to take conquered Kheldour as part of Gwynedd, to protect and defend it from the likes of those who have lately ruled, then I, Sighere, will be your man of life and limb, serving you in all things as are within my power. In return, I ask only that Your Grace grant unto me, and all the heirs of my body whatsoever, such titles and lands as Your Grace may deem fitting for one who has thus enlarged your kingdom. As Your Grace's viceroy in Kheldour, I would rule in Your Grace's name, governing Kheldour's people in justice, to the greater good of all your people of Gwynedd."

As the herald finished speaking, Sighere drew his sword and kissed its blade, then knelt and laid it on the top step of the dais before him, the hilt toward Cinhil's throne. He bowed his head, still kneeling, as Cinhil leaned to consult with his chancellor, also beckoning Jebediah to approach. Sighere's knights had also knelt as their overlord did, and Cinhil glanced at all of them thoughtfully.

"He blusters, as was always his wont, but what think you from a military point of view, Jeb?" he whispered, as the marshal crouched beside the throne.

Jebediah gave a slight nod. "Acceptance will mean a summer campaign, at least in Rhendall, and there remain many details to be worked out, but the offer is a princely one, Sire. With Sighere's strength added to our own, we can hold what he has won and greatly reinforce our eastern front. A lesser campaign of this sort would also give us an opportunity to test our new military organization before we must answer a more serious threat in the future."

"My thoughts precisely," Cinhil murmured. "Alister?"

Camber also nodded. "The offer *is* princely, Sire. And I have heard naught but good of Sighere, despite his blustering façade. If he gives his word, then he is your man, come what may. I think you could find far worse viceroys than Sighere of Eastmarch, for any of your lands."

With a nod, Cinhil sat straight in his chair, giving Jebediah time to get to his feet, then stood and let his gaze brush Sighere's kneeling men, settle on the earl himself, who now gazed up stolidly from his place at the foot of the dais. The sword of promise lay bright on the dais between them.

"My Lord Sighere," Cinhil said, in a voice which carried to the farthest reaches of the hall, "we are greatly moved by this noble offer, and are minded to accept your allegiance under the general terms specified. But take up your sword, I pray you. No oaths are yet required, and certainly no surrenders. We must speak further on the details of what you propose."

Sighere had started to retrieve his sword at Cinhil's bidding, but then he hesitated and stood instead.

"Your Highness." His voice was a pleasing tenor, unexpected in so large and robust-looking a man. "I have no wish to defy you so early in our relationship . . . " There was a rustle of discontent among Cinhil's knights. "But, I pray you, let me bind myself in oath."

The knights relaxed, with a few audible sighs.

"I concede that further negotiations will be necessary," Sighere continued, "but in the meantime, your assistance in Kheldour is much needed. I would not have formalities lose either of us what we desire. The word of Cinhil Haldane is sufficient to me to ensure that all are fairly treated."

There was a murmur of approval at that last, and Cinhil bade Camber come closer. Camber could see the king's satisfaction, and suddenly he wondered whether Cinhil had worked this all out before, unbeknownst to any of the rest of them. Perhaps they had all underestimated Cinhil.

"My Lord Bishop, are you prepared to witness Lord Sighere's oath, since he does desire it?"

With a bow, Camber beckoned for a young sub-deacon, who held a jewel-encrusted Gospel book.

"I am prepared, Sire."

Nodding, Cinhil turned to face Sighere once more. "Sighere, Earl of Eastmarch, you may approach us. My Lord Marshal, please bring his sword."

As Sighere slowly climbed the dais steps, sweeping back his coif at last to bare his head, Jebediah moved behind him and took up his sword. Sighere, easing himself down on greaved and mailed knees, lifted his hands to Cinhil, palm to palm. Cinhil took Sighere's hands between his own and let his eyes meet Sighere's brown ones as Jebediah knelt on one knee with Sighere's sword.

"I, Sighere, do become your liegeman of life and limb," the kneeling man said in a low but steady voice. "Faith and truth will I bear unto you, in living and dying, against all manner of folk, so help me God."

With that, he leaned forward to touch his forehead to their joined hands.

Cinhil, obviously much moved by the gesture, drew a steadying breath before returning the oath.

"This do I hear, Sighere of Eastmarch. And I, for my part, pledge the protection of Gwynedd to you and all your people, to defend you from every creature with all my power. This is the word of Cinhil Donal Ifor Haldane, King of Gwynedd and Kheldour, Lord of Meara and Mooryn and the Purple March, Overlord of Eastmarch. So help me God."

With that, Cinhil released Sighere's hands and leaned to kiss the Gospel which Camber extended with a bow. The Book was then presented to Sighere, who also touched it reverently with his lips. As Camber was withdrawing the Book, Cinhil took Sighere's sword from Jebediah and held it with the blade up, signaling for Sighere to remain kneeling.

"Sighere of Eastmarch," Cinhil said, glancing along the length of the blade, "in token of the oaths we have just exchanged, I shall return your sword—but not before it, too, becomes a symbol of the bonds we have forged this day."

Deftly he brought the flat of the blade down on Sighere's right shoulder. The earl flushed with pleasure and bowed his head as he realized what Cinhil was doing.

"Sighere of Eastmarch, I confirm you in your present rank and titles—" He moved the blade to strike Sighere's left shoulder lightly. "—with the understanding that more suitable forms have yet to be decided."

He brought the flat of the blade down lightly on Sighere's bowed head, then raised the sword and laid it across both his hands to present it to Sighere. The earl, receiving the sword with another bow of his head, kissed the blade and then slid it back into its sheath with a resounding click.

The sound was the signal for loud and spontaneous cheering all through the hall, as Earl Sighere of Eastmarch was raised by the king's own hands and taken to meet his new brothers.

CHAPTER TWENTY-ONE

And let us not be weary in well doing:
for in due season we shall reap, if we faint not.
— Galatians 6:9

The alliance with Sighere somewhat changed Cinhil's summer plans. Instead of remaining at Valoret to continue his administrative reforms, he accompanied his army into Kheldour with Jebediah and Sighere, observing with increasing interest how those two able generals subdued and consolidated the lands which Sighere had given largely in name.

His chancellor he left at the capital, to assist Queen Megan in her duties as regent during his absence and to direct further work on the judicial reforms which Cinhil proposed to treat at his Winter Court, when he returned. Rhys and Joram also stayed in Valoret, Rhys to attend the expectant queen and Joram to continue his service to the chancellor-bishop.

Almost as an afterthought, Cinhil sent a lesser portion of his army with Earls Fintan and Tamarron, to patrol the Eastmarch-Torenth borderlands and prevent any Torenthi invasion force from cutting off his main van in Kheldour. It was a wise move; for if Nimur of Torenth *had* contemplated such an invasion with his ransomed men, he did not follow through. In any case, all was quiet on Gwynedd's new eastern border that summer of 906. Cinhil could never know whether or not his deterrent had been necessary.

In the north, Cinhil's forces encountered little re-

sistance. The greater part of Kheldour had accepted
Sighere's liberating army the previous autumn, and by
now greeted the almost-legendary King Cinhil as a
long-awaited friend. Rhendall was more difficult, for
the rugged terrain of that mountain region afforded
ample hiding places for Festillic forays against the
occupying Gwynedd army. But by the end of August,
even the last of the Kheldour Festils had been ferreted out of their hiding place between Rhendall's
twin lakes, the young niece and nephew of the slain
Termod finally surrendering their fortress stronghold of
Rhorau.

Cinhil would not allow the two to be killed, though
Sighere urged it and Jebediah counseled the same; for
they were, both of them, hardly more than children.
Nor could he allow them to go free and breed future
Festillic threats. God knew, one such threat in Torenth
was enough to anticipate. Reluctantly, he consigned
them to the wardenship of Sighere's eldest son, Ewan,
to whom he also gave the lordship of the entire
Rhendall region. Ewan would keep the two in close
but honorable captivity until the end of their days—a
grim fate, but not so grim as some which Cinhil had
considered.

Further consolidation was also accomplished during
that summer's campaign. Hrorik, Sighere's middle son,
so distinguished himself in battle that he became a
chief vassal of Cinhil in his own right, receiving most
of the lands of his father's former earldom of Eastmarch as his holding. Sighere's youngest son, also
named Sighere, was granted the new earldom to be
called Marley, carved out of the northern portions of
old Eastmarch, for he had also served Cinhil most
valiantly. In all three of Sighere's sons, Cinhil counted
himself fortunate. He could not conceive of more loyal
and powerful allies to hold this newest extension of
his kingdom.

But for Sighere himself was reserved the greatest
honor of all: to be created a duke—the first ever in
Gwynedd—and to receive for himself and his heirs

the royal Duchy of Claibourne, so named for the principal city of the northwesternmost portion of old Kheldour. Duke Sighere also became Viceroy of the Kheldish Riding, that office to become the hereditary due of the Dukes of Claibourne for as long as Sighere's line should last. Rhendall, now held by Ewan, would be the secondary title of the Claibourne dukes, borne during the duke's lifetime by his eldest son but functioning as a separate earldom under that son so long as father and son both lived. On Sighere's death, Ewan would become Duke of Claibourne as well as Earl of Rhendall, until he had a son to administer the lesser title. Of course, the viceregal office also went with the ducal inheritance. Sighere had great reason to be pleased as the summer days began to shorten.

And in Valoret, the weeks and months passed as quickly for Camber as they did for his king, if with less dramatic excitement than what Cinhil daily faced in Kheldour. The shift from spring to summer brought Queen Megan's condition to the notice of anyone with the eyes to see, her blossoming happiness the delight of all who loved their usually sad-faced young queen. Evaine, too, began to show unmistakable signs of impending motherhood, to be delivered shortly past Christmas. Rhys, physician to both women, could hardly decide whether he was more pleased with the improved health and spirits of Megan or the splendid progress of the son his wife carried beneath her heart.

Of course, Megan's son would be another heir for Gwynedd—and God knew, they needed another. But thought of his own son brought a tremor of excitement to Rhys's mind whenever he thought about him. In fact, he sometimes found it difficult to reconcile his own joyous wonderment with the utter calm and serenity which Evaine increasingly displayed. Her entire outlook took on a mellowness which was quite alien to the Evaine Rhys knew so well. Even Joram ceased the occasional sharp comments which he and his sister had sometimes exchanged in the past.

Camber, too, noticed the change in his daughter,

and the corresponding change it wrought in Rhys and Joram. He cherished his time with Evaine and tried to be a sounding board for both his sons' wonder, helping his daughter ease into this new phase of her life and becoming less demanding of her time as the child within her grew. Many hours they spent together, father and daughter, sometimes translating the ancient records and discussing what they had found, speculating on the enigmatic ward cubes, but more often simply relaxing in each other's minds.

Together they explored the implications of the role Camber had chosen to assume. The matter of sainthood they especially considered, not only from its impact on Gwynedd's future but from its possible effect on Camber himself. Almost, they could justify the public side—if not to Joram's satisfaction, at least to their own. But Camber continued to brood on the inner morality, and what effect the common acclamation of Camber as saint might have on the living Camber's mind. There was simply no way of knowing. He hoped they would never have to know.

Cinhil's absence allowed them far greater freedom than they would have had, to meet and plan and try to decide what to do. Little by little, pieces of information did begin to sift together.

For example, through a chance encounter with Dom Emrys, the abbot of the Order of Saint Gabriel, who had come to court to complain of encroachments on the Order's fields near Saint Neot's, Camber learned that Queron Kinevan had left the Gabrilite Order in April. Emrys seemed still to be surprised at this, for the Healer-priest had held an enviable reputation both in his community and in the secular world. Emrys could offer no explanation as to why Queron had left or where he had gone.

From another source, Rhys discovered that Queron had been involved in the purchase of a partially fortified and much ruined manor called Dolban, which lay on the road which ran northeast out of Valoret along the river toward Caerrorie. Further investigation revealed only that Dom Queron had been seen in the area once or twice, no longer wearing the white robes of his former Order, and that extensive building activity was now being carried on behind the restored walls of Castle Dolban.

That last fascinated Camber, for he could not imagine where Queron had gotten the money to pursue such a project, the priest having previously sworn vows of poverty to his Order; but increasing pressures at court prevented him from pursuing the investigation overmuch. Even though Cinhil was still in Kheldour, and not expected back until mid-September, the council—or such of it as was in residence—was required to meet twice weekly and send detailed reports to the king. The queen was increasingly unable to sit through the meetings, her time coming due about the same time that Cinhil was expected home; and Anscom, who had always handled a great portion of the ecclesiastical liaison, had suffered recurrent illnesses throughout the summer, and was more often absent than present.

As the archbishop's condition worsened, Camber felt obliged to spend more and more time at his side, not out of duty, but out of genuine affection. The long years of battling a recalcitrant digestive system had finally taken their toll on the aging prelate. Even so skilled a Healer as Rhys could do little other than to ease Anscom's discomfort—and that, Camber could do as well as he, and Anscom preferred Camber's touch.

Accordingly, and at the insistence of Anscom, Camber sent Rhys and Joram out, ostensibly to visit Caerrorie but in fact to survey the situation at Dolban. They camped near the manor for nearly a week in mid-August, disguised as itinerant merchants, observing the comings and goings of various workmen and questioning those they dared.

They learned that the manor had been bought through a factor named John, who had paid in gold. A bailiff named Thomas now paid the laborers and dealt with the villagers who brought increasing amounts of supplies for the manor's upkeep. For the gold and silver which the bailiff dispersed, the peasants were asked not to talk about what they saw inside—though, under Rhys and Joram's careful prodding, some allowed as how the buildings looked like monastic ones. Certainly, the manor's old chapel had been restored and, some said, greatly enlarged. Vast amounts of fine-cut stone and timber had been brought through the gates at midsummer, and one old carpenter told of a great statue of a hooded man which stood close beside the new rose-marble altar.

If there was a master of the place, then it was surely the small, wiry man in gray robes who sometimes walked the rampart walls at night. The man's description fit Queron to perfection, right down to the fat reddish-brown Gabrilite braid hanging down his back. Rhys and Joram never saw him themselves, but the man they had Truth-Read for the information could not have lied. Queron was surely at Dolban.

In a last effort to gain more insight before returning to report to Camber and Anscom, the two paid a quick, nighttime visit to Caerrorie to check on the tomb. Elinor was away for the present, gone with her new husband and the two boys to visit her new in-laws; but Umphred, Caerrorie's old bailiff, admitted the two young men quite readily.

Yes, visitors had continued to pray at the dead master's tomb, Umphred told them. And many left gifts of flowers and prayers still. He even took them there, through the secret passage which had always connected the family chapel with the main house. But no one had approached the young master Davin's mother with any proposals to build a shrine, so far as Umphred knew. Nor had anything been changed about the tomb itself. Did Father Joram and Lord Rhys *really* think their father had been a saint?

They never did get to check the actual tomb closely, though Umphred insisted that it had been undisturbed. On their way back to Valoret, close by the road from

Caerrorie, they found several illicit Camberian shrines, evidently erected by the common folk, who had good reason to remember their late lord with love; and they brought back several copies of prayers and devotions to "Saint Camber" which had been left there and in the chapel near the tomb.

But, again, it was impossible to determine from this slender evidence whether these were isolated items or part of an organized movement. The hand on several of the prayers looked a great deal like Guaire's, but Camber himself could not be sure. Too many others had handled the parchment, and Guaire's hand was not particularly distinctive.

Nor did Camber have a chance to pursue the matter further, for on the night of the first of September, Anscon of Trevas died in his arms—the culmination of several months of worsening bouts with nausea and loss of weight and finally vomiting of blood. He died peacefully enough, under the circumstances, suffering no pain under the relieving hands of his Deryni comforters; but they could not cure him.

Camber, as Bishop of Grecotha, celebrated Anscom's Requiem Mass—one of the most difficult things he had ever had to do. It had not been deemed meet, in that hot and humid September weather, to delay burial until the king might return; even a preserving spell had time limitations. So Anscom was laid away in a vault beneath the cathedral floor but two days after his death.

More momentous to Gwynedd than Anscom's funeral, however, which had not been entirely unexpected in light of the archbishop's known failing health, was the election of his successor. The unanimous choice, with some reservations, was one Jaffray of Carbury.

Jaffray, one of Gwynedd's six itinerant bishops, and a former member of the Gabrilite Order, had been under consideration for a titled see for some time, being Deryni and moderate in his politics and a man in whom even humans placed a great deal of trust. He had been very popular all through the Purple March, which was his current assignment. He seemed to have a knack for bringing together dissident factions—a not-unwelcome talent for the years ahead.

Unfortunately, Anscom had not necessarily been considering Jaffray for Valoret, since, if he *must* predecease Camber, he had hoped to ease his friend's burden by nominating someone in whom Camber could confide his true identity. Any other arrangement might open the way for the Servants of Saint Camber to press their suit, if the new archbishop did not know why it should be denied.

But any other candidates Anscom might have considered grooming for the primacy were years away from having the necessary experience for so critical a position, and Anscom had simply run out of time. One absolute requirement for any successor was that the man be Deryni. Under no circumstances would Anscom surrender the primate's chair to any human priest, no matter how otherwise qualified. The survival of his people might one day hinge on the strong intervention of a Deryni advocate in Valoret.

And so Anscom had ended up choosing Jaffray by default: Jaffray, who was at least Deryni and otherwise qualified, but who could not be relied upon as a confidant for Camber. In the final week before his death, Anscom sent the name of his nominee to Cinhil in Kheldour. By the time Cinhil's approval came back, Anscom was dead. Archbishop Oriss of Rhemuth convened the Council of Bishops and presented the name of Anscom's nominee. When he announced that King Cinhil had approved, the bishops also approved.

Camber had some doubts, for the same reasons as Anscom, of this man whom he did not know, either as Camber or as Alister—but he had no alternative suggestions, so he, too, must say "yea" with all the rest. And because Jaffray did not and must not know of Alister Cullen's true identity—both Camber and Anscom had feared Jaffray's and Queron's former ties with the Gabrilites—he would not know to be wary of the Servants of Saint Camber, whenever they might rear their heads. Camber dared not tell him.

Nothing untoward happened during the first week of Jaffray's tenure. No one came to court from Dolban; and once the king returned, both to mourn Anscom and to recognize Gwynedd's new primate, normal activities of the court quickly resumed. For the next few weeks, Camber was so caught up in a succession of meetings and conferences with Cinhil that he almost forgot to worry.

Megan's son was born in late September—named Rhys, for the Healer who had brought him safely into the world—and Cinhil, pleased at the new baby's perfect form and health, declared a week of celebration. Megan recovered much more quickly than after the previous birth, and seemed to thrive on Cinhil's mere presence in the same city again. The new little prince grew stronger with each passing day.

It was more than a month after Anscom's death that the new archbishop summoned his first consistory, bidding the attendance of as many of his brother bishops and masters of religious orders as could attend. Their meeting place was the same chapter house where Camber had first faced the Michaelines as Alister Cullen—only now Camber sat as only one of eight bishops present, in the last of three episcopal chairs to Jaffray's left, not Chancellor of Gwynedd within these walls, but Bishop of Grecotha only, and junior to every other prelate present.

Joram sat behind and slightly to his left on a backless stool. Each bishop was entitled to a single attendant, and Joram was Alister Cullen's logical choice, as confidental secretary. But other than Joram, there was not one man in the chamber whom Camber had known before he became Alister Cullen.

The morning session went routinely enough. During the first hour, Archbishop Jaffray received the homage and credentials of those abbots and priors who had been unable, for one reason or another, to attend his enthronement a few weeks earlier. After that, following a short address in which Jaffray outlined his expectations for his tenure, he invited preliminary discussion of possible successors to the bishopric left vacant by his election to the See of Valoret.

Camber listened a great deal and said little. The entire morning was quite uneventful. At noon, the entire company adjourned for a light midday meal.

But the afternoon session held a different promise, which Camber noticed soon after he reentered the chapter house following their break. It was not immediately apparent as he crossed the tiled floor, for he was initially absorbed in a merry conversation with the wire-thin Bishop Eustace, who sat next to him and could make light of almost anything. Joram followed a few respectful steps behind, chatting casually with Eustace's secretary.

However, as Camber took his seat, still chuckling at one of Eustace's wry comments, he made an automatic scan of the room and realized that the chamber was nearly filled to capacity, where there had been only half that number in the morning. Men in the habits of most of the great orders of Gwynedd were crowded onto the tiered seats behind the thrones of his colleagues, white and brown and black and burgundy and blue among the purple of the bishops. Crevan Allyn and a handful of his Michaelines had slipped into places on the first level, directly behind Bishop Dermot O'Beirne. On the second tier, closer to the dais, sat Dom Emrys and a score of Gabrilite priests.

Camber had just glanced behind him to confirm that a similar array of clergy lined his side of the round hall when the archbishop's chamberlain rapped on the floor with his iron-shod staff for silence. All came to their feet as Archbishops Jaffray and Oriss entered and took their places on the dais.

As the room settled down again, Camber saw Jebediah slip in and join Crevan and the other Michaelines, strangely wearing the garb of only an ordinary Michaeline knight—no badge of his secular office. Jebediah flashed what Camber took to be a curious glance in Camber's direction; but before Camber could speculate on his meaning, the chamberlain was rapping for attention again, his voice strong in the silence which his staff commanded.

"Your Grace, Reverend Lords, brethren of a new religious order beg leave to present a petition."

An icy chill slid down Camber's spine as the great doors swung back, and suddenly he *knew,* beyond any doubting, just who was about to enter.

He felt Joram stiffen and mentally bristle beside him as a gray-robed Queron Kinevan strode slowly into the chamber, flanked by several other gray robes whom Camber had never seen before—and Guaire of Arliss.

Now Camber knew where Queron had gotten the money for his building project at Dolban, and what that project must be. How could he have forgotten that Guaire was wealthy in his own right?

He watched with curious detachment as Queron paused in the precise center of the chamber to bow deeply, hands folded piously out of sight in deep sleeves, then approached the dais to kiss Jaffray's ring. The former Gabrilite nodded respectfully to Dom Emrys as he straightened from his obeisance to the archbishop and backed off a few paces. Behind him, Queron's companions sank to their knees and bowed their heads. Several, including Guaire, wore the beginnings of a Gabrilite-style braid like Queron's.

Joram caught his breath and sat forward in horrified fascination as Queron withdrew a scroll from his sleeve and began to unroll it. Without betraying all, there was nothing he or his father could do to stop Queron Kinevan.

"My Lord Archbishop, worthy Reverend Fathers, I will speak plain," Queron said, glancing at his scroll and then letting the hand which held it fall to his side. "I and my brothers seek your blessing to form a new religious community, dedicated to the service of a yet-unrecognized saint. We have already established his first shrine at our monastery of Dolban, and would build a second here in the cathedral where his body once lay. Eventually, we would have his burial place enshrined as well, so that all may visit his relics and benefit from his sanctity. To that end, we here present formal petition for the canonization of the late Earl of Culdi, Camber MacRorie."

There was an instant of total silence as the sense of Queron's words penetrated, and then the hall erupted in excited exclamation. Joram came to his feet almost involuntarily, his anguished "No!" drowned out in the din but stated all the more emphatically by his stricken expression.

Attention started to shift from Queron to Joram, for most present knew who Joram was, but Queron was determined to retain the advantage he had gained by speaking first. He had known Joram would be an opponent. Moving a step closer to the episcopal dais, he brandished his scroll to catch their gaze once more, his voice rising above Joram's protest and even overpowering the clergy's voices.

"Your Grace, I beseech you, may I speak?" he shouted. "I beg leave to present our case without interference. I assure you that it cannot be refuted!"

As discussion subsided and seats were resumed, Queron swept his audience with his hard Deryni glance and lowered his scroll, once more in command. Joram stood mute and pale before the older man's gaze, one hand clenched white-knuckled on a finial of Camber's high-backed chair. Camber dared not react as Queron measured his son.

"I thank you, my lords," Queron finally said, in a normal conversational tone, turning his attention back to Jaffray. "Your Grace, may I now proceed?"

Jaffray, who alone of the bishops had not joined in the excited reaction to Queron's pronouncement, sat back thoughtfully in his throne, one ringed hand absently stroking his chin as his eyes flicked from Queron to Joram, then to Camber.

"Please ask your secretary to be seated, Bishop

Cullen. We know Dom Queron, and will hear his petition."

Robert Oriss, seated to Jaffray's right, leaned closer to his colleague, to speak without taking his eyes from the stunned Joram.

"The young man is Lord Camber's son, Your Grace. Are you aware of that?"

"I have been so informed," Jaffray replied, not unkindly. "Regardless of that fact, I must ask him to hold his peace until Dom Queron has elaborated. Please be seated, Father MacRorie. You will be given ample opportunity to speak later on."

At Camber's touch on his elbow, Joram sank slowly back to his stool, to perch on the edge with taut attention. In vain Camber tried to breach the wall of his son's resistance, not daring to maintain the physical contact or the force necessary to insist upon the communication. Perhaps later. However he did it, he must be certain that Joram did not overreact. They dared not risk the slightest slip under Queron's perceptive gaze.

With a slight sigh, Camber half rose to bow slightly in Jaffray's direction.

"My pardon for him, Your Grace. My secretary is young and overwrought. I shall try to see that it does not happen again."

"We shall thank you for it," Jaffray replied. He returned his gaze to Queron. "You have our leave to speak now, Dom Queron. Please continue."

Queron bowed, rerolling the scroll he had used with such effectiveness a few minutes before. He still had not disclosed its contents. Perhaps it was only a stage prop, at that. Whatever, it had served its purpose even if it was blank. Camber wondered which other of the vast Deryni arsenal of persuasion Queron would use next.

Feigning only dutiful interest, and a little concern for the young priest crouched miserably beside him, Camber settled back in one of Alister Cullen's favorite poses of stone-faced concentration, fingers steepled so that the hands could rise casually to mask his expression if necessary, no line of his body betraying his inner tension. He watched Queron pivot gracefully to scan his audience, the scroll tap-tapping lightly against a tapering hand as the rapier mind weighed their emotions. With his first words, reassuring, confidential, the assembly began visibly to relax.

"Your Grace, learned Fathers, Reverend Lords. For those who may not know me, I am Queron Kinevan, Healer and sometime priest of the Order of Saint Gabriel. Healer I am still, and priest also; but as you can see, my garb proclaims me no longer Gabrilite. There is a reason for that. Not a failing of my old Order, which I shall always cherish." Here he bowed slightly to Dom Emrys. "Rather, a calling to another task which is for me and, I believe, for Gwynedd a more important one. I hope to help you understand the reasons for my change of heart, and to enlist your support."

He drew a leisurely breath as his audience settled down to listen.

"As all are aware, the Earl of Culdi was slain in battle last year. More precisely, Camber MacRorie was slain: a gentle and pious man, as all do know; the restorer of our gracious king—long may he reign; the Defender of Humankind, as many do call him now, and with just cause—for he fell defending all of us from the Festillic destroyers.

"He was cut down in the fullness of his service to this land—cut down long before his work could come to full fruition. But as we believe now, who call ourselves his Servants, he was not content to leave us with his work thus unfulfilled, and with this land in danger. He died in body, but he is not gone! His hand is still felt upon this land and upon its people, to the greater good of all of us. To a certain few, he has even spoken directly, giving guidance and promise of hope, when all earthly comfort had failed; even giving the gift of healing in his miracles."

He had them now, and knew it. He let his volume

drop to a barely audible level and watched all present hush and catch their breath to hear him better. Camber, forefingers absently stroking his nose to hide his growing apprehension, knew the awful stomach-churn of fear as he wondered at Queron's reference to healing.

Could Queron know of Cinhil's experience?

"I spoke to one such man last spring," Queron continued. "He is in this room today." Camber allowed himself to relax slightly; Cinhil was not present. "He told me of a miracle: how Blessed Camber came to him as though in a dream—but *it was not a dream!* Those of you who know me or my reputation will believe me, I hope, when I say that I have questioned this man closely, to the fullest extent of my abilities—and I am convinced that the Blessed Camber did appear to him as he describes. This I shall demonstrate. Nor is he the only unimpeachable witness to similar events."

There: another possible reference to Cinhil—for who else involved in what had happened was truly unimpeachable? And Cinhil's testimony was by far the more dangerous of the two.

"But I believe that the evidence will speak for itself, Reverend Fathers. I believe that Camber MacRorie has been given God's grace to continue his work upon this land, even in death. I believe that this august assembly will have no choice, in the end, but to declare Camber MacRorie among the blessed, and a saint.

"If I offend any with my plainness, I apologize."

As he bowed his head, to all outward appearances spent for the moment—though Camber knew that he was just beginning—there was an instant of profound silence and then an incoherent murmur as the assembled bishops and clergy conferred among themselves. Jaffray let them go for several minutes before holding up a hand for silence, which was immediately given.

"We thank you, Dom Queron. Father MacRorie,

do you wish to make a statement before Dom Queron begins presenting his evidence?"

Joram stood slowly, tearing his gaze upward to meet Jaffray's. He had permitted his father's mental touch during the last minutes of Queron's impassioned plea, and given reassurance that he would not betray their cause. Still, he felt bound in conscience to tell as much of the truth as possible without endangering the man for whose sake he had already compromised so much for love.

"Your Grace, I loved my father," he said steadily. "I loved him, and still do, more than I can say." He glanced at the floor, his mind once more closed to Camber's, then looked up at Jaffray again. "But he was a man, like other men: gentle and pious, as Dom Queron has said; a loving father, a wise counselor—gifted beyond the ken even of most others of our race. He sacrificed much to accomplish what he believed in, and was content to pay the price because he loved this land and its king—perhaps too much.

"But he was no saint. I only hope I may persuade you that he would be horrified if he knew what went on beneath this roof!"

With a sigh, Jaffray looked at Queron again. Jaffray was a handsome man for his years, his dark Gabrilite braid hardly touched by gray, but in the past minutes he had aged a great deal as he realized the extent of Joram's opposition. As Queron looked up, hands clasped thoughtfully behind his back, Jaffray frowned and tapped his bishop's ring against his teeth several times. The archbishop was clearly considering what to do next.

"Dom Queron," he said, after another sigh, "I am constrained to remind these reverend Fathers that you and I were ever friends and brothers when I was yet a Gabrilite, and that I want very much to believe what my friend and brother has just told this august assembly—though I should point out that I, like they, am hearing your testimony for the first time. However, I must also recognize that the distinguished son of the man you seek to make a saint does not share your enthusiasm. Are you prepared to prove your contention with witnesses, as is the custom in such proceedings?"

"I am prepared, Your Grace."

"Very well. You have said that one such witness is present. I should like to hear his testimony. On that basis, we shall determine whether the case warrants further consideration. Is that agreeable to you?"

Queron bowed.

"Good. Father MacRorie, you may be seated. I charge you to hold your peace until Queron's witness has had his say."

Nodding, unable to speak for sheer despair, Joram sank to his seat and leaned his head against the side of his father's chair. Once more the mental barriers fell, permitting Camber's cautious touch. As Camber slipped into his son's mind, soothing, thanking, reassuring, Queron turned to face his still-kneeling brethren. Guaire rose as though on cue, the promptness of his response leading Camber to suspect that he and Queron were already bonded in some kind of magical rapport. Now they would see whether Queron was as skilled as his reputation would have him to be. From a purely objective stance, it would be interesting to learn how much Guaire remembered.

"Your Grace." Queron handed his scroll to one of the men still kneeling and bowed formally toward the archbishops' thrones. "I present Lord Guaire of Arliss, a great benefactor of our Order and, if Your Grace will permit it, soon to be one of the Servants of Saint Camber—for so we mean to call our company."

Jaffray gazed across at Guaire thoughtfully. "I have heard of your family, Guaire. You are not yet in holy orders?"

"No, Your Grace."

Taking in hand the jeweled pectoral cross which hung on his chest, Jaffray extended it toward Guaire.

"Guaire of Arliss, do you swear by this symbol of our faith and the holy relics it contains that the testimony which you are about to give shall be only the truth, fully cognizant of the consequences of perjury to your immortal soul?"

Guaire came forward to kiss the cross. "I swear it, so help me God."

At Jaffray's nod of approval, Guaire rose and backed into place at Queron's side, eyes downcast. Queron, hands clasped easily before him, nodded slightly to Jaffray again before glancing briefly at his audience.

"Guaire, please tell these Reverend Lords whether you have ever seen aught in this room before today—other than our brethren, of course."

"Yes, Dom Queron. I know Father Joram and Lord Jebediah—and Bishop Cullen, of course."

"Very good. In what capacity, please?"

"I was a friend of Father Joram's brother Cathan, before his death at the hands of King Imre. I worked with Father Joram and Lord Jebediah and the Bl—and the Lord Camber during the year before the Restoration. I was Lord Camber's squire after Cathan died—until his death. After that, I entered the service of Bishop Cullen."

"I see. And there is no one else here whom you have seen before?"

"Seen, yes. That was inevitable while I was in Bishop Cullen's service. But not to talk to. I was only a clark and sometime valet to His Grace of Grecotha."

"But you left Bishop Cullen's service. Why?"

Guaire studied the sandaled toes protruding from beneath his gray robe.

"Last spring, I approached His Grace about permission to build a shrine to Saint Camber in the cathedral. He—was not in favor of the shrine—and Father Joram was vehemently opposed—so I decided that our cause could be better served if I left His Grace's service, so as not to embarrass him or cause strife within this household. I hoped that eventually the Bl—Blessed Camber would make him change his mind."

At this point, Queron cleared his throat.

"Your Grace, Reverend Lords, I think it would be helpful at this time if Guaire related the reason for his entry into service with Bishop Cullen. On that tale hangs the first miracle we intend to prove."

"A miracle?" Archbishop Oriss exclaimed. "You mean, this—this young Guaire went to Cullen because of a miracle?"

"Guaire, please tell the Reverend Lords what happened," Queron said calmly.

Guaire raised his head, his eyes focusing on some invisible point midway between himself and Jaffray's disbelieving eyes, and Camber knew that his recall would be perfect. Queron had seen to that.

Patiently he settled back into his chair to listen, resolved to let his own heightened senses take in everything they could. This would be a more telling probe than Camber had first believed, for it was obvious that Queron had groomed his witness well. Now he must hope that Queron's very perfection would trip him up, that too precise a recall would cast doubt on Guaire's testimony rather than strengthening it—though Camber entertained no false expectation of such a miracle.

"It happened on the night of Lord Camber's funeral," Guaire murmured, softly at first, but gaining volume as he spoke. "As many can attest, I was distraught at Camber's death. That night found me weeping by his coffin in the chapel as if I could not live. I must have been there for several hours by the time Father Cullen came and found me. I think the guards were worried, and asked him to check on me."

His audience gave an engrossed sigh as it settled down to listen again.

"He took me back to a room—it belonged to Brother Johannes, who was then his valet—and he and Johannes tried to get me to sleep. I—think they were afraid to leave me alone, for fear I might do myself injury. Much of that part of the evening is still unclear in my mind.

"At any rate, I couldn't sleep until Father Cullen

gave me some hot wine to drink. Later I surmised that there must have been a sleeping potion in it. I'm not sure how long I slept."

As Guaire paused to draw breath, Queron eased casually around behind him, eyes averted, listening rather than watching. Guaire did not seem to notice.

"In any case, I was very much awake for what happened next," Guaire continued. "I remember waking and being aware that I was in the bed, that the wine I had drunk must have been drugged, so calm was I —and then having the distinct feeling that there was someone else in the room—as if the door to the outer corridor had opened and closed, though I heard nothing.

"When I opened my eyes, I fully expected to see Brother Johannes or Father Cullen moving about. But Brother Johannes was sleeping peacefully in a chair beside the fire; and when I turned my head toward the door, I—knew instantly that it was not Father Cullen."

He swallowed and closed his eyes briefly, drawing a deep breath as though to gather courage for his next words. But before he could continue, Queron laid his right hand on Guaire's neck and passed his left over the younger man's eyes. Guaire breathed out with a sigh and relaxed, going very still, his head nodding forward slightly as Queron took away his left hand.

Queron, with a deep breath of his own, looked up at Jaffray, brown eyes hooded under thick lashes, his right arm still laid protectively across Guaire's shoulders.

"Your Grace, I wish to pause here for just a moment to suggest a better way than words to tell what happened next. With Your Grace's indulgence, I should like to *show* what Guaire saw that night."

As questioning murmurs passed through the assembly, Camber thought he saw a faint smile flick across Jaffray's face, found himself wondering whether Jaffray and Queron had set all of this up in advance, despite what Jaffray had said.

No, impossible. Even Queron was not capable of that. Or was he?

"Please tell our brothers what you have in mind," Jaffray said quietly.

Queron bowed. "As Your Grace knows, but many of this assembly may not, there is a process taught by our Gabrilite Order which enables an adept to reach into another's memory and project a visible image of that other's recollection which anyone may see. We Healers sometimes use it in treating certain sicknesses of the mind." He shifted his attention to his audience. "The process is not precisely magic, though it does seem to be a skill found solely in Deryni, and it is not dangerous for the subject, the Healer, or observers—though the Healer does expend a great deal of energy. What I propose, with His Grace's permission, is to work this recollecting now, that all of you may see with your own eyes what Guaire himself saw that night."

There was a whispering of fearful wonder, much nervous coughing and shuffling of feet, and then silence as all eyes turned toward Jaffray.

"Let the doors be barred," the archbishop said. "We will have no interruptions. Dom Queron, you may proceed."

CHAPTER TWENTY-TWO

For thou shalt be his witness unto all men
of what thou hast seen and heard.
                                        —Acts 22:15

As the chamberlain saw to the barring of the door, stationing two nearby ecclesiastical knights to guard it, Queron directed the rest of his brethren to seats in the first tier, only he and Guaire remaining in the center of the chamber. Camber shifted uneasily in his chair as a cloak was called for and procured. His outward expression was only commensurate with the general excitement and suspense of his colleagues, but his mind churned with misgiving.

He had heard of what Queron proposed to do, of course, though he had never seen it. He was sure that Rhys probably even knew the procedure, for Rhys had received part of his Healer's training from the Gabrilites, and was acknowledged as one of the most skilled young Healers in Gwynedd.

Camber had never even considered trying it for himself, however, having neither Gabrilite nor Healer's training, and he was both intrigued and apprehensive at the prospect of watching his own actions mirrored through another's mind. What made matters worse, and would tax his acting ability even more, was the fact that Queron was now laying out the cloak on a spot only a short distance from Camber's feet, obviously intending it as a surrogate bed from which Guaire would reenact his part.

As Queron led the compliant Guaire to lie upon
that cloak with his face toward Camber and Eustace,
Camber suspected that the choice of position had not
been entirely coincidental; for Alister Cullen had already been mentioned as having knowledge of the
incident about to be depicted. Queron could not be
aware of his true involvement, of course, but that
would not prevent him from noting the reactions of
whoever had connections with the incident, however
far removed. Camber had to appreciate the Healer-
priest's foresight. He must never underestimate Queron
Kinevan.

Beside him, Joram, too, had finally regained his
equilibrium, his usual curiosity thoroughly reengaged
at the thought of witnessing a Deryni skill which he
also had never seen. Joram sat forward almost
eagerly, his previous despair replaced by alert interest.
Even though he had shared his father's remembrance
of Guaire's "miracle," and was well acquainted with
the care and skill which had gone into the encounter
from Camber's point of view, that was different from
seeing it through the eyes of the one for whom it had
been intended. Besides, Joram had never been able
to resist an opportunity to watch his talented father
in action, even when he did not agree with what was
being done. Most certainly, he did not approve of what
Queron was about to do; for successful re-creation
of Guaire's experience would almost certainly prove
the very thing Joram had been trying to avoid. It
could only be interpreted as a miracle.

Joram watched with hushed mind, in tandem with
his father, as Queron knelt beside the reclining Guaire
and sat back on his haunches, facing toward the archbishops and in profile to Camber. As the room quieted
down, Queron laid his hand lightly on Guaire's forehead and began to extend a heavier control, his own
manner stilling and centering as he breathed slowly,
in and out. At one point he glanced up dreamily at
Jaffray, who nodded minutely, then returned his attention fully to Guaire.

After a moment, Guaire curled up on his side, as though asleep, and moaned, pulling the edges of the cloak more closely around him. As Queron sat motionless, all stillness now, Guaire opened his eyes hesitantly and appeared to look around.

Camber knew what must happen next. Shifting his gaze out to the center of the room, toward which Queron now slightly turned his face, he watched a tendril of smoky luminescence begin to coalesce, gradually becoming a motionless figure cloaked and hooded in gray.

Was that what he had looked like? No wonder Guaire had been frightened at first!

Guaire rolled over and blinked, staring in amazement as the tall, light-shrouded figure glided a little closer. Alarm animated his face for just an instant as he started to sit bolt upright, but then he froze halfway up, leaning on one elbow, to breathe the ineffable name:

"Camber!"

The apparition moved a few steps closer still, then stopped as the hood fell back from silver-gilt hair familiar to nearly everyone in the hall. There was a deep, scarcely breathed, "Ah!" as the face was seen and recognized.

Camber stared at his own image, transfixed. The face seemed younger than he remembered looking for some years, and Camber realized that this must be the way Guaire had seen him, through idolizing eyes.

"Don't be afraid," his own voice said, spoken by Queron, but projected to sound from the figure's lips, and almost exactly in Camber's tone. "I return but for a moment, to ease your grief and to assure you that I am at peace where I now dwell."

Camber nodded slightly as Guaire did, caught up in the recollection of that other night, and missed conscious registry of the next few exchanges.

". . . With you gone, the king will endure unchecked," Guaire was saying earnestly, when Camber snapped back to full awareness. "I fear him, Lord."

"Pity him, Guaire," the apparition replied gently. "Do not fear him. And help those who remain to carry on our work: Joram, and Rhys, my daughter Evaine —my grandsons, when they are older. And Alister Cullen, who brought you here. He, most of all, has need of your support, if you will only give it."

"Father Alister?" Guaire shook his head in bewilderment, his voice almost plaintive. "But he is so gruff, and sure of himself. How could I possibly help him?"

"He is not so self-sufficient as he would have men think," the response came, a familiar smile playing about the lips. "Gruff he may be, and sometimes far too stubborn for his own good. But he, even more than my children, will miss that companionship we used to share. Will you help him, Guaire? Will you serve him as you served me?"

All attention focused back on Guaire and waited for his reply, living the moment with him, wondering, awed. Camber could not help admiring the artistry of the man named Queron, who could call so dazzling a recall from Guaire's drug-fogged memory of that night and now held an undrugged audience equally spellbound. He hid a smile behind one casually raised hand as Guaire looked up shyly at his visitant.

"I could truly help him?"

"You could."

"To serve him, as I served you?"

"He is more than worthy, Guaire. And too proud to ask you for your help."

As Guaire swallowed, half the audience swallowed with him.

"Very well, Lord. I will do it. And I will keep your memory alive, I swear it!"

"My memory is not important," the figure replied, more humbly than Camber remembered. "The work we began is. Help Alister, Guaire. Help the king. And be assured that I shall be with you, even when you are least aware." That much was certain, Camber thought. "I count on you to carry out my work."

"I will, Lord!" Guaire's eyes went round as he realized the vision was about to leave. "No! Wait, Lord! Do not leave me yet!"

The apparition paused to gaze at him with compassion.

"I may not stay, my son. Nor may I come to you again. Be at peace."

Staring at the figure forlornly, Guaire scrambled to his knees and raised his hands in a last, desperate supplication.

"Then give me your blessing, Lord. Please! Do not deny me this!"

The familiar face became more solemn, the head tilting slightly as though considering the request, and then a graceful hand was lifting to trace the sign of blessing over Guaire's bowed head.

"Benedicat te omnipotens Deus, Pater, et Filius, et Spiritus Sanctus," the apparition whispered, its form beginning to fade even as Guaire breathed a fervent "Amen."

A last vestige of a ghostly hand seemed to touch the trembling head and then disappeared entirely. Guaire remained motionless for several seconds before opening his eyes to emptiness.

But as he gasped and started to scramble to his feet, Queron roused from his own silence and lightly touched Guaire's shoulder. Instantly Guaire subsided and collapsed back on his heels, eyes closing, head lolling forward slack on his chest.

A concerned "Oh!" whispered through the watchers as Queron himself sank back momentarily, passing a slightly trembling hand across his forehead in a gesture which Camber knew masked a fatigue-banishing spell. But then the Healer-priest drew a deep breath and got slowly to his feet, leaning heavily on Guaire's shoulder for support. His touch brought Guaire back to normal consciousness, to blink and look around bewilderedly as he tried to reorient himself.

A sigh of relief rippled through the chamber.

"Your Grace, the thought will occur to some within

this company that if I could produce the effect which you have just witnessed, then Guaire's experience could also have been magically induced," Queron said, helping Guaire to his feet with a hand under one elbow and picking up the cloak from the floor. "I assure you, this was not the case. Even though his conscious memories were blurred by the effects of the sleeping draught he was given—and I mean to cast no aspersions on the good Bishop Cullen. Sir, you gave him precisely what I myself would have given him, had I been in your place—still, his unconscious mind recorded details of which even he was not aware at the time.

"What Guaire saw was not a magical projection; Camber was physically present in some way which I cannot explain other than through supernatural intervention. It was not Brother Johannes, who was sleeping in a chair behind Guaire—who has been questioned about his own memories of that night and remembers nothing—and it certainly was not Bishop Cullen. I am willing to submit to Your Grace's full examination, to be Truth-Read before this entire company at any depth Your Grace may choose to employ, to confirm that I speak the truth and have in no way embellished what Guaire saw."

To the murmurings of his colleagues, Jaffrey let his gaze sweep over the chamber, obviously much moved. "I think that will not be necessary, Queron, unless — But would you have this done, my lords? Would you prefer that I confirm Queron's testimony, for form's sake? I have no objection, nor does Queron, and will gladly do it if that will ease your minds. I see a few looks of doubt."

Young Bishop O'Beirne, who had seen mainly the back of Queron's Camberian projection, glanced uneasily to some of his colleagues for support and stood. "Forgive me, Your Grace, but the ways of Deryni are often mystifying to us humans. I think we would all rest easier if Dom Queron's story were confirmed by one of our own number—by another bishop, that is—such as yourself—if it please Your Grace."

As O'Beirne sat down, there were nods of agreement and a few murmurings in his support. Queron bowed as Jaffray's eyes flicked back to him, handing his cloak to Guaire and coming forward immediately to kneel at the archbishop's feet.

Queron inclined his head in submission, and the room grew hushed. Jaffray, with a slow, deep breath to prepare for the merging with his former brother's mind, reached out to touch his right fingertips lightly to Queron's temple. His eyes closed and he breathed out slowly, and for a little while nothing disturbed the quiet of the chamber.

After a moment, Jaffray drew another breath and raised his eyes, blinked, let his hand drop to clasp Queron's hand briefly. Some of the serenity he had gained from dipping into Queron's mind stayed with him as he glanced around the room and Queron stood.

"Dom Queron speaks the truth," he said quietly, his voice reflecting a little of his awe. "Guaire did see what we have seen, and through no Deryni beguilement. I can only agree with Queron's judgment that it was a genuine miracle."

Whispered comment murmured through the chamber, then eased as all realized that Jaffray was not finished.

"Other things I have read also," Jaffray continued, "which have considerable bearing on this case, and I will allow Dom Queron to present them in the due course of this hearing. However, at this time, I would bring to your attention another piece of information which tends to confirm our speculations concerning Camber's sanctity."

The lords glanced at one another, some sitting forward in their seats, and Camber felt himself tense. Was Jaffray going to reveal the second "miracle," which Cinhil had witnessed?

"Dom Queron relates that he and his brethren have conducted further investigation into the matter of the

Lord Camber's status," Jaffray continued, "including several visits to Camber's burial place in Caerrorie."

Beside Camber, Joram shrank down in his seat. Both of them knew what must be coming next, and if it was not the feared revelation concerning Cinhil, the alternative was nearly as bad.

"Camber's tomb is empty, my lords," Jaffray said. "Queron believes Camber to have been bodily assumed into heaven!"

The chamber erupted into excited speculation at that, for such a miracle was unheard of in recent times, and surely betokened Camber's sanctity. Only Joram and Camber did not join in, Joram sitting stunned, eyes wide with horror, his bishop gazing at him in what appeared to be deepest sympathy.

As the chaos died down, Jaffray slowly turned his attention to Joram. Queron still stood on the dais at Jaffray's left, his gaze following the archbishop's.

"Father MacRorie." The archbishop's words silenced all further conversation. "Your expression would seem to betoken disbelief. Can it be that you were unaware of the body's disappearance?"

Joram stood, too shaken at the discovery to do more than try to stall.

"I—cannot imagine how Dom Queron can have learned such a thing," Joram stammered. "M-my father was buried in a private family vault, beside the tomb of his wife, my mother. If Queron has violated the sanctity of his final resting place—"

"The sanctity of his final resting place appears to be assured," Jaffray interjected. "Unless, of course, you can offer some other explanation for the empty tomb."

Joram stared at the floor, his eyes blurring with unbidden tears but remembering the justification they had concocted when they first spoke of moving Cullen's body.

"I—I moved his body," he whispered in desperation.

"I didn't quite catch that, Father."

"I said, I moved his body," Joram repeated, louder as he looked up into Jaffray's eyes.

"A convenient explanation," Dom Queron murmured, to Jaffray, but loud enough that everyone could hear it. "I trust that Father MacRorie can substantiate it."

"Well, Father?"

Joram swallowed and nodded, thinking fast. "It—was necessary, Your Grace. M-my father requested it."

"He *requested* it?" Jaffray gasped, obviously inferring a further miraculous occurrence.

"*Before* his death, Your Grace," Joram corrected hastily. "He—was concerned that when he died—and he realized that at nearly sixty, that might be sooner than he hoped, whether in battle or of some other cause—he was concerned that there might be—difficulties. He—feared that the tomb of any Deryni as well known and controversial as himself might be desecrated," he continued, gathering confidence as his explanation began to take more credible shape. "Perhaps he even feared the very sort of thing which is taking place here today, and did not wish his mortal remains to become a focal point for some well-meaning but illicit cult activity. I but followed his instructions," he ended lamely.

"And moved his body to another tomb." Jaffray nodded. "Which means, then, Father, that you can produce his body for this court?"

With a sinking feeling, Joram shook his head. He and Camber both knew that what remained of Alister Cullen's body no longer wore its previous disguise, and could be all too readily identified if it were subjected to the close scrutiny of a Deryni master such as Queron or Jaffray.

"No, Your Grace, I may not."

"Pray, why not? Or is it that you cannot?" Jaffray asked. "Is it because the body was never moved by you at all, and you can account for its absence no better than Dom Queron can?"

Before Joram could frame a reply, Queron seized the initiative.

"Your Grace, I fear that the good Father MacRorie is a victim of his own filial piety. I do not know why he is trying to deceive this court, though I believe it to be out of a genuine love for his father, whose sanctity he is disinclined to accept, for some reason known only to himself. But I say to him, either produce Camber's body or retract the story. I maintain that he cannot produce the body, because he did not know until a few minutes ago that it was gone!"

Joram bowed his head, unable to refute Queron's logic. To correct any of the misconceptions could ultimately betray all. He had already said too much. Even now, he was treading on the narrow edge of disobedience to his archbishop.

"Father, please be reasonable." Jaffray's tone was almost conciliatory. "For your sake, I want to believe you. I am not insensitive to what an emotional experience this must be for you. However, I cannot allow your personal sensitivities to interfere with the rightful business of this court. Will you submit to my Truth-Read, as Queron has done, if I agree to keep its results confidential as to details? This would also be useful for a future matter which I'm sure you are aware must eventually be brought before this court."

Joram could not help an involuntary gasp, now virtually certain that he was trapped. Under no circumstances could he submit to Jaffray's Truth-Read, though it cost him his life! The removal of Alister's body, his part in the incident which Cinhil had witnessed— He did not care to think what might happen if Jaffray tried to force him to submit and he had to resist the Gabrilite-trained Deryni.

But as he opened his mouth to refuse, prepared to endure whatever consequences might befall as a result, Camber's presence surged into his mind with a force which made him stagger, hands clapped to his head in pain.

You are under a compulsion not to reveal my final

*resting place—which, of course, you do not know,
since I am not yet dead,* Camber's thought boomed
in his mind. *If Jaffray tries to force you, the attempt
could shatter your mind. The compulsion is very
strong. Tell him!*

Groggily, still reeling a little from the force of the
communication, Joram straightened to look at the
archbishop again, grateful for the physical diversion,
which had brought looks of alarm to the faces of
Jaffray and Queron and everyone else watching. He
could feel his father's support more passively now,
knew that Bishop Cullen was staring up at him with
as much concern as anyone else in the chamber. He
realized that Camber must have something in mind,
but he did not know what it was. He must simply follow orders and trust that he would be guided to do the
right thing.

"It—it seems that I may not permit your reading,
Your Grace," he said, even his voice sounding a little
shaken. "I have just been reminded quite painfully of
certain—ah—compulsions placed upon me by my
father not to reveal his final resting place. In truth, I
cannot consciously recall it," he added, by way of reinforcement. And all of that was true.

Jaffray pursed his lips suspiciously. "Such lapses of
memory can be overcome, Father." The words were
neutral enough, but they carried an edge of threat,
nonetheless.

"To do so, in this case, could shatter my mind.
Please do not force me, Your Grace," Joram
pleaded.

Camber stood and laid both hands on his son's
shoulders.

"Your Grace, my secretary is very upset. May I
speak?"

"Only if you have something constructive to offer,
Bishop Cullen," Jaffray said irritably. "Father Mac-
Rorie's excuse is a little too timely, and I am strongly
considering calling his bluff."

"Then allow me to offer an alternative, Your

Grace," Camber soothed. "Joram and I have been close since his first entry into our Order. He has been almost a son to me, and I suspect that I know him better than any in this room—and knew his father better, too. Since taking him on my staff a year ago, I have been his confessor, as well."

All this was true, both as Camber and as Alister, and Camber drew confidence as Jaffray raised no immediate objection.

"Your Grace, permit *me* to Truth-Read Joram, if you will—if he and Camber will," Camber continued. "If he is, indeed, under some compulsion to resist the probing of an outsider in this matter—and to his emotionally wrought mind, you *are* an outsider, even though you be his spiritual father as archbishop—perhaps he can permit my touch instead. Forcing his compliance might, indeed, do great damage. Camber possessed more than passing skill in the guarding of his secrets."

Jaffray scowled impatiently as he considered what his bishop had said.

"Well, will you permit it, Father MacRorie?"

"I'm not sure that is wise, Your Grace," Queron interjected, for the second time cutting Joram off before he could respond. "We have already seen that Bishop Cullen figures somewhat in Guaire's visitation, though I will concede that His Grace did not learn of it until after the fact. However, I suggest that His Grace might not be the most objective of Readers in this case. We have information that he, as well as Joram, was involved in another miracle attributed to Blessed Camber—though we are informed through other testimony that His Grace was unconscious during this intervention."

There! Another reference to an additional witness. Cinhil? Or was it Dualta? Yet, for some reason, even Queron had not dared to mention the king by name or even by position. Perhaps he, too, was afraid to gamble on Cinhil's possible response.

Measuring the possibility, Camber turned his attention to Jaffray. The archbishop was looking at him expectantly, one eyebrow arched in question.

"Is this true, Bishop Cullen?"

"I am told that it is, Your Grace. I remember nothing of the alleged incident."

"Did Joram tell you of it?"

"No, Your Grace."

"Then who did?" Jaffray insisted.

"I may not say, Your Grace. That was a privileged communication, whose source I may not reveal unless that witness is called before this court and gives me leave. However, regardless of how this matter is decided, I maintain that I have nothing to gain or lose. My own knowledge of Camber's alleged sanctity springs solely from hearsay."

"Yet Your Grace refused Guaire's request to build the cathedral shrine, when he came to you last winter," Queron interjected.

"I suggested that Guaire might be mistaken in his interpretation of what he thought he saw," Camber amended. "He had not come to ask *me* for permission, but to ask my intercession with Archbishop Anscom, may he rest in peace. It was Guaire's decision not to present your petition to the archbishop at that time."

"But you *did* discourage Guaire's endeavor?" Jaffray asked.

"Yes, Your Grace. At that time, I had no evidence of what he claimed, other than his somewhat agitated recounting of what I then believed to be a dream. Also, Your Grace should consider that I was trying to ease the distress of young Joram, whom I love and whose father I respected greatly, and who was present when Guaire presented his request. I only seek justice done, Your Grace. Surely that is sufficient to ensure that my examination of Joram would be sufficiently impartial. But, of course, the question may well be academic. We do not yet know whether Joram can permit even my touch."

"Well, Father MacRorie, how say you?" Jaffray

asked sternly. "Will these 'compulsions' permit you to yield to Bishop Cullen's Reading?"

"I—don't know, Your Grace," Joram whispered, feigning uncertainty. "I think so. I feel—some resistance, even to that, but I would trust Bishop Cullen above all other men to try to read beyond it. Believe me, Your Grace, I have no desire to disobey you, but I am even less inclined to have my mind ripped from me by force."

He and Camber watched Jaffray turn to consult with Oriss, Queron leaning down to add his input. Then Jaffray shook his head and turned back to them.

"Very well. I warn you that there are still misgivings, but you may proceed. Will you require any special preparations?"

"None, Your Grace."

With a bow, Camber grabbed the stool Joram had been using and carried it out into the center of the chamber. Bidding Joram come and sit there, facing the archbishops, he took his place behind his son and laid his hands lightly on the tense shoulders, his mind sending a quick, emphatic message to the other's.

Make this look good, son. We have real work to do, and I want them to think you're putting up a fair resistance, even to me. I'll put you to sleep when you're finished, so you won't have to answer any more questions. Just trust me.

Go, was Joram's only reply.

"Very well, Joram," Camber continued on a verbal level, gently massaging the tense shoulder muscles as his eyes roved casually around the room. "I know it's a little more difficult to let go in front of all these people—it's difficult for me, too, for this is a very private thing we're about to share. But we've done this kind of thing before, even if not on this level. So I want you to just relax and find that familiar centering point again."

Joram took a deep breath and let it out, willing himself to relax into the trust which he and his father had always shared. Here, with the close rapport which was growing through their physical contact, there would be no danger of any other Deryni "over-hearing" what passed between them. This was private in the very midst of the enemy, a momentary escape, a surrender to Camber's sure, capable direction.

Joram felt his eyelids flutter, a sure physical sign that Camber was insisting even as Joram was allow-ing. He let his father's words wash through his con-sciousness and carry him, transcending all physical awareness in the stillness of what was fast becoming an empty room, so far as he was concerned.

"That's right. Let your eyes close and flow with me," Camber was saying, directing his gaze to the floor before Joram as he became aware of Joram's yielding and the increased absorption of his audience. "I know it takes a little time, but you can do it. You can ignore everything except my voice and touch and the familiar closeness of my mind."

This he voiced to reassure the humans in his audi-ence, who had never seen so open a demonstration of deep Deryni probing. On a more superficial level, he was aware of several of them slipping into trance with Joram.

No matter. In a moment, words would pass and they would perceive only what they could see.

"Let go, now, and let me enter," he murmured, hands easing gradually from Joram's shoulders to his neck, thumbs resting against the spine beneath the bright hair. He could feel Joram's pulse, slow and steady beneath his fingertips, as he slipped them up to touch the temples.

"That's right. No more words now. No sound to dis-turb you, no physical sensations to break the binding. Be one with me, Joram."

As Camber himself closed his eyes, there was not a sound in the stilled chamber; and in a way, this was an even deeper magic than that which Queron had woven. Deftly, Camber merged his thoughts with Joram's, the two of them instantaneously reviewing all that had been said, formulating a new plan of action. The while, they were safe from any other prying mind. Not Queron nor Jaffray nor any other Deryni in the room had an inkling of what really passed between them.

Several times during the next few minutes, Joram physically squirmed beneath Camber's touch, his face seeming to mirror some inner struggle which appeared to surge between them. In reality, the two of them were isolating all Joram's memories of Camber's true identity where they could not be touched, in case of further probing by Jaffray's court, blocking those memories from all conscious recall until Camber himself should release that block.

When they were done, and Joram's only conscious knowledge of his interrogator was what it ought to be, Camber touched a point controlling consciousness and exerted pressure. Joram's body went slack as the contact was severed. Camber, slowly opening his eyes, dropped his hands to Joram's shoulders and looked up, supporting the sleeping Joram against his body.

"He spoke the truth, Your Grace," Camber murmured, his words jarring several rapt listeners who had drifted under his spell. "He did move the body, shortly after the original burial, and he did receive instructions from his father ahead of time to do so." That much was literally true. "However, his memory of the final burial place has been erased." That was also true, for Camber had himself just erased it.

Jaffray studied the bishop and his unconscious charge through narrowed eyes.

"Has he been harmed in your questioning, Father?"

"Not permanently, Your Grace. There was very deep resistance to be overcome, but the aftereffects are mainly fatigue. I've but made him sleep. He should be fit by morning, provided he has an undisturbed night."

Jaffray nodded, apparently satisfied by the answer.

"And your conclusion regarding Camber's body?"

"None possible, Your Grace. There being no way to produce the body, we may only state with certainty that the claim of miraculous bodily assumption, as put forward by the Servants of Camber, can be neither proved nor disproved."

"But the matter of Guaire's vision—" Queron interjected. "Father MacRorie's testimony does not refute that."

"That is true," Camber replied. "And Joram has no knowledge of that incident beyond what everyone in this room has seen. Of course, he knew something about it, since he was a witness to my conversation with Guaire last winter, but that is all."

Jaffray stared searchingly at the gray-haired bishop, still supporting the sleeping Joram, then shifted in his throne and sighed.

"Very well, Bishop Cullen. We thank you for your assistance. You may retire to see to your secretary's comfort. In the meantime, I shall adjourn this council for today, as it grows late. We will continue this inquiry tomorrow, when all of us are rested. Dom Queron, I shall expect you to present your additional witnesses at that time."

"Yes, Your Grace. Several of our major witnesses could not be present this afternoon for various reasons, but we can ensure their presence for tomorrow."

"Then this council is adjourned."

Camber felt a sickening stirring in his stomach as the council began to disperse, for he well knew whom Queron must have in mind. Joram would be questioned again, of course, though Camber had no doubt now that he would reveal anything. And he himself would probably be called, though loss of memory would stand him in good stead.

Rhys and Dualta would also be summoned. About Dualta he could do nothing, but he would call Rhys to him tonight, ostensibly to minister to Joram, and thus alert the Healer to what lay ahead. No one would dare to ask entry to a Healer's mind, nor could insist, if they did ask, so Rhys was safe so long as he said nothing incongruous.

But the prime witness, if Queron dared to call him,

would be Cinhil—and no one knew how he would re-act. At least there was one witness Queron would *not* be able to call, Camber thought as he and several Michaelines picked up Joram to take him to his quarters. Not even the clever Queron Kinevan would be able to find a Michaeline monk named John.

Word of the afternoon's events spread even more quickly than Camber had feared. By the time he had seen the groggy Joram safely to bed, and briefed Rhys, and turned away nearly a dozen well-meaning colleagues avid for his personal insight on what had transpired, both Vespers and Compline had come and gone and it was becoming obvious that he was not going to get any privacy so long as he stayed where people could find him. If he was to have any chance to regain his mental equilibrium, to prepare for tomorrow's further ordeal, he would have to go elsewhere, if only for an hour or so.

He did not move quickly enough, though. One demand he could not put off with excuse of fatigue, and that was Cinhil's. The king's page arrived just as he was preparing to slip away, his master's message couched in courteous terms, but carrying the unmistakable force of a royal summons.

So, muffled in the anonymity of a black mantle, the folds of the hood drawn close to shield his identity from the light of the page's torch, Camber followed the boy out of the archbishop's palace and through the cathedral yard, to enter the keep through a postern door in the great south gate. Soon he was climbing the spiral turnpike of the King's Tower, to be admitted by the king himself, almost before the page could knock.

Without speaking, Cinhil invited his guest to a seat beside the fireplace, himself standing on the hearth, hands resting on the mantel beam, half looking over his shoulder at Camber. He was dressed for bed, in a long, fur-lined dressing gown, but it was obvious that sleep was far from his thoughts.

"So they mean to make him a saint," he said.

"It does seem inevitable," Camber replied.

Cinhil looked at him shrewdly. "Why, Bishop Cullen, you sound less than enthusiastic. Can it be that you don't approve of what your fellow clerics are doing?"

"I hardly think my approval is the issue, Sire," said Camber. "I've simply never known a saint before. The thought that one might have crept upon us unawares is frankly unnerving. But I gather you've already been given a full report on what happened this afternoon?"

Cinhil nodded, turning to lean against the side of the fireplace, cold hands pressed between his body and the fire-warmed stone.

"Jebediah came and told me, as soon as the council had adjourned. He says this Dom Queron intends to call additional witnesses tomorrow. Of course, Jebediah doesn't know about what happened that night in your quarters, but what about Queron? Or does Jebediah know, too?"

"Not unless Dualta told him, though I don't think he did. Jebediah would have said something to me. However, I'm almost certain that Queron knows. He has carefully avoided mentioning you by name, but he made several references to a high-ranking witness, not present, whose word is unimpeachable. Who else could he mean?"

"Then Dualta must have told *him*," Cinhil concluded.

"Probably. Dualta wasn't there today—in fact, I haven't seen him for months—but Queron did indicate that he would produce absent witnesses tomorrow. One can only assume that Dualta will be among them. Rhys received a summons."

"Blast the man's competence!" Cinhil hissed. "Does anyone else know?"

"About you? Jaffray, for certain."

"*Jaffray?*"

"Of course. After all, he could hardly have Truth-Read Queron and not be aware of all Queron's arguments. However, he, too, has declined to bring your name into evidence yet, for reasons best known to himself and Queron. He's apparently content to let Queron present the case in his own good time, to feign ignorance of any but the matter directly at hand, until Queron is ready for it to be revealed."

"I fail to see the logic in that," Cinhil muttered.

"Why, to enhance his credibility with the human contingent, I should imagine. Whether he means to or not, that's what's happening. All the bishops appear to trust Jaffray, and especially the human ones. It was Bishop O'Beirne who urged Jaffray to perform the Truth-Read and confirm Queron's original testimony, after Queron had suggested it. I doubt there are half a dozen men who were present who are still unconvinced that Guaire did, indeed, see Camber MacRorie." *And none of them realizes that he really did,* Camber added to himself.

Cinhil harrumphed and threw himself into another chair beside Camber.

"Jaffray. He's going to be a problem, isn't he? He was here briefly, too, you know."

"Oh?"

"Yes. He asked permission to move tomorrow's session into the great hall here at the castle, to accommodate the increased attendance he expects, once word of this gets out."

"And he invited you to attend," Camber guessed.

"Well, I could hardly refuse, could I? After all, I'm the king. Your precious Camber saw to that. If the kingmaker is going to be canonized, then the king should obviously support the measure. It would be highly disrespectful, not to mention ungrateful, if His Highness did not grace this august assemblage."

Camber could not help a small Alister smile. "Jaffray said that?"

"Not in so many words, but the meaning was plain enough. He'll force me to testify, too, won't he?"

"Well, I hardly think that 'force' is the proper word, but, yes, he'll certainly try to persuade you. Or Queron will. He'd be a fool not to. Your value as a witness is inestimable. Everyone knows that Cinhil Haldane would never dare to lie under oath. And if the king attests to a miracle regarding Camber MacRorie, who can gainsay him?"

Cinhil looked down at the floor, silent for some seconds. When he finally stirred, it was to gaze into the dancing flames on the hearth before him.

"Was it a miracle, Alister? What did I really see? I've asked myself a thousand times since then, but I'm still no closer to an answer. I'm not even certain I'm capable of objectivity, where he's concerned. How can I feel so many conflicting emotions about one man? In some respects, I have to admit that I respected and even admired him, but another part of me hates him for what he did to me."

Camber dared not meet the king's eyes.

"He gave and demanded much, Sire. He did what he thought he must, but the cost was great, for you and for him. I think he would not fault you for your uncertainty, though. I suspect that he, too, had mixed emotions about what he felt he had to do. He would not have hurt you, had there been any other way to save Gwynedd."

"But was he a saint?" Cinhil whispered. "They will ask me, Alister. How can I speak of what I do not know?"

"Then, if you must speak, speak of what you saw and do not make a judgment, Sire. Let that be upon the bishops' heads. Such things are no longer your concern."

"Are they not?" Cinhil replied softly.

A strange, almost awkward silence settled between them, with Camber receiving the definite impression that Cinhil was struggling with himself, that there was something else bothering the king which he had not yet revealed. After a few minutes, Cinhil rose and began pacing a brisk, nervous track between the two chairs and the hearth, back and forth, only a few steps to either direction. Finally, he stopped to face the watching bishop.

"There's something I wish to confess to you, Alister. I have wanted to tell you for some time, but I —was afraid you wouldn't approve. You probably still won't."

Camber furrowed his bushy Alister brows. "If you seek absolution, you have your own very capable confessor, Sire."

"No, I wish to confess to you, even if you cannot grant absolution, once you've heard. Will you hear me, Alister?"

"Very well, if you wish."

Camber felt distinctly uncomfortable as he rose and followed Cinhil across the room to a lighted candlestick which the king picked up and carried toward his bed. Camber was wondering where they were going, for the oratory was behind them, when Cinhil paused at the foot of the bed and knelt before a large, metal-bound trunk. He handed the candlestick up to Camber and then manipulated the locking mechanism and opened the lid. As he turned back the top layer of brown wool, the rich tracery of ecclesiastical embroidery gleamed in Camber's candlelight.

Camber caught his breath as Cinhil lifted that layer, for beneath lay a chalice, paten, and other priestly accoutrements. He knelt down to lay one hand on the edge of the trunk in disbelief, somehow knowing that these did not belong to Cinhil's confessor, not daring to articulate what he was thinking. If what he suspected was true . . .

Almost as though he were no longer aware of Camber's presence, Cinhil pulled out a neatly folded bundle of fabric and shook out the folds of a chasuble, white silk and gleaming gold. He stared at the cruciform orphrey bands limning the shoulders and breast, as though trying to divine some new justification for his conscience, then laid the garment over his arms for the bishop's inspection.

"It's beautiful, isn't it?" he whispered.

Chapter Twenty-Three

I desire to be present with you now,
and to change my voice;
for I stand in doubt of you.
                              —Galatians 4:20

"I'm—not sure I understand, Sire," Camber said, after a slight pause, afraid that he understood far too well. "Aren't these Father Alfred's vestments?"

"No, they're mine. Father Alfred has never used them."

"But you have," Camber said, in a flat, stunned voice.

"Yes—since the day you were consecrated bishop, every day, faithfully, even as I used to do."

With a sigh, Camber leaned one elbow on the edge of the trunk and rubbed his forehead, trying to decide how to respond. How had he not foreseen this? No wonder Cinhil had seemed to settle down, of late.

He knew what his response *should* be, of course. Alister Cullen could quote chapter and verse of canon law and why Cinhil, as a laicized priest, was courting serious sanctions by resuming the exercise of his office. Even Camber, in the relative newness of his own year-old priesthood, was well aware of the ecclesiastical implications of what Cinhil had done. Any priest would be.

But he could not find it in his heart to condemn Cinhil. Had he not already brought enough unhappiness to the pious king? What harm did it do for Cinhil to resume his priestly functions in private? A priest was a priest forever, never mind the words of a now-dead archbishop who had commanded this particular priest to set aside his office and assume a crown. If celebration of his love for God helped to ease Cinhil's mourning for his stolen vocation, and made the bearing of his royal exile easier, then who was the supposedly dead Camber MacRorie, in his own hypocrisy, to tell the king he must not do it? Could this not be Cinhil's secret, as Camber had his?

"You're shocked, aren't you?" Cinhil whispered, when he could stand the silence of Camber's contemplation no longer. "God, you must think me some kind of a monster!"

Camber looked up at the king with a start. He had not realized how his silence must be feeding Cinhil's guilt—as if the poor, beleaguered king needed a further portion of remorse. What Cinhil had done was unwise, and could have drastic repercussions if his secret were ever learned by anyone else, but he must not be allowed to add this failing to what he already considered to be a shattered life.

"Monster?" he murmured. "Good God, no, Cinhil! That was the furthest thing from my mind, believe me. I confess, I was surprised. You know the law in this regard as well as I—better, perhaps, for you surely considered very carefully before doing what you did."

Cinhil nodded miserably, too overcome to make a verbal response.

"Tell me, does it give you comfort, what you do?" Camber asked gently.

"It—is my life's blood!" Cinhil choked, head bowing over the chasuble in his arms.

For a moment, Camber said nothing, not daring to disturb the balance which Cinhil was so precariously maintaining between longing and near despair. He watched Cinhil's thumb caress the folds of creamy silk, caught the trembling of the hand Cinhil thought he could not see. He wondered whether Cinhil thought he would try to take the chasuble away from him.

"Cinhil?" he finally said, leaning closer but not touching the tensed body. "Cinhil, I want you to realize that I understand what has brought you to this. I understand, and I do not condemn you for it. I will not even forbid it. Nor can I think that Our Lord, in His infinite comprehension of all men's hearts, would hold such love of Him against you."

Cinhil swallowed and raised his head slowly, dazed eyes seeking visual confirmation of what he had just heard.

"Do you really mean that?"

"I do."

Cinhil seemed to ponder that for a moment, but then he glanced at Camber's bishop's ring and sighed as he began folding the chasuble once more.

"Well, you may be right about Him—I want to believe that you are. But what about the bishops? What will they do to me when they find out?"

"Why, how should they find out, Sire?" Camber asked, his brow furrowing as Cinhil laid the vestment back in the trunk. "You've confessed to me. Do you intend to confess to the rest, as well?"

"You won't tell them, then?" Cinhil said hopefully.

For answer, Camber reached into the trunk and felt among the folded vestments until he found what he had seen before: a wide, embroidered stole of violet silk. This he pulled out and held across the fingers of his right hand, his eyes rising to meet Cinhil's.

"Do you see this, Sire?"

"Yes."

"Well, there is another like it, which you cannot see. It has lain around my neck since I rose from yonder chair beside the fire. How should I tell anyone what you have confided? Do you think my vows less binding than your own?"

They prayed together after that; and in a little while, Cinhil shyly asked his brother priest to help him celebrate a Mass. With some misgivings, Camber consented, serving as deacon and making the responses as Cinhil moved through the rite. But his hesitancy soon melted away in the fire of Cinhil's devotion; and partway through the Mass, the king's thoughts and prayers began to soar with the same fervent clarity which Camber had not seen since a long-ago night in a hidden, rock-bound chapel. So open and single of mind was Cinhil that Camber could almost have read him like a fine-penned scroll at noon, without the king being any the wiser. The experience confirmed that Camber had been right in taking an accepting stance on Cinhil's technical disobedience, and helped to cement even further the rapport which had been building steadily between king and bishop all through the past year.

But for all its reassurance, the incident was strained for Camber. By the time he left, an hour later, he was even more in need of the solitude he had originally sought. Taking a torch from one of the guards at the foot of the King's Tower, he made his way back through the castle yard and out the southern gate once more, hardly daring to let himself think about what he had just learned. When finally he re-entered the wing of the archbishop's palace where his own apartments lay, he went down instead of up, into the older levels, passing at last through a modest oak door onto a stone-paved landing. A small chapel lay below him, accessible by a wide, man-high flight of stairs which ended in the center of the chamber.

It was not Camber's favorite retreat, especially at this winter time of year, but it was out of the way and usually deserted, as it was tonight: a fitting refuge for one who must wrestle ancient wars of conscience. The simple barrel vaulting had originally been lime-washed, in hopes that the white would help to gather the scant daylight which filtered through the three arched lights set high and deep above the door; but time and the dampness had made the lime flake off in unsightly patches. The walls, once frescoed with scenes from the life of the Virgin, had long since been abandoned as a lost cause and mostly chipped back to the bare stone.

Still, the chapel was not in ruin. The floor was kept scoured clean and the altar maintained, for the place was still used by the occasional overflow of visiting priests who must find somewhere to celebrate their daily Office. But there were no frills. The altar was bare of ornament except for the necessary linens, two candles in nondescript holders, a plain wooden crucifix, almost crude in its execution, and a graceful but time-grayed statue of the Virgin which stood with downcast eyes beside an unpretentious tabernacle, arms folded across her breast in an attitude of perpetual adoration. No place for high-flown grandeur, this.

With a sigh, Camber started down the steps, his torch casting a circle of ruddy light around his feet as he descended, the only illumination besides the sanctuary lamp burning red above the altar. He bowed and crossed himself at the foot of the steps, then shoved his torch into a cresset set in the rough north wall. Then he returned to the space before the altar and lowered himself to the floor, to lay prostrate as he had on the night of his ordination, only the layers of his mantle somewhat insulating him from the cold and dampness of the stone.

God help him, where did he now stand? What had he done today, in the furtherance of his own perhaps misguided judgment? Was he going to be able to live with what he had wrought, in the days and months and years ahead?

What about Cinhil, for example? Camber had told him that an infinitely compassionate God would not hold his loving disobedience against him—but suppose Camber was wrong? By reassuring Cinhil, perhaps Camber was plunging the already foundering king into even deeper disfavor with a God who was also infinitely just.

And while he was on the subject of justice, what would a just God have to say, in the final reckoning, to a man who was allowing His Church to be led astray and call holy one who knew himself not to be as he appeared, whose entire present existence was based upon a grand deception?

Was he wrong to let the charade continue? Had he now involved God's honor? Had he really been motivated by the betterment of the kingdom, or was he a victim of his own pride, seduced by the arrogant belief that his guidance, and no other, could save the kingdom and the king?

And yet, his original justification still *seemed* solid. Without Cinhil, coolly plucked from his monastic life and forced to assume his destined role as king, Gwynedd would probably still lie under the cruel and negligent rule of Imre of Festil. And without the continuing temperance of Alister Cullen, whoever the guiding mind behind the external façade, Cinhil would have been expending far too much energy in sullen resentment of the man who had placed him where he still did not wish to be.

Now Cinhil was beginning to function as a king should function, especially as he found his own personal stride within the framework of the part he had been dealt. Already, awesome gains had been made in the governance of Gwynedd, not to mention the expansion in size and alliances. If Camber had not done what he had done, where would Cinhil be today? Where might Gwynedd be tomorrow?

The opening of the chapel door intruded on his inner dialogue at that. His first thought was to wonder whether someone had sought and found him, or if it was simply someone else looking for a quiet retreat, who had also known that this chapel was not often used at this hour.

He did not move as footsteps entered and paused on the landing, hoping that whoever it was would have the good sense to go away and leave him in peace, seeing his attitude of prostration and realizing that he did not wish to be disturbed.

But the intruder did not move from the top of the

landing. Camber could hear him breathing lightly, caught the hollow scrape of boot on stone as the watcher shifted weight minutely. The total absence of any psychic impression told him that the intruder was Deryni, too, his mind carefully shielded from any intrusion. The door closed, but the footsteps had not moved back through the doorway first.

With a sigh, Camber raised his head and got stiffly to his knees, the cold which had permeated him suddenly achingly apparent. His hood fell back from his head as he turned to look up.

Jebediah stood there on the landing above him, handsome face turned to a grim mask by the light of the torch he held, white sword belt gleaming against the dark of the rest of his raiment.

"I thought I might find you here," he said in a low voice.

Camber felt a shiver of apprehension ascend his spine, a chill unconnected with the tomb-coldness of the room itself. Why had Jebediah sought him out, and why so grave of mien? Could the grand master possibly suspect that Alister Cullen was not all he seemed? Had Camber made some fatal error in council this afternoon?

No, that was paranoia slipping into his thinking. As serious as the possibility of suspicion was the probability that Jebediah had finally decided to press him for the reasons for their decreased personal relationship in the past year. While that could prove distinctly awkward, it was far preferable to suspicions of Alister himself.

Camber got clumsily to his feet, giving Jebediah an open, welcoming smile.

"Ah, Jebediah. And here, I thought I'd found a refuge, safe even from you," he said lightly. "After this afternoon, and several hours with the king, I felt the unmistakable need for solitude. But you are always welcome."

"Am I?"

Turning, Jebediah dropped the door bar into place

with an ominous thud and then moved rapidly down the steps to put his torch on the wall opposite Camber's.

"Actually, I thought we might talk," he continued, bending his knee to the Presence signified by the altar lamp. "We really don't get much chance any more, you know—except officially, of course. Frankly, I find our joint planning sessions with Cinhil and the council a poor substitute for the times we used to share."

"Well, our various duties—"

"Are perhaps not the real reason for our distance," Jebediah interrupted. He leaned both hands on the hilt of his sword and looked at the floor. "Strange, but I have the recurring notion—and I pray I'm wrong—that being the bishop's secretary is perhaps more important than merely being His Grace's friend of many years' standing. I'm sorry if that sounds petulant, Alister."

Camber, hands clasped behind his back in an unconscious Alister gesture, was so startled at the bitterness in those last words that he could only stare in amazement. Why, Jebediah was jealous of Joram!

"My God, Jeb, you surely don't think that, do you?" he asked softly, when he had recovered from his initial shock. "Why, we've both been so busy this past year, I in Grecotha and here, and you here and on campaign—I thought you understood that. Joram was *with* me, almost like a son. Surely you don't begrudge him my support now, when he needs it most?"

"Begrudge him? No," Jebediah whispered. "I envy him, though. It's a fault, I know, but I can't help it. I envy his time with you, his interaction with your life, the way we used to be. We were both busy in the old days, too, Alister, but we still managed to find the time to share our problems and successes." He looked up, hardly able to meet Camber's eyes, in his misery. "Oh, I understand that you're a bishop now, and cannot, in your office, open all to me. I understand that." He looked away again. "But I always thought you realized how much your friendship meant to me.

Sometimes it's almost as if you had died instead of Camber."

All but gasping inwardly, Camber wondered whether Jebediah realized what he had said. The statement had to have been a chance one. Jebediah was concerned about his apparent replacement in Alister's affections by Joram. He was not worried about the year-dead Camber, at least for now. Jebediah could not know the truth, or even suspect. He was too blunt to pretend innocence on that important an issue.

But suspicion could grow, if Camber did not do something, and quickly. Jebediah was a very astute observer, and might even guess the truth, in time. And in his present bitter state, if Camber could not immediately ensure his cooperation and silence, then he could not be allowed to leave this room.

That judgment was a harsh one, Camber knew. It was not one he even wished to consider, but there might eventually be no other way around it. Jebediah was strong, both physically and psychically. If it came to a purely physical confrontation, Camber doubted very much whether he could beat the battle-fit younger man. At one time, Alister and Jebediah had been well matched in speed and skill; but Camber, though competent, had never been the swordsman Alister had been, and certainly had not been able to keep up his practice in these past grueling months.

Even an arcane confrontation was not a certain victory, though here Camber would have the decided edge. Jebediah would not be expecting a psychic ambush. Alister had always been somewhat reticent about using his Deryni abilities except for inner exploration, whereas Camber had honed all his talents to a fine edge.

But Jebediah knew Alister's mental touch intimately. Part of the great attraction between the two men had always been their similar levels of potential and intuition, the groundpoint for frequent communion of minds in deep spiritual sharing—a sensitive side to the grand master which few other warriors even suspected.

Yes, given the alternatives, a psychic approach was undoubtedly the best; but it would have to be on Camber's terms from the beginning. If Camber were to succeed, he must overwhelm Jebediah's defenses before he even realized that battle had been engaged —and that would depend upon how much control he could secure before Jebediah realized he was not dealing with Alister. Total success would enable him to take Jebediah into his confidence and win him as an ally; even partial failure would make of Jebediah a prisoner or, worse, a casualty. Camber did not even want to think about the latter possibility.

Whatever the outcome, the task must be begun. Only a few seconds had elapsed while Camber weighed the possibilities, but now he must make his move or risk complicating an already delicate situation. Shifting his weight uncomfortably, he chanced a hesitant, sidelong glance at Jebediah, allowing the pale, sea-ice eyes to mirror some of the real pain which Alister would have felt at Jebediah's jealous words.

"I'm—sorry, Jeb. I hadn't realized."

"No, I don't suppose you did," Jebediah whispered, head still bowed.

Wetting his lips nervously, Camber continued, letting the part of him that was Alister come to the fore, there at the most surface level of his awareness.

"Can you forgive me?" he asked. "It's a fault to become so wrapped up in one's own affairs that one hasn't time for comfort. It must have been terrible for you."

Jebediah dared to lift his head, though he still could not bear to meet the sea-ice eyes. "Aye, it was terrible. I doubt you can even imagine how it hurt to see you struggling alone, before Camber's funeral. You wouldn't share your burden. You totally shut me out. I never did understand why."

As he finally looked Camber full in the face, Camber realized that this was the opening he had been trying to build, to set Jebediah up for the psychic encounter which would decide both their futures.

Swallowing, Camber returned Jebediah's gaze, letting just a trace of Alister's most surface levels, of concern and remorse, open to the other's query. Instantly he saw a spark of hopefulness igniting in the other's eyes, caught Jebediah's quick intake of breath as he finally met something in his friend's mind beyond rigid shields.

"Dare I hope?" Jebediah murmured.

"You know it cannot be as it was before," Camber breathed, neither opening further nor shutting down what contact had been made. "I have promises to guard now which were not mine before."

Jebediah nodded, wide-eyed, accepting without question.

"But if you are willing to yield control," Camber continued, "to let me be the one who guides the depth of our exchange—then perhaps I can share some of what has occupied my mind these many months of separation. Later, when I am more certain of my own limitations, perhaps a more equal sharing will be possible."

A shy, hopeful smile twitched at Jebediah's mouth, almost out of place on the rugged, handsome face. "Hardly the promise of our former communion, but I understand the reason. You will forgive me if I mourn that necessity just a little?"

"I should always forgive you, Jeb," Camber answered quietly, himself mourning the necessity as he acknowledged his own intentions. "Shall we sit here on the steps? It's been a long day, and my bones ache from the cold."

As Camber drew his mantle closer and sat on the second step, easing his back against the next, Jebediah folded his lean body to a seat on the bottommost one without a word, the tooled scabbard of his sword stretched between them along the length of his outstretched, booted legs.

"This will be rather different from the old days," the grand master said, taking a deep breath as he raised his eyes to Camber. "I'm as nervous as before a battle."

"I know," Camber replied.

He dropped his hands to Jebediah's shoulders and pulled him back to lean against his knee, at the same time gathering his own essence deep within him, so that only the Alister part of him might show at first. As he raised his right hand, the one which wore the bishop's ring, he hesitated for just an instant to clench and unclench his fist as though warming his fingers—long enough for the purple gemstone to catch Jebediah's eye and remind him, if only on some deep, inner level, of the reason for this unequal sharing.

Then he brought that hand to the back of Jebediah's neck, to cup the already tilting head in the fan of his fingers. Jebediah responded immediately to the familiar touch, breathing out with a sigh and letting his head loll against Camber's hand, eyes fluttering dreamily as he began to open to the contact. Camber let a little more of Alister's personality seep through the bond being forged and felt Jebediah's consciousness stilling in further response, no hint of suspicion yet fogging the clarity of that well-ordered mind.

"Let go now," Camber said softly, as much a thought as a whisper, as he stretched to the furthest limits of revealment which he dared, using only Alister's memories.

And to his amazement, Jebediah did let go, taking the sparseness of the Alister contact for natural caution as his old friend explored the limits to which he might share and still retain the security of his office.

Camber marveled at the naive trust, at the same time hating himself for having to betray it. Gathering all his resources for one massive onslaught, quick and without warning, he poised and then swooped, seizing so many avenues simultaneously that Jebediah never had a chance to realize what was happening until it was too late to resist effectively.

Jebediah gasped and flinched under Camber's hands at the force of the contact, mind staggering with the shock of an alien consciousness overwhelming his own. He could not do more. Physically and psychically blind now, he struggled helplessly against the bonds already formed, shrinking from the constant new incursions, fruitlessly trying to prevent the imposition of knowledge which he had not expected, had not wanted, would not have considered, had he retained control of his own mind.

Only in sheer body reflex was he at all able to resist Camber's bidding, warrior's muscles responding to the threat even if the warrior's mind could not. Almost independent of his mind's frantic struggling, his right hand crawled to the dagger at his right side, closing half-paralyzed fingers around the ivory hilt, dragging the blade slowly from its sheath.

Camber saw the movement, and shifted quickly to block the rising hand. Relenting not one iota from his task of education, he twisted around to straddle the now-sprawling Michaeline and redouble his assault, left hand locked around Jebediah's powerful wrist in a separate war of strength as his will forced knowledge into Jebediah's mind, giving all the necessary details, from Alister's death to the present.

Jebediah shook his head in denial and cried out, a despairing animal moan of grief, as he stared up at Camber with blank, unseeing eyes. His left hand lashed out to twist itself in the neck of Camber's mantle, pulling Camber down closer as the dagger hand rose slowly against the grasp of Camber's, nearer and nearer to Camber's throat.

But Camber would not be distracted. Relentlessly he drove home the final realizations: the benefits already accrued to Cinhil; the smallness of their numbers who knew the truth of Camber-Alister; the consequences if the play did not go on, in terms of anti-Deryni backlash already brewing in small ways among the restored human nobility; the trap of all of them who were now committed to play out the charade—and that Camber and his children were willing to make any necessary sacrifice for the sake of Gwynedd. Was Jebediah?

With that, Camber disengaged from all controls save one: a touch which would bring swift unconsciousness and, if necessary, death. At the same time, he bade his long-borrowed shape melt away from him, his own Camber face gazing down at Jebediah in hope and compassion. The dagger was resting against his throat now, near to drawing blood, but he ignored its deadly pressure, praying that Jebediah's good common sense would keep him from rejecting what had been revealed and forcing Camber to use his ultimate weapon.

And Jebediah, sensing his release but not yet the full significance of what had happened, arched his body from under Camber's in that first instant of freedom and rolled with him to the floor, to straddle his former captor and sit upon his chest, dagger pressed close against the quickened pulse, his other hand twisted in the mantle to choke out what life the dagger spared.

Camber went totally limp, quicksilver eyes beseeching as they stared calmly up into Jebediah's crazed ones, arms outflung to either side in an attitude of total physical surrender.

And finally Jebediah saw, and knew, and realized what he was about to do. With a strangled gasp, his eyes once more reflected reason and his hand opened in reflex horror at what it held. Camber could almost see the succession of memories which flashed through Jebediah's mind as he froze there, open-palmed hand still poised beside Camber's neck, though the dagger now lay on the floor beside the silver-gilt head.

Then the staring eyes closed, and the frantically working throat choked out a single sob, and Jebediah was collapsing to weep unashamedly in Camber's arms.

Slowly Camber eased from under Jebediah's weight, struggling to a cramped sitting position, the while cradling the sobbing Jebediah in his arms as he would have soothed one of his own children, as Jebediah mourned the loss of his friend and brother. After a while, when the sobs had subsided somewhat, Camber stroked the trembling head lightly, calling Jebediah back to the present.

"I'm sorry I had to do that," he finally whispered, when he was sure that Jebediah's reason was once more regaining control over sheer emotion. "I suppose I should have told you sooner. You, of all people, had a right to know.

"But we were paranoid, all of us. We thought— and rightly, for most, but not for you—that the fewer people who knew, the safer we would be. I almost didn't tell you, even tonight, but I was afraid you were about to guess and that I wouldn't be able to control your anger if you did. I almost couldn't, as it was. I know now that I should never have done what I did in that hall this afternoon in front of you. I was afraid you might see something not of Alister in me."

With a loud sniff, Jebediah drew away, to wipe a sleeve across eyes and nose and sit up against the bottom of the stair, knees drawn close against his chest. Camber, too, took advantage of the opportunity to ease to a less-cramped position, though he would not have moved before that and disturbed Jebediah's settling for all his body's ease.

"I—didn't, really," Jebediah murmured, responding to Camber's last statement. "I mean, I realized that something was different, and I—I *was* jealous of Joram—but I never dreamed that it wasn't Alister— or that it was you."

As he looked up, he made a visible effort to regain control of at least his expression, swallowing with difficulty and taking a deep breath to steady himself.

"What—" He gulped and began again. "What would you have done, if you hadn't been able to make me accept—this?"

As he gestured toward Camber's face, Camber pursed his lips and glanced down for an instant, then reached out to his final control and exerted the slightest amount of pressure as he looked up again.

"I'm afraid I was not as honest as you would like to believe," he whispered, as Jebediah felt the effect and reeled on the edge of unconsciousness. He released the pressure and the final control and grasped Jebediah's upper arm in a steadying hold. "As you can see, I held back one last, desperate weapon. If I'd really had to use it—I'm not sure what I would have done."

Jebediah winced, nodding slowly in acceptance of that revelation. "You would have killed me," he said, quite dispassionately. "And you would have been right. You couldn't let me leave here as anything less than an ally. The cause you've been working for is far too important to endanger by my angry betrayal." He paused. "My God, what agonies you must have endured in these past months since his death! Why, my disappointment was nothing beside your—"

"Hush." Camber held up a hand and shook his head. "You had a right to feel the way you did. Your grief was no less real for being based on a lie unknown to you. I wish I could have been more bold, to give you truth before today. *He* would never have subjected you to the loneliness and rejection which I forced upon you."

"No, but he would have understood the things you did," Jebediah whispered. "And—had he been you, I think he might have done the same."

"Perhaps."

A moment of thoughtful silence, mutually shared, and then Jebediah drew breath and spoke again.

"A year and more ago, I made you an offer, Camber-Alister," he breathed, hardly daring to speak aloud in the solemnity of the moment. "I did not know you fully then, though I thought I did, but I offered you my help, to ease the burden which you carried. You refused me. And now I find I know you even less than I did then. But please do not refuse me again. Let me help."

For an instant, Camber searched the sorrowing eyes —bloodshot now, with their former weeping—reading the trust and loyalty which he had always known was there for Alister, and which he had sensed he might find for himself but had never dared to verify, for fear of losing all. As he stretched out his arm, to lay his right hand on Jebediah's open palm, he let first Alister and then Camber flow out and mingle with the timidly offered Jebediah, gasping with the sheer delight which the unexpected three-way interaction evoked.

He had not realized the fullness of the Alister part of him before this very instant, feeling it interact with the mind of the man who had known and loved Alister Cullen perhaps better than any other living person. Jebediah, too, was astonished at the contact, his own memories and experiences of Alister merging and fusing with the pseudo-Alister almost as if a physical presence held that essence and urged its participation in this strange sharing which neither Jebediah nor Camber had dreamed possible.

They sat there, wrists clasped across the space between them, for nearly an hour, delighting in their mutual discoveries, sorrowing at their disappointments, even laughing aloud from time to time as some new facet of sharing fell beneath their scrutiny. Then finally they stirred, Camber to resume the shape of the man he now understood far, far better than he had ever dreamed possible, and Jebediah to watch in awed fascination as a new friend took back the form of an older one who was not totally lost after all.

Chapter Twenty-Four

For neither at any time used we flattering words,
as ye know, nor a cloak of covetousness;
God is witness: nor of men sought we glory.
                                        —I Thessalonians 2:5–6

The tale of Camber's sainting was not finished, much to Camber's distaste. The Council of Bishops, when it reconvened early the next morning in the castle's great hall, showed every sign of being as awful as Camber had feared. A festival atmosphere prevailed. He even overheard one monk remark to another that today's testimony would probably be almost boring, the question no longer being *whether* sanctity should be accorded Camber of Culdi, but *to what degree!*

That bothered him, as he and Joram wound their way among the milling clerics and tried to reach their seats, though he had forced himself to accept the probability that canonization was now a foregone conclusion. He had consoled himself by ensuring that, if it was inevitable, further testimony by those who knew the truth could not be turned in such a way as to reveal the secret they were preserving at such cost. His principals, now including Jebediah, had all been briefed as thoroughly as he dared the night before. Unless something totally unexpected happened, the hearing would progress to the logical conclusion which Queron and the Servants of Saint Camber had planned all along. Compared to the day before, he felt almost safe—at least from discovery by mortal agents involved in the situation. Immortal agents were quite another story; he still had not resolved where he might stand with his Creator as a consequence of what he was allowing to be done.

As he took his seat, he saw Jebediah come onto the dais with Jaffray's chamberlain, apparently arguing over the arrangement of additional stools for clarks who would take down the proceedings. He could not hear what they were saying, but after a few minutes Archbishop Oriss got up from his chair to the right of the dais—he having been relegated to a lower position to accommodate the king's throne—and suddenly there was no argument. The chamberlain bowed, Jebediah bowed, and the stools were returned to the places they had occupied before the argument started. Jebediah, with a shrug and a quick glance in Camber's direction, melted back into the crowd still milling in the center of the hall and disappeared through a side door, through which the king would shortly enter.

Many seemed to take their cues from that, moving noisily into the three rows of chairs along each side of the hall and beginning to settle in their places. In the packed gallery above the far end of the hall, Camber thought he saw a flash of Rhys's red hair, but he could not be certain.

He was not given time to ponder further, though, for at that moment, Bishop Eustace slipped into place beside him with a hearty greeting. The jocular Eustace could not fail to notice his colleague's subdued response, and, on pursuing the matter, learned that his distinguished fellow had spent much of the previous night in prayer for guidance—which was true, if not in precisely the sense that Eustace understood it— and had concluded that he should accede to the will of the majority of the Council of Bishops when it came to the vote, counting himself too personally involved, however indirectly, to pass objective judgment. Eustace, human that he was, could hardly be faulted for not catching all the shades of Camber's meaning and thinking he was only tired.

Nor was Eustace content to stop at that. Garrulous as ever, he noted that even Joram seemed to have gained a certain resignation with his recovery from the previous afternoon's ordeal. Of course, Eustace was quick to point out that Joram's sister and brother-in-law, present, so he understood, in the gallery with the queen and various other of the nobility, could hardly be expected to appear as resigned as Joram, not having had the benefit of witnessing the previous day's remarkable testimony. But if today was anything like yesterday, Eustace had no doubt that they, too, would soon be convinced of the sanctity of Camber Mac-Rorie.

Eustace was. So were at least three of his esteemed colleagues. Surely Evaine MacRorie Thuryn, devoted daughter of the late earl, as everyone knew, could not for long deny her father's saintliness in the face of such conclusive evidence; and all knew of the Healer Rhys Thuryn's lifelong loyalty to the man who had become his father-in-law. Why, the queen herself had been Camber's ward before her marriage to the king. How could any of them doubt that Camber had been a very holy man?

A trumpet fanfare silenced further verbal speculation, much to Camber's unqualified relief, and then king and primate-archbishop were simultaneously entering from opposite sides of the hall to the chanting of a spirited *Te Deum*. As all rose to bow, the two passed to the dais with their several attendants, the king in a robe of somber but formally cut forest green, the state crown of leaves and crosses gleaming on his white-winged raven head. Jaffray, not to be outdone, had donned full ecclesiasticals for today's session, down to the jeweled cope and miter, where the day before he had been content with the purple and simple skullcap of any other bishop.

The point was not lost on the assembled company as the two men sat, Cinhil a trifle before the archbishop. Though this was Cinhil's hall, it was still Jaffray's court. As Primate of All Gwynedd, Archbishop Jaffray of Valoret held total precedence in matters spiritual.

The morning's business progressed smoothly enough at first. Following Jaffray's introduction and a brief summary of what had been established the day before, Queron presented two of his brother Servants of Saint Camber who had accompanied him on a certain visit to Camber's tomb at Caerrorie and had them relate their findings—or lack of findings—to a spellbound court.

The two men told a chilling story: how they, with Queron, had secretly gained entry to the MacRorie family chapel one dark, moonless night the previous summer and stolen into the crypt where lay the tomb of their revered master. Queron had countered the standard Deryni-set spells customarily placed on a Deryni grave to protect it from grave robbers, and then the three of them had pried open the door to the tomb.

But when they had lifted the lid of the sarcophagus and held their torches close, fully expecting to see the lead-wrapped coffin of the Earl of Culdi—there was nothing there! The tomb was empty!

The audience breathed sighs of wonder, as if that information had never been explored the day before, so caught up were they in the unfolding story. Queron noticed the effect, but did not dwell upon it, turning instead to a scholarly examination of his two witnesses: How did they know that Camber had *ever* been in the tomb? Perhaps the tomb had always been empty.

But, no, one of the witnesses reminded him—one Charles, who had been a baker in the village below Caerrorie at the time of Camber's death. He had seen the burial with his own eyes, the day Camber's body came home from Valoret. Of course the tomb had been occupied.

Further, neither of the men could explain how the body might have been removed by any human agency

—human here being taken to mean mortal, as opposed to supernatural. Nor could they discern any motive for some secret removal by Father Joram MacRorie, as the young priest had claimed. On the contrary, the same Charles had seen Father Joram and the Lord Rhys come to visit the tomb several months ago, he having been sent by his brethren to watch for any sign that someone knew the body was no longer there. Why, after so long, should Joram and Rhys come disguised to look at the tomb, if they had known that the tomb was empty as Joram claimed? Charles could only conclude that Joram and Rhys *had not known*.

On that point, Queron rested this portion of his argument, there being no way to determine whether Charles's subjective judgment had or had not been valid. Rhys, having been thoroughly briefed by Camber when he attended Joram the night before, denied any knowledge of the removal of Camber's body by Joram or anyone else, deriving moral justification from the fact that they had not moved Camber's body, but Alister's. His denial also tallied with Joram's implication that he had worked alone, at his father's command, such a request obviously having been made before Rhys had become a member of the immediate family.

Queron even questioned the expectant Evaine on the matter, feeling that perhaps Camber might have confided something of his burial wishes to her, as well as to Joram. But of course, Camber had not; and Evaine could truthfully say that she had neither moved nor known of moving her father's body. Since the Lady Evaine had no connection with any of the other evidence which Queron proposed to present, and since she was obviously in a delicate condition, Queron permitted her to retire once more. Camber could not help a small smile of satisfaction, deftly shielded behind one hand ostensibly raised to cover a yawn, as Evaine curtsied innocently and made her way back to the gallery with the studied gravity so often exhibited by very pregnant ladies. Had Queron only known her true part in the matter of "Saint Camber," he would not have been so quick to be so gracious.

All of this took half the morning; and those who had not been present the day before and seen the arcane presentations of evidence were beginning to fidget with boredom by the time Queron had finished his cross-examination regarding the disappearance of Camber's body. But the next presentation brought evidence new to all the observers save those who did not wish to talk about it. From a door by the left-hand fireplace entered at Queron's summons one Lord Dualta Jarriot, his garb proclaiming him a Knight of the Order of Saint Michael.

Dualta approached the thrones stolidly, bowing with formal correctness to Cinhil before kneeling to kiss the archbishop's ring. He avoided the king's gaze, being very much aware that he was disobeying Cinhil's direct command by coming here to testify and praying that Queron could indeed protect him from the king's wrath when it was all over. Naturally, Cinhil dared do nothing to stop him now.

Queron did not employ any Deryni pyrotechnics in his initial examination of Dualta, confining himself to a normal question-and-answer format while he established Dualta's identity and his connection with the incident about to be related. Because of the number of other witnesses who had been present, Queron admitted that he was unable to repeat his energy-draining technique of the day before and *show* what Dualta had seen; but he did reveal that he had, with Dualta's consent, earlier Truth-Read Dualta's testimony and found the young knight to be telling the literal truth.

But he would let Dualta tell his story. The young man was not Deryni, but he did have remarkable recall, having been trained to the Michaeline military discipline which was as legendary in its field as Gabrilite training was to Deryni. Queron was certain that the court would find Lord Dualta's testimony of interest.

So was Camber.

The hall grew hushed as Dualta related the events leading to his "miracle": how he had entered his vicar general's chamber with an unnamed companion to find Cullen unconscious, apparently striving against some overwhelming force which seemed to be affecting everyone in the room.

Camber noted with curiosity that Dualta, too, had refrained from mentioning Cinhil by name as yet. It could only mean that Queron was saving Cinhil's identity as a tour de force; for there was no way that this testimony could be completed without revealing the unnamed observer.

Rhys and Joram had tried to ease the stricken man's distress, Dualta continued, but it was obvious that what fought for him was far stronger than they. Lord Rhys had hinted that it was some vestige of the evil Ariella, which had been continuing to threaten Cullen ever since he had defeated her that night at Iomaire.

Then Cullen had stopped breathing, his face slowly going blue as Rhys and a horrified Joram lowered his body to the floor and began to breathe for him, trying to keep him alive.

And as Dualta told his tale, it was as if he had slipped back to that time somewhat the way that Guaire had, though without the apparent aid of Queron or any other agent, now recalling his own part as though the struggling victim again lay before him in the hall which had become no longer hall but bishop's bedchamber in his mind's eye.

"O God, if Camber were only here!" Dualta cried, falling to his knees and reaching out his hands in supplication. "O God! Camber could save the vicar general!"

For a few seconds, Dualta knelt there as though transfixed, his audience frozen with him in anticipation and gasping as his expression changed from despair to awed wonder.

Then Dualta was describing what he had seen in a low, trembling voice, how Cullen's face had misted over for just an instant and then begun to shift, had seemed to change to the face of Camber MacRorie, as if the one had been superimposed over the other!

The apparition had not lasted long, Dualta finally told them. Rhys, his hands on Cullen's chest, had seemed least affected by what had happened, seemingly accepting the intervention as an assistance so that he could resume his healing work on his patient. As the Healer had closed his eyes and bowed his head, apparently entering his healing trance, the image had faded, the mist dispelled, and the familiar features of Alister Cullen reasserted themselves. Joram, stonily observant while the apparition occurred, had collapsed with his face in his hands and wept when it was all over.

Dualta's face was whiter than the belt he wore, and his eyes still stared at a spot on the floor before him, where some who watched could almost fancy that they also saw what he still saw in the eyes of his own memory. His hands hung in the air, as if he gripped the arm of someone else kneeling there beside him. He turned his head slightly, as if in response to what that person had said, then swallowed and released his hold on air.

"The Lord's Name be praised!" he whispered fervently, crossing himself and then clasping his hands in reverence. "He sent the blessed Camber to help us!" he cried. "The Lord sent Camber to save His servant Alister!"

As he bowed his head in thanksgiving, Queron moved quietly beside him and laid a hand on his shoulder, bending to speak a few words in his ear which the spellbound audience could not hear. In a few seconds, Dualta raised his head and looked at Queron, then at the king, the archbishop, the watching audience. He flashed a nervous, self-conscious ghost of a smile as he got to his feet with Queron's aid.

"I pray you to forgive me, Reverend Lords, Sire," he murmured earnestly, especially beseeching Cinhil as he straightened his mantle with shaking hands. "I had not intended—"

Jaffray waved his hand in negation. "No apologies are necessary, Lord Dualta. Your testimony has been quite enlightening, thus far. Dom Queron, do you intend to have Lord Dualta continue at this time?"

"I am not certain, Your Grace." Queron bowed and turned slightly toward Cinhil. "Sire, we come here to a very delicate matter, for the next portion of the testimony can be better told by another witness of whom Your Highness is doubtless aware. I can, of course, ask Lord Dualta to continue, if you wish, but . . ."

Cinhil had been following the entire examination to this point with tight-lipped concentration, his eyes at least half the time covered by one hand, as if to shade them from the light—though there was precious little in the hall other than from torch and fireplace. Of course, Camber knew that Cinhil was not trying to hide from the light—and he was sure that Queron knew that, too. Jaffray, who also knew what Queron was doing, did not make a point of turning to stare at the king; but he did not have to, for all the other bishops and, indeed, everyone else in the hall were staring for him.

Camber's heart went out to the king. Queron had set this up quite mercilessly. There was no way that Cinhil could avoid testifying now. Queron would make the matter as graceful as possible, but he would not relent.

"Your Highness?" Queron asked softly, as if unsure whether Cinhil had heard his question.

Cinhil toyed with a signet ring on his thumb, still managing to appear nonchalant.

"I was not aware that the king had any jurisdiction in the archbishop's court," he countered, not looking up.

Archbishop Oriss looked at Queron, then at Jaffray, who still had said and done nothing, then at Cinhil.

"Sire? Is this witness known to Your Grace?"

Cinhil nodded slowly, not daring to lift his eyes and thus risk meeting those of any other who had been there. Camber wondered whether Queron and Jaffray had set this up deliberately, baiting Oriss to do their dirty work for them and so force Cinhil to testify—for Cinhil would not lie, no matter what it cost him.

With a sigh, Cinhil turned his face toward Oriss.

"He is well known to me, Archbishop."

"Then should we not hear from him?" Oriss persisted.

When Cinhil did not answer, Eustace, sitting beside Camber, cleared his throat and stood.

"Sire, forgive me, but I do not understand what is happening here. I am a simple man. I do not like intrigues and mysteries. If there is another material witness, then he should be made to come forth. Friendship with Your Grace should not grant him immunity from speaking the truth in so important a matter."

"You are certainly correct, Bishop," Cinhil began evenly, making one last, game try to avoid the issue while he still had the nerve. "It should not. But—confound it, man!" He looked up at Eustace with eyes blazing. "You must be aware of my mixed feelings about Camber. *I was that other witness!* I had not wished to be drawn into this dispute!"

There were many gasps of surprise, for up until that instant, most of the men in the hall had not guessed that Cinhil himself was the unnamed witness. Amazement rustled through the hall like an errant wind, gradually subsiding when Cinhil did not speak further. After a moment of awkward silence, Queron essayed the breach.

"Your Highness, I must apologize. I did not intend for you to be forced into this testimony against your will."

Camber nodded to himself and restrained a bitter smile, knowing that that was *exactly* what Queron had intended.

Queron returned his attention to Jaffray. "My apologies to Your Grace, as well. I should not have mentioned this. With your permission, I should like to ask Lord Dualta to—"

"No."

Cinhil's word was not loud, but it cut Queron off as effectively as though it had been shouted. To the sound of low-voiced murmurs of surprise, Cinhil stood, curtly signaling with his hand for them to remain seated when they would have risen in respect. Removing his crown with steady hands, he laid it gently on the cushion of his throne. Awed silence followed him down the three shallow steps of the dais as he turned to face Jaffray. Without his crown, in his somber robes of near-black green, he looked almost like the ascetic monk he had always wished to be.

"I am prepared to give my testimony in this matter, my Lord Archbishop. Since I do not speak from the throne, you may dispense with regal titles for the duration of this examination."

Jaffray half-stood and bowed, then resumed his seat, glancing at Queron.

"I think we need not place His Grace under oath," he said, half questioning, and then shaking his head as Queron minutely shook his. "Dom Queron, you may proceed with the witness."

Bowing deeply, Queron turned to face Cinhil. This was the witness he had been waiting for, who would confirm all that had been said, even in his understandable reluctance. In fact, that very reluctance would make his testimony all the more telling, for Cinhil had not been exaggerating when he had spoken of his mixed feelings regarding Camber. Cinhil was truly the unimpeachable witness whom Queron had promised, for all that he did not physically wear his crown. Camber could almost read Queron's triumph in his very stance. God, if he but knew what he was really doing!

"I shall try to make this as brief as possible, Father —if I may call you by that title without causing undue pain. All here know that you were once a priest."

Cinhil winced at that, as Queron had intended, reminding all that this was at least one reason Cinhil had for not wishing any honor for Camber. Queron glanced at the floor, considering his next barb.

"Very well, Father. You affirm, then, that you were,

indeed, present in Bishop Cullen's chamber on that night before the Blessed Camber's funeral?"

"Yes," came Cinhil's whispered reply.

"And that you witnessed something quite out of the ordinary concerning Bishop Cullen on that night?"

"Yes," Cinhil said again.

"Excellent," Queron said, scanning his audience and gauging their response. "Now, Father, please tell these Reverend Lords what you saw that night, in as much detail as you can remember. We wish specifically to hear of anything relating to Camber."

Cinhil closed his eyes and swallowed, then looked at the floor and began to relate what he believed he had seen.

His initial testimony did not take long. Glossing over what Dualta had already related, for Dualta's recollection differed very little from his own as far as sequence of events, Cinhil dwelt instead on his own reaction to the alleged miracle: his white-faced disbelief at first, and then his growing awe and almost fear as he realized that he was not mad, and that the others had seen the same thing.

"I did not want to believe it," Cinhil whispered, "even though Dualta had stated what I suppose we were all thinking. I told myself that we must have been mistaken, that miracles do not happen any more. Even Lord Rhys would not commit himself; and Healers are probably the closest thing we know to miracle-workers on an everyday basis. He said that Bishop Cullen seemed to be out of danger, but he declined to speculate on how that had come about. When I asked whether it could have been through Camber's intervention, he said he was not qualified to judge.

"It was then that I realized that there was another witness I hadn't noticed before." The audience sat forward, for from here, Cinhil's testimony was new.

"There was a young Michaeline monk kneeling in the doorway of the oratory. Rhys told me that his name was Brother John, and that Bishop Cullen had asked to see him on a minor matter of discipline. They'd forgotten about him in all the confusion."

Here, Queron cleared his throat. "For the record, Father, though Lord Dualta confirms the presence of this Brother John, neither he nor any other member of the Michaeline Order whom we have questioned, has been able to locate this Brother John since the night in question. There appears to be no record that he ever existed. We know that you also tried to find him. Were you more successful?"

Cinhil shook his head, to a few rumblings of disapproval from among the bishops.

"Thank you, Father. Please continue. We'll come back to this point a little later."

Cinhil bowed nervously and seemed to steel himself to speak again. Not a sound came from his rapt audience.

"This—Brother John was kneeling just inside the oratory. I asked him whether he'd seen what had just happened. He replied that he was only an ignorant monk, and not learned in such matters, but I insisted that he answer. I remember that when he looked up, he had the most incredible eyes I'd ever seen— a sort of smoky black."

"Go on, please," Queron urged.

"Yes, sir. He—admitted that he had seen something. And when I pressed him for details, he said, 'It was *him.* He drew *his* shadow across the vicar general.'"

"And by '*him*,' what did you take him to mean?" Queron asked softly.

"I—asked him," Cinhil breathed. "I asked him, and he said—he said, 'It seemed to be the Lord Camber, Sire.'" Cinhil took a deep breath and closed his eyes, almost speaking to himself. "I shall remember his words until the day I die. He said, '*It seemed to be the Lord Camber. Yet, he is dead. I have seen him! I—I have heard of goodly men returning before, to aid the worthy . . .*'"

A great sigh swept through the hall as Cinhil's voice trailed off. Even Queron did not press him further.

After a moment, Cinhil slowly opened his eyes, though he still did not appear to see. He raised his hands to stare at them, willing the clenched fists to relax, then let them fall slack at his sides as he sighed and looked up at Queron. Queron had drawn out of him what he had not wished to say, even though it was the truth. Now Cinhil wanted only to escape, to be quit of this public testimony for a man he had at once resented and feared.

Queron let out his own breath and gave Cinhil an acknowledging nod.

"Thank you, Father. Would you please tell the court what, if anything, happened after that?"

"Little more," Cinhil murmured. "I had to get away and think. I still did not want to believe what I had seen and heard. I—told them not to discuss the matter, and then I left."

"And went . . . ?"

"To—to the cathedral for a little while, to—pray beside *his* body." He hung his head again. "After that, I returned to my apartments," he whispered.

"And nothing noteworthy occurred in the cathedral?" Queron persisted, though gently, for beyond this point, even he did not know what to expect.

But Cinhil only shook his head, raising his eyes to Queron's with such determination that even Queron's aplomb was a little shaken. The Healer-priest bowed profoundly, one hand sweeping in a gesture of "as you wish," patently acknowledging Cinhil's shift back from witness to monarch. He seemed to regain most of his poise as he returned his attention to the archbishop. He had, after all, accomplished his purpose.

"Your Grace, I think we need not cross-examine this witness further. May he be excused?"

"Of course," Jaffray said. "Sire, if you wish, we can adjourn for the rest of the day. I realize that this has been very difficult for you."

For answer, Cinhil turned his Haldane gaze hard on the archbishop, then pivoted slowly to scan the hall. His audience shrank under his scrutiny—all except

Camber—not daring to speak or even to move as he finally ascended the three dais steps to pick up his crown and take his seat. Though he was a little pale as he replaced the crown on his head, his face now betrayed no hint of what he had just been through. That, in itself, was enough to give him a vaguely foreboding air. It did not help that he avoided looking at Jaffray as he laid his hands formally on the arms of the throne.

But Camber, reading resignation as well as resentment for what had just transpired, did not share the apprehension of his colleagues. In a flash of vivid insight, he knew that even Cinhil, in his anger and frustration, had finally realized that one did not always have a choice of games which must be played. Not himself; not the bishops; not even Queron.

And so, there would be no reprisals. Now Cinhil was simply going to reassert the proper balance between king and Church, to ensure a viable working relationship for the future. Cinhil had lost this particular battle, but he would not always lose. He had won a minor victory only the night before, when he had gained an understanding ally in his struggle to be what he wanted to be, as well as what he was forced to be. Cinhil had learned much in the past year.

"We thank you for your concern, Archbishop, but no recess is necessary on our account," Cinhil said, every inch the gracious monarch. "We would not have it said that the King of Gwynedd in any way impeded the functioning of this august court, regardless of any personal biases which he himself might hold. As a dutiful son of the Church, the king sits here at Your Grace's invitation, and by your leave. Pray, continue, and accept our apologies if we seemed less than cooperative earlier."

To that, Jaffray had no choice but to make placating noises and assure the king that the court sympathized with his personal involvement, and certainly understood his seeming reluctance to testify, either for or against the matter under consideration. Cinhil accepted his reassurances graciously, and everyone seemed to relax.

After a few false starts, Dualta was recalled to complete his testimony and to verify Cinhil's story of the mysterious Brother John; and then Rhys and Joram were also recalled, though they could add nothing to what had already been said. Rhys had never seen Brother John before that night in Cullen's chambers, and Joram claimed that the monk had come to him that evening with a story that Bishop Cullen had summoned him. Bishop Cullen, of course, could neither confirm nor deny Joram's statement, having lost any precise memory of whether he had summoned a Brother John or not.

That about wound up the morning's testimony, other than to speculate on the significance of the elusive Brother John. The scant evidence regarding his existence, other than the testimony concerning his one-time appearance, furthered the air of mystery surrounding him, and even raised in one listener's mind the possibility that said John had actually been an angel, sent to bear witness to God's most recent miracle. That theory, voiced by the human Bishop of Nyford, who was by now an avid Camberian supporter, could not have been disproven except by those who dared not reveal the truth. And so, since the monk could not be produced, and it could not readily be proven that he had ever existed—perhaps he *had* been an angel. The possibility certainly did not detract from the growing Camberian hagiography.

Similar speculation continued after a late lunch break, with numerous lesser witnesses coming forward to attest to changes wrought in their lives by the supposed intercession of the Blessed Camber: miraculous cures at his tomb, petitions answered, protection derived from calling upon the *Defensor Hominum*— the Defender of Humankind. Of course, none of the claims was necessarily provable by the rigorous criteria set in the morning's testimony—but by then it did not really matter. The Council of Bishops was convinced.

By the end of the afternoon, it was clear that only formalities remained to be performed before Camber's sainthood would be officially recognized.

Camber himself could only sigh and accept the inevitable, casting his required vote with a silent prayer that the God Who had sustained him through so much already, and had allowed this to happen, would also accept this final bit of hypocrisy on his part.

The vote was unanimous, the response to its announcement almost universally joyous. On the fourteenth of the month, two weeks away, Camber Kyriell MacRorie would be formally canonized, to be known henceforth as Saint Camber of Culdi, *Defensor Hominum*—and other titles to be determined in the intervening days before the official celebration.

Camber said little as the company dispersed, drawing solace from the companionship of Joram and Jebediah, who could legitimately be with him at such a moment, and casting one long, sorrowful look at Evaine and Rhys in the gallery, before he passed out of the hall. He took no supper that night, and spent the evening in seclusion after hearing Vespers with his son and Jebediah. His new status was going to take some getting used to.

CHAPTER TWENTY-FIVE

*How is he numbered among the children of God,
and his lot is among the saints!*
—Wisdom of Solomon 5:5

The season changed, and it was true autumn, and
Saint Camber of Culdi was proclaimed in all the par-
ishes and cathedrals of Gwynedd. The season changed
again, and the Feast of Christmas came and went, and
then it was the new year, though the Three Kings had
not yet come bearing gifts.

And in the early hours of a day midway between
the coming of the Sun of Justice and the feast known
as Epiphany, the Bishop of Grecotha knelt in the
chapel now dedicated to the new-made saint and pondered what he had become—this man whom the
world knew as Alister Cullen, but who knew himself
to be the very Camber of the legends.

Or, not the Camber of the legends, precisely, for
that man was now a man who had never really lived,
lauded with tales of miraculous doings never wrought
by him in life, and now expounded when the man himself could not refute their claims. Or, he could have,
but he would not. So far as the world was concerned,
Camber Kyriell MacRorie was dead and must remain
so.

Resignedly, Camber gazed at the shrine his adherents had built to the man they had made of him, trying
to understand at a level of the heart what his mind and
reason had been forced to accept months before. All

Gwynedd was talking about Saint Camber now. This was the first time he had found the new shrine empty in the nearly two months since the formal canonization, and this was only because it was snowing bitterly outside, and in the deepest dark of the night. What was it that drew them?

He searched the face of the image they had made of him, the life-sized figure of a Camber who had never been, carved in a pale gray marble the way Guaire had seen him, cowl fallen back from gilded hair, the painted face upraised to gaze at hands which held a royal diadem, a replica of the crown of crosses and leaves which Camber had set on Cinhil's head that night which seemed so long ago.

Sanctus Camberus, Defensor Hominum, Regis Creator, the legend read on the altar front. Saint Camber, Defender of Humankind, Kingmaker. To either side of the altar, in hand-deep pans of sand set on wrought bronze stands, scores of candles blazed in tawny golden splendor, illuminating the chapel without any taint of colored glass. The entire chamber had been refaced with white stone, carved alabaster screens replacing the old wooden ones, even the floor being retiled in a white-and-gray cross pattern which some said was destined to become the badge of the Servants of Saint Camber, who had commissioned the entire work. It was rumored that the Camber shrine at the Servants' abbey in Dolban was even more sumptuous, though Camber had not yet summoned the courage to go and see it.

His own trepidations aside, he wondered what it all meant in terms of the world's reality and not his own. As a cohesive force in the society of Gwynedd, he knew that the cult of Saint Camber was already showing incredible gains, drawing together humans and Deryni in ways which Camber himself could never have foreseen in the days when he had tried to prevent what had happened. Who could have dreamed that Saint Camber, as well as being the Defender of Humankind, would now be hailed as the patron of

Deryni magic, a proponent of responsible use of that power—which was all the human population had ever asked of the Deryni anyway: that they not be exploited by their more gifted brethren. Certainly, no one resented the ministrations of the Healers, for example.

But that did not explain the other things that had begun to happen: the increasingly miraculous occurrences ascribed to a saintly Camber's holy intervention. The results being obtained were obviously real—cures and turns of luck and other answers to men's prayers —but Camber knew that he was not responsible. Could it be that faith alone *could* work miracles, even if the agent being credited—in this case, "Saint Camber"—did not exist?

Or did "Saint Camber" exist after all, because he was present in the beliefs of men? Perhaps the cult of Camber had passed beyond even the Deryni sphere of understanding, into that realm of Deity which transcended mortal ken. Why should an omnipotent God *not* work through the name of Camber, if He so chose? Was not one name as good as another? There must be *some* plan to account for what had happened, or Camber could not have managed to succeed thus far.

But suppose he was wrong? Perhaps God was playing with him, building him up only to let him fall from even higher . . .

He shuddered at that, leaning his elbows on the armrest of the prie-dieu and burying his face in his hands and wondering, not for the first time, whether he had gone too far. He heard a rustling sound behind him, from the doorway of the chapel, and suddenly realized that he was not alone, though he had heard no one approach. Even as he started to turn to see who it was, for he could detect no specific psychic identity behind close-held shields, a voice spoke softly.

"Saint Camber, eh?"

Almost, and Camber reacted physically as well as mentally, before he realized that it was Cinhil who had spoken and that the words were not an accusation. He looked back to see Cinhil leaning against the doorjamb, arms folded across his chest, snow glittering on the shoulders of his dark cloak and powdering his hair. Camber started to get up, but Cinhil shook his head and waved him to stay where he was as he came to kneel beside him. The king blew on his bare hands to warm them as he glanced around the chapel, an ironic smile playing about his lips.

"You surprise me, Alister. I think I actually took you unawares. You didn't even hear me approach, did you?"

"You're learning to shield quite well," Camber smiled, relaxing. "I'm sorry. I was—preoccupied."

"So I gathered."

Cinhil glanced up at the statue towering above them and raised a wistful eyebrow, then looked back at Camber. His manner had become more serious, the gray eyes darker in the few seconds since he had knelt. Camber wondered what had brought him here at this hour, and in the falling snow. He suspected he knew.

"Tell me, do you still doubt him, too?" Cinhil asked, his voice hardly more than a whisper.

Camber averted his eyes thoughtfully, suspicions confirmed, painfully aware that this was the one area in which he could not be open with the king.

"What does it really matter?" he answered. "His cult exists. No one can deny the positive effects his followers are exerting on Gwynedd. Perhaps that is the true criterion for sainthood, after all."

Cinhil thought about that for a moment, then nodded slowly. "You may be right. And yet, there's something more to it than that. At times, I—God help me, Alister, I almost think I feel his presence, as if he—still wanted me to do something, only I don't know what it is." He looked down in embarrassment. "That sounds totally irrational, doesn't it?"

"Not necessarily," Camber replied, a little amused at the double truth which Cinhil had unwittingly spoken. "But what does your heart say to you? Never mind your reason."

Cinhil gave a little sigh and shrugged. "I don't know. I've even tried to ask *him*. That night that he—saved you, I—came here to the cathedral and tried to pray beside his bier. I stormed the heavens; I demanded that he tell me what he was doing, what he wanted of me—but he never answered. He still hasn't."

"If he did, how do you think you would know?" Camber asked softly. He almost held his breath, waiting, for Cinhil's answer would tell him much about how he must proceed in the times ahead.

With another sigh, Cinhil sat back on his heels and gazed up at the statue of the saint in question. He thought in silence for so long that Camber had about decided that he was not going to answer. Then Cinhil shook his head and glanced at Camber.

"I'm not sure I can answer that," he finally said. "In the simplicity of what I used to believe, when I was only a simple, cloistered priest, spending my days in prayer, I suppose I would have expected—oh, I don't know—perhaps a vision or a dream, such as Guaire experienced. I've tried to let something like that happen—believe me, I have, Alister—but nothing has. Besides, after all that's happened in these past two years, I'm not sure that would suffice any more. I don't know what would."

"Well, perhaps that *is* too simplistic an expectation." Camber said after a moment. "I suspect that as we become more sophisticated in our view of the world, we tend to become more demanding too. We want more rational reassurances, when what we *need* is a reawakening of that childlike wonder that we all once had: that awesome ability to see the miracles in every waking moment, to believe what our senses tell us we see, to hear God's voice speaking in His people and their deeds."

"And through His saints?" Cinhil asked cynically, glancing up at the statue once again.

"Perhaps. Perhaps that's even sufficient for most men. But as we grow and change, perhaps He changes His way of reaching into us, as well. Maybe for you, a Saint Camber isn't necessary. All of the bitterness aside, you have a job to do now, and you're learning to do it well, whether or not any saint continues to be a guiding factor in your life. Your conscience will tell you whether you're doing His will. Perhaps that's another language God speaks, after a time."

"Is my conscience God, then?" Cinhil grinned. "Blasphemy, Bishop, blasphemy!"

"You know that's not what I mean," Camber chuckled, getting to his feet. "But come. 'Tis too late and too cold to continue this philosophical discourse tonight. Over breakfast tomorrow, if you insist, but I, for one, am tired of talking about our friend Camber."

As he gestured toward the statue, Cinhil also stood, and together they made their way to the doorway of the chapel, where Cinhil paused to look back a final time.

"You know," the king said, as they walked on toward the northern door, where a guard waited with his horse, "I think I've realized something tonight, after all."

"Oh?"

"Yes. I think I've learned that I can let him be. Mind you, I haven't forgotten or forgiven what he did to me. That will take a while, if it ever happens. But I think I *can* cope with what he's become. The saint back there in that chapel is not the man I feared and respected."

Camber smiled as he held the door for Cinhil to pass through into the snow.

"Then, you've learned a great deal, Sire," he said softly, tempering his next words for the waiting guard. "Shall I come to you early, then, to celebrate Mass? Afterwards, we can continue our discussion over breakfast—or whenever you would like."

Cinhil nodded casually enough, but Camber knew that he, too, was seeing in his mind's eye that beloved trunk full of vestments, that he was appreciating Cullen for his recognition of that bond and secret which the two of them shared. Falling snow sputtered in the torch the guard held as Cinhil swung up on his horse, the fire making his eyes glitter in the darkness.

"That would be fine," he said, raising a hand in salute. "God bless you, Bishop Cullen."

"And God bless you, Sire," said Camber of Culdi, as the king moved away in his glowing sphere of torchlight.

(Camber's story will be concluded in the third volume of the legends of Camber, Camber the Heretic.*)*

APPENDICES

INDEX OF CHARACTERS

ALFRED, Father—Cinhil's human confessor.

ALISTER CULLEN, Father—*see Cullen.*

ALLYN, Crevan—Alister Cullen's successor as Vicar General of the Order of Saint Michael; human.

ALROY, Prince—infant son and heir of King Cinhil, twin to Javan; in poor health.

ANDREW—farrier at Grecotha.

ANSCOM of Trevas, Archbishop—Deryni Primate of All Gwynedd; Archbishop of Valoret.

ANSEL MacRorie, Lord—younger son of Cathan; age five.

ARIELLA of Festil, Princess—elder sister of the former King Imre and mother of his son, Mark.

BAYVEL de Cameron, Lord—uncle of Queen Megan.

BENEDICT—King Cinhil's name in religion.

BEREN, Sir—a Michaeline knight.

CAMBER Kyriell MacRorie, Lord—Earl of Culdi: canonized as Saint Camber in 906; *Defensor Hominum* and patron of Deryni magic.

CAMERON—family name of Queen Megan.

CATHAN MacRorie, Lord—Camber's eldest son and heir; murdered by Imre in 903.

CHARLES, Brother—a Servant of Saint Camber; formerly a baker in village at Caerrorie.

CINHIL Donal Ifor Haldane, King—restored King of Gwynedd; formerly a priest of the *Ordo Verbi Dei* under the name of Benedict; kidnapped from his monastery by Joram and Rhys.

COEL Howell, Lord—brother of Elinor, Cathan's wife; member of Imre's council; executed by King Cinhil in 905.

CRINAN—Cathan's squire; doubled for Rhys under a shape-changing spell.

CULLEN, Father Alister—Deryni Vicar General of the Order of Saint Michael; later, Bishop of Grecotha and Chancellor of Gwynedd.

DAVET, Bishop—one of Gwynedd's six itinerant bishops.

DAVIN MacRorie, Lord—elder son of Cathan; age seven; Earl of Culdi after his grandfather's death.

DERMOT O'Beirne, Bishop—human Bishop of Cashien, in west Gwynedd.

DOTHAN of Erne, Lord—former Festillic minister imprisoned by Cinhil for trial; son and daughter killed in assassination attempt on Cinhil.

DUALTA Jarriot, Lord—a Michaeline knight.

ELINOR MacRorie, Lady—widow of Cathan; mother of Davin and Ansel; later, wife to James Drummond.

EMRYS, Dom—Deryni adept and Abbot of the Order of Saint Gabriel.

EUSTACE of Fairleigh, Bishop—one of Gwynedd's six itinerant bishops; human.

EVAINE MacRorie Thuryn, Lady—daughter of Camber and wife to Rhys.

EWAN, Lord—eldest son of Duke Sighere; later, Earl of Rhendall.

FINTAN, Lord—human earl on Cinhil's council.

GABRILITES—priests of the Order of Saint Gabriel, an all-Deryni esoteric order based at Saint Neot's, in the south Lendour mountains; especially noted for training Healers.

GELLIS de Cleary, Father—acting Precentor of the Order of Saint Michael.

GUAIRE of Arliss, Lord—friend of Cathan; former aide to Camber and Cullen; finally, a founding Servant of Saint Camber.

HALDANE—surname of the ancient royal family of Gwynedd.

HILDRED, Lord—human baron on Cinhil's council; expert on horses.

HOWELL, Coel—*see Coel.*

HOWICCAN, Pargan—classic Deryni lyric poet.

HRORIK, Lord—middle son of Duke Sighere; later, Earl of Eastmarch.

HUMPHREY of Gallareaux, Father—dead Michaeline priest responsible for death of Cinhil's firstborn son, Prince Aidan.

ILLAN, Lord—a Michaeline knight.

IMRE, King—fifth Festillic King of Gwynedd, reigned 900–904; died after defeat by Cinhil.

JAFFRAY of Carbury, Archbishop—successor to Anscom as Archbishop of Valoret; Deryni and former Gabrilite.

JAVAN, Prince—infant son of King Cinhil, twin to Alroy; born with a clubfoot.

JAMES Drummond, Lord—grand-nephew of Camber; former suitor to Elinor and later her second husband.

JASPER Miller, Father—a Michaeline priest.

JEBEDIAH of Alcara, Lord—Deryni Grand Master of the Order of Saint Michael; later, Earl Marshal of Gwynedd.

JOHANNES, Brother—lay Michaeline monk, servant of Vicar General Alister Cullen.

JOHN—factor who bought Dolban for the Servants of Saint Camber.

JOHN, Brother—an alias of Evaine.

JORAM MacRorie, Father—youngest son of Camber; priest and knight of the Order of Saint Michael; later, confidential secretary to Bishop Alister Cullen.

JOWERTH Leslie, Lord—formerly a Festillic minister; Deryni; now on Cinhil's staff.

KAI, Bishop—one of Gwynedd's six itinerant bishops.

KYRIELL—Camber's name in religion.

LAUREN, Sir—a Michaeline knight.

MacGREGOR, Bishop Ailin—one of Gwynedd's six itinerant bishops.

MacRORIE—surname of Camber's family.

MARK of Festil—infant son of Imre and Ariella and carrier of the Festillic line in Torenth after his parents' deaths.

MEGAN, Queen—wife to Cinhil; mother of Alroy, Javan, and Rhys Haldane; formerly Camber's ward.

MICHAELINES—priests and knights of the Order of Saint Michael, a militant fighting and teaching order, predominantly Deryni.

MURDOCH, Baron—human Baron of Caithane, of an ancient human family in power before the Festillic Interregnum.

NATHAN, Father—a Michaeline priest.

NIALLAN Trey, Bishop—Deryni Bishop of Dhassa; formerely of the Order of Saint Michael.

NIMUR, King—Deryni King of Torenth; connected to the Festils of Gwynedd through the female line.

ORIN—Deryni mystic and magician; author of the Protocol of Orin, a collection of four scrolls containing extremely potent spells of Deryni magic.

ORISS, Father Robert—human Vicar General of the *Ordo Verbi Dei;* boyhood friend of Anscom of Trevas; later, Archbishop of Rhemuth.

PORRIC Lunal, Father—a priest of the Order of Saint Michael and a candidate to succeed Alister Cullen as Vicar General.

QUERON Kinevan, Dom—Deryni Healer-priest, originally of the Order of Saint Gabriel; a founding Servant of Saint Camber.

RAYMOND, Bishop—former Prince-Bishop of Dhassa and maternal uncle of Alister Cullen, whom he ordained.

REVAN—lame former carpenter's apprentice saved by Cathan; now a clark to Evaine.

RHYS Thuryn, Lord—Deryni physician and Healer; developer of the Thuryn technique of concentration; husband of Evaine and son-in-law to Camber.

SIGHERE, Duke—former independent Earl of Eastmarch; later, first Duke of Claibourne.

SIGHERE, Lord—youngest son of Duke Sighere; later, Earl of Marley.

SORLE—Cinhil's squire.

TAMMARON, Lord—human earl on Cinhil's staff.

TERMOD of Rhorau, Lord—Deryni princeling, cousin of Imre, killed by Willimite terrorists in 903.

THOMAS—bailiff at Dolban, for Servants of Saint Camber.

THURYN—see Rhys.

TOBAN—hospice page.

TORCUILL de la Marche, Lord—Deryni baron, formerly a Festillic minister; now on Cinhil's staff.

TURLOUGH, Bishop—one of Gwynedd's six itinerant bishops.

UDAUT, Lord—a human earl; Constable of Gwynedd.

ULLIAM ap Lugh, Bishop—human Bishop of Nyford.

UMPHRED—Camber's bailiff at Caerrorie.

WILLIAM—farrier at Grecotha.

WILLIM, Saint—child martyr to Deryni ill-use; patron saint of the Willimite movement.

WILLIMITES—terrorist group sworn to punish Deryni who escape justice through normal legal channels; mostly suppressed in 904 under Imre.

WILLOWEN, Father—human Dean of Grecotha Cathedral and assistant to Bishop Cullen.

WULPHER, Master—Cathan's steward; doubled for Joram under a shape-changing spell.

INDEX OF PLACES

CUILTEINE—potential site for a new Michaeline Commanderie.

CULDI—central city of the Honor of Culdi, on the Gwynedd-Meara border.

DHASSA—free holy city in the Lendour Mountains; seat of the Bishop of Dhassa.

DOLBAN—ruined manor bought by Guaire of Arliss as a site for the first monastery of the Servants of Saint Camber; on the main road between Valoret and Caerrorie.

EASTMARCH—independent holding of Sighere, Earl of Eastmarch; later given to Hrorik, Sighere's middle son.

GRECOTHA—university city, site of the Varnarite school; seat of the Bishop of Grecotha. Camber, Anscom, and Cullen all attended school here at one time or another.

GWYNEDD—central of the Eleven Kingdoms; seat of the Festillic Dynasty, 822–904; restored to the Haldane Line in 904.

HAUT EIRIAL—a Michaeline establishment destroyed by Imre in 904.

HOWICCE—kingdom to the southwest of Gwynedd; loosely allied with Llannedd.

IOMAIRE—site of battle with Ariella, on Gwynedd-Eastmarch border.

KHELDISH RIDING—viceregality broken off Kheldour after annexation of Kheldour by Sighere and Cinhil in 906.

KHELDOUR—small kingdom north of Gwynedd, famous for textiles and carpets; associated with Rhendall and the Festils through Termod of Rhorau.

LLANNEDD—kingdom to the southwest of Gwynedd; loosely allied with Howicce.

MARLEY—small earldom carved out of Eastmarch and given to Sighere, youngest son of Duke Sighere, in 906.

MEARA—kingdom/princedom to the northwest of Gwynedd; nominally a vassal state of Gwynedd.

MOLLINGFORD—a Michaeline establishment destroyed by Imre in 904.

MOORYN—petty kingdom at the southeast of Gwynedd; formerly a powerful ally under Imre's reign.

NYFORD—river town in central Gwynedd, near Saint Illtyd's Monastery; seat of the Bishop of Nyford; site of Imre's abortive new capital.

RHENDALL—lake region north of Gwynedd; formerly the Festillic holding of Termod of Rhorau; given to Ewan, eldest son of Duke Sighere, in 906 as the secondary title of the Duke of Claibourne.

RHEMUTH—ancient capital of Gwynedd under the Haldanes; abandoned during the Festillic Interregnum; slated to be restored under Cinhil.

RHORAU—fortress seat of Lord Termod, cousin of King Imre, in the Rhendall lake region.

SAINT FOILLAN'S ABBEY—establishment of the *Ordo Verbi Dei*, in the mountains, three days' ride southeast of Valoret, where Camber and Rhys found Prince Cinhil Haldane.

SAINT LIAM'S ABBEY—a Michaeline-staffed abbey school, four hours' ride northeast of Valoret.

SAINT NEOT'S MONASTERY—stronghold of the Order of Saint Gabriel, an esoteric, all-Deryni order, in the Lendour Highlands.

TORENTH—kingdom to the east of Gwynedd; ruled by the Deryni King Nimur.

VALORET—Festillic capital of Gwynedd, 822–905.

PARTIAL LINEAGE OF THE HALDANE KINGS

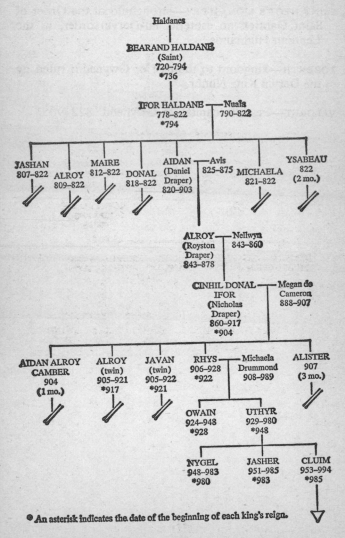

Haldanes

BEARAND HALDANE
(Saint)
720–794
*736

IFOR HALDANE — Nuala
778–822   790–822
*794

JASHAN   ALROY   MAIRE   DONAL   AIDAN — Avis   MICHAELA   YSABEAU
807–822   809–822   812–822   818–822   (Daniel   825–875   821–822   822
                                                      Draper)   (2 mo.)
                                                      820–903

ALROY — Neilwyn
(Royston   843–860
Draper)
843–878

CINHIL DONAL — Megan de
IFOR   Cameron
(Nicholas   888–907
Draper)
860–917
*904

AIDAN ALROY   ALROY   JAVAN   RHYS — Michaela   ALISTER
CAMBER   (twin)   (twin)   906–928   Drummond   907
904   905–921   905–922   *922   908–989   (3 mo.)
(1 mo.)   *917   *921

OWAIN   UTHYR
924–948   929–980
*928   *948

NYGEL   JASHER   CLUIM
948–983   951–985   953–994
*980   *983   *985

* An asterisk indicates the date of the beginning of each king's reign.

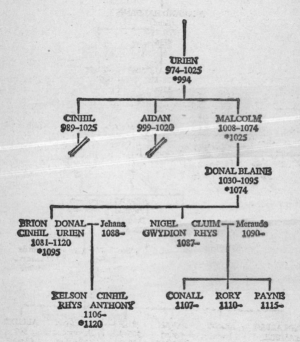

URIEN
974–1025
●994

CINHIL
989–1025

AIDAN
999–1020

MALCOLM
1008–1074
●1025

DONAL BLAINE
1030–1095
●1074

BRION DONAL——Jehana
CINHIL URIEN 1088–
1081–1120
●1095

NIGEL CLUIM——Meraude
GWYDION RHYS 1090–
1087–

KELSON CINHIL
RHYS ANTHONY
1106–
●1120

CONALL
1107–

RORY
1110–

PAYNE
1115–

THE FESTILLIC KINGS OF GWYNEDD AND THEIR DESCENDANTS

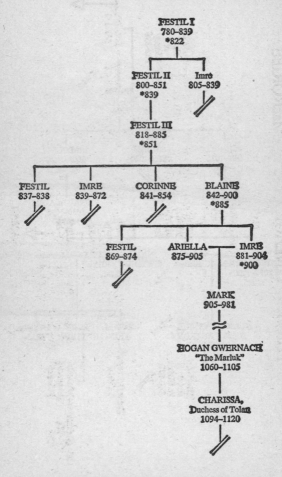

FESTIL I
780–839
*822

FESTIL II
800–851
*839

Imre
805–839

FESTIL III
818–885
*851

FESTIL
837–838

IMRE
839–872

CORINNE
841–854

BLAINE
842–900
*885

FESTIL
869–874

ARIELLA
875–905

IMRE
881–904
*900

MARK
905–981

HOGAN GWERNACH
"The Marluk"
1060–1105

CHARISSA,
Duchess of Tolan
1094–1120

* An asterisk indicates the date of the beginning of each king's reign.

PARTIAL LINEAGE OF THE MacRORIES

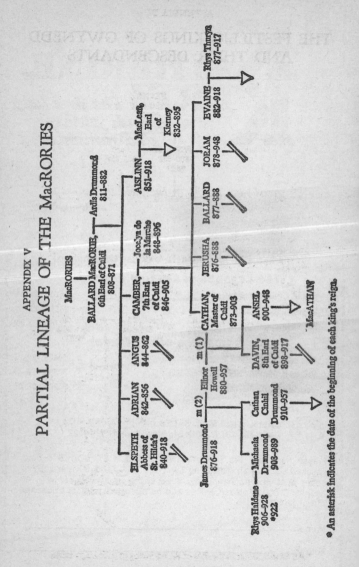

* An asterisk indicates the date of the beginning of each king's reign.